DESIRE'S DETERMINATION

"What are you afraid of, Kentir?" Reaching up, Laura touched his face, skimming her fingertips over his cheekbones and his hard jaw. With the lightest pressure she outlined his lips. She was rewarded by his swift intake of breath.

"You distract me from my work." His voice was a low growl.

"Perhaps you need distraction," she whispered. Her hands were on Kentir's shoulders, so she felt the shudder that went through him when she moved closer to press herself against him. "This evening has been designated as a time for pleasure and relaxation. If the others can accept Seret's decree, why can't you?"

"Laura, don't," he said, as if in warning.

"Don't what?" she asked. "Would it destroy you to put your arms around me?"

"It might." He took another long, shuddering breath. "Do you know what you are doing to me?"

"Yes," she whispered, her lips still curved into a smile. She met his eyes squarely, certain for the first time in her life that she wanted a man—this man, and no other. A heated melting began deep within her. "Yes, Kentir, I know exactly what I am doing."

Love

ONCE & FOREVER

FLORA SPEER

LOVE SPELL BOOKS   ◆   NEW YORK CITY

*This book is dedicated to the
memory of Immanuel Velikovsky.*

LOVE SPELL®

January 1999

Published by

Dorchester Publishing Co., Inc.
276 Fifth Avenue
New York, NY 10001

ISBN 0-505-52291-8

The name "Love Spell" and its logo are trademarks of Dorchester
Publishing Co., Inc.

Printed in the United States of America.

The world was all . . . a seething sea . . .
The stars began to fray, and time and earth
Washed hands in mischief . . .

> *Shah-nahmeh*
> by Firdausi, circa A.D. 1010

Cape Canaveral, Florida: NASA launched a spacecraft
Saturday on a three-year voyage to an asteroid. . . . The find-
ings . . . should contribute to the study of collision avoidance—
how to keep asteroids from crashing to Earth. . . .

> From an Associated Press story in
> *The Hartford Courant,*
> Sunday, February 18, 1996

Love

ONCE & FOREVER

Chapter One

Ventnor, New Jersey
August, 1998

"Laura, you can't be serious," Alberta Morrison cried, casting a look of irate disapproval at her daughter. "Roger Greydon is a fine man, an up-and-coming politician. With the right woman behind him, who knows how far he can go? He's sure to win the Senate seat in the November election. Why, he might even be president one day. How can you change your mind like this?"

"Because I don't love him," Laura said. "He doesn't love me, either."

"I never heard such nonsense! Why would he ask you to marry him if he doesn't love you? And

11

just look at that gorgeous engagement ring! How can you bear to give it back?"

"Because it doesn't mean anything. Oh, Mom, why can't you understand? Dad does."

"You told your father about your decision before you told me?" Mrs. Morrison's eyes filled with tears. "A girl ought to tell her mother these things first."

"I'm sorry, Mom," Laura said with a sigh. "Last night after you went to bed Dad started asking questions. I think it was because he sensed how unsure I was about Roger." Her father had always been quick to perceive Laura's unspoken emotions. He was also an expert at getting her to talk about what was troubling her. Unlike his wife, William Morrison always listened to what his children were saying—and he seemed to hear the things they chose to leave unspoken.

"All girls are unsure about taking such a big step," Laura's mother said. "I'll just have a word with your father. Roger is too good a catch for you to let him get away. I won't allow you to make a mistake you are sure to regret later."

"Knock it off, Mom! Just listen to yourself; you sound like an overly ambitious, pre–World War II mother. Come down to earth. It's the end of the twentieth century, and rising politicians are no longer considered good matrimonial catches. A woman who has ambitions in that direction is expected to become a politician herself, instead of depending on a man to do it for her. Why do I have to tell you this? You are usually so up-to-date on modern trends."

"It's different where one's own daughters are concerned. With Susan finishing her internship and about to set up her office in that dreadful neighborhood in Philadelphia, I just know her future existence is going to be a tale of drudgery and unending work. Family practice, indeed! What is your sister thinking of?

"Why am I talking about Susan?" Mrs. Morrison went on, shaking her head. "She's a hopeless case. She won't listen to a word I say on the subject of men or marriage. But you, Laura—I had such hopes for you, especially after you went to work for Roger. Oh, my dear, I want you to have the glamorous life I never had."

"As far as I can tell," Laura said, "you've had a very happy life, with a husband who adores you, and a son and two daughters who all think you are the best mom ever. We even have this wonderful house at the beach! You know you love coming here each summer."

"I do," Alberta Morrison admitted. "And I am happy with our life in Philadelphia and the house there. It's just that I want something more exciting for you. I could just wring your father's neck!" she ended with a burst of renewed irritation.

"Don't blame Dad," Laura said. "And don't you dare scold him, either. He didn't actually say anything against Roger."

"I'm sure I know him well enough to guess exactly what methods he used," Mrs. Morrison said. "He asked questions deliberately slanted to make you think before you answered them."

"That's exactly what he did, and I am glad of it." Silently, Laura blessed her father for his direct and unflinching questioning. He had made her say out loud what she had not wanted to admit. Having spoken the truth about her feelings, she could no longer deny what was in her heart.

"He does the same thing to me," her mother said. "All the time. It can be so annoying."

"He keeps you out of trouble, Mom."

"I suppose he does, even when I don't want him to." Mrs. Morrison sniffed and looked annoyed all over again. Then she said, "I know I am sometimes foolish and much too impulsive, but I do want what's best for all of my children."

"I know, Mom. Bill and Susan know it, too. And Dad loves your impulsiveness. He says you keep his life interesting." With real affection and a patience born of her twenty-four years of dealing with her mother, Laura bestowed a warm hug on the older woman.

They were standing in the front hall of the Morrisons' summer house, where Mrs. Morrison had accosted Laura just as her daughter was leaving. It was a big, old-fashioned house with a wide porch across the front, the kind of place few people wanted to bother with anymore, but Alberta Morrison had made it into a welcoming summer home with plenty of room for her family and their guests.

Until recently Laura, her older sister Susan, and her brother Bill, who was the eldest of the three Morrison children, had been happy to spend every summer of their lives at the beach

14

house. Now Susan was preparing to open a medical office in Philadelphia and Bill was married and living in Texas. With her only son settled and her older daughter refusing to listen to her mother's dire warnings about the nastiness of a medical practice in one of the poorer sections of a large city, Alberta Morrison had been left at loose ends. It was perhaps inevitable that she would begin to interfere in her youngest child's life.

Laura had been working as an executive assistant to Roger Greydon, who two days ago had asked her to marry him. Laura had said yes, but no sooner had Roger slipped the two-carat diamond on her finger than she began to have second thoughts. Her father's persistent questions the previous evening had only crystallized Laura's doubts.

Knowing her mother would object vigorously to what she was going to do, Laura had called Roger at the hotel in Atlantic City where he was staying for a political meeting, and had asked him to meet her two hours later, on the beach. Laura had insisted they meet discreetly and without reporters or cameramen in attendance. She thought the open sand was probably the only place where no one could eavesdrop on the senatorial candidate who was rapidly becoming famous and the young woman about whom there had been many rumors in recent days. At least no formal announcement of their engagement had yet been made. Roger could avoid awkward explanations to the press.

Laura had been on her way to join Roger when her mother had waylaid her and started asking probing questions.

"Well, Laura," said Alberta Morrison, sounding like a tragic heroine who was about to expire from sorrow, "if you feel you really must make this unfortunate break with a man who could one day lay the world at your feet, then I suppose you must do what you think is right."

"I don't want the world at my feet. This will work out for the best, Mom. You'll see." Laura dropped a quick kiss on her mother's cheek and started out of the house. She had reached the porch when her mother's voice stopped her again.

"You will be back in time for dinner, won't you?"

"Dinner?" Laura repeated, frowning a little. "Probably. Mom, please don't worry about me."

"Your sister called," Mrs. Morrison said, somewhat irrelevantly. "The painters finished their work on her office this morning and there is nothing more Susan can do there until the equipment is delivered the day after tomorrow, so she is driving down from Philadelphia this afternoon. I was hoping we could gather at dinner for a family celebration. Now, of course, there is nothing to celebrate, but I would like to have my daughters with me at this sad time." She sounded as if there had been a death in the family.

"Sure, Mom," Laura said, as patiently as she could manage. "I'll be home in plenty of time for dinner. I'll even dress up for it. Let's have shrimp cocktail. Susan loves it." Laura hoped the suggestion, which involved a trip to the supermarket, would take her mother's mind off what Laura was planning to do that afternoon.

"Oh, dear," said Mrs. Morrison, "I haven't even begun to think about the menu." Closing the screen door, she disappeared into the house.

"Good," Laura said to herself, "that'll keep her busy for a while." Laura headed for the beach. It was only half a block away, but her mother's protestations and arguments as to why Laura should not break off her engagement to Roger had caused a delay of a good half hour or more.

Laura broke into a trot, not wanting to be late, fearing that if she was, Roger would decide to come to the house. If that happened, she'd have to cope with both her mother and Roger, and she did not want her mother to know what she had discovered about Roger. Laura was convinced that her mother simply would not understand. Her father was a different matter entirely. Laura smiled, thinking of the way her father had listened without objection when she had revealed her conviction that Roger was not the man for her.

"Aside from what I have recently learned about him," Laura had said to her father the previous evening, "I think you are a large part of the reason why Roger proposed to me in the first place. Roger wants to be seen as being on the cutting edge of science, the perfect candidate for the coming century. It would improve his image im-

17

measurably to have such a famous father-in-law."

"On the contrary, it could only improve his image to have a lovely and intelligent young wife on his arm," William Morrison had responded. "Don't sell yourself short, Laura. You have been a great asset to Roger during the time you have worked for him."

Laura regarded her father with deep love and respect. William Morrison had begun his career by inventing an accurate and almost indestructible timing device that was small enough to be used in rockets. The Morrison Timer had caused a sensation at NASA, and was later adapted for use in electronic gear for the general public. Other inventions had followed the first; all of them had been accepted for use on either the space shuttle or on NASA's unmanned interplanetary spacecraft, and all of the inventions had also had civilian applications. William Morrison, a quiet, unassuming man, had become famous as a forward-looking genius.

Laura was sure her father's fame was the reason she had been chosen over a dozen other applicants for the job as Roger Greydon's executive assistant, and she was convinced that Roger had begun courting her for the same calculating reason.

None of that would have mattered to Laura if Roger had actually loved her, but he didn't—as she had learned to her humiliation just one day after agreeing to marry him. Now she was on her way to tell him she had changed her mind.

Laura ran up the wooden plank ramp to the boardwalk and paused there, looking along the beach for Roger. She saw him standing by the water. Contrary to the agreement they had made over the telephone, he was not alone. Of course not; she should have known better than to expect Roger to do as he had promised.

Laura crossed the boardwalk to the steps that led down to the beach. While she stood at the top of the steps scuffing off her sneakers, she took an extra minute to watch Roger and his companion. And she wondered why she had ever imagined she could marry him. For the truth was that, while Roger had lied and betrayed her, Laura had betrayed herself and her dreams.

All her life Laura had known in her deepest heart that somewhere there existed a man who would love her with his entire heart and soul, a man whom she could love forever in the same way. But, caught up in the glamour of Roger's whirlwind courtship, of parties with famous people, of sudden trips to Washington or New York, where rooms awaited them in the best hotels, dazzled by the expensive presents Roger gave her, amid the excitement and exhaustion of a fast-paced political career, Laura had almost forgotten her most secret, most cherished hope. Almost, but not completely.

Her father's gentle interrogation had been the reminder she needed. What did it matter if a man could give her the world, if his heart was closed to her? And how could she marry and live with a man whom she did not truly love? In the end, those had been the questions William Morrison had insisted that his daughter must answer with scrupulous honesty.

Down on the beach, Roger had seen her. He waved and started toward her. Laura motioned to him to wait where he was and then she ran down the steps and across the sand to meet him.

"So that's it, Roger," Laura said half an hour later. "I can't marry you. I never should have accepted your proposal in the first place. I'm sorry if I've hurt you." She didn't think he was hurt at all. She could see that he was trying to look unhappy but, after a year of increasing familiarity with his moods, Laura knew Roger pretty well and she could tell he was acting. He wasn't happy at the sudden alteration in the carefully laid plans that he intended would lead him to the United States Senate, but he wasn't heartbroken, either.

"Are you absolutely sure about this?" Roger asked, bouncing the engagement ring up and down in his palm, looking at it as if he couldn't believe she had actually dared to return it.

Laura bit her tongue. As she had done so often during her time with Roger, she did not say what was on her mind. She knew that she ought to have ended the relationship months ago, well before he had proposed to her. Her only regrets were that it had taken her so long to do it, and that she had given herself to Roger, had willingly let him make love to her. She knew now that she should have placed her own value higher.

"I am positive that I am doing the right thing." Having spoken as firmly as she could, Laura watched Roger's fingers close around the ring. Wondering what he would do with it, she risked a glance at Marlene, Roger's public relations assistant, who had come to the beach with Roger and who had listened in silence while Laura ended the engagement.

Marlene was incredibly beautiful, with shoulder-length golden curls and large sky blue eyes that at the moment were soft with unshed tears of sympathy for her friends.

Laura, whose own hair was short, medium brown and straight, whose eyes were also brown and not remarkable in size or color, often felt invisible when she was with Marlene. Laura had always wondered why Marlene had so readily become her friend, why Marlene had listened to everything Laura said with such dedicated interest, and why she had so willingly dispensed advice on how to deal with a man like Roger. Now Laura knew why. She had learned the truth on the previous day. Thinking that the truth was enough to make anyone forever cynical and distrustful of men, Laura looked away from her handsome companions.

She had been so intent on what she wanted to say to Roger that she hadn't paid much attention to her surroundings. She loved the seashore, and now she saw that it was late afternoon on an ideal August day. The scene before her could have been painted by a great artist. The ocean was several shades of dark blue, with sparkling white foam where the waves crested and rolled toward the sandy shore. Not a cloud marred the sky. Even the beachgoers had distributed themselves across the pale sand in picturesque groups punctuated by gaily colored umbrellas.

A few yards away from Laura a young couple in matching sweat suits walked with their hands linked, their heads close together. A teenage girl in a skimpy bikini stood at the red-and-white lifeguard stand talking to one of the guards, who looked down upon her affectionately from his high perch. Laura knew both of the lifeguards. They had been assigned to the same beach every summer for several years. The younger man sitting on the stand was Ben. Beside the lifeboat that was pulled up on the sand next to the stand, Jim, the older lifeguard, was chatting with his wife, while their little girl played around their feet, digging holes in the mud. Up on the boardwalk an elderly couple strolled, seemingly content after years of living together. Couples were everywhere; only Laura did not have a partner.

For the space of a single minute, Laura wondered if she would ever find an honest man whom she could love for a lifetime, a lover to hold her hand and stroll along the boardwalk with her when they were both old. Then she brought her attention back to the couple standing before her.

"Of course," she said to Roger, "I can't continue to work as your assistant. It would be too awkward for both of us, especially with the election campaign just moving into full swing. You'll be getting my resignation letter in the mail. I won't return after my vacation is over. I'm sorry, Marlene, but you are just going to have to pick up the slack until Roger finds someone else."

"How sad this is for both of you," Marlene murmured.

"These things happen," Laura said to the friend who had betrayed her trust. "No one is to blame. I don't have it in me to be the perfect political wife that Roger needs. The Washington social scene is not my thing." She fell silent, wishing she did not feel an obligation to smooth over any unpleasantness she might have caused, yearning to say what she really thought. But years of training in good manners by her mother prevented Laura from speaking her mind.

"Well," Roger said, clearing his throat, "if you're sure you'll be all right, I ought to be leaving. I have to make an announcement to the press about your resignation."

"I'll be just fine." Laura struggled to keep her face straight, to force back the giddy, relieved laughter that suddenly threatened to overcome her sense of propriety.

"Good-bye, then," Roger said. He gave Laura a long, hard look, as if he still could not quite believe that she had ended their engagement. Or maybe he couldn't believe that she had done it without an emotional scene.

"I'll go with you, Roger," Marlene offered. "I'm sure you are going to need your public relations assistant when you meet the media. Good-bye for now, Laura, dear." As Marlene spoke she lifted her arms, almost as if she intended to embrace Laura. Perhaps the look in Laura's eyes stopped her, for a faint, puzzled line appeared on Marlene's smooth brow.

"Good-bye," Laura said. She stayed where she was, as the two of them walked across the beach toward the boardwalk. They did not touch. They were too savvy about public appearances for that, but they moved in unison, a remarkably good-looking couple of equal height, and only now did Laura realize that they were dressed very similarly. Both of them were wearing tan chino slacks rolled up at the ankles to keep them dry. Roger had on a navy polo shirt and Marlene wore the same style of shirt in pale blue.

A matched pair of cobras, Laura thought watching them. *I ought to be furious, but I don't give a damn about either of them. Which, I guess, tells me something about my true feelings for Roger.*

She turned her back on her ex-fiancé and his lover, to face the ocean instead. She took a few steps into the water, letting the salty coolness wash over her bare feet and her ankles, hoping the sea would carry away all unpleasant thoughts. But it didn't and her thoughts kept running round and round.

Something was wrong in her own life and the lives of the people she cared about. All of them were constantly on edge, worried, and never truly happy. Her father was all but retired at too early an age and he was bored with his inactivity. Laura suspected that he and her mother were no longer as content in their marriage as they had

24

once been. Her mother managed two households, one in a Philadelphia suburb and the other at the shore during the summers, but housekeeping didn't use up all of her energy and so she interfered in the lives of her children. Laura's brother, Bill, had joined a law firm in Texas in part to get away from his mother. Susan was doing something similar by immersing herself in the family clinic she was setting up, and Alberta Morrison was right when she protested that it was in a dangerous part of town. Susan was right, too, when she pointed out that people in that neighborhood deserved easy access to medical care, but she was trying to escape her mother as surely as Bill had done.

Laura herself was drifting through life. She knew she ought to be making better use of her talents than she had been doing in her job as Roger's assistant, and her emotional life was basically empty. Even Roger, who possessed a large fortune and had a brilliant future ahead of him, wasn't a happy man, either. He couldn't be, not when his life was so filled with dishonesty.

Each one of them—intelligent, well educated, and certainly not economically deprived—had somehow taken a wrong turn in life, had gotten lost along the way. Laura wished she could change things for the better, but she didn't know how. There was a vital piece missing from all of their lives, and she had no idea what it was or where it might be found.

At least I won't have to deal with Roger anymore, Laura thought. *No more watching everything I say or do. No more trying to turn myself into Roger's perfect fiancée, so I can later turn myself into his perfect wife. I can be me again, and plan my own life, to suit myself. Today I have taken the first step.*

But a step to where? she asked herself. *What will I do now? What happens next?*

Putting off another confrontation with her mother, who was probably lying in wait back at the house, ready for another argument, Laura lingered at the water's edge. She knew she was procrastinating, but she could not summon enough energy to leave the beach. A strange lassitude had fastened upon her. She put it down to emotional stress. Lazily, she swung first one foot and then the other through the water. The waves were getting higher as the tide came in. Water splashed up onto the white shorts and the gray sweatshirt Laura was wearing over her bathing suit. The water was agreeably warm, and she was contemplating the notion of taking a swim when her swinging foot struck something hard and she looked down.

"Sea glass," she said, poking at it with one toe. Pieces of old glass were a common sight along the shore. With their jagged edges worn smooth by the combined action of water and sand, the more brightly colored specimens were popular trophies among beachcombers. Laura's mother kept an ornamental glass jar filled with small pieces of sea glass on a table in the living room of their summer house.

This particular piece of sea glass was half-covered by sand, and when the wave lapping over it drew back toward the sea, the pale, blue-green color of the glass shone up at Laura with an unusual luster. A new wave rushed toward shore, bringing with it a long strand of brown seaweed that wrapped itself around Laura's ankle as if to keep her where she was when she would have retreated to drier ground. Bending down, she brushed the seaweed away. From this closer vantage point she could see that the odd piece of sea glass had been uncovered a little more by the sucking motion of the last wave. Thinking she could give it to her mother as a peace offering, Laura dug the glass out and sloshed it around in the water to remove the clinging sand.

That's funny; it looks as if there is a piece of gold caught inside the glass. Turning toward the afternoon sun, Laura raised the piece of glass to the sky, letting the sunlight shine through it.

The thing was the size and shape of a large hen's egg. Its surface was smooth and polished, with none of the usual cloudiness of sea glass, and showing no sign at all of abrasion by the sand in which it had been buried. The color was a clear aquamarine, the shade of tropic water near a southern island. Except for the tiny speck at its core, Laura could see no flaws in the strange object.

This can't be sea glass. It's something else. She continued to move the piece of glass about, trying to make the sunlight bounce off it from different angles so she could get a better view of the bit of gold inside it. The gold appeared to be the same shape as the glass itself. How could a piece of gold become embedded deep inside a chunk of glass? If hot, liquid glass had been poured into a mold to make the egg shape, wouldn't the heat have melted the gold? What was the temperature at which gold melted? Asking herself these questions, Laura frowned, staring into the aquamarine egg while she turned it around in her fingers.

Finally she got the angle just right, and a ray of sunlight struck the inner gold. Laura heard a clicking sound and the metal began to glow, turning from gold to red and then to white. Within a few seconds, the mysterious inner mote of foreign material was burning blue-white. The intense light began to hurt her eyes, while a low, whirring noise grated on her ears.

Acting on instinct, Laura tried to drop the glass egg, only to discover that she could not. It would not leave her fingers. She wanted to turn toward the lifeguards, to call to them for help, but she could not move. She was immobilized there on the beach, with the incoming waves swirling around her calves, with her hand raised and the egg-shaped piece of glass still held toward the sun between her thumb and forefinger.

Suddenly a ray of focused white light was projected outward by the strange object. The light seared across Laura's retinas, making her head spin, making her feel sick . . . and then the world around her exploded into light and devastating heat and pain. . . .

Chapter Two

The heat was unbearable. Perspiration covered Laura's face and throat. It dripped down her sides and her arms, and pooled between her breasts. Her sweatshirt was damp and sticky. Her first impulse was to remove the shirt, but the sun was so bright and hot that she feared its intense rays would soon burn her exposed skin. She settled for pulling the sweatshirt away from her body and flapping it to try to generate a slight air current. It was a useless effort. The air that brushed across her skin felt as if it had come directly from a furnace.

Where are my sunglasses? Lacking that vital piece of equipment, she was forced to squint in order to see. *Why is the sun so big? What just happened?*

She was still holding the aquamarine egg. The mysterious light inside it was extinguished and it looked like a piece of ordinary glass once more. Not knowing what else to do with it, Laura deposited the glass egg in the front pocket of her sweatshirt. Then, with a growing sense of confusion, she used both hands to shade her eyes while she looked around.

Everything she saw was colored in torrid shades, as if the entire world were on fire. The sky appeared to be made of burnished brass, and the sun flaming at its zenith was unquestionably larger than the sun Laura knew. The Atlantic Ocean was gone and so was the familiar strip of pale beach. From where she stood all Laura could see were orange-gold sand dunes, the cloudless, brazen sky, and the blistering sun. There was no shade, not a breath of wind, no sight or sound of seabirds or of any other life-forms, not even a bit of dune grass.

She soon discovered that she could not walk on the sand. It was too hot for her bare feet. When she took a step in any direction she felt as though she were walking on burning coals. With a yelp of pain she jumped back to the area, only about two feet square, where she had been standing when . . .

"When what?" she cried. "What is going on? Where am I? How did I get here?" There was no way to answer her questions. Another quick, squinting scan of the immediate area showed her that she was standing in a bowl-shaped depression in the sand, with the dunes forming an irregular border that blocked her distant view.

Maybe there's someone on the other side of the dunes, she thought. Raising her voice, she called, "Help! Help! Can anyone hear me?"

There was no response to her cries, though a faint murmur came to her ears, a sound as if the wind was rising.

"Great. All I need is a sandstorm," Laura muttered to herself, recalling movies she had seen in which giant whirlwinds of sand scoured everything in their path, leaving once-living animals as nothing more than mounds of bleached bones. To stave off the panic fluttering in her chest at that fearsome thought, she continued to talk to herself.

"Wouldn't you know it? Just when I start to get my life straightened out, something crazy has to happen! This is not what I had in mind when I was thinking about future possibilities. What in heaven's name am I supposed to do now?" She ended with a laugh that verged on hysteria.

"Stay calm, girl," she told herself. "Getting upset won't solve your problem. It doesn't matter how you got here, so don't worry about that right now. Deal with what you do know. You are apparently stranded in a desert. Therefore, you need water and shelter from the sun if you are going to survive. And you aren't going to find either if you just stay where you are. For all you know, there is an oasis on the other side of those dunes. What you have to do is walk to the top of the nearest dune and look around. To get there you have to balance the certainty of sunburn against the possibility of cool water and palm trees. Preferably, they'll be date palms, so you will have something to eat. You always did like dates. And who knows? When you reach that oasis, maybe there'll be a handsome sheik waiting for you."

While she talked to keep her courage up, Laura stripped off her only protection against the sun, her sweatshirt. The action left her wearing a pair of white shorts and a blue one-piece bathing suit. The perspiration on her skin dried almost the same instant that she removed the sweatshirt, proof to her that she would soon be badly dehydrated if she did not locate some kind of shelter.

Throwing the sweatshirt onto the sand a foot or so away from where she was, Laura stepped on it. Using the arms of the shirt to hold on to the fabric, she began an awkward, jerky progress toward the sand dune she had chosen, keeping the body of the shirt as a mat between her feet and the sand. The sand was so hot that the fabric was soon heated, but at least Laura could move without burning her feet. Her progress was slow, but she had a goal and she would not stop until she had reached it.

The sides of the sand dune were steep and the sand was loose. As she climbed, Laura slid back a step or two for every three steps she took toward the top. She was panting, breathing in hot, dry air, and she knew she was giving up vital body moisture with each breath she expired. But she would not stop, not even when she grew dizzy and tiny lights began to flash before her eyes. She could hear the wind rising. Apparently the sandstorm was moving closer, though she still could not feel a breeze, and the sky remained clear of dust clouds. Laura redoubled her efforts, determined to find shelter, or die trying.

When she reached the top of the dune and looked around, all she could see from horizon to horizon was more sand dunes. In all that desolate landscape there was no sign of life, and nothing that could possibly serve as shelter. In despair, Laura crouched atop her sweatshirt with her head bowed, telling herself not to cry because tears would deprive her of body fluid she could not afford to lose.

The windy sound was growing louder, but still no air brushed across her exposed skin. In her exhausted, emotionally overwrought state, it took Laura several minutes to realize that what she was hearing was not wind at all. It was a machine, and it was coming nearer.

Machines mean people, she thought, lifting her head. *People who can rescue me. I have to make them see me. I don't care if the soles of my feet burn right off; I'll stand on this hilltop and wave my sweatshirt to attract their attention.*

But she wasn't ready to burn her feet just yet. First she had to sight the machine. She stood up to search the dunes for a glimpse of it. She soon discovered that the machine wasn't on the ground. It was in the air. It was round and flat, with a dome in the middle of the upper side. Lights seemed to be blinking around the circular edge, but Laura couldn't be sure of that, because the sun was reflecting off the silvery surface of the ship. The closer it came, the larger the strange vehicle appeared to be, though there was no way for her to estimate its size with any degree of accuracy, since the only other objects in view were the sand dunes.

"Oh, my God!" Laura cried in a cracked voice. "It's a flying saucer, and it's landing right in front of me!"

In her alarm at the unexpected sight, she took a step backward, moving off the protection of her sweatshirt. At once the hot sand sent a painful signal through the soles of her feet. She tried to return to the fabric, but her feet tangled in the sleeves. The next thing she knew she was tumbling down the side of the sand dune, falling back into the bowl-shaped area from which she had so tediously climbed. Hot, stinging sand whirled around her, burning her skin until, with a cry of pain and fear, she landed on the exact spot from which she had begun. She knew it was the same place because it was the one small area where the sand did not scorch her badly burned skin. But it made no difference whether she was burned or not. The appearance of the alien ship had ended any hope she had of getting safely out of her predicament.

Laura watched in horror as the saucer-shaped vessel descended until it vanished from her sight behind the dunes. She was trapped—trapped and doomed, for if the creatures aboard the UFO now landing on the other side of the dunes did not find her, she would soon die of exposure to the heat and the sun. And if the aliens aboard that terrifying ship did discover her, what would they do to her?

They knew where she was. They must have seen her from the air, because she could hear them coming. How they climbed the sand dune without slipping and sliding as she had done she did not know, but she could hear steady footsteps crunching on the sand, as if a band of them was marching up the hill. After an agonizing few minutes she saw their helmets appearing over the rim of the nearest dune—oval, white helmets with black faceplates. As they advanced on her, Laura could see that they wore white suits, white gloves, and white boots.

They were humanoid in shape, and they seemed to be slender, for their suits were not bulky. There were six of them marching relentlessly down the near side of the dune from which Laura had just fallen. She stared at them, terror holding her transfixed, keeping her in a crouching posture as the six came onward.

Then, abruptly, something deep in Laura's heart rebelled against her fate. If she was to be captured by aliens, taken aboard their ship, and subjected to the humiliating examination she had read about in accounts of such abductions, then she would show these creatures what humans were really made of. There would be no screaming, no cringing, no tears from her. She reached across the burning sand for her crumpled sweatshirt. After shaking as much sand as possible out of it, she pulled it on again. Never taking her eyes from the oncoming aliens, she rose to her feet to stand firmly on the one little patch of sand that was a tolerable temperature. She held her arms at her sides, squared her shoulders, and lifted her chin in a gesture of defiance.

The six aliens stopped, as if they were startled by her action. Laura stared them down one by one, looking from one blank, black faceplate to the next, letting her searching gaze encompass each of her unwelcome visitors. There was silence for a long moment, until Laura decided to seize the initiative and speak first. To her frightened mind only one sentence seemed appropriate to the occasion.

"Take me to your leader," she said.

Chapter Three

One of the white-suited strangers stepped forward with arms spread wide, gloved hands held out, palms up.

"Sure," Laura said, nodding. "I get it. You come in peace." She pressed her lips firmly together so she couldn't scream in terror. Then she lifted her chin another notch and glared at the aliens. She hoped she looked stern and forbidding, but she was uncomfortably aware of how unprotected she was with her head and legs uncovered and no weapon available to her. If the strangers decided to attack her, there was no way for her to defend herself.

Another gesture from the creature who appeared to be in charge indicated Laura's midriff.

The gloved hand described an unmistakable shape.

"You have five fingers," Laura noted, watching the white glove move. "And I guess you're saying you want that piece of glass I found on the beach. Is it some kind of homing device? Is that how you found me?"

When the alien repeated the gesture, Laura folded her arms across her midriff, holding her sweatshirt close to her body. She could feel the glass egg deep in the pocket where she had put it. The rough handling the sweatshirt had received during her climb up the sand dune and, later, her fall back down it, had not dislodged the piece of glass from its fleecy nest.

"No way are you getting this," Laura said to the alien, speaking with sufficient forcefulness to make her point clear despite any language barriers. "As far as I can tell, this gadget I'm hiding is the only bargaining chip I have. If you want it, first you have to give me shelter, preferably air conditioned, and a large pitcher of cold water."

The aliens stood as if contemplating what to do next. Laura watched them warily, unsure what to expect and knowing she could not fight them. Much of her strength had been expended on the pointless climb up the sand dune. Her throat was parched and dry, and she could tell that her face and legs were already badly sand-burned and getting worse with each minute she spent beneath the blazing sun. Her arms and back weren't in much better condition, though at the moment her sweatshirt provided some protection. But she refused to back down. She was not going to hand over the mysterious egg. She might, however, consent to enter the spaceship, if only for the sake of getting into a shady spot before she succumbed to sunstroke.

As if the alien leader had read her mind, the white-sleeved arms reached out and caught Laura. She grabbed for the glass in her pocket, but it wasn't what the alien was after—at least, not at that particular moment. Laura was swung into the air, seized in alien arms—very strong alien arms—that held her securely. When she bit back an alarmed cry and instinctively wound her own arms around the neck of the impersonal black-and-white helmet, Laura discovered that the shoulder muscles beneath the white suit were remarkably well developed. From that moment on, she thought of the creature who held her as male.

Still carrying Laura, he retraced his route up the side of the sand dune and down the other side, heading for his ship. His five companions surrounded them, staying close, but as far as Laura could tell, they did not speak among themselves. As if Laura were weightless, the alien marched onward to where the circular ship awaited them. Laura regarded it with fear, knowing she could not avoid being taken inside. When the white-suited creatures and their captive approached the ship, a door slid open with a soft hiss of air, and a ramp descended. As soon as they were all inside the ship, the ramp retracted and the door closed again, smoothly, quietly, and without any action on the part of the six strangers.

The transition from the dry, ovenlike heat and glaring orange sunshine of the desert to the inside of the ship was pure bliss. Almost forgetting her fear in her relief at being out of the hot sun, Laura took a long breath of cool, slightly moist air, letting it fill her aching lungs. Soft lighting eased the burning discomfort of her eyes. The inside of the UFO was silver, like the outside, and there was a pale green stripe running along the floor. Laura decided it was a directional sign. She wriggled around, trying to stand, but her captor refused to release her.

The other five aliens began to divest themselves of their helmets and white suits. Before Laura could get a good look at them, the creature holding her started along the green-striped corridor that spiraled upward through the ship. Still silent, he continued at a steady pace until they reached an interior chamber. Again a door slid open at their approach and closed immediately after they had passed through it. The alien set Laura down on a high table, one of two in the center of the room. She was glad he wasn't going to make her stand. She wasn't sure her legs would hold her.

"I suppose this is the famous examining table I have read so much about?" Laura said, her voice high-pitched and quavering with barely suppressed fear. "Isn't this where you aliens shine bright lights in my eyes and stick needles into me?"

Her captor did not answer. Having released her from his arms, he moved to the far side of the room. And now a voice from the second examining table caught Laura's attention.

"Hua Te," someone said.

Laura was too surprised to respond. She had been so concerned with what the alien intended to do to her that she had not noticed there was someone else in the room.

Sitting cross-legged on the other examining table was an Asian man. His short black hair was lightly streaked with silver and he wore a loose, dark blue caftan. Laura was sure the man was human, but he did not look frightened. Perhaps he was better at hiding his fear than she was. At any rate, his expression was distinctly sympathetic.

"Hua Te," the man said again, touching his chest.

"Is that your name?" Laura asked. When the man remained silent, she touched her own chest. "Laura. I am Laura."

"Laura," the man repeated, pointing at her. Then, touching himself again, he said, "Hua Te."

"I'm pleased to meet you, Hua Te. I'm pleased to meet anyone who looks human. Do you speak English?" Swinging her legs over the side of the table, Laura sat facing Hua Te while she continued to ask questions. "Did they capture you, too? Do you know what they plan to do with us?" She halted when Hua Te shook his head to indicate that he did not understand her. Or perhaps he meant that she could not understand his language if he were to answer her.

Unfolding his legs, Hua Te jumped down from the table to cross the narrow space separating him from Laura. He took her hand and patted it in a kindly way. He continued to hold her hand when Laura jerked around in response to a noise behind her.

The alien who had carried her aboard the UFO had removed his white suit. Laura had expected to see a gray-skinned, big-eyed, hairless creature with thin arms and a delicate frame, like the aliens described by self-proclaimed UFO abductees, the same kind of aliens who were so often vividly portrayed on the front pages of supermarket tabloids. The person approaching her was neither gray-skinned nor hairless, and he was anything but delicate. He did not look like any alien Laura had ever read about or seen portrayed in the movies or on television.

He was about six feet tall, with flinty gray-blue eyes and dark hair. His tanned skin stretched smoothly over high cheekbones and a square, determined jaw. The body beneath his deep red tunic and the matching trousers that were tucked into calf-high boots indicated strong, flexible muscles. There was a raw, masculine energy contained within his smoothly controlled movements, and Laura had experienced his strength in the ease with which he had carried her across the sand and into the ship.

His eyes met hers, cool mystery boring into her frightened brown gaze. The shock of that startlingly intimate contact made Laura stop breathing for a moment. In fact, it seemed to her that everything had stopped, as if the world itself had halted its eternal spinning. Only when the man averted his gaze from hers did Laura begin to breathe again; only then did the earth resume its normal motion.

She was still sitting on the side of the examining table, with her legs hanging down and Hua Te holding her hand. As her captor drew nearer, Hua Te dropped her hand and stepped back.

"This is it, isn't it?" Laura asked, seeing the needle and the small silver device the man approaching her was holding. She knew what the needle was for, but she did wonder about the unknown device, which looked like a computer chip. "This is where you start examining me. But why? You are human, aren't you? Or are you some special kind of robot that only looks human? What do you want with me?" Despite her intention to be brave, the last question came out as a terrified squeak.

Laura looked at Hua Te, who was indicating with gestures and by his expression that she should not be afraid. But she was afraid. She had never been so frightened in her life. Then her captor put out a hand, caught her chin in his warm fingers, and turned her face until she was once more gazing into the gray-blue depths of his eyes.

He spoke to her in a low, compelling voice. She could not understand what he was telling her, but she found that she did not want to tear her eyes from his. For some reason beyond her comprehension, she trusted him. Not his mysterious, white-suited companions. Only him. He was breathing slowly and deeply, and she discovered that she was involuntarily matching his breathing, looking into his smoky, fathomless eyes. . . .

She felt a needle prick behind her left ear, then a quick, jabbing pain. Laura winced. The man stepped away from her.

"The discomfort should be minimal," he said. "It will cease to be uncomfortable in a few moments, as your body adjusts to the implant."

"What did you do?" Laura asked. "I can understand you now."

"I have inserted a translation device just behind your ear," he said. "Does it still hurt?"

"No." Laura rubbed at the spot. "I can't feel a thing back there."

"Good." He moved away, going to a table laden with metal instruments.

"Was the little chip I saw the device you implanted?" Laura asked.

"Yes." His voice was clipped, abrupt.

"Does it work for every language?" Now that she was able to understand what he was saying, her fear subsided to a manageable level. If she could talk to this man, and to his companions, then she might be able to reason with them and convince them to let her go.

"As far as we know, the translator is universally effective," the man said.

"The creation of such a device is a remarkable

achievement," Laura said, thinking it would be a good idea to flatter him a little.

"It was a necessary achievement." He continued to speak in the same abrupt manner.

"You are a scientist," Laura said. "You must be, to be so dispassionate."

"Dispassionate?" Having laid down the needle next to others of varying sizes, he faced her again, one eyebrow cocked in a quizzical way, one corner of his mouth lifted in sardonic humor. "I assure you I am anything but dispassionate, especially about my work."

"Does your work include experimenting on fellow humans?" Laura demanded. When he did not respond but merely stood gazing at her, she asked, "You are human, aren't you?"

"Yes." The corner of his mouth lifted upward again. "Are you?"

"Of course I am!"

"That is what Hua Te said. Yet it is plain to see that the two of you are very different." He looked from Laura to Hua Te and back again, and something flickered in the depths of his eyes. "I find the disparity interesting. Among the Kheressians, we do not have such differences."

"Kheressians," Laura repeated. "I've never heard of them before. Are they your people?"

"Yes." Again his response was abrupt and peculiarly disinterested.

"Are we on Earth?" Laura asked.

"Where else would we be?" His gaze sharpened. "Do you know souls from other worlds?"

"Not personally," Laura answered him. "Some

45

people say aliens have made contact with us. Other people say that's nonsense, that those who claim to have met aliens are lying, or imagining things."

"And what do you say?" he asked, as if her answer was of great interest to him.

"I don't know what the truth is. When I first saw you and your friends in those white space suits, I thought you were aliens. But you're not, are you?"

"Not space suits; desert suits," he said.

"What?" She stared at him, not understanding.

"We wear them when we journey to the arid portions of the earth," he explained. "The suits protect us against the heat and the dryness."

"I could have used one while I waited for you to find me," Laura said. She regarded him with wary interest, unsure what his next move would be and trying to convince herself that the effect his nearness was having on her heart rate and her breathing had more to do with her fear than with his masculine strength or the aura of carefully controlled emotion that surrounded him.

"I will take the timestone now," he said.

"The what?"

"The blue, egg-shaped object that you found. I want it." He held out his hand, waiting.

"Finders, keepers," Laura said, irritated by his abrupt manner. "It's mine now."

"It has served its purpose and will not function again without extensive repairs," he said. "Give it to me."

"If it's not functioning, why do you want it?"

46

But, under the compulsion of his intense eyes, she reached into her sweatshirt pocket and pulled out the glass egg. She put it into his outstretched hand, her fingers brushing against his skin when she released her grip on the egg.

She had the answer to one of her many questions. After touching and being touched by him, she had no doubt that there was warm blood pulsing through his strong, masculine body. He had told her the truth. He was human, or something very close to human. And he was the most magnetic male she had ever encountered.

"Is it a homing device?" Laura asked, tearing her eyes from his face to glance at the glass egg he now held. "Is that how you found me?"

"Your questions will be answered later," he said, and pocketed the timestone. "You will want to replenish your fluid levels." Turning to a niche built into the wall, he pressed a button. Liquid gurgled into a tall, crystalline cup.

"I am thirsty," Laura admitted, "and I'm sure I have a bad sunburn." Accepting the cup from him, she drank deeply of its pale blue contents. She was too dehydrated to worry about what was in the liquid. Her body craved the moisture, and it tasted like cold, clean water. At the moment, the blue liquid was all that mattered to her.

"I regret that you were kept waiting in the desert for so long," the man said. He watched her drink, his eyes on her slender throat. "Our arrival was delayed because we were retrieving Hua Te."

"You mean you were kidnapping him at the same time you were kidnapping me," Laura said.

"With the help of that timestone of yours."

"Kidnapping?" he repeated, looking astonished. "What a strange word to apply to a scientific project."

"Are you saying this is one of those weird, expensive, top-secret government projects I keep hearing about on television exposé programs?" Laura cried. "As a taxpayer, I have a right to know what is going on here! Where am I? Where are you taking me? And what are you going to do with me when we get there? For that matter, why was I chosen to be part of your cursed project? I most certainly did not volunteer!"

"You would not have become dehydrated if you had remained where you first found yourself," he told her, ignoring her angry questions. "The area of sand where you arrived was cool enough to prevent physical harm to you. You should have stayed there."

"Well, I had no way of knowing that I wasn't supposed to move," she snapped at him. "No one bothered to inform me that I was supposed to stand on a tiny patch of sand and await your blessed coming."

"I apologize for your inconvenience." There was laughter in his voice and in the depths of his eyes.

"What is your name?" she asked, speaking as if she intended to report him to his boss. And she just might, if she could discover who his boss was. She could see his growing amusement at her anger, and that made her even angrier.

"I am Kentir." With that, he started toward the

door. "I'll see to it that you have food, adequate liquid refreshment, and a private place to rest. And suitable clothing," he added, with a lingering glance at her bare legs and sandy feet.

"Am I to consider myself a prisoner?" Laura demanded, fear rising anew in her heart.

"Say, rather, a guest. An honored guest," Kentir replied. "You and Hua Te are free to speak together, and you may explore the ship as you wish, so long as you do not interfere with its operation."

"Will you be listening to everything we say?" Laura asked.

"Eavesdropping is a rudeness to which I would not descend," Kentir said.

"People who would descend to kidnapping will descend to anything." Laura's snappy response elicited a genuine smile from him. It transformed his harsh, rather solemn features. Just for a moment, he looked younger, boyish, almost mischievous. Then the smile was gone and he was serious again.

"It is natural for you to have many questions," Kentir said. "They will be answered when we have reached our destination and all of us have assembled."

"Assembled where?" Laura wasn't going to back down. She didn't want to wait for answers. She wanted them right away. If she was left without an explanation she knew she would soon give in to the panic that was threatening her ability to think.

"At Issa," Kentir said in response to her ques-

49

tion about their destination. "We are going to Issa."

"What is Issa?" Laura asked Hua Te a few minutes after Kentir had gone. She had spent the interval experimenting with the button in the wall niche and had succeeded in producing another cup of the blue liquid. Having consumed it, she felt much restored. She was still frightened but, since she hadn't been hurt or even examined yet, she was beginning to hope that what had happened to her was all a mistake. She could not believe Kentir meant to harm her. Surely she would be returned home soon. If Kentir and his companions wanted her to swear never to reveal anything she had seen or heard while aboard their ship, she would gladly make such a promise. "Hua Te, do you know what Kentir was talking about?"

"He has revealed more to you than he has to me," Hua Te replied.

"You don't seem to be very upset at finding yourself forced aboard a UFO," Laura said, turning from the wall niche to face him. Now that she was standing right next to Hua Te, she discovered that he was just her height and slender in build. She sensed a quiet strength in him that was more a matter of mental attitude than muscle power. She could not discern his age. There was silver in his black hair, but his face was unlined and his dark eyes held a youthful sparkle.

"What has happened, has happened," Hua Te said with calm composure. "I am certain there is much to be learned while I am here. Kentir has promised that the purpose behind my abduction to this remarkable vessel will soon be revealed. I believe him to be an honest man. Therefore, for the present, I will practice patience and careful observation."

"Yes, well, Oriental philosophy may be fine for you, but I'm afraid I am not a very patient person," Laura said rather sharply.

"You will learn, in time. You are still very young."

"I am twenty-four years old," Laura said, still in the same sharp tone of voice.

"An age that seems remarkably youthful to me." Hua Te's smile took away any reproach for the rudeness of Laura's words. Fine lines crinkled around his eyes, as if he smiled often, and he exuded such warmth and good humor that Laura began to relax.

"I'm sorry if I have been behaving badly, Hua Te," she said. "I find it frightening to be snatched away from my ordinary life and set down in a strange place among people who won't tell me what is going on, or why they have brought me here. I guess the excitement has made me forget my manners. All I want is to go home." But if she was allowed to return home, would she ever see Kentir again? The question entered her mind with disturbing force, surprising her. She didn't even know the man; what could it matter whether she saw him again or not?

"The day has been disconcerting," Hua Te said, nodding his agreement with Laura's sentiments.

"Perhaps, if you will tell me about your ordinary life, the information will shed some light on our present situation. There may be a connection between the two of us, some reason why we were selected by these strangers."

"That's a good idea." Laura made herself stop thinking about Kentir, so she could pay attention to Hua Te's suggestion. "We'll exchange information." She was about to launch into a description of how she had found the glass egg at the edge of the sea, when the door slid open to admit a woman.

"I am Imilca," the newcomer said, advancing into the room. She appeared to be a few years older than Laura. Her curly, reddish blond hair was pulled back at the nape of her neck in a simple style, and her slender form was clothed in a dark red tunic and matching trousers very similar to the outfit Kentir had been wearing. "If you will come with me, I'll show you to cabins where you may rest.

"You will require medical attention," Imilca continued, her soft gray eyes skimming quickly over Laura's face and legs. "I suspect that beneath your clothing, your back and arms are also burned. I will send for Renan, who is the doctor of the project."

"What project?" Laura asked.

"Did Kentir not tell you that everything will be explained after we reach Issa?" Imilca said. Gesturing toward the door, she added, "If you will follow me, please."

"I want an explanation now." Laura planted

her feet firmly on the floor and refused to move.

"I can explain this much to you," Imilca said. "I am a teacher and a behavior specialist. I was accepted into the project because of my skill at explaining difficult subjects to students who do not have the necessary educational background for complete understanding."

"In other words, you think Hua Te and I are stupid," Laura said in an unpleasant tone.

"Not at all. But I am constrained to obey the orders I have been given," Imilca responded with a smile. "While I cannot immediately answer the questions that most perplex you, I can introduce you to the other members of our ship's crew, and I can tell you a little about our civilization and our history. However, I do think you will be more comfortable after a bath and fresh clothing have been provided—not to mention treatment for your burned skin and perhaps something more to drink."

Laura had the distinct feeling that she was being manipulated by Imilca's apparent concern for her well-being into doing what her captors wanted her to do. She glanced at Hua Te to see how he was taking Imilca's instructions. The corners of Hua Te's mouth curved upward and he had a definite twinkle in his eyes, as if he was enjoying himself.

"Imilca's suggestions seem reasonable to me," Hua Te said.

"Thank you, Hua Te." Imilca beamed at him. Returning her attention to Laura, she went on, "You have no reason to fear us. Have we threatened you? Or harmed you in any way?"

"Aside from snatching me away from my home, no," Laura conceded. "At least, not yet."

"Then will you accept my invitation to make yourself more comfortable?"

"All right," Laura agreed, somewhat ungraciously. "I'll go along with whatever your arrangements are. Just for the time being, you understand. I reserve the right to change my mind and raise objections later."

"For the time being," Imilca repeated with a little laugh. "What an interesting phrase. Time being what it is, your decision is a wise one." She moved to the door, which immediately slid open. Imilca waited patiently while Laura and Hua Te exchanged a glance of silent agreement before they went with her into the corridor.

Imilca and her charges followed the green direction line on the floor until they reached a lower level of the ship. There, Imilca showed Laura to a small cabin that was just across the corridor from where Hua Te was housed. Laura was glad he would be nearby. She was beginning to think of him as a friend.

Promising to return soon, Imilca left Laura alone. As soon as she was gone, Laura tested the door. It opened with no difficulty, and when she stepped into the corridor there were no guards posted to prevent her from going wherever she wanted. Encouraged by this sign that she was not a closely guarded prisoner, Laura returned to her cabin and began to explore it.

The floor, walls, and ceiling of the cabin were

all made of the same silvery metal. The only furniture was a narrow bed built into one wall and three empty drawers built into the opposite wall. There were no portholes, nor was there any object in the cabin that might provide an answer to any of Laura's many questions.

Since she was feeling gritty from the sand clinging to her skin and still a bit overheated from sunburn, Laura decided to follow Imilca's instructions on how to use the shower in the bathroom that opened from her cabin. As warm water sluiced the sand and salt from her hair and body, she tried to make her mind a blank, to relax and let herself accept that she had no control over her immediate future. Perhaps she would do well to adopt Hua Te's attitude that what could not be changed ought to be accepted, and that there was something to be learned from what had happened to them.

She came out of the bathroom in an improved state of mind, wearing only the pale green towel she had found hanging from a hook on the wall, to discover Imilca waiting for her. With Imilca was a man whom she introduced as Renan, the project physician.

Renan appeared to be in his midthirties. Not a person who would stand out in a crowd, he had brown hair and gray eyes and was of medium height and build. Though he was pleasant enough, he lacked Kentir's compelling magnetism, and he was no more forthcoming with information than either Kentir or Imilca had been. Yet something about Renan's plain face and quiet manner soothed Laura's lingering apprehensions, even as the lotion he provided eased the discomfort of her sunburn. She watched in fascination as the redness and blisters disappeared from her legs and from her shoulders and arms. When she reentered the bathroom to dress, Laura saw in the polished section of wall that served as a mirror that the skin of her face also appeared to be healed. On closer scrutiny she noticed that a couple of minor blemishes that had annoyed her for days were gone along with the sunburn.

By the time she finished pulling on the dark red tunic and trousers made of a soft, silky fabric, and the comfortable flat sandals Imilca had provided, Laura began to think that whatever these people intended for her and Hua Te, it would not be as terrible as she had first feared. It might even prove to be an interesting adventure. Hoping that a bit of diplomacy would lead to information about what awaited her, she apologized to Imilca for her earlier sharpness of tongue.

"Of course you are angry and frightened, in spite of our assurances that you will not be harmed," Imilca said. "I understand, and I thank you for your apology. Now, would you like to visit the bridge? Hua Te has asked me to conduct him there. We will be delighted if you will join us."

Believing Imilca's offer could be the opening she sought for the answers to her questions, Laura at once agreed.

Chapter Four

It seemed to Laura that she, Imilca, and Hua Te walked along miles of silvery, upward-spiraling corridor before they reached the bridge. They passed several men and women on the way. Each was dressed in dark red tunic and trousers, and each smiled and offered a polite greeting. Imilca scarcely slowed her brisk pace, so there was no opportunity for Laura to ask questions of anyone. While there were many doors along the corridor, all of them were closed, allowing no glimpses inside the various compartments and cabins. Laura's initial fears had been muted by the kind way in which Imilca and Renan treated her, but her curiosity was rapidly approaching an intolerable level.

"Imilca, can this ship be taken into outer space?" Laura asked.

"It is not meant for long-distance travel, though it can be converted for space," Imilca answered. "Once, we made great spaceships, but all of them are gone now."

"What do you mean, gone?" Laura asked.

"You will learn later about the Great Departure," Imilca said. Her voice and smile were tinged with sadness. "We have reached the bridge. From it you will be able to see where we are flying."

They stepped through a sliding door into the uppermost, domed area that Laura had noticed on her first sighting of the ship. The clear windows all around the dome provided an unobstructed view of the sky, and beyond the edge of the saucer, Laura could glimpse the land over which they were passing. Despite her curiosity, she gave these interesting surroundings only a cursory glance, for her full attention was at once caught by the tall, broad-shouldered figure standing in the center of the bridge next to a large chair secured to a swiveling mechanism. By the number of controls surrounding it, the chair could only be the captain's position.

"Is Kentir the captain of this ship?" Laura asked Imilca.

"He is also the project leader," Imilca answered her.

Kentir heard them and turned. He looked a little startled to see her. Laura couldn't tell whether it was because she was on the bridge, or because by his standards she was at last decently clothed.

While Imilca began to explain the purposes of the various auxiliary control consoles set about the bridge, and Hua Te followed her, listening intently to what she was saying and asking the occasional question, Laura moved toward Kentir as if pulled by a magnet. Her gaze was on his face and she could not make herself look away. He was staring at her as if he wanted to devour her. She halted when she was just a few inches away from him.

Kentir did not touch her, but Laura had the sensation that his hand had reached out to stroke along her cheek and push back a lock of her short hair that had fallen across her face. She could almost feel the errant lock of hair moving back into place. When Kentir broke the eye contact and turned his back on her, Laura began to tremble.

"You will find the bridge interesting," he said, speaking over his shoulder.

"Yes, it's very interesting." Laura told herself not to read more into Kentir's intense scrutiny than he meant. She was an oddity to him, perhaps a laboratory specimen to be observed, but that was all. There was nothing personal in his regard of her.

Kentir bent forward to check the controls. He spoke a few words to a woman who sat at a console a few feet away. The woman answered him. Kentir checked the controls again.

Laura grasped the back of the captain's chair to steady herself while she watched the way the movement of his shoulder muscles stretched the thin red fabric of his tunic. She knew he had dismissed her from his thoughts, that all of his attention was on his ship, yet the sensation of his fingertips caressing her cheek lingered in her mind. Then Hua Te called to her to come and see the land over which they were flying, and Laura put her foolish idea away.

"I am familiar with many maps," Hua Te said when Laura joined him and Imilca at one of the large viewing ports, "yet I am unable to determine our present location."

"Are those the Alps?" Laura asked, looking across the downward-sloping surface of the ship's body to a series of jagged gray peaks that thrust skyward.

"I do not think so," Hua Te answered. He shook his head in perplexity. "I have seen the Alps. The mountains below us are different, not only in their shape, but in the color of the bare rocks at their peaks. Furthermore, I see no ice or snow on these mountains. We are flying over some other part of the world than Europe."

"You're right," Laura agreed. "When I was kidnapped, I was on the American side of the Atlantic. We haven't been flying long enough to reach Europe. Not at our present speed. What is that gigantic lake?" She paused to look more closely at the landscape far below, and then at the sky and the position of the abnormally large sun, before continuing, "Imilca, is that Canada beneath us? We are heading north, aren't we?"

"Perhaps a global view will help you to locate

yourselves correctly," Imilca said. She glanced toward the captain's chair. "Kentir, may I have your permission to show them the Earthchart?"

"Certainly," Kentir responded with a quick nod, not taking his eyes off his instruments. "There is no reason why they shouldn't receive a geography lesson."

Laura was about to tell Kentir that she, too, was familiar with maps and did not need any lessons. Then Imilca pressed a button on a nearby metal column that served as a waist-high table. At once Laura's attention was diverted from Kentir to the display Imilca had produced.

A light set below the surface of the table sent a beam upward to touch a spherical silver object attached to the ceiling. In the light a holographic image of the earth appeared, rotating in the air midway between table and ceiling. The detail on the image was remarkable. Laura saw blue oceans, green land masses, tall mountains rising in relief, and red-gold deserts that formed a wide, unbroken ring around the equator.

"We use the holographic images to navigate our ships," Imilca explained. "Arad is our expert, but today he is flying with Kentir's brother, Thuban.

"We are approximately here," Imilca said, pointing to a spot between the equator and the North Pole. "As you guessed, we are flying northward. Issa lies here." She pointed again, this time to a long peninsula that jutted into the sea near the North Pole.

"But this is not a map of the earth!" Laura

cried, just as Hua Te made a similar exclamation.

"Of course it is Earth," Imilca said, but she looked upset and her face was drained of color.

"Imilca," Laura insisted, "something is wrong with the image. Why does it show so much desert? Where's North America? Where is Africa? And I don't see Antarctica."

"Is there anything you do recognize?" Kentir asked. There was nothing indifferent about his attitude now. He left the captain's position to join the three who stood around the table.

"Well," Laura said, watching the globe rotate, "if we are looking at a historical map—or, I should say, a prehistorical map, the kind geologists invent on computers to use as illustrations for television shows—then the biggest land mass might be South America and Africa, joined together and just beginning to separate here, where this long river runs southward." She traced the line of the river with a finger before continuing.

"I know some geologists have a theory that the two continents were once one large continent. But the whole thing is too far north. And I suppose the piece of land on the other side of the globe might be Australia, or maybe a distorted version of Antarctica." She pointed to a gigantic island in what seemed to be the South Pacific Ocean. "It's hard to tell. Nothing on this globe looks familiar to me. The continents are out of place and none of them are the right shape."

"I have the same impression," Hua Te said. "Every point of reference with which I am familiar is absent from the image before us. By the way, Imilca, I should like to know how this marvelous image in the air is produced. There is nothing like it in my time."

"Your time?" Laura exclaimed, shocked by the implication of his last words. "Hua Te, are you saying that you believe we have traveled through time?"

"Certainly," Hua Te answered her. "It is the only explanation for what has happened to us. In the time into which I was born, there are no flying machines, nor are there maps like the remarkable globe we see here, though wise men everywhere are aware that the world is round. Therefore, I conclude that I have been transported to a different time, or to a different world, or both. And so have you been transported, Laura.

"You have assured me that we are flying over Earth," Hua Te went on, speaking to Imilca, "which eliminates the possibility that we are visiting another world. The only other possibility is that Laura and I are now in a time so distant from our own that the face of the earth is altered beyond our recognition. I would like to know whether we have been moved into the past or sent to the future."

Laura decided an adherence to Oriental philosophy offered advantages that she ought to investigate at her first opportunity. While her head was spinning faster than the holographic globe in front of her and she feared she would faint at any moment from the stress of trying to comprehend the enormity of Hua Te's conclusions, he appeared to be perfectly calm and completely accepting of what had been done to him.

"You have been brought to the past," Kentir said.

"The timestone!" Laura exclaimed. "That's how you did it. The glass egg I found is a miniature time machine."

"That is correct," Kentir said. "The timestones also contain tracking devices, as you guessed, so we can locate our visitors."

"Your gadget almost got lost," Laura told him. "I discovered it buried in the sand at the edge of the ocean."

"Whereas my timestone appeared on a table in a room high in a city house," Hua Te said.

"That's not a very efficient way to use what must be an expensive device," Laura said to Kentir.

"On the contrary," he said, "it is the simplest means of employing a timestone. One of the most dependable characteristics of an intelligent human being is curiosity. A human who finds a peculiar object will almost invariably pick it up and then lift it toward a light source in order to see it better. The inner mechanism of each timestone is set to be activated when a ray of natural light strikes it. The timestone then returns to its time of origin, carrying with it the person who is holding it."

"However," Imilca said when Kentir paused for a moment, "because of the rotation of the earth during the hour or two when the timestone is away from us, it will return to a different place.

The mechanism does need refining. We are working on that."

"I am glad to hear it!" Laura said, as sarcastically as she could. "Would it be too much to ask why you have done this to us?"

"You are here because we need your help," Imilca said. "Truly, we mean no harm to you."

"Help?" Laura repeated. "What kind of help can you possibly expect after you have kidnapped us?"

"You will learn more later," Kentir said, in a way that indicated he would have no more to say on the subject until he was ready.

"Later isn't good enough," Laura cried. "I want to know exactly how far into the past you have brought Hua Te and me." She was beyond the calming effects of Oriental philosophy, beyond anything but fear and horror. At that moment, all she wanted to do was run across the familiar beach at Ventnor, then down the street to her family's summer home, to race up the porch steps and into the living room and find her parents sitting there. She tried to tell herself she was in the middle of a terrible nightmare, but somehow the familiar southern New Jersey shore seemed very far away.

"We believe you have come to us over a distance of perhaps half a million years," Kentir said.

"You *believe?*" Laura yelled at him. "Don't you *know?*"

"Over so vast a stretch of time, it is impossible to be precise, though we are working on a more accurate timing device for the timestones," Kentir said. With a wave of one hand toward the spinning globe, he went on, "You tell us that the map of Earth is greatly changed in your time. It is possible that the length of a year has also changed. Our year is three hundred and sixty days long."

"Ours is three hundred and sixty-five days long," Laura said. It took all of her courage to put aside her outrage and her fear so she could answer him in a rational way. "Plus an extra quarter day. Plus a few more seconds here and there."

"So." Kentir's dark eyebrows rose at this information. "My prediction was correct."

"Is this a true representation of the way the earth rotates in this time?" Hua Te said, indicating the constantly moving holographic image.

"It is." Kentir looked from the globe to Hua Te. "Why do you ask?"

"In my time," Hua Te said, "the earth's axis is not upright. It is tilted."

"He's right," Laura put in, her interest caught in spite of the chill pervading her heart. "The axis is inclined twenty-three degrees and twenty-seven minutes to the plane of the earth's orbit around the sun. The tilt is what gives us our seasons. I earned a perfect grade in Earth Science in high school," she added defiantly when they all stared at her in surprise at the exactness of her knowledge.

"In this time, it is different." Kentir's lips closed tightly on the short sentence. He touched the button on the table, and the holographic globe vanished. Without another word Kentir returned to the captain's chair. There he sat, his long fingers gripping the chair arms, his dark brows drawn together in frowning concentration.

"If you would like to observe our approach to Issa, you may sit in any of the chairs near the viewports." Imilca's gentle voice broke the strained silence.

"Thank you." With calm aplomb, Hua Te took the chair by a viewport that Imilca indicated. She sat next to him and they began to talk in low voices.

Laura stayed beside the table, watching Kentir, wondering if his frowning attention was entirely directed toward his ship, or whether some of it was centered on the information she and Hua Te had just provided. Or was he contemplating the problem that was so desperate, so pressing, that he had been forced to stoop to kidnapping in order to solve it?

What Laura had learned in return for the information she had given to Kentir and Imilca was an impossible story. It was ridiculous. It must be lies. People could not travel through time.

And yet, she believed Kentir's claims. An innocent piece of sea glass had proven to be a time machine in disguise. It had transported her into a past so distant from her own world that Laura could barely comprehend the time span involved. It was enough to reduce any thinking person to a state of whimpering terror. But Laura refused to give in to that encroaching terror. She hoped she could learn to accept the terrible facts with the same calm spirit Hua Te was displaying. She did not see that she had much choice in the matter.

When Imilca beckoned to her to join them, Laura went to sit between Hua Te and the woman from the distant past, and she spent the rest of the flight staring through the nearest viewport at a world she did not recognize.

Chapter Five

The contrast between the desert where Laura had first landed and the city of Issa was remarkable. Where the desert had been a dead place painted in shades of brassy orange and red, Issa was the cool blue and white of northern latitudes, decorated by the vivid greens of fresh plant life and the bright colors of flowers.

As Laura had seen on the holographic globe, Issa was set so far north that it lay just within the Arctic Circle—except, Laura reminded herself, that no Arctic Circle had yet been thought of or described on any map. She had asked Imilca about it and Imilca hadn't understood. According to Imilca, the Kheressians didn't use latitude or longitude, but had developed their own system for determining position while navigating.

Despite Issa's northern location, the temperature was definitely not arctic. Laura wore only the red tunic, trousers, and sandals Imilca had given her, with no outer coat, yet she was not cold. The climate of Earth in the distant time in which Laura found herself was as different from that she had known as was the map.

Kentir brought his ship to a stop on a bare field that served as a landing area, and which boasted only a single, oblong stone building as control tower and passenger terminal. Once the final details of shutting down the ship were completed, they all disembarked, and Kentir led the company on a walk of a mile or so into the city. No one seemed to think it odd that they should walk, and Laura was so interested in what she was seeing that it did not occur to her to question the fact that they went on foot. She found it a wonderful way to get a close look at the landscape.

The road they took was wide and paved with finely cut stones that were worn and rutted from long use. From the look of them the ruts had been made by wheels, yet there were no wheeled vehicles to be seen. Nor were there any other people on the road.

The way lay up a slight incline, and at the top Laura halted to look around. Behind her in the distance a low range of mountains rose, their sides heavily forested. The airfield was located on a rolling plain that stretched from the base of the mountains to the horizon on either side. In front of Laura, just a short distance away, lay the open sea. The unobstructed view gave the impression of boundless space, and the lack of any outstanding geographical features produced a sense of enduring serenity. It was a pleasant setting for a city, particularly if the climate was always as balmy as on the present day, when the sky was a clear and cloudless blue.

In those first, brief moments of her contemplation of Issa, Laura experienced an odd contentment, as if she were where she was meant to be. Afterward, she thought about the initial impact Issa had made on her and wondered if it had been no more than an illusion, for her next reaction was less positive.

The hill on which Laura and her companions stood sloped downward to the city and the sea. To Laura's left, white waves foamed upon a sandy shore, while on her right lay a stone wharf that defined a harbor, where the water was apparently much deeper. At the end of the wharf rose a stone tower that could only be a lighthouse. But lighthouse and wharf were both crumbling and there were no ships in the harbor. There was not even a rowboat or a small sailboat.

"No fishing, no shipping, no pleasure craft," Laura said to Hua Te. "And, therefore, no need to keep the seaport in good repair. I wonder why? I'm sure if we ask, they won't tell us."

"Are you coming?" Kentir called. He had walked ahead of them and now he paused, waiting until Laura and Hua Te caught up with him. Then he proceeded down the hill and into the city along the stone-paved road, with the others following at their own pace.

71

Once they left the low crest of the hill, they were within the suburbs of Issa. On either side of the road stood large villas, each separated from its neighbors by a shoulder-high stone wall. From the overgrown villa gardens long branches of flowering shrubs tumbled over the tops of the walls. Weeds and grasses, and even a few saplings here and there, sprouted out of chinks in the broken stones. The houses behind the walls were obviously deserted. There was no one to stare at the two strangers from another time who walked into the city in company with a group of Kheressians, using a route that, to judge by the depth of the ruts in the stone paving, had seen centuries of constant use. Laura wanted to stop and look at the riotous plant growth and at the houses, but Kentir maintained a steady pace that did not permit dawdling.

Laura could see that Issa was a city at least as ancient as the road that led into it. Possibly it was far older. Some of the buildings at the outskirts of town looked as if they had been there since the very beginning of time and were currently in the process of decaying and returning to the earth from which their stones had originally been quarried. The buildings in the center of the city were in better condition, though all of them showed signs of long exposure to the elements.

Every building Laura saw in Issa was constructed entirely of gigantic blocks of stone. Despite the size of the individual stones, many of the buildings conveyed a lightness and delicacy that was remarkably pleasing to the eye. They passed one structure with an outline reminiscent of the silhouette of the Taj Mahal. Laura slowed to gape at it, impressed by the elegance and beauty wrought out of the stone. A little farther on, another building boasted a soaring steeple like that of a Gothic cathedral. When they came to a crossroad, Laura looked down the final, gently angled slope of the hill toward the sea and saw a domed, columned edifice that struck a note of recognition in her memory, though she could not think where she had seen anything exactly like it. Off to one side in a parklike open space stood a small pyramid with its top lopped off to make a flat platform. In a neat line flanking it were three smaller pyramids, and these all boasted the pointed tops that usually crowned a pyramid shape.

"Hua Te," Laura said, "do you recognize any of the architectural styles we see here?"

"Indeed," Hua Te answered her at once. "During my travels I have seen pyramids, as well as buildings with graceful columns similar to those." He indicated the domed building that Laura had already noticed.

"Would it be overly fanciful of me to think we are observing the precursors of the various architectural styles that still exist in the twentieth century?" Laura asked. "Is such a thing possible? After all, most of our buildings are based on architecture from previous eras." She was a little surprised at the way Hua Te went still at her words and stared at her intently for a moment or two before he responded to her question.

73

"The twentieth century," Hua Te said, speaking slowly and with an odd absence of emotion, as if he was trying hard to prevent his feelings from spilling over into his words. "No, Laura, I do not consider your observation at all fanciful. After what has occurred to us on this day, I believe anything is possible.

"Have you noticed the masonry?" Hua Te asked, speaking more briskly than before as he revealed his interest in their remarkable surroundings. "All of the stones used in the construction of these buildings have been cut so perfectly that they fit together without mortar."

"I wonder where they got the stones," Laura said. "I didn't see any sign of a quarry when we flew in over the plain, which means the builders had to transport each block of stone from somewhere else. Just as the builders of the pyramids in Egypt did. And, like the pyramids, this city was built to last for eternity. But it looks as if it has seen happier days. Imilca, where is everyone?" Laura asked of the woman who was walking beside Hua Te.

"They have gone," Imilca answered, sighing. "With only a few of us left, we no longer have either the time or the spirit to make the city a cheerful place. I can remember when there were flower sellers on every corner in Issa, when the harbor was filled with ships loaded with cargoes from all over the world, and the streets rang with voices speaking in the tongues of many lands. In those days, folk came from far places to visit Great Issa."

"What happened to change all of that?" Laura asked, knowing as she spoke that she probably wasn't going to receive an answer to satisfy her curiosity.

"The end is drawing near," Imilca said. "Most of our people have fled. Only we who serve under Kentir's command are left."

"Repent, for the end of the world is at hand," Laura murmured. She looked around, half expecting to see someone carrying a sign through the beautiful, yet gloomy city to announce just such an event.

For Issa was a place of gloom, its past glories vanished, living on only in the memories of the few who remained there. The stillness of the streets through which they walked, the acres of high stone walls, the emptiness of the buildings they passed, the sighing wind that blew dead leaves and particles of dust around the wayfarers' feet, and, most of all, the smell of dry decay, depressed Laura. In all of that once-great city the only sign of life aside from their little group of eight was in the sky. A duplicate of Kentir's ship suddenly appeared, a saucer-shaped vessel that flew above the city on a low trajectory, heading toward the field where their own ship had landed.

"Good," Kentir said, looking upward. "The others are arriving while it is yet early in the day.

"What others?" Laura asked.

"There will be two additional visitors to our time," Kentir replied. "They will be housed with you."

"Do you mean to say that you have kidnapped other people besides Hua Te and me?" Laura exclaimed. The sense of outrage she was trying to control threatened to overtake her once again. She sent a cold stare in Kentir's direction.

"I wish you would not use that word, *kidnapped*," said Kentir, frowning at her.

"Can you think of a better word to fit your actions?" she demanded.

Laura was walking with Hua Te and Imilca, Kentir a step or two ahead, and the others following in no particular order. At Laura's challenging words, Kentir stopped abruptly and swung around to face her.

"There is no other way," he said, his voice low and harsh. "We have tried everything else. You four who come to us by the timestones are our last hope."

"You had no right to steal us away from our homes!" Laura cried, trying her best to ignore the pain she heard in his voice. At that moment, she didn't want to hear any explanation that would dissolve her anger. It was far better to be angry with Kentir than to be the panic-stricken victim of a criminal act. She was almost glad to see Kentir's face darkening with unconcealed irritation and his mouth opening, no doubt to blast her with his own anger.

"Don't argue here," Renan, the physician, said. He clapped a hand on Kentir's shoulder, interrupting what Kentir would have said next. "Take them inside, Kentir. Let them see the remnants of the life we are trying to preserve. Then they may begin to understand. After they know everything, they may even find it possible to forgive us."

"As usual, your advice is good, Renan," Kentir said. "These people have a right to be angry with us so long as they remain ignorant of our great purpose."

"And just what is that purpose?" Laura demanded of Kentir.

"Please," Renan said, answering for his friend, "do not judge us until later. For the moment, simply come with us and observe."

Dropping his hand from Kentir's shoulder, Renan approached a heavy wooden door set into a massive stone wall. As soon as the door swung inward, fragrance wafted toward Laura's nose. She inhaled deeply, not recognizing individual scents, but aware of the sweet smells of living, growing things that challenged the dusty emptiness on the side of the wall where she still stood. Eagerly, she passed through the door Renan was holding open for her.

"Here, in the compound where we live, we have preserved a small part of what Issa used to be," Imilca said, following Laura through the door.

They entered a garden of profuse greenery and spectacular flowers. Ferns grew in the shady spots, while palm trees towered above, their fronds mingling with the leaves of deciduous trees and the long, thin needles of evergreens. At least, they looked to Laura like palms and evergreens and trees that would lose their leaves in autumn. On closer inspection, none of the trees or plants she saw were familiar to her. Nor was she able to recognize any of the flowers. Tiny white blossoms starred the moss beside the path where Laura and her companions were walking. Large red and yellow flowers bloomed in the sunnier, open areas. But in all that luxurious growth the only thing even slightly familiar to Laura was a small tree bearing pale pink flowers. She thought it was an almond tree, though she wasn't absolutely certain.

In her own time, Laura was not much of a gardener. But, thanks to her mother's insistence that Laura help with the weeding, she had enough of an acquaintance with plants and flowers to know that what she saw in the strange garden did not grow in the twentieth century. The garden that spread its marvels to delight the senses of those who walked along its paths was otherworldly. Or ancient. No, not ancient—it was prehistoric. Possibly, even *pre*-prehistoric.

Breathing in the sweet fragrance of flowers and the fresh scent of green leaves, hearing the gurgle of water in a small fountain and the buzzing of unknown insects as they worked their way from blossom to blossom, looking from beautiful flower to delicate leaf to clear blue sky above, Laura at last comprehended in her heart and mind and in every cell of her body that she was in a time and place completely alien to her. She was on her own in an unknown environment, with neither family nor friends to support her. In a way, it was a relief to be so far removed from the problems and the quiet discontent that pervaded her ordinary life, but she felt guilty to be so relieved.

And the chances were excellent that she would remain in an alien time and place for the rest of her days. Temporarily paralyzed by that realization, Laura stood unmoving on the garden path while those around her walked on, Imilca and Hua Te engaged in conversation, Renan and the others spread out along the path in small groups.

Except for one other person. Kentir remained at Laura's side, as if he alone understood what her thoughts were. When she turned to him, unable to speak, he put his arms around her and let her rest against his strength until her trembling had stopped and she was in control of herself once more.

It took quite a while, for in addition to fear and the wrenching loneliness that were the results of a jarring displacement in both time and space, she had also to deal with her personal reaction to Kentir's closeness. He smelled wonderful. Laura breathed in the scent of warm masculinity tinged with a leafy-green smell that reminded her of the garden itself. At first she thought it was a fragrance from the garden, until he tightened his arms for a moment and her nose was pressed against his chest. Then she knew for certain that it was Kentir's own body scent, and she experienced a breathtaking sensation in her own bosom, as if she had come home after a long journey.

She told herself she was being foolish. She did

not know the man who held her. He was a kid-napper. And yet it did not seem to matter. It had not mattered since the moment when she had first gazed into his remarkable gray-blue eyes.

"I'm sorry I broke down," she said when she could speak. "It's just that everything in this garden is so strange, and when I saw it, I finally understood once and for all that this is real. It isn't a nightmare. I won't wake up in my own bed at home."

"I had not thought before about the effects of what we are doing on those whom we bring to us," Kentir said. "Our need is so urgent that I blocked out consideration of the life you would leave behind, of loved ones who would miss you and whose loss you would mourn. I closed my heart when my own loved ones left Issa, and since that day I have not allowed emotion to speak to me. Now I begin to fear that I have done a great injustice to you, to Hua Te, and to the others who will soon join us at our headquarters."

"Headquarters?" Laura pulled a little away from him so she could look up into his face. At once Kentir dropped his arms and stepped back, an action Laura immediately regretted. She wanted him to embrace her again. But her common sense told her that Kentir had just provided her with a valuable clue to what was going on. She would be a fool to let any information pass without questioning him about it, without learning everything she could. "Headquarters for the project you spoke of earlier today?"

"I have said too much," Kentir told her. "We are both required to wait until the meeting, when all of us are gathered."

"Fine," she said. "If you can't talk about this mysterious project of yours, then tell me about your life. Renan is right when he suggests that understanding will bring forgiveness for what you have done. You say your loved ones have left Issa. Why did they go away?"

"For their safety," he said. "Though neither they nor I can be certain they will be safe." His craggy features were softened by an unmistakable grief.

"Why are they in danger?" Laura asked. When he did not reply at once, she added, "Is there a war going on? Is that why Issa has been evacuated? Forgive me for saying so, Kentir, but you and your friends don't look like much of an army to me."

"We are not soldiers," he said. "We are scientists."

"All of you?" Seeing his nod of confirmation, Laura fell silent. Then a new concern rose in her heart and she could no longer keep quiet. "Has the city been quarantined because of a plague?"

"No. We are all healthy. You do ask many questions, don't you?"

"It's human nature to be curious," Laura responded. "You said so yourself."

"You need not remind me. Before we sent the timestones into the future, we assumed it would be so during all other times in which humans live. It has become clear that we were correct in our supposition. All humans are, indeed, possessed of a remarkable degree of curiosity." He chuckled, then sobered. "Stop guessing, Laura. I cannot tell you more than I have, because we of the project have agreed that Seret should be present when you are told."

"Who is Seret?"

"She is our leader," Kentir answered.

"Your leader is a woman?" Laura grinned at him. "Now, that is an interesting fact. Not to mention an encouraging one."

"It is also the last fact I will provide until the meeting," Kentir said, his faint smile softening the blunt declaration. "If you and I are to continue speaking, we will converse on a different subject." Taking Laura's elbow, he began to walk through the garden once more, along the path Hua Te and Imilca had taken. The others were far ahead of them. Laura and Kentir were alone, surrounded by sweet fragrances and the soft sounds of insects going about their work.

"All right, then, let's return to the subject of your loved ones," Laura suggested, eager to learn all she could about him. "Are you married?"

"I was betrothed," Kentir replied.

"Was?" Laura asked, knowing she was prying, yet insatiably curious about the man who trod the garden path beside her, his fingers warm upon her arm.

"Yes, was," Kentir repeated. He took his hand from her elbow, and it seemed to Laura that he withdrew his attention from her, that his thoughts were somewhere very far away. Then, before she could speak again, he went on, "I will anticipate your next questions by telling you that Nivesa and I grew up together and she and I always knew that when the time was right we would marry. Our families were close friends and expected it of us."

"But you didn't marry."

"We ended our betrothal the day before she left Issa. We knew we would never see each other again. Her duty was to take her parents and mine, and the small children of our families, away from Issa, while my mission was to remain here and lead the project. I wanted her to be free to find happiness with someone else."

"That's so sad." Laura's eyes filled with tears at the thought of a life broken apart for the sake of duty, and of a man who cared enough to free the woman he loved. Whatever the project was that he was leading, it must be vitally important if it could cause such disruption between lovers. "Kentir, just answer one more question and then I promise, I won't ask any more. Where did Nivesa take your family?"

"Off-world," he said.

"Off . . . ?" Laura stared at him, her jaw dropping. "You mean, into space? In a spaceship? They left Earth?"

"Yes. She was the pilot of the ship."

Laura could see by the set of his jaw and the firm line of his mouth that he thought he had said too much. She would keep her promise and not pry any more into his personal life. She shouldn't have pried in the first place. It wasn't her business. Yet a small, quiet voice buried deep in her heart murmured, "It is, it is, it is . . ."

Chapter Six

"This is the house where you will live while you are with us," Kentir said, leading Laura out of the overgrown garden and onto a broad swath of roughly cut grass.

A white stone seawall served as boundary between the lawn and the water and as protection for the buildings in the compound. On the far side of the lawn several low buildings were just visible behind a screen of trees and tall bushes. Laura gave them only a cursory glance, for they paled in comparison to the main structure. On a little rise in the center of the lawn sat a building three stories high, graced with tall windows that stood open to the soft breezes, and surrounded by flowering shrubbery similar to the landscaping of the houses they had passed on their way into Issa. Unlike the gardens of those other, crumbling houses, the bushes around this well-kept building were neatly pruned.

"Oh, how lovely," Laura exclaimed. "It could be a beach house in my own time. A house owned by a very wealthy family," she added, noting that the building before her was much larger than her parents' house at the seashore.

The solid, white stone blocks of which the house was made were beautifully fitted together without mortar, like the other stonework Laura had seen. The house was lighter in scale than the public buildings within the city proper. Here, the architect had constructed a dwelling situated so each large window opened onto a bright vista of sea or garden or, at the back side of the house, on a view of lawns and gently rolling hills.

"Come," Kentir said, starting up the crushed stone path to the blue front door. "Imilca will be waiting for us."

Eager to discover what awaited her behind the blue door, Laura hurried after Kentir, through an entrance that opened directly into the large main room.

Inside the house, all was serenity. The interior walls of the main room were painted with murals depicting flowers and trees copied from those in the real garden. The upper walls and the ceiling were sky blue, while the floor was made of inlaid blocks of stone in various shades of green, in imitation of grass. After taking note of the garden decor of the room, Laura was not at all surprised to discover a rocklike fountain built into one wall. From the rock a stream of water issued like a miniature waterfall, to fill a small pool. Tubs of flowers were set around the edge of the pool, and tiny blue and red fish darted through the water. Before Laura had a chance to get a good look at the fish, to see if they were like fish in her own time, Imilca approached her with a bright smile and outstretched hands.

"Welcome," Imilca said. "This is a more proper way to greet guests than our first meeting in the desert. Laura, you are free to explore both house and grounds as you wish, for you are an honored guest here, not a prisoner."

"I will rejoin you later," Kentir said, speaking to both Laura and Imilca. "I should meet the incoming party and our new guests." With that, he was gone.

Imilca showed Laura up a wide stone staircase to an airy room on the second floor that had a view of lawn and sea. The bed set against one inner wall was large and comfortable, with a pale green coverlet and lots of inviting pillows. A wardrobe had been provided for Laura to use, and there were cosmetics and various other feminine necessities in the bathroom next door.

Laura did not have much difficulty identifying the purpose of each jar and bottle. She lingered over a tall, silvery glass bottle containing perfume. Inhaling the delicious scent, she decided it must be distilled from a combination of all of the flowers in the garden, for she could not distinguish any one fragrance. She rubbed a little of the perfume on her wrist and sniffed it again, aware that her mood was improving with each breath she took.

"It's my perfume," Imilca said. "I prepare it myself. Fragrances are so important. They can make us happy or sad, and the right scent can recall a forgotten memory. Of course, that particular perfume will smell different on you, since we do not have the same body chemistry. But I have always loved the scent, and I thought you would like it, too."

"I do. Thank you, Imilca." Laura rubbed her wrist again. "It smells like a thousand flowers all mixed together."

"I am glad it pleases you," Imilca said. She walked about the room, checking on the pale green draperies that could be pulled across the windows, straightening a pillow on the bed, showing Laura the low chest where clothing was kept, lingering instead of leaving Laura to her own devices. "I sent a message about the clothes after you were aboard the saucership, so the garments you find in the chest ought to fit you."

Imilca actually used a different word than *saucership*. Laura heard the word, which made no sense to her, but, thanks to the translator behind her left ear, she was able to make a connection between the Kheressian language and her own experience, to come up with a term that had meaning to her.

"Imilca," Laura asked, "does the translator work by teaching a foreign language to the person in whom it is implanted?"

"How clever of you to understand so quickly,"

Imilca said. "Before long you will be speaking our language and you won't need artificial assistance."

Laura was delighted to find that Imilca was willing to stay and talk. With her, Laura felt no compunction about asking questions. She decided the time was right to try to learn more about why she had been brought to Issa.

"Kentir told me he was betrothed, but his fiancée took his family and escaped off-world," Laura said.

"Yes. They have all gone," Imilca responded to the implied question. Her soft gray eyes swam with moisture. "Nivesa is my sister."

"Then your family is gone, too," Laura said. "Imilca, I didn't know. I didn't mean to raise the subject of a tragic parting."

"I will not consider it a tragedy, nor do I think Kentir will, either, if only our project succeeds," Imilca said. "We who remain behind have freely chosen to do so."

"Forgive me for asking what may be a painful question," Laura said, "but I am curious. Kentir mentioned that Nivesa took children with her, as well as his parents and hers. Did you have a husband who left in that group? Or children?"

"My husband was killed in one of the first attempts to fly a saucership converted for use in space," Imilca answered. "I was left with an infant daughter, whom I gave into my sister's custody because, like Kentir, I am needed here. Nivesa will raise her niece as if she were her own daughter."

"I can't imagine how it must hurt to give up a beloved child," Laura whispered, sympathizing with Imilca's pain and loss.

"You would give her up readily if you believed sending her away was her best chance to live," Imilca responded with a quiet dignity that touched Laura's heart.

"Everything I hear about this project you are involved in indicates that it is of earthshaking importance," Laura said.

"That is exactly right," Imilca told her.

Laura intended to add that she was beginning to realize that decent people like Kentir and Imilca would not have resorted to kidnapping without good reason, and that she was no longer angry, but would reserve judgment about what had been done to her until she had heard the explanation their leader, Seret, would provide. But as Laura began to speak, her conversation with Imilca was interrupted by loud voices coming from the direction of the garden outside.

"That will be Kentir and Thuban with our new guests," Imilca said. "Please excuse me. I do believe Kentir will require my assistance."

"From the sound of things, Kentir will require a weapon," Laura said. She followed Imilca out of the bedroom and along the corridor to the top of the stairs that led down to the main room. There Laura halted, while Imilca ran down the steps.

Hua Te, who had also heard the voices, came out of a room farther down the corridor to join

Laura. Together they watched the action below as three men in red tunics and trousers brought a fourth man into the house. In fact, they dragged him inside, for the fourth man was putting up a mighty struggle and was shouting at the top of his lungs. To Laura's amazement, she saw feathers in gaudy colors flying out of the confused melee. The feathers floated about the room for a while on the air currents generated by swinging arms and legs. The man was eventually subdued and, in the quieter atmosphere, the feathers drifted slowly downward to rest like bright, broken flowers scattered upon the green stone floor.

"He fought so strongly," one of the men said to Imilca, "that we have been unable to implant the translator. Our sedatives have had no effect on him. Since he cannot understand what we say, he persists in fighting us."

"Let me try to communicate with him, Thuban," Imilca said. "Tone of voice can sometimes convey what actual words cannot. No doubt the poor man is terrified by what has happened to him." Imilca stepped forward, smiling, holding her hands out, palms up. She spoke in her softest, most reassuring tones. "Sir, you are welcome here. We mean no harm to you."

With a wild roar the man lunged at Imilca, spouting an obscene oath that made Laura wish her translator was not working. Those who were holding him barely managed to restrain the struggling, yelling man.

"Now see what you've done," Thuban shouted at Imilca. A tall, muscular man, he looked as if he wanted to strike both Imilca and the raging stranger out of sheer frustration.

Kentir had followed the violent group through the front door. He brought with him a slender woman with close-cropped black hair, who wore a dark blue jumpsuit with a red patch on her left sleeve and a heavy belt with an empty weapon holster. The woman looked angry, but she remained blessedly silent while almost everyone else in the main room was shouting.

"Kentir," Thuban said in a fierce voice, "were it not for your explicit order to keep alive whomever the timestones bring to us, I swear to you, I would have killed this madman before we reached Issa. He injured two of my crew. I've had to send them to Renan for treatment."

While attention was momentarily diverted from the man who was being restrained, he uttered a loud cry and renewed his efforts to break free.

"Enough of this," Kentir said. He held out his hand to Thuban. "Give me the translator. Then you, dear brother, may hold his head steady while Nirod and Arad hold his arms. If the translator must be implanted without anesthesia, then so be it."

"I could have done it myself," Thuban said.

"Then why didn't you?" Kentir demanded.

The brothers stood with locked gazes until Thuban put into Kentir's palm a device just like the one Kentir had used on Laura. Thuban reached beneath the man's feathered headdress to grab his long, black hair and hold his head immobilized. Thuban's companions took a tighter grasp of the man's arms.

Kentir stepped forward and, with a quick, efficient gesture, implanted the translator behind the man's left ear. He howled with the pain of it and Laura clapped her hands over her own ears to muffle the sounds of the man's outraged curses.

"I know you can understand me now," Kentir said to the man. "Tell me your name."

"By what right do you steal a high priest away from his official duties?" the man demanded.

"On your knees, you fool." Speaking in a loud, commanding voice, the woman in the blue jumpsuit, who had come into the house at Kentir's side and whom Laura took to be the fourth visitor from another time, strode forward to glare at the man who claimed to be a high priest. "You are in the presence of gods. Are you so full of your own importance that you do not recognize a god when you meet one? Who else but a god could touch your ear with fire and thus allow you to understand the sacred language?"

An instant of surprised silence followed these astonishing remarks. The Kheressians looked at each other as if they could not believe what they had just heard, while the unknown man gave up his struggle and stood still. When those holding him loosened their grip, he pulled away from them and prostrated himself on the stone floor before Kentir.

"Most revered holiness," the man said, "I beg you to have pity upon your faithful servant, Chacatlipichi. At the moment when your sacred egg appeared before me, I was so engrossed in the ceremony I was conducting that I did not understand your wish to call me away to your own country. If you will but forgive me, I promise to do whatever you ask of me."

"Chacatlipichi," Kentir responded to this plea, "stand up and look me in the eye. I am no god, but a man like yourself, who needs your help."

"He won't believe that," said the dark-haired woman, her voice dripping contempt for Chacatlipichi. "He's an Aztec priest. I recognized him by his outlandish costume and by the smell of blood that hovers about him. He was apparently in the middle of an important ceremony and was just beginning to remove the heart from a sacrificial victim when he saw your timestone on the altar and picked it up. He would have finished the ceremony aboard ship, using me as a substitute victim, if Thuban had not taken away his obsidian knife as well as the timestone, and ordered him confined him to a cabin."

"Aztec priest?" murmured Hua Te to Laura.

"I believe it," Laura said, noting the brightly colored, feathered anklets and wristbands that Chacatlipichi wore, his disordered feather headdress, and his cloak, all of which explained the broken feathers lying about the floor, which had been torn off during the skirmish between the priest and the Kheressians. "I've seen illustrations of Aztecs in *National Geographic* magazine.

He certainly looks like one of them. What that woman says about him is further proof. The Aztecs routinely practiced human sacrifice," Laura ended with a shudder.

"I suggest you lock him up and keep him confined," said the dark-haired woman to Kentir. "He cannot possibly be of any use to you."

"I will decide what is to be done with our visitors," Kentir told her. To the men who had been holding the Aztec, he said, "Take Chacatlipichi to a guest room and see that he is made comfortable. If he is hungry or thirsty, provide for his needs. I want two of you to keep him company at all times.

"Chacatlipichi, you will not be harmed," Kentir continued, speaking to the Aztec. "Please go with these men. You and I will talk together later."

"Call him Chac," suggested the dark-haired woman. "It's easier to say. Now, as to my own situation, I repeat what I have already told you and your brother. I am Lieutenant Marica, of the Presidential Special Forces. I am also permitted to provide my identification number to my captors, and I will do so if you wish, but I do not think the number will have any meaning for you."

"Thank you for the information, Lieutenant Marica," Kentir responded to the woman with careful politeness. "You are right about the number. I do not need to know it."

"I insist that you return me to my guard post at once!" Marica said. Indeed, she looked ready to engage in battle with Kentir if he did not do as she demanded.

"Name, rank, and serial number," Laura said, keeping her voice too low for those at the bottom of the stairs to hear her. "Hua Te, Lieutenant Marica is a member of the armed forces. The question is, what armed forces? I have never heard of the Special Forces she mentioned, so she must not be a United States citizen, unless she is from some later century." Considering that possibility, Laura fell silent again, to listen to what was going on in the room below.

"Imilca, will you conduct our lady guest to a room?" asked Kentir, turning away from the hard-faced Marica without responding to her questions or her demands.

"If you will follow me," Imilca said to the dark-haired woman.

"Lead on, then, but don't think I will give up my insistence that I be sent home. You are holding me without legal cause. I will expect appropriate compensation for what you have done." Marica responded to Kentir's instructions and Imilca's request with an angry look at both of them, but she did follow Imilca up the stairs. When she reached the top of the stairs, Marica stopped to confront Laura and Hua Te. "Are you two also honored guests here?" she asked in a sardonic drawl.

"I guess you could say that," Laura answered.

"Who are you?" Marica said in a demanding tone. Then, a little less abruptly, she asked, "Do you know what these people want with us?"

"I am Laura Morrison. This is Hua Te. And no, I have no idea why we are here."

"From when do you come?" Marica asked, still using the clipped diction of an officer who expected to be obeyed.

"I'm from the twentieth century," Laura said, "though I'm not sure if that will mean anything to you."

"It does. I am familiar with your calendar system. You're not entirely a barbarian then. Or, I should say, not the kind of barbarian that Chac is. According to your system of reckoning time, I have come here from the twenty-second century—and I can tell you that I expect to realize a profit for my inconvenience. A good financial gain is worth almost any trouble." When Laura made no immediate response to these statements, Marica turned to Hua Te.

"What about you?" Marica said, looking at Hua Te with a definite air of arrogance. "You're Chinese, aren't you? From what historical era did they pluck you?"

"As you have guessed, I was, indeed, born in the Middle Kingdom," Hua Te answered. "I was taken from the twelfth century of Laura's calendar." He smiled at Laura's gasp of surprise at this information.

"So far in the past? What use can you to be to these Kheressian abductors?" Marica asked in unconcealed disdain. "Well, the Chinese were civilized long before anyone else was, so it is possible that you will be considered useful in some way. Certainly your people were civilized before that fellow and his kind," she added, watching as the guards led Chacatlipichi past them and down the hall.

"I thank you for the compliment you have paid me," Hua Te said, bowing to Marica. She did not respond to the courtesy, apparently having dismissed Hua Te from her thoughts.

"Well, Imilca," Marica said in a voice more commanding than polite, "you are supposed to show me to a guest room. Take me there at once."

"She's a real sweetheart," Laura commented, looking after Marica.

"I am not familiar with the term," Hua Te said, "though your tone of voice explains its meaning plainly enough."

"Do you really think those two newcomers will be of any help to our hosts in their mysterious project?" Laura asked, glancing down to the main room, where Kentir and Thuban stood quietly talking.

"That," said Hua Te, also watching the two below, "depends on what it is our hosts expect us to do for them."

Laura wasn't wearing a watch, so she couldn't be certain of the time, but she guessed it was about half an hour after the scene in the main room. Kentir and Thuban had gone off somewhere, their heads close together in conversation. When Imilca had emerged from Marica's room looking distraught, both Laura and Hua Te had insisted she join them for a relaxing walk.

The three of them strolled across the lawn toward the seawall. The ground sloped gently downward in a broad sweep of grass, with trees and thick shrubbery off in the distance to Laura's right. Through the leafy screen she could see the low stone buildings she had noticed earlier in the day. To her left was the garden, then the tall stone wall that enclosed the property, which was built right down to the seawall. Beyond the walls, where the shoreline curved, lay the deserted city of Issa, with its ruined lighthouse at the end of the long wharf. Laura found the city too depressing to look at, so she kept her eyes on the dancing ocean waves or on Hua Te's serene face.

"Hua Te," Laura said, "why didn't you tell me when you lived? You heard me say I come from the twentieth century."

Hua Te did not respond at once. He appeared to be contemplating the ocean view. Or perhaps he was deciding exactly how to answer Laura's question.

"Well?" she said to him after a minute or two. "Did you think I'd look at you the way Marica did if you told me where and when you were born?"

"Never," Hua Te answered her. "Even on such short acquaintance, I know you have a generous soul and will not scorn anyone merely for being different from you. But I am accustomed to keeping my own counsel and so I do not say what it is not necessary to reveal."

"So you're playing your cards close to the vest, are you?" Laura said with a grin. "Oops—sorry, Hua Te. You are probably receiving a very peculiar translation of that phrase. May I ask a better question? You mentioned that when you discovered the timestone that brought you here, you were in a house in a city. Were you in China?"

"No," Hua Te said. "I was in Baghdad."

"Oh," Laura said. "Marco Polo in reverse."

"I do not know the name," Hua Te said.

"Of course you don't. Marco Polo lived after your time. He was a famous traveler who went from Europe to China and then wrote a book about it."

"Whereas I traveled from China to Europe," Hua Te said. "I understand the reference now."

"Why were you in Baghdad?" Laura asked. "Was it just a stop on your travels?"

"I had been living there for some years, with two young Englishmen who were my pupils as well as my traveling companions," Hua Te said.

"How fascinating! I can think of at least a dozen questions to ask about that statement," Laura said. "But I'll only ask the most obvious question. What were you teaching those two twelfth-century Englishmen?"

They had reached the seawall. Hua Te sat down upon it and gazed at the sea and the waves tumbling in toward the narrow, sandy beach. He did not speak for a while. After exchanging a glance, Laura and Imilca sat together near Hua Te.

The sun was gentle on Laura's face; the breeze was scented by salty sea and garden flowers. There was even a faint fragrance rising from the grass at her feet. It was pleasant to sit quietly while Hua Te pondered her question. Laura could see that the frown had eased from Imilca's brow, and she appeared to be much more relaxed than she had been immediately after leaving Marica's room.

Laura discovered to her surprise that she was content to be where she was, sitting between Imilca and Hua Te, without anything urgent to do. The nagging difficulties of her former life were slowly evaporating from her mind, leaving her with the hope that all problems would resolve themselves if only she kept her thoughts on what was occurring at each moment of her extraordinary adventure. There was no logical reason to back up her feelings of peace and relaxation, but she embraced them all the same.

Perhaps Hua Te was experiencing the same sense of contentment, for when he finally began to speak his low voice blended with the murmur of the surf and the sighing of the breeze.

"In the time from which I come," Hua Te said, "I was considered a learned man."

"A scholar," Laura said. "The Chinese are famous for their love of learning."

"And a mage," said Hua Te.

"I do not understand that word," Imilca said, touching her left ear. "It does not translate into Kheressian."

"Do you wear a translator, too?" Laura asked.

"All of us do," Imilca answered. "Our project team must communicate frequently with members of other teams in many lands around the world. We cannot work together unless we un-

101

derstand each other. It was the invention of the translator that brought peace to our world long ago, when we feared we would destroy ourselves in bitter wars caused by misunderstanding. But Hua Te, I have never heard the word you used, or anything like it. *Mage*," Imilca repeated, twisting her mouth and mispronouncing it.

"I am not surprised to hear you say the word is unknown to you," Hua Te said. "Since my arrival in this time, I have attempted a few experiments. None of them have been successful. I did lay down my staff in Baghdad, when I picked up the timestone, but I believe the difficulty is not caused by the lack of a staff, but rather, it is the result of a fundamental difference between my time and this."

"Are you talking about magic?" Laura asked, intrigued by Hua Te's mention of a staff.

"So some name it," Hua Te said. "May I try another experiment now, with the two of you?"

"Be my guest," Laura exclaimed. "Oh, sorry. That probably didn't translate well, did it? Go right ahead, Hua Te. It will be interesting to see what you can do."

"The point is," Hua Te said, "that in the sense you mean, I have not been able to *do* anything in this time. Imilca, have I your permission to attempt this experiment? It will not hurt you in any way."

"Very well," Imilca said, though she looked doubtful.

"Look at me, Imilca," Hua Te instructed. "Look straight into my eyes." When Imilca's gaze was locked on his, Hua Te made a gesture with his left hand. Imilca continued to stare at him, and Hua Te made the same gesture a second time.

"Yes?" said Imilca. "What are you going to do, Hua Te?"

"Remarkable," Hua Te murmured. "Did you observe nothing, Imilca?"

"What should I have seen?" Imilca asked.

"I saw something," Laura said. "I was watching you, Hua Te, and you got blurry."

"Just so," Hua Te said. "Now it is your turn, Laura. Look into my eyes as Imilca did."

Laura did as he directed. Again Hua Te made the gesture with his left hand. The air around him wavered, his form grew indistinct, and, suddenly, Hua Te vanished. Before her startled exclamation could leave Laura's lips, he was back again.

"What did you do?" she cried. "That's amazing! I couldn't see you at all. You were invisible for a minute or two. Was it some kind of hypnotic suggestion?"

"An interesting concept," Hua Te said. "Suggestion is certainly a part of the skill, which is simple enough to learn. Believing in its efficacy is another matter altogether. Magic cannot work properly without a belief in it.

"The point of my demonstration," Hua Te went on, "is that while you, Laura, are susceptible to the suggestion that I could not be seen, Imilca is not. Nor are the other Kheressians susceptible. My magic is useless here. It simply does not work on these people."

"Which seems to indicate that their thought processes are different from ours," Laura said. "Or else their brain structure is fundamentally different."

"And yet the Kheressians are human," Hua Te said. "I am certain of it."

"A world without magic," Laura whispered. "How strange. How boring."

"We are not boring!" Imilca exclaimed. "Never say so. We Kheressians are an interesting people."

"As you have proven by inventing the timestone," Hua Te said, smiling at her. "Only minds capable of great leaps of imagination could realize such a concept. There are aspects of the Kheressian mind that I would very much like to explore. In the interests of greater learning, of course."

"Of course," Imilca agreed. "Knowledge is always useful."

"As you are a teacher," Hua Te said, still smiling at her, "perhaps you will be able to help me."

"I will be glad to try," Imilca murmured.

Just then, Laura noticed Kentir walking toward the house with Thuban. Seeing the way Kentir moved, with the easy grace of one in complete control of his body, it occurred to Laura that there was magic in Kheressia after all. It was just a different kind of magic from that practiced by Hua Te—though, to hear the soft conversation now being conducted between the Chinese mage and the Kheressian lady, Laura suspected that Hua Te was as much aware of that different magic as she was.

Chapter Seven

"The meeting has been postponed until morning," Kentir announced during the evening meal, "in hope that Chacatlipichi will be able to join us then."

"Surely you don't imagine that barbarian will be any help to you," Marica said, scoffing at the idea.

"Must we really postpone learning what you want of us?" Laura asked Kentir.

"It can't be helped," Kentir answered. "Seret made the decision, not I."

"Of course it can be helped," Marica snapped at Kentir. "Never mind this Seret person; just tell us what we need to know about the mysterious problem you claim to have. We will then decide if we have any information that might be of use to you, after which you will reverse the action of the timestones and return us to our own proper times."

"I am afraid it won't be that simple," Kentir said.

"I don't see why not," Marica responded, her dark eyes flashing with irritation. "Don't you understand what you have done to me? And to these two?" she asked, tilting her chin to indicate Laura and Hua Te.

"Marica, please," Imilca said, "could we discuss something other than your displeasure at being here?"

"I do not wish to change the subject," Marica retorted. "It is plain to me that neither you, nor your other so-called guests, have any comprehension of the seriousness of what you have done."

"We do understand," Kentir said. He sounded weary, and as he spoke, he rubbed the back of his neck, as if the muscles there ached. "We would not have brought any of you here if we did not believe it will ultimately be as much to your benefit as to ours."

"Hah!" As she uttered this sound of disbelief, Marica leaned across the dining table toward Kentir. "My people are also capable of time travel, as we have often proved by tests with animals and with inanimate objects, but we consider it immoral to attempt to move humans around in time. Everyone in my time knows why it can't be done. Shall I explain the matter to you?"

"I am sure you are going to do so without my asking," Kentir said in a voice so soft and dangerous that Laura looked at him in alarm.

Marica, however, did not seem to notice the warning in Kentir's voice. She continued to speak with unabashed relish for her subject and with undisguised contempt for a man and a culture unaware of the facts as she perceived them.

"Based on research with animals, our scientists have developed a theory," Marica said. "The theory of transdimensional disorder." She paused, looking around the table from face to face as if to gauge the effect of her pronouncement.

"And what might the symptoms of this disorder be?" Renan asked from his place at the far end of the table. "As a physician, I am always interested in newly discovered illnesses."

"The symptoms are rapid aging and death," Marica answered with obvious satisfaction at the shocked reactions her words were causing. "Every animal used in our experiments has died within hours of its return, or was already dead when our researchers retrieved it. Based on those results, there can be no doubt of the fate soon to befall all of us whom you have kidnapped."

Laura pushed her plate aside. Until Marica had taken over the conversation, she had been enjoying her meal. It had begun with a creamy soup, which Imilca informed her was made of vegetables. The second course had consisted of tiny pastries, each one no larger than a single bite, filled with a mixture of spices and a round, slightly crunchy grain. The final course was fruit. Throughout the meal they drank a cold beverage that tasted like some kind of herbal tea.

Though all of the tastes and many of the textures of the meal were unfamiliar to Laura, and even the crockery and utensils required some thought on her part to use them correctly, still she found the food delicious and the company pleasant. Even Thuban, who earlier had impressed Laura as a colder, harder version of Kentir, was exerting himself to make polite conversation and to praise the tasty food. Only Marica seemed determined to be as unpleasant as possible.

"All of our time-traveling guests appear to be in excellent health," Renan said to Marica. "I include in my assessment even Chacatlipichi, who has exerted himself in constant, strenuous resistance since his arrival."

"The theory of transdimensional disorder states that every being is attached to a specific time line, which begins unwinding at the moment of birth," Marica said, speaking as if she was explaining to uneducated children. "Travel through time results in a loss of important reference points on the traveler's individual time line. This loss, in turn, results in the rapid aging and death I have mentioned. The result is inevitable. There is no known cure."

"Then you are fated to a prompt demise," Thuban remarked, not bothering to look up from his plate. "It will be a blessing for all of us. Marica, you have been complaining since first we located you. I begin to think that only death will silence you."

"Thuban! Marica is our guest!" Kentir exclaimed, glaring across the table at his brother. Thuban scowled back at him, but did desist from his uncharitable remarks to Marica.

"Has it occurred to your researchers that the only evidence they have found for this affliction rests upon experiments with animals?" Renan asked Marica. "Animals are not thinking beings and, therefore, they cannot be made to understand what has happened to them. Thus, their deaths may have been caused by extreme fear.

"Humans are capable of understanding," Renan continued. "Once the situation is explained to them and they realize they are under no threat of physical or spiritual harm, they should be able to find new points of reference on an alternate time line. I am assuming, of course, that the time line your scientists theorize about actually does exist. Speaking for myself, I require more proof than you have offered."

"Tell your objections to the theory to Chac and see how he reacts," Marica said with a sneer. "As the unwilling guest with the least ability to comprehend what has happened to him, he is the most likely candidate for mental deterioration and prompt death."

"As it happens, I have spoken to Chacatlipichi in private," Kentir said, "and he does appear to understand, in his own terms. He has asked for

109

time in which to fast and to prepare himself to hear our problem."

"How does he intend to prepare?" Marica asked. "By ripping the living, beating heart out of one of your servants?"

Laura could not supress her gasp of shock at Marica's crude statement. When she looked at Marica, she thought she detected a wicked gleam in the other woman's eyes. Laura's immediate dislike of Marica was based upon instinct, rather than on reason. Out of that same instinct, she could not help wondering if Marica was operating on some secret agenda of her own, and if that was why she was so insistant about the dire effects of time travel.

Laura could not tell what Kentir's true impression of Marica was. He spoke to her in the same contained, quiet way he had been using all through the meal.

"We do not have servants here, Marica," Kentir said. He looked around the table, then rose from his seat. "I believe we have finished our meal. Let us call an end to this gathering. I wish you all a good night's rest. Until tomorrow, then."

"Until tomorrow, Kentir," Imilca said.

"Until tomorrow," Renan echoed his friends.

The party began to disperse. Renan and a few of the dozen or so others who had been at the table headed toward the back of the house, talking among themselves in a companionable way. Marica stalked out of the dining room and up the stairs to the second floor without looking at or speaking to any of the company, all of whom she clearly regarded as her inferiors. Kentir and Thuban left together, engaged in what appeared to be a contentious, if quiet, discussion. Only Imilca and Hua Te lingered at the table.

"Excuse me, Imilca," Laura said, interrupting their conversation. "Is it all right if I take a walk in the garden?"

"Of course," Imilca answered with a smile. "There are many fragrant, night-blooming flowers to be enjoyed. Shall I join you, or would you rather be alone?"

"After the last hour, I think a little quiet contemplation is in order," Laura responded.

"I understand," Imilca said. "Until tomorrow."

"Until tomorrow," Laura repeated. It seemed to be the standard evening farewell in Issa.

Laura was not actually interested in being alone. She had seen Kentir and Thuban separate when they reached the main room, after which Kentir had left the house by the front door. Laura followed him. She stood on the front step until her eyes had adjusted to the darkness enough to allow her to see Kentir's tall, broad-shouldered shape moving across the lawn. She went after him, not hurrying, not even sure she wanted to catch up with him. She told herself she only wanted to know where he was going. She was not ready to admit that she wanted to be with him, to hear his low-pitched voice and share his thoughts about the disturbing revelations Marica had made.

Kentir hurried past the low building Laura had noticed earlier. He continued walking at a rapid pace until he reached the top of a small, grass-covered hill. There he paused for a while, looking up at the night sky. Then he dropped down to sit facing the sea with his arms wrapped around his knees.

"Come and sit with me, Laura," he said.

"How did you know I was following you?" She climbed the hill to join him. "I thought I was being quiet."

"I was aware of your footsteps. Perhaps my senses are sharper than yours."

"I saw you looking at the sky." She sat beside him, not touching him, but close enough to feel his warmth. "I thought you were probably remembering your fiancée. I didn't mean to interrupt a private time."

"You did not interrupt," he said. "Each evening when the stars begin to shine I think of Nivesa, and I wonder how she and the others who went with her are faring. But there is no purpose to be served in dwelling on loss. I can only hope they are all safe. And well. Especially Imilca's daughter. Children sicken so easily."

"I have been looking at the sky, too," Laura said. "Like everything else in this time, the stars are all askew. I'm not sure I could pick out any of the usual constellations. Another reference point on my personal time line is lost." She ended on a bitter laugh.

"What have we done to you by bringing you here?" he asked, his voice filled with doubt and worry. "For the first time, tonight I have begun to question our decision to use the timestones.

What if Marica's theory is correct and we, in our great need, have caused your deaths?"

"What if she's wrong?" Laura asked.

"Do you think she is?" A faint note of hope crept back into his words.

"I'm inclined to agree with Renan when he says the results of experiments on animals can't be extrapolated to humans," Laura answered. "Heaven knows, we've seen enough of that kind of bogus science in my own time."

"Heaven knows," Kentir repeated, looking at the sky again. He sighed. "Heaven, indeed."

"Personally," Laura said, "I would like to believe Marica is wrong just because she is a dreadful person. She doesn't have a kind word for anything or anyone. She criticized the entire dinner."

"You were angry, too, when we first found you," Kentir reminded her. "Your anger came from fear."

"I don't think Marica is afraid. She's just full of bravado and nastiness."

"Are you sure that's what it is?"

"Not entirely," Laura admitted. "But I don't like her, and I can't help wondering what the real truth is about transdimensional disorder.

"I don't think Hua Te likes Marica, either," Laura continued, "but he's too deep-minded to say anything slighting about her on such short acquaintance. Hua Te will wait for further evidence about Marica's character."

"And you are not deep-minded?" Kentir asked, his voice taking on a teasing note.

"Not me," she said, matching her tone to his. "I am generally considered to be a flighty type. And I don't have any specialized training, so I don't know if I will be of any help to you. In my own time I was an executive assistant, a position that cannot have any meaning in this time. In the hour just before I found your timestone, I broke my engagement and lost my job, too, since I was working for my fiancé," she ended, not knowing exactly why she felt compelled to reveal those facts about her personal life to Kentir.

"Perhaps you will be more useful than you think," he said, adding, "You do not appear to be unhappy at the end of your betrothal. I sense no great sorrow in you."

"You're right about that. I think now that I never loved Roger, that I said yes to his proposal chiefly because my mother was so eager to see me married to an important man. I'm glad it's over and done with." Laura decided it was time to change the subject to something less personal. Looking at the star-strewn sky she asked, "Will the moon rise later? Or has it already set?"

To Laura's mind it was an innocent enough question, an inquiry similar to a casual remark about the weather. She did not expect Kentir to catch his breath and then to sit perfectly still for a long, long time. Something about his rigid posture told her he was deeply disturbed. After a few minutes his continued silence began to frighten her.

"Kentir, talk to me, please," she begged. "What is it? What have I said to upset you?"

"Were you speaking of a satellite?" he asked with deliberate carefulness. "A small celestial body similar to those that orbit around certain other planets?"

"That is exactly what I mean," she said. In an attempt to lighten his tense mood she went on in a teasing way, "I was speaking of the moon, the rocky chunk of real estate that shines in the sky each night, that changes from a crescent to a full circle and back to a crescent again each month. The month is named for the moon. Or do you have a different name for it in this time?"

"We have no month," he said, very quietly. "We have no moon."

"Of course you have," Laura said, then stopped, one hand at her mouth as the importance of Kentir's statement sank in. "Oh, my God. There's no moon?"

"No," he said.

"Then I am on the wrong planet."

"You are on Earth," he said. "I am certain of it."

"But it can't be, unless—unless the moon arrives from somewhere in space and goes into orbit at a later time."

"Exactly." Kentir's voice was grim.

"But how?" Laura cried.

"I do not know. We will discuss it with Seret tomorrow," Kentir said.

"Don't pretend you aren't upset by this information," Laura said. "I can tell you are."

"I have heard worse news in the past three years," Kentir replied, "and I know there is still worse to come. But this night, at least, is peaceful. Do not disrupt it further, Laura. If you cannot appreciate the beauty around us, then leave me."

"Fine. If that's what you want, I'll go." She started to rise, but Kentir caught her wrist, keeping her where she was.

"You do not understand," he said, "how easy it would be to drift into madness, to forsake my obligation to this world. There are those among the Kheressians who have lost their sanity. There are many—too many, and relatives of mine among them—who have lost their lives trying to prevent the approaching disaster. If I can find some measure of peace by sitting on a hilltop, gazing at the eternal stars for an hour, is that so wrong?"

"It's not wrong at all," Laura said. She stopped trying to pull away from him. "Imilca says you are the leader of the project. Whatever the project is, the responsibility is obviously a heavy one."

"You provide a pleasant distraction," Kentir said, lacing his fingers through hers. "Look at the sky now, Laura."

She glanced upward at his bidding. At first she saw the stars, more of them than she could ever remember seeing in her own time. She knew it was because there were no city lights—and no moonlight—to obscure the stars, but she had never realized before how much light the stars shed upon the earth. The long curve of the shoreline was made visible by starlight on the ocean and the white sand. Perched at the edge of the sea, Issa lay silent, reflecting a pale light from its stone buildings, haunting and disturbing in its emptiness. With a shiver, Laura removed her gaze from the city and returned it to the sky. After a while she noticed a flicker of faint green light.

"What is that?" she asked.

"The aurora," Kentir answered.

"We call it the northern lights," Laura said. "I've only seen the aurora a couple of times before tonight. Where I live, the city lights prevent us from seeing most objects in the sky. Look, Kentir, it's growing brighter."

"Every night now it colors the heavens," Kentir said. "Seret tells us the aurora will become more brilliant in the near future, until it is visible in the daytime. At the end, there will be frequent lightning, too."

Laura scarcely heard his last remarks. She was watching the aurora suffuse the sky with billowing folds of light, as if a sheer green drapery were being drawn between Earth and the stars that continued to twinkle behind the light.

"It's beautiful," she murmured, entranced by the heavenly display.

"It will be one of the last beauties of Earth to endure," Kentir said. "When all else is gone, Earth's magnetic field will still glow in a final burst of radiance before the darkness."

"What darkness?" she asked, turning to look at him. The light in the sky was slowly changing from green to golden rose as it grew stronger, and Kentir's uplifted face was clearly visible. She noted his sharp, clean-cut profile before he, too, turned his head. She saw his mouth set in a stern line and she knew she had overstepped an unrecognized boundary. "I do ask the wrong questions, don't I?" she whispered.

"Not the wrong ones. Just the right ones at the wrong time," he said, his voice as low as hers.

"I'm spoiling your quiet time," she murmured.

"You could retrieve it for me."

"How?" Her voice was just a whisper of sound. His mouth was so close to hers that she could taste his breath. Around them the faint fragrance of the scented grass rose with their slightest movements. "Tell me how to restore your peace, Kentir."

"Like this." Lightly, Kentir brushed his lips across hers. "And like this." His mouth returned, more firmly this time.

They were still sitting side by side, close, but with only their mouths touching. Laura wished he would put his arms around her. She had never wanted anything so much in her life. She smothered a cry of disappointment when Kentir sat back, watching her.

"That was wrong," he said. "And foolish of me."

"I don't think so," Laura whispered.

"It should not have happened."

"Why not, Kentir?"

"Tomorrow you will understand why I cannot allow anything to interfere with my duty," he said. In a swift, fluid movement he was on his feet, looking down at her. "For me, the pleasure of the evening is gone. You may feel differently. Remain here as long as you wish. You will be perfectly safe and no one will disturb you."

"Don't go, Kentir. Stay and talk to me. There is so much I want to know." But he was already gone, striding across the lawn toward the house, leaving Laura alone with the blazing beauty that shimmered across the sky.

Chapter Eight

The guests gathered in the main room early the next morning. Chacatlipichi came in with a guard on either side, though he appeared to be restored to calmness by his talk with Kentir and by a night of quiet reflection. He had repaired his costume, so the feathers on his wristbands and anklets were smoothed into bands of glowing color. His bright cloak hung loosely from his shoulders, and his plumed headdress rose high above his sloping forehead. His dark eyes burned with a fierce intelligence. Altogether, Chacatlipichi was an impressive figure, and if Laura had not known about his bloody priestly activities, she would have admired his quiet dignity. Hua Te bowed politely to the Aztec priest, and Laura followed suit, but Marica turned her back on him.

A large chair had been placed on a dais at the opposite end of the room from the fountain that Laura had noticed on the previous day. From dais to fountain two rows of straight-backed chairs faced each other.

"They don't look especially comfortable," Laura said, regarding the chairs.

"Hard seats make for brief meetings," Hua Te responded, his words bringing a laugh from Laura.

"As my anger and my fear subside, my curiosity rises," she said. "Kentir told me a few things last evening that really surprised me." She had remained on the hilltop for several hours after he had left her, watching the sky and the tideless sea, thinking over all that Kentir had said. She wanted to tell Hua Te what she had learned and ask if his conclusions about the new information were the same as hers, but there wasn't time.

Imilca and Kentir appeared, both of them wearing the dark red tunics and trousers that Laura by now recognized as the uniform for those who were working on the mysterious project. She was wearing the uniform, too, her sweatshirt and shorts having been discarded while she was still on the saucership. With Imilca and Kentir came a small, elderly woman who was wearing a bright yellow robe that flowed about her spare figure.

"Surely that is Seret," Hua Te murmured, his

voice audible only to Laura. "In the Middle Kingdom, yellow is the color reserved for the emperor. According to Imilca, Seret is the ruler of the Kheressians."

Laura had previously noted the respectful way in which Kentir and Imilca always spoke of Seret. She studied the woman with great interest. Seret's face was deeply wrinkled with age, yet she walked with an upright, dignified grace. Her thick white hair was bound into a single braid, and her eyes were a clear, sky blue that missed nothing when they scanned the four guests who awaited her presence. Just behind Seret came Thuban and Renan, and then the rest of the red-uniformed members of Kentir's project. Laura recognized Arad and Nirod among them, the two men who had dragged Chacatlipichi into the house the previous day.

Seret took her seat in the large chair on the dais and the others sat in whatever order they wished, though Laura noticed that, despite the apparent casualness of the seating arrangements, each of the guests was between two members of the project team. She was between Imilca and Thuban, with Hua Te sitting opposite her, between Kentir and Renan. Marica and Chacatlipichi were in chairs set farther down the rows, at a distance from Seret. Seeing this, Laura guessed that Kentir believed they might present a danger to Seret, so he had ordered them kept as far as possible from her.

"As those of you who are strangers here have likely guessed, I am Seret, leader of the Keressians," the elderly woman said into the quiet that fell as soon as all were seated. "I welcome you to Issa, and I thank you for coming to us."

"As if we had a choice," said Marica in a loud, rude voice.

"You will, of course, be curious as to why you are here," Seret went on as if Marica had not spoken. "And some of you will be concerned about your personal safety."

"Forget the polite nonsense and get to the point," Marica interrupted again.

At Marica's remark Thuban made an annoyed sound. Leaning forward to look past Laura as if she did not exist, he turned his dark, cold gaze on Marica. Laura shivered to see that look, but Marica glared right back at Thuban, her face set in lines of anger and outrage.

"We have all been made aware of your fears," Thuban said to Marica. "You must learn to live with them, as the rest of us live with our own fears. I assure you, it will not be for long."

"I am not afraid," Marica said. "I am enraged by the way I have been used. I demand to be returned to my home at once. And I warn you, I expect to profit in some way from this unpleasant experience."

"Marica, you will keep silent and listen to Seret," Thuban told her.

His voice and expression were so threatening that Laura, watching and listening to him, shook with a nameless dread. She wished she had nerve enough to get up and move away from Thuban. She sent a pleading look in Kentir's direction, but all she got from him was the tiniest glimmer of a smile and a slight shake of his head, which Laura interpreted as a signal to stay where she was. With a sigh she reluctantly obeyed Kentir's silent command and sat back in her chair, returning her full attention to Seret.

"None of you would be here if we were not desperate," Seret said, choosing to ignore the exchange between Marica and Thuban. "Our problem is simply told. Nor will it be difficult to explain its significance to each of you within the context of your own times. It is the solution to our problem that has so far eluded us."

"We will do what we can to assist you," Hua Te said when Seret paused.

"Of course we will," Laura said, her eyes on Kentir rather than on Seret.

"Your assurances are appreciated," Seret said. "The problem is this. Three years ago, our astronomers discovered a large asteroid moving through space on a trajectory that will bring it directly toward Earth. The astronomers believe there is only a slight chance that the asteroid will pass extremely close to Earth without colliding with it. It is far more likely that the asteroid will crash into the earth. When it does, most forms of life now existing will be instantaneously destroyed."

"Excuse me, Seret," Laura broke into the elderly leader's remarks. "I want to be sure I understand what you are saying, and that you and I mean the same thing when we speak of an asteroid. Do you mean a chunk of rock that is moving through outer space?"

"That is correct," Seret said. "In this case, we are speaking of a very large rock, indeed."

"And this rock has no source of illumination except for light reflected off it from a star or our own sun?" Laura asked.

"Yes," Seret said.

"Then how can you see it?" Laura asked.

"Furthermore," Hua Te said, adding his own question to the discussion, "how can you be certain the path your astronomers have plotted for this object is the correct path?"

"In Kheressia, we have two important sciences," Seret answered them with no sign of annoyance. "The first science is medicine, and we are proud of the accomplishments of our physicians in eliminating the diseases that once plagued us, often to our deaths. Thanks to medical science, no longer do we become ill," Seret said with a smile for Renan.

"Our second important science is astronomy," Seret said, continuing her explanation. "Our star-searching lenses are the finest our people can produce, and Kheressian astronomers have made many important discoveries about the universe beyond our immediate planetary system. Just prior to the first news of the asteroid, we had begun to send explorers into space. As soon as we understood the gravity of what the astronomers were saying, we applied all of our knowledge of space travel and of other worlds in the effort to save as many of our people as possible.

I am only grateful that our astronomers were able to provide three years' warning."

"I don't mean to question your claim," Laura said. "I just want to be sure I understand exactly what you are saying."

"Laura, I would be surprised, and disappointed, if you did not have any questions at all," Seret told her with a smile.

"Please go on, Seret," Hua Te said. "Tell us all you know about the approaching catastrophe."

"It is my intention to do exactly that," Seret said. "Should the asteroid collide with Earth, any life that survives the impact and the worldwide firestorms ignited by it will very likely succumb to asphyxiation from the smoke and the vast dust clouds that will billow from Earth's surface into the upper atmosphere, or to the cold that is certain to follow when the dust and smoke block the sunlight. A long age of ice and snow will then begin.

"Nor will the story be appreciably different if Earth suffers a close encounter with the asteroid instead of a direct strike," Seret continued. "In that case, we can expect severe earthquakes, volcanic eruptions on a scale never imagined before, and enormous waves that will sweep far inland, destroying everything in their paths."

"I don't care what your scientists claim; they are obviously wrong," Marica said, interrupting Seret. She waved a hand, indicating the other guests who had been brought through time. "The four of us are proof that human life did survive. *If* your scientists were right about the asteroid in the first place," she ended with a rude sound that conveyed all too plainly her lack of faith in Kheressian astronomers, despite Seret's endorsement of their scientific abilities.

"I have peered through the finest star-searching lenses to see with my own eyes the doom approaching us," Seret said, her serenity unfazed by Marica's disbelief. "We are determined to discover a way to forestall that doom, either by averting it entirely, or else by surviving it."

"It's your problem," Marica said. "Why should we care about it? I repeat, I demand to be sent home at once—with handsome compensation for my trouble and suffering, of course."

"Marica, if you have nothing useful to say," Thuban commanded in a voice like thunder, "then be silent and allow others to speak."

"The approaching cataclysm augurs the end of the age," Chacatlipichi stated in a loud voice. He rose from his seat near the fountain to stand between the two rows of chairs, facing Seret at the other end of the room. "So it has repeatedly happened since the world began. The sacred books of my people tell how Earth and Sun function in great cycles, each cycle several thousand years long."

"What nonsense!" Marica exclaimed. "Don't listen to him. The man is a barbarian. He has no advanced science to offer. All he knows are pagan rituals that can have no meaning to intelligent, educated people."

"I perceive that you believe in no gods," Chacatlipichi said to Marica.

"Of course not," Marica responded with undisguised contempt for such an idea. "The people of my time have grown beyond superstitions."

"If your people have no belief in anything greater than themselves," Chacatlipichi said, "then their lives are without purpose or meaning." While Marica sputtered in outrage at his statement, Chacatlipichi once again addressed himself to Seret.

"From what you have said, great Seret, I believe you speak of the Age of the Fourth Sun, Tzontlilic. The sacred books tell us how, at the end of that ancient age, men died of starvation after a deluge of blood and fire."

"That," said Seret, "is what I wish to avoid. I want as many humans as possible to survive."

"As a high priest, I am well versed in the wisdom of the sacred books," Chacatlipichi said. "I know how to avert the coming catastrophe."

"Tell us, Chacatlipichi," Seret commanded. "If you know of a way to help us, then speak, and we will listen without mocking your words or your beliefs." This gentle reproof brought a derisive snort from Marica, but she raised no further argument.

"Blood sacrifice is required to prevent the end of the age," Chacatlipichi said. "I do not have the calendar of my people available to me here, but you, Seret, as the leader of your people, as one who watches the sky for portents—you can determine the exact, propitious times for sacrifice. Prepare the sacred fire with your own regal hands, give me back the obsidian knife I carried with me into your land, and supply me with enough slaves or war prisoners, and I will undertake to prevent what you do not wish to occur."

Laura listened to Chacatlipichi's words with horror. Yet there was about the Aztec priest such an air of honest belief in what he said, such a brave willingness to aid Seret in saving her world, that, in spite of Laura's revulsion at the idea of human sacrifice, she could not feel disgust for the man. Chacatlipichi was trying to help in the only way he knew, the way sanctioned by his people. There was something admirable in Chacatlipichi's attitude, and Laura found that she liked him a great deal more than she liked the coldhearted, disdainful Marica.

"Now you have all heard from his own lips that what I have been saying about him is true," Marica exclaimed, pointing an accusing finger at the Aztec. "This creature is a disgusting barbarian. Take him away and lock him up permanently. He cannot have anything to suggest that will be of practical use to you, Seret. All he knows are prayers and incantations and dreadful sacrifices."

"In the Middle Kingdom, where I was born," Hua Te said, interrupting Marica when it seemed she was about to continue her argument against Chacatlipichi, "Chinese sages speak of perished ages that they call *kis*. The sages say there have been ten *kis* from the beginning of the world until the time of K'ung Fu-tzu. I have been told that the age into which I was born is the eleventh *kis*."

"My people know K'ung Fu-tzu as Confucius," Laura said. She had seen Seret frown as Hua Te spoke, as if she did not entirely understand what he was saying. Laura decided a bit of clarification was in order. "I'm not sure how the name translates for you, Seret, but the man is revered as a great philosopher. I confess, I don't know anything about the *kis* that Hua Te mentioned, but I do know that many groups of people throughout history have believed legends about past ages that vanished in great floods or other catastrophes. Unfortunately, the few scientists who have tried to explain how the catastrophes occurred and what the results were have too often been ridiculed and their work discounted as wild imaginings."

"Thank you, Laura," Seret said. "You, Hua Te, and Chacatlipichi have provided information that confirms Kheressian beliefs."

"They have provided you with insane fantasies," Marica declared. "No one with a bit of sense could possibly believe such rubbish. There is no scientific proof of what they say."

"In fact," Seret said, "all three of them speak accurately when they talk of cyclic ages that end in worldwide destruction. We know from the writings of our historians that similar celestial catastrophes have happened in past ages, with great loss of life. They will certainly occur again in the future."

"If I understand you correctly," Laura said to

Seret, "you are suggesting that if we can prevent this disaster, or figure out a way to survive it, then we can take the information we gain here back to our own times, to use it there if necessary."

"It is so." Seret looked at her with approval. "I am pleased to hear you use the word *we,* for the goal we have set for ourselves will require cooperation if *we,* together, are to succeed. And all that we learn during the project, the Kheressians are willing to share with those who will come after us in later ages."

"Just recently," Laura said, "a comet broke into pieces and plunged into the planet Jupiter. The event was big news in my country. I saw the pictures taken by our astronomers. I have also seen a meteor crater in Arizona, and my father has told me about an asteroid that shattered when it hit the atmosphere above Siberia decades ago. The explosion caused terrible damage for miles around. So, based on my own knowledge, I don't have any difficulty believing what you say about the devastation the asteroid will cause.

"I do think it will make our task easier, and save time," Laura went on, "if you will tell us what methods you have tried so far to prevent loss of life. That seems to me to be the primary issue here."

"You have correctly understood the problem facing us," Seret said. "Since Kentir is the leader of the project, I suggest that you ask of him anything you want to know about the work. I am certain he will answer your questions honestly."

"Kentir," Laura said, looking at him, "you told me yesterday that your family and your fiancée have gone off-world. Is the asteroid the reason why they fled?" She was sure it was so, but she wanted to hear him say it. She also wanted Hua Te to hear Kentir's response.

"We sent away as many of our people as we could, believing from our astronomical studies that they would discover other, hospitable planets where human survival will be possible, even if all life ends here on Earth," Kentir answered her. "They left more than two years ago, and they are all far out of contact with Earth now, scattering throughout the galaxy."

"From what Imilca said to Laura and me yesterday, I know that you who live in Issa are not the only humans left on the planet," Hua Te said, looking around at those in the room. "Tell us about the others."

"There are a few groups of about the same size as this one, who remained behind after the great evacuation," Kentir said. "They are scattered around the world and, like us, they are engaged in a quest for survival. We have pledged to exchange any useful information we discover."

"Why didn't you all just leave?" Laura asked.

"As Seret has explained to you, the people of Earth were at the very beginning of their ability to move into space when the asteroid first became apparent," Kentir said. "For several centuries now, Earth has been ruled by a loose confederation of leaders, Seret being the eldest and most respected. As soon as she learned of the approach of the asteroid, Seret called for an immediate conference of all the leaders.

"The first decision to come out of that conference was the order to evacuate as many people as possible," Kentir said. "To do so, we used every spaceship we had. Every earthbound vessel that could be converted for space travel was also used, until each country ran out of ships. There is no time left to build more ships, no workers left to build them, and no more materials available, even if we had the time and the workers. We expended all of our scientific and manufacturing resources in the one great effort to save humankind."

"You should have used your cursed timestones to send yourselves into the future—or far into your own past, where you would be safe—instead of abducting us," Marica said.

"Until you came to us," Kentir responded, "we could not be certain there was a future for our planet. As Seret has explained, we had no way of knowing if life on Earth would survive, or if this beautiful world we love so much would become a charred cinder. And if life did survive, we asked ourselves what sorts of creatures might emerge in that latter time, or whether intelligent life would ever develop again. In the end, after the timestones were invented by one of our group, we decided to send four of the stones into the future, each to a different place and era. It is difficult to convey to you the joy we experienced when four living, intelligent humans appeared in our world."

"Well," said Marica, "now that you know it can be done, you don't need us. Just use the cursed timestones to save yourselves."

"No," Kentir responded, very firmly. "We have a responsibility to do everything we can to save Earth. We are all pledged to give our lives to that goal, if it becomes necessary."

"It is possible," Seret said, "that you who have come to us from the future exist only because of what we will do in this time as the asteroid draws near. The lives of future generations may well depend on us. We are determined not to fail them."

Seret's strong purpose was clear in the tone of her voice as well as in her words. When Laura glanced at Kentir she saw a corresponding certainty that what the Kheressians were doing was the right thing. Laura's respect for both of them increased dramatically. Aged and frail Seret might be, but nothing would sway her from the course she had chosen. Nor would Kentir weaken. He had spoken no more than the simple truth when he declared his willingness to die rather than give up the effort to save Earth.

Laura saw Hua Te nodding his approval of the words spoken by Kentir and Seret. She also saw that Marica was not impressed.

"Instead of wasting your time loading people into spaceships and inventing timestones," said the ever-contentious Marica, "why didn't you concentrate some of your energy on building a weapon that could blast the asteroid into atoms?"

"I am leading the work on such a weapon,"

Thuban said, breaking into the discussion when it seemed as if Marica would continue asking rude questions only to criticize the answers she was given. "Perhaps you would care to assist us in the effort. But Seret, in her wisdom, has decided that several alternate plans ought to be devised, since there is always the possibility that the few weapons we have time to make will not succeed when we use them."

"Alternative plans?" Marica repeated scornfully. "Why don't you just find yourselves a large, deep cave, pack it full of food and water, seal it up, and hide in it until the danger has passed? That is my advice. Now, send me home. I've done my bit for your cause."

"I don't think your idea would work, Marica," Laura said. "Haven't you been listening to Seret? The impact of a large asteroid, or even the effects if it comes close but misses Earth, will cause earthquakes and tidal waves, and certainly volcanic eruptions, too—which means a cave will probably be destroyed along with so much else. From what we have just heard, it sounds as if the scientists expect an ice age to begin shortly after the first effects of the catastrophe have ended, so anyone who survives the initial impact will likely die of the cold."

"All the more reason to send us home at once," Marica responded. "By the way, Seret, you can give me a few of your extra timestones to take with me when I go. I know a couple of scientists who will be happy to buy them from me for enough money to allow me to retire in comfort.

Really, it's the only way for you to soothe my deeply distressed feelings."

"We do not have extra timestones," Seret said, her voice cold with disapproval.

Laura looked from Marica's angry face to Seret's aged, solemn visage, to Thuban's glowering expression. Then she turned her attention back to Kentir. He was the person to whom she was most drawn. She was beginning to comprehend the extent of the burden he bore, the responsibility of discovering a way for human life to survive, while at the same time dealing with conflicting personalities. Marica was probably not the first person to question everything Kentir did. Laura had the feeling that Kentir's own brother often challenged his authority.

The story Laura had just heard sounded like the plot for a science-fiction movie. Yet it was a true story. She did not doubt it. Because of the comet that had recently struck Jupiter, many magazines and newspapers of her own time had carried articles containing the warnings of famous scientists about the dangers of comets or asteroids crashing into the earth. Even without confirmation from her own reading that such dreadful events were possible, Laura was inclined to believe Seret. And Kentir. He spoke with such intensity on the subject that she could not doubt him.

Kentir met her eyes with a steady gaze. Laura wished she could smile at him, but the situation was too serious. All she could do was promise to help him. Perhaps she could find a way to lighten his burden a bit.

"Send Marica back to the twenty-second century," Laura said to Kentir. "But I am staying right here. You have asked for my opinion and it is this: the only way to keep Earth habitable is by stopping the asteroid before it comes close enough to cause the upheavals Seret has described. Because I was born onto this planet, your problem is my responsibility, too. I will do anything I can to help you."

"And so will I," said Hua Te. "I could not do otherwise."

"No one of you will be returned to your own time until the last possible moment," Thuban said in a cold, hard voice. "All of you will be pressed into service. Even you, priest," he ended with a glare at Chacatlipichi.

"I have dedicated my life to the service of the gods," Chacatlipichi responded to Thuban's challenge with grave dignity. "I will do all you ask of me. But why is it that you do not require the spilling of blood to stave off the coming end of this present age?"

"We'll save the bloodletting for a last resort," Thuban answered, moderating his harsh voice, as if he understood that Chacatlipichi was only trying to help. "There are too few of us left. We have no one to spare for sacrifice."

"As you wish, my lord," Chacatlipichi said. He bent his head briefly in the direction of the dais and Seret, then resumed his seat.

"Kentir," Seret said, "I leave you in full command of the project. Make use of our visitors in whatever capacity seems best to you. I will expect you to continue your daily reports to me."

When Seret rose to leave the room everyone else stood, too, the meeting having ended. But Marica wasn't going to leave it at that.

"You, Thuban!" she shouted after Kentir's brother when he started for the door with Seret's hand on his arm. "Wait just a minute. I have more to say to you."

"Later, perhaps," Thuban answered her. "I must attend Seret."

"Not later. Now!" Marica went after him, following him out of the room and past the blue front door. She could still be heard outside the house, arguing with Thuban.

"Oh, dear," said Imilca, shaking her head. "I am sure there will be more trouble between them."

"I believe I ought to attend Seret, too," Renan said. "She may require a physician after Marica is through." On that, he hastened after Marica and the others.

"Kentir," Laura said, putting out a hand to stop him when he would have left the room. "I expected you to mention the lack of a moon in this time, and also the difference in the length of the year between now and my own century."

"We do not have time in which to discuss either calendars or nonexistent celestial bodies," Kentir said, taking another step toward the door.

"Just how big is the asteroid?" Laura asked. "Is it possible that if it hits Earth a glancing blow, it might knock this planet into a wider orbit around the sun? And then, could the asteroid be caught by Earth's gravity and become the moon?"

"If you continue to allow your imagination to run away with you in that way," Kentir said, "you will be of little practical use to us."

"I thought you intended for all of us to use our imaginations," Laura shot back at him. "I thought our differing views were exactly why you needed us."

"I do not have time to argue with you," Kentir said. He turned his head, listening to the loud discussion going on between Thuban and Marica. They were talking about weapons, and from the sound of their voices they were moving toward the back of the house, an area where Laura had not yet been.

"Imilca will begin testing you," Kentir said, sparing a quick glance that included both Laura and Hua Te. "Go with her and follow her instructions." With that, he was gone. A minute later Laura heard his voice added to the dispute going on outside between Thuban and Marica.

"I am not happy about these arrangements," Laura said to Hua Te as the two of them followed Imilca through a series of interconnecting rooms on the ground floor of the house. She had hoped Kentir would stay with her, that he would be the person to whom she would talk about the oncoming asteroid. Beyond her disappointment at Kentir's cool treatment of her, the meeting just ended had generated a new worry.

"I see in our situation the opportunity to acquire great knowledge," Hua Te responded in a remarkably tranquil way.

"That's not what I meant," Laura said. "Now that we know why we are here, I think you are right; we ought to learn as much as we can from the Kheressians, just in case we ever do get home again. Hua Te, I am disturbed by Marica's behavior. You heard her, so you must understand how hostile she is. I have a feeling that Marica will do whatever she can to prevent us from helping these people."

"Those who are consumed by fear are often difficult to deal with," Hua Te said, looking thoughtful.

"That's what Kentir said, too," Laura responded. "He thinks Marica is acting out of fear. But I think Marica has her own agenda."

"Do you believe she could be a danger to our hosts and to us?" Hua Te asked.

"I think it's possible," Laura replied. "Everything she says or does indicates selfishness and a lack of concern for others. She says she just wants to go home again, but I'm not sure that's all Marica is thinking about. Not after the remarks she made about wanting to take some timestones home with her."

"Here we are," Imilca said, interrupting the conversation. She had been walking ahead of Laura and Hua Te, and Laura could not be sure how much of their talk Imilca had heard. Imilca showed them into a small, square room with unornamented white walls. An open door looked out on the lush garden. A white stone table sat in the center of the room, with cushioned stone benches along either side.

"I note," said Hua Te, moving to one of the benches as he spoke, "that here we have more comfortable seating. This indicates a longer meeting than the one we have just had with Seret."

"If you will sit also," Imilca said to Laura, "we will begin at once."

"Begin what?" Laura asked, seating herself on the bench beside Hua Te.

"Before you begin your work here," Imilca said, "I will determine the areas in which you possess knowledge that will be of greatest help to us."

Imilca took a place across the table from Laura and Hua Te. With a smile and a mild expression, she began to ask questions. Her manner never varied; Imilca was always polite, but the next few hours proved to be more grueling than any college final exam Laura had ever taken. Imilca did not use pen and notebook, or even a recorder to tape the responses of the two she was testing. Instead, she appeared to absorb every word spoken by either Laura or Hua Te. She frequently returned to previous responses, recited them exactly from memory, and then asked for clarification on some minor point.

Imilca soon learned that Laura spoke a little Spanish and a smattering of French, that she had majored in English literature at college, that she had been fascinated by the American space program for most of her life. Except for a few facts about the space program and her father's work for NASA, Laura could not imagine what use the Kheressians might be able to make of the information she was providing. To her, none of it seemed pertinent to the problem they were all facing.

Nevertheless, Laura discovered that under Imilca's gentle, yet relentless questioning she could not hide anything about herself, and so she revealed the details of her job as an executive assistant to Roger, her desultory romance with him, his political ambitions, and the way in which her mother had urged her to accept Roger's proposal of marriage. On and on the questioning went, with only one very brief break at midday for a cup of herbal tea and a snack. By the time Imilca was finished with her, Laura felt as if her brain had been turned inside out and squeezed dry. Everything Imilca wanted to know, Laura had told her.

She was not so sure Hua Te had told everything about himself. To Laura, it seemed that Hua Te was choosing his answers with care, and sometimes avoiding direct responses. Having often listened to politicians who talked without giving straight answers to probing questions, Laura recognized dissimulation when she heard it.

"That will be all for now," Imilca said when the sun was sending low shafts of gold light through the open door. "You may rest for the remainder of the afternoon and evening. Kentir will meet with you in the morning to assign you to your work."

Imilca left them and headed back through the house, while Laura and Hua Te, by mutual but unspoken consent, took the opposite way. They went through the open door, walking out of the house and into the garden.

"My head is aching," Laura complained. "I feel like a laboratory specimen that has been dissected and examined right down to its last little cell."

"You have not learned to hide your deepest thoughts," Hua Te said. "What interesting people our hosts are proving to be."

"*Determined* would be a better word for them," Laura said, rubbing her forehead and temples. "I wish I were able to sidestep prying questions as easily as you do."

"It is a learned skill, practiced over many years," Hua Te said. "The knowledge I possess was committed to memory during decades of study. My goal was to become a learned man, and among my friends I am considered a sage. Yet the power of Imilca's memory astounds me. I have no doubt that at this moment, Imilca is reciting to Kentir all that you and I have revealed to her."

"I'm not sure I like that idea," Laura said, thinking of what Kentir would learn about her, additional facts that she had omitted during her talk with him about the life she had left behind. "I spoke about some pretty personal stuff. I couldn't seem to stop talking."

"First, evidence of an immunity to my magical arts," Hua Te said, "and now, Imilca's apparent ability to absorb everything that is said to her. My observations make me wonder again if the minds of these Kheressians are different from our minds. If it is so, remarkable possibilities present themselves."

"Remarkable possibilities, indeed," Laura said, seizing upon a subject that would distract her from thoughts of Kentir learning all about her personal affairs. "Hua Te, in all your studies, did you ever discover a legend about a mysterious, long-ago land that vanished?"

"There is a tale," Hua Te answered, "of a great civilization that existed even before the Middle Kingdom came into being. During my travels, I have heard the story in several lands."

"My people have the same story," Laura said. "We call the land Atlantis. According to the tale, Atlantis was an advanced civilization set on an island continent. The story says Atlantis vanished in a single day, in a great cataclysm. A lot of sensible people throughout history have believed in the idea of an extremely ancient, lost civilization. Do you suppose we are in Atlantis now? Could the asteroid be the cause of the legendary catastrophe?"

"If we are in that far-distant place," Hua Te said, "then, according to the tales I have heard, there will be survivors who will escape to other lands, and their stories will keep the legend alive for many thousands of years."

"What an amazing adventure," Laura exclaimed, "to find ourselves in Atlantis. I wish we could be certain it is where we are. But if the legend of Atlantis is true and if we are there, then . . ." Unable to accept the inevitable conclusion, Laura left the thought unexpressed. But she was just beginning to learn how rigorous Hua Te could be when it came to facing unpleasant truths. He finished the thought for her.

"In this remarkable world in which we find ourselves," Hua Te said, "we cannot be certain of anything, except that it will soon end."

Chapter Nine

Imilca having completed her testing of the four guests, they were all put to work the next day. Laura went with the others to the single-story building she had noticed on two previous occasions. In response to her questions, Imilca told her it was Kentir's headquarters, the place where the work of the project was carried out.

The building sprawled across the landscape in a series of interconnected rooms similar to the arrangement of the ground floor of the main house. Upon entering the building, Laura and her companions found themselves in a large, low-ceilinged space. Work niches opened off the sides of the room, and a round stone table sat in the center of the floor. A holographic image of the world hovered over the circular table. Another image representing the oncoming asteroid was being used to depict the various possibilities for the future of the planet, depending on the exact path taken by the asteroid. Arad, the navigator, was manipulating the images, while Kentir and Thuban stood together at the table, observing the motions of the two celestial bodies.

"Why do you bother?" asked Marica when she saw what the men were doing. "From what Seret says, you are all going to die anyway."

"Not so," Kentir said. "There is a way to prevent the catastrophe, and we are going to find it."

"Do you really think so?" said Marica with her customary sneer. "And just how do you plan to reward us for assisting you in this impossible task?"

"The knowledge that you have helped to save the planet on which you live ought to be reward enough," Thuban responded, fairly growling the words at her. His face was as dark as a thundercloud, and his gray eyes looked daggers at Marica.

"Ah, altruism. How romantic," Marica said. "And how foolish. Don't expect me to do anything for you without proper recompense."

"Imilca tells us you boast of being a weapons expert," Kentir said to Marica.

"I am educated in the use of any and all weapons," Marica said proudly. "I am also well trained in fending off attacks made by stealth, and I have an aptitude for uncovering nefarious intrigues of any kind."

"Are those skills part of your training for work

in the Presidential Special Forces?" Laura asked.

"What do you know about the Special Forces?" Marica demanded, turning fierce eyes on Laura.

"When you first arrived, you said you are a member," Laura answered. "I was only wondering if you are among those assigned to protect important people, like the Secret Service of my time. Surely you've heard of it."

"I am under no obligation to reveal any information to you," Marica said. "What reason do you have for questioning me?"

"Just curiosity and personal interest," Laura said. "I was hoping to know you better, that's all."

"Don't try it. And don't think for a moment that I believe your flimsy excuse, either," Marica said. "No one asks such questions without a hidden cause. I'll uncover your intentions soon enough."

Laura was tempted to accuse Marica of paranoia, but she thought better of it and kept quiet. She wasn't interested in starting a fight with the woman. Marica's hostile remarks produced a moment of uncomfortable silence, until Thuban spoke to her again.

"Imilca reports that you are also knowledgeable about laser technology."

"That is correct," Marica snapped at him. "Do you expect me to explain to you what a laser is?"

"We already know," Thuban said. "In your boasting you told Imilca enough about the subject for us to recognize that we use a similar technology. We focus sunlight through crystals to provide the power we need. We call the crystals firestones, for the heat they generate."

"Is it the same technology that powers the timestones when they are raised to a light source?" Laura asked, remembering what had happened to her when she had innocently lifted the blue stone she had found on the beach at home.

"It is. The timestones are a special kind of crystal," Thuban answered. He used a milder tone with Laura than the one he employed when speaking to Marica, but there was a certain edge to his next remark. "You did not inform Imilca of your knowledge of lasers."

"That's because I don't have any real information," Laura said. "What I know about producing lasers is very general and probably inaccurate. If I knew anything about them, I'd be happy to tell you, Thuban. I want to help."

"I believe you," Thuban said. He then turned his attention back to Marica. "But I do not believe everything *you* say. However, let us discover if you are as knowledgeable about weapons as you claim to be. Come with me."

"Why should I?" Marica demanded, not moving from where she stood.

"You will go with Thuban and follow his orders," Kentir said.

"Why?" Marica asked again, still not moving.

"Because if we don't learn to work together," Kentir said, "we will all die together. Go with Thuban, Marica. Now!"

"Come on, Marica. You are wasting valuable time," Thuban said. He jerked his head, indicating the door to a side room. In response to his repeated summons, Marica stalked toward him at a slow pace deliberately calculated to annoy the impatient, glowering Thuban. Marica brushed roughly against Thuban as she went past him and into the room. The door slid shut behind them.

"I do not think Thuban will find such an unwilling worker helpful," Chacatlipichi remarked to no one in particular. "Marica may contrive to produce more harm than good."

"Leave Marica to Thuban," Kentir said. He checked the door to the room where Thuban and Marica were, making sure it was completely closed before he returned to the three remaining visitors. "Hua Te, I would like you to work with Imilca. She thinks you can be of use to her."

"I shall be delighted," Hua Te said. "May I ask what Imilca and I will be doing?"

"I am making more timestones," Imilca said. "There are two other project members working with me, and I believe you are particularly suited to assist us. Our task is to produce a timestone for every person who lives here in the compound. If all else fails, Seret has decreed that we are to use the timestones to remove ourselves to other times. But we do not have adequate time to make enough of the stones, and the technology is so new to us that we cannot be sure of the accuracy of our product, especially when we are forced to work in haste. Look, Hua Te, I'll show you what we have been doing. I hope you will be able to offer suggestions for improvement."

Imilca led Hua Te to one of the niches at the

far side of the room. There they quickly became engrossed in the displays produced by what appeared to be a miniature computer screen set into one wall of the niche.

"I am trusting the two of you not to mention the nature of Imilca's work to Marica," Kentir said, looking from Laura to Chacatlipichi.

"I wouldn't think of it," Laura responded at once.

"I would think of it," Chacatlipichi said, "but, having thought, I would never speak of the matter to one with a spirit as ungenerous as Marica's."

"I knew I could depend on you," Kentir said. "It may look as if I am ignoring security precautions, but I assure you, Marica will not discover what Imilca's work is by observing the information displayed on the screen in Imilca's work niche. Nor will Marica be able to call up data. Only Imilca holds the key to extracting material on the timestones, and the stones that are finished and ready for use are well hidden.

"Now, Chacatlipichi," Kentir went on, "Imilca's testing of you has shown you to be adept at astronomical calculations and at working with calendars."

"Kentir, I wish you would call me Chac," he said. "Kheressian tongues are continually stumbling over the pronunciation of my full name, so I will adopt the shortened version Marica has bestowed on me."

"As you wish," Kentir said, and then proceeded to make clear his intention to treat the Aztec as a full member of his team. He assigned Chac to work with the two astronomers of the project, a man and a woman who were also mathematicians.

"The astronomers constantly track the asteroid and immediately report any deviation from its expected path," Kentir explained.

"I am honored to know the gods find me worthy to be entrusted with so important a task," Chac said, bowing to Kentir. He had removed his ornate feather costume in favor of the uniform of dark red tunic and trousers worn by all the project workers. With his black hair pulled to the top of his head and fastened into a neat ponytail, the Aztec priest looked little different from the other men on Kentir's team, some of whom also wore their hair long.

When they were introduced to Chac, the astronomers showed every sign of being delighted to work with him. At once they began to show him how the Kheressian version of a computer worked. Convinced that he was aiding the gods, Chac showed no fear of a technology unimagined in his homeland. Instead, he applied himself to learning how to use the computer. Laura had no doubt that he would decipher the workings of the machine, not by understanding the technology involved, but by his skill with numbers, for Chac could perform multiple computations in his head. His vast knowledge of observational astronomy and of the movements of heavenly bodies would further increase his value to his fellow astronomers.

Throughout the discussion of assignments Laura watched Kentir closely, as she had begun to do whenever they were in the same place. She enjoyed looking at him. His features were too boldly carved for him to be considered a handsome man in the classical sense, but the play of expression across his face was fascinating to Laura, and she took note of the way in which he hid his thoughts while dealing with Marica, then let Hua Te and Chac see both his pleasure at their interest in his project, and his gratitude for their willing help. However, with the other three visitors assigned to their tasks, only Laura remained without a job.

"What shall I do?" she asked Kentir. "As I told Imilca, I don't have any advanced technical skills."

"Nonetheless, I can use you." Kentir regarded her soberly. "Imilca reports that you possess general knowledge of a wide range of subjects."

"That's me, a wide-ranging generalist," Laura said, hoping to make him smile. She longed to see amusement brighten his face and make his eyes dance. She wasn't successful.

"You are to be my assistant," Kentir said.

"I am? Do you think that's a good idea?" Laura asked.

"Why not? It's what you were before, when you worked with the man who was your betrothed. You explained to Imilca how you dealt with many different kinds of people, some of whom were difficult or impatient, and how you compiled and organized information before imparting the pertinent facts to your superior. You will do the same for me."

Laura could not decide whether to be pleased with this arrangement or not. Kentir's cool manner did not soften as he began to give her specific directions on her duties as his assistant. She could easily discern his feelings toward each of the other three visitors, yet she had no idea what his opinion of her was. Perhaps he did not like what Imilca had reported to him about her private life.

"In all the talk I've heard about the asteroid, no one has told me how much time we have until it arrives," Laura said, interrupting Kentir's instructions.

"A quarter of a year," Kentir said. "Eighty-nine days, to be exact."

"That isn't very much time." Laura tried to keep the tension out of her voice, but she didn't think she had succeeded.

"Then let us not waste what time we have." Kentir's voice was almost as cold and abrupt as his brother's.

Under other, less stressful circumstances Laura might have been amused to discover herself at the far reaches of time, yet still acting as an executive assistant to a powerful man. Kentir had divided the people working on the project into several teams, and each team made reports to him twice a day. He also received daily information from the leaders of other, similar projects that were scattered around the globe. Kentir needed someone to keep the wealth of information in some sort of order and, Laura soon discovered, he also needed someone to weed out repetitious material so the reports he passed on to Seret each morning were concise.

The weeding and consolidation were Laura's tasks. The translator implanted behind her ear, which made it possible for her to understand the speech of the Kheressians and of the other time travelers, also enabled her to decipher written material. She worked hard on the constant stream of reports, always doing her best, but she earned little thanks from Kentir.

Gone was the sympathetic, concerned man whom Laura had glimpsed on her first evening in Issa. She began to wonder if that man, who had told her of the sad departure of the woman and the family he loved, the man who had kissed her, was a false personality, invented by Kentir to rouse her sympathy and her support for his work. The Kentir she dealt with each day allowed no hint of emotion to color his manner toward her. He functioned like a well-oiled machine, systematically doing what must be done, seldom taking a break, though he insisted that others must periodically rest if they were to do their best work. The passing days fell into a routine marred only by the growing tension of the team members, who knew only too well how short their remaining time was.

They were exploring all possibilities for survival. Marica's sneering remarks about hiding in a cave were an idea that had been thought of long before she arrived in Issa. Seret and Kentir considered an underground hiding place to be a last, forlorn hope, but one that could not be overlooked. One of Kentir's teams was preparing such a retreat in a distant, geologically stable mountain range, and the two saucerships based at Issa, all that was left of the Kheressian fleet, made regular trips to the cave with supplies. The head of this special team was Nirod, who was a close friend of Thuban.

Occasionally, when he could find the time for it, Thuban himself piloted one of the saucerships to the cave, for Thuban liked nothing better than to fly, and he had a reputation for daring and risk taking. As time went on, Laura began to suspect Thuban of using the flights as a relief from Marica's taunting presence.

Marica was apparently determined to be as unpleasant as possible with anyone who spoke to her. On one occasion, while Laura, Imilca, and Marica were all three in the dining room after the midday meal, Laura tried to draw Marica into the conversation she was having with Imilca.

"I have been explaining to Imilca the way in which women are traditionally associated with the moon," Laura said, "and how the feminine menstrual cycle is believed to reflect the lunar cycle. With no moon at this period of history, the Kheressians have no such tradition and, from what Imilca has told me, there is a completely different attitude toward women as a result. Marica, you might be interested in what Imilca has to say on the subject. Tell me, do the women of your time still make the same connection with the phases of the moon that twentieth-century women do?"

"My people have advanced well beyond such primitive nonsense," Marica declared, not troubling to hide her disdain for the subject under discussion. "Only those women who wish to bear children allow themselves to be bothered by the annoyance of a monthly cycle. The rest of us have been entirely freed by medication."

"I suppose the same medication also keeps you infertile," Laura said.

"Certainly. I have no interest in the discomfort of childbearing, or the time-consuming business of child rearing," Marica said.

"In Kheressia also, the choice is left to each woman," Imilca told them. "I, for one, am thankful I accepted the discomfort and the inconvenience of having a child."

"And what thanks did you get in return for all your trouble?" Marica demanded. "Your child was sent off to live in an unknown place beyond the solar system—if she lives long enough to reach such a place—while you have been left behind, to perish in a futile attempt to stop an unstoppable asteroid. I see no profit to you, nor any personal benefit at all from the arrangement—which, I am sure, was ordained by a man."

"I made my own choice to have a child," Imilca said quietly.

"I doubt it," Marica said. "You were certainly influenced by a man's wishes. You don't impress me as being strong enough to stand up against a determined male."

"Imilca's husband is dead and she will never see her daughter again," Laura cried in exasperation. "Marica, why can't you show a little sensitivity? What is your problem, anyway?"

"My problem is a simple one," Marica said. "I want to go home before I fall ill and die of transdimensional disorder. I don't intend to go home empty-handed, either."

"Renan doesn't believe in transdimensional disorder," Laura said.

"What does Renan know of the advanced science of a future century?" Marica asked. Without waiting for an answer, she jumped up from the table and left the other women.

"Never mind her," Imilca said. "Laura, please tell me more about the interesting effects of the moon on your world and on the attitudes of your people. I have a little time left to listen to you and learn, before my midday rest ends and I must rejoin Hua Te in the project building."

Hua Te had told Laura in private that he and Imilca were laboring on an improved version of the timestones. If they were successful, the new, more precisely calibrated timestones would open the possibility of a group of people traveling through time together. Hua Te and Imilca were also trying to perfect a reversing action for the stones that had brought Laura and the other time travelers into the past. Their hope was that the timestones could be reset to return the visitors to the exact moment and place of their initial departures.

But the mechanism of the stones was delicate, and there was still a lot of work to be done. Neither Hua Te nor Imilca ever spoke in great detail about what they were doing, and never when there was a chance that Marica might be within earshot.

While the timestones were regarded as objects to be used as a last resort, the Kheressians looked upon the weapon Thuban had invented, and on which he continued to work, as their best chance for reducing the deadly effect the asteroid would have upon Earth. From her daily reading of the reports handed in to Kentir's desk, Laura learned some of the details of Thuban's weapon. If the weapon functioned as well as Thuban assured everyone it would, the asteroid could be diverted to a path that would cause much less devastation to Earth and to the people living on it.

An alternate possibility, and the one Kentir and Thuban favored, was to direct an intense light beam upon the asteroid for so long a time that the heat of the beam would shatter the asteroid into small pieces. The pieces would either burn up in the atmosphere as they approached Earth, or else they would race off into space again, causing little or no harm.

At Marica's suggestion, an explosive device was also being added to the weapon. Marica insisted it was an improvement, a backup system in case the light beam proved to be inadequate. Laura did not understand how the new addition was to work, but Kentir said he was satisfied with the changes that Thuban and Marica were making. The project members worked on in grim hope, while the asteroid came steadily closer.

As Laura began to know the various personalities involved with the project, she became friends with some of them. Imilca was easy to know and like, as was Arad, the youthful holographic expert, who had an eye for any pretty female. Thuban and his friend Nirod were slightly more distant, but Laura hoped to be on warmer terms with them before much longer.

Renan was more difficult to approach. He was a quiet man and usually stayed in the background. Laura suspected the physician suffered from shyness except when he was speaking about the art of medicine. Then he became eloquent and animated. Laura wished her sister, Susan, could come to Issa and meet Renan. She thought the two of them would have much in common. They were so engrossed in the practice of medicine that each would at once recognize in the other a kindred spirit.

Unfortunately, there was no chance that Susan and Renan would ever meet—and Laura feared there was very little chance that she would ever see her sister again, though she refused to give up hope that it could happen, if Hua Te and Imilca were successful in their work on the timestones. For the most part, Laura tried not to think about her family. It was more important to concentrate on her daily tasks.

Unlike some of the other project members,

who worked in shifts, Laura was free after her evening meal. Each night after eating, she walked to the hill where she had discovered Kentir on her first evening in Issa, and there she scanned the heavens. Seldom were there clouds to obscure the view. Always the aurora colored the sky, while the stars shone brightly. To the unaided eye there was no sign of the asteroid.

It was not until the tenth night that Kentir again came to the hill while Laura was there. She had begun to think he was deliberately avoiding her, perhaps delaying his nightly arrival until after she had retired, so he wouldn't have to talk to her about anything but work. She thought it was possible that he sought solitude on the little hill, relief from the constant pressures he must feel as leader of the project. Watching him approach through the shadows, Laura jumped to her feet, poised to leave at the first hint that he would prefer to be alone.

"It all looks so peaceful," she said when he drew near, "but it's a false peace."

"Thuban tells me the weapon will be ready in just a few more days," Kentir said. "Marica has been a great help to him."

"I am glad one of us has proven useful," Laura responded. "It's too bad that we all couldn't provide the scientific knowledge you need."

"Don't you understand yet?" Kentir exclaimed. He stood facing her, fists planted on his hips, and he sounded annoyed. "It is true that we would have been glad to receive the assistance of a great scientist, but your mere presence gives us hope.

We look at the four of you and we know that, no matter what effect the asteroid may have on our own world, all is not lost. Seeing you, we can believe that, whatever happens, life will continue to renew itself."

"The problem," Laura said, "is that the life that does continue may not be the life of Issa, or any of the other cities of this time. From what I have seen of the Kheressians, I think the loss of your culture would be a great tragedy." She paused to look more closely at Kentir. In the greenish glow of the aurora, his face was haggard.

"You tell everyone else to take periodic breaks, but you never rest," Laura said.

"I will rest when this is over," Kentir said. "If we fail, I will rest for all eternity."

"We can't fail," Laura cried, frightened by the weary despair she heard in his voice. "I can't bear the thought of losing you. Of losing any of my new friends," she hastily added when she saw him staring at her.

"Very well, then," he said. He smiled a little at her impassioned words and corrected himself. "*When* we succeed, then I will sleep well, knowing we have saved our world. And after I awaken from that sweet rest, we will begin to restore Issa to what it once was. We will rebuild the city first, and in time we will repopulate all of Kheressia."

"Tell me about the city," Laura begged. She stared through the twilight to where the dark shape of the empty city lay. "Tell me about the way it used to be."

"In the beginning, Issa was no more than a

small fishing village," Kentir said. He waved an arm toward the stone buildings in the distance. He did not let his arm fall to his side again. Instead, he laid it across Laura's shoulders. She moved nearer, reveling in his closeness, but Kentir's thoughts were on the deserted city.

"The first Issa was left in rubble at the end of a long and deadly war," Kentir said. "When peace was finally established, the leader of Kheressia, a great general who had been born in Issa, made it her capital and rebuilt it."

"A woman general," Laura murmured softly, so as not to disturb his mood.

"Why not?" Kentir asked. "A woman can be as fierce as a man, in war as well as in love."

"I guess that's true enough." Laura was aware of her own fierce feelings. The warmth emanating from Kentir's body, and the strength of the arm casually draped upon her shoulders, were having a surprising effect on her. She wanted Kentir to draw her closer still, to put both of his arms around her. She wanted to him to kiss her as he had done on their first evening on the hill. She felt a sharp tug at her heart as she acknowledged that she, who had never found sex very exciting and had often tried to avoid it, actually wanted Kentir to embrace her with passion.

The thought startled her. She did not want to trust or depend on any man, and Kentir was, after all, a kidnapper. Laura told herself she would be wise to keep that little detail in mind. Yet Kentir was so compelling a personality that when she was with him she tended to forget what he had taken from her by snatching her away from her home and family.

His deep voice coming to her out of the darkness put an end to thoughts of her home and of the reasons why she was unwilling to trust any man too easily. Kentir, unaware of her confusion, was still talking about Kheressian history.

"At the time when Issa was rebuilt after the war," Kentir said, "its citizens still feared attack, which is why the walls are so massive. But as decade upon decade, and then hundreds of years, passed and the peace continued undisturbed, places such as this compound were established on the outskirts of the city, with walls intended for privacy, rather than defense. Within the solid city walls, protective roofs were removed so inner courtyards could be constructed and gardens planted. When I was a boy, there was no city on Earth so filled with greenery and flowers, with music and fine art, no place so full of laughter and joy as Issa. There were schools, museums, government buildings set in flower-filled parks, great halls for public gatherings, and beautiful temples." Kentir paused, and Laura could tell by the look on his face that, as Imilca had once done when discussing the same subject, he was remembering a lost era of youthful happiness.

"Temples built for your gods?" Laura prodded gently, wanting him to continue, because if he did, he would stay with her for a while longer.

"Early in our history, the Kheressians worshiped many gods, but, because the first Kheressians were fisherfolk, the god of the sea was considered the greatest of all," Kentir said.

"Poseidon," Laura whispered, recalling the tales of Atlantis and of the great temple of Poseidon that supposedly stood as its centerpiece.

"Do you call him by that name?" Kentir asked. "In the last few hundred years, our old gods have gradually been discarded. A new philosophy has arisen, and now most men and women believe in the All-Knowing One, the being who orders the universe and guides our lives, who requires no temples of stone and gold, and no statues."

"Do you believe this being sent the asteroid to destroy you?" Laura asked.

"Only a fool would think such a thing," Kentir answered her. "The motion of the asteroid obeys the laws of nature. We Kheressians no longer believe, as Chac does, that a blood sacrifice can alter immutable laws. But we do believe that strong, intelligent action on our part can produce a counteraction in a large body that is moving according to nature's laws. Thus, our attempt to prevent the damage the asteroid will wreak on us."

"The Lord helps those who help themselves," Laura said. "In my time, that is a well-known adage."

"I am pleased to learn we are not so far apart in philosophy," Kentir murmured, his arm tightening on her shoulders. For just a moment his cheek rested on Laura's hair.

She put her arms around his waist, and when she lifted her head to gaze into his shadowed eyes, he looked back at her as if she held the answers to all of the troubling questions about the future that he dared not ask himself, or her. They stood that way for a long time before, with a groan, he gathered her closer and kissed her.

Kentir's mouth was hard and demanding, forcing her lips apart, his tongue thrusting into her. Laura met his sudden display of passion with her own urgency, holding him more tightly, pressing against him. She was aware of his hands on her back as they slid from her shoulders, along her spine, to her hips. With her mind awash in delight, and her qualms about trusting him dissolving in a rush of desire, Laura joyfully acknowledged that the men of Issa—or, at least, the one hot-blooded male who was holding her— were as hard when aroused and as determined upon what they wanted as were the men of her own world. Locked in each other's arms, Laura and Kentir sank to the grassy ground.

"We should not be doing this." Kentir gasped, his lips on Laura's throat, his hands caressing her breasts. "There is work to be done and you are distracting me from it."

"Everyone deserves a break now and then," Laura whispered. She ran her fingers through his dark hair, and when she felt his weight on her she put her arms around him, fully expecting his passionate advances to continue. She was ready to accept and return them, ready to do anything Kentir wanted of her.

"I haven't slept for days." His words were

slurred. With a deep sigh he rested his head on her breasts.

"Kentir?" Laura waited for him to touch her again, perhaps to lift the edge of her tunic and begin kissing her breasts. She moved restlessly in expectation. Kentir did not move. Laura stroked his shoulders, but when he did not respond she finally realized what had happened.

"I don't recall ever putting a man to sleep before," she said with a wry chuckle, "but I'm not insulted. You do need to rest, or you won't be able to continue leading the project."

Kentir stirred, murmuring her name. Then he grew still once more. And suddenly, with an odd little settling around her heart and a rush of moisture to her eyes, Laura knew she was in the one place in all the world and in all of time where she truly belonged—in Kentir's arms. It no longer mattered to her that he had stolen her away from all that was familiar to her. Only one thing mattered: Kentir was the man for whom she had been waiting all of her life, the man she could love forever. But, having found him on the very edge of time, she could not imagine how they were ever going to discover a safe future. It was entirely possible that fate and the Kheressian timestone had brought them together only to tear them apart again.

"Was this evening too soon for us, Kentir?" she whispered. "Or is it already too late?"

The sleeping Kentir did not respond. Laura did not know whether he cared for her or not. Perhaps he was capable of loving only Nivesa, his lost fiancée. But, for this brief time, while he slept with his head on her breast, he was hers. Laura held him in her arms until she, too, drifted into slumber.

Chapter Ten

Laura wakened later in the warm, summerlike night, when the sky began to lighten toward dawn and Kentir lifted her into his arms to carry her to the house. She put her arms around his neck, nuzzled her face into his shoulder, and dozed off again. The next thing she knew, Kentir was tucking her into her bed.

"Stay with me," she murmured, reaching for him, though she was still half-asleep.

"I cannot. I have work to do." He smoothed her tousled hair off her face. "Go back to sleep, Laura."

Kentir kissed her lightly on the cheek, then stood by the bed, gazing down at her. Laura was already drifting into a deeper slumber, but she heard each word he spoke.

"Thank you," Kentir whispered, "for the first respite from worry that I have enjoyed in too many days. And for the first passionate kisses I have exchanged with any woman since my Nivesa went away." Bending, Kentir traced a fingertip across Laura's lips."

"Until tomorrow," he said, keeping his voice soft as he spoke the traditional Kheressian farewell. "Before the end of all we know, I will try to make a time for us, Laura, so we can finish what we started on the hilltop. Even if we join together only once, still we will carry the sweet memory with us into whatever lies beyond the day of the asteroid."

For what remained of the night, Laura slept more soundly than at any time since she had come to Issa. When she wakened the sun was high. Knowing she should have been at work some time ago, she hurried through her morning toilette. She paused in the dining room just long enough to gulp down a cup of herbal tea and grab a piece of fruit to eat on her way, before she set out at a fast walk for the building where the project team worked. As she expected, she found Kentir there before her.

Whenever she was with him, Laura focused on Kentir to the exclusion of anyone else. It was to his boldly sculptured face and tall figure that her eyes were immediately drawn. On this morning, Kentir was unshaven, his tunic was wrinkled, and he looked as if the brief period of rest he had spent with Laura had never happened at all.

He was arguing with Thuban, while several other Kheressians stood about the room watching them in silence, as if they were too shocked by the dispute to intervene in it. Marica was standing next to Thuban and she looked as if she was enjoying the quarrel between brothers.

"I tell you, it is the best way!" Thuban shouted at Kentir. "And it may be the only way."

"You want to risk not only your own life and the lives of your crew members," Kentir said, "but you are also willing to put at risk a ship we cannot afford to lose."

"Risk?" Thuban yelled. "We are all at risk! You are too cautious, Kentir. You always have been. All right, then, I'll pilot the ship without any crew."

"I won't allow it. My cautious attitude is one of the reasons why Seret chose me over you to lead this project," Kentir declared. "You have just proven how right she was, for you know as well as I do that a crew of six is required to fly a saucership properly."

"Two skilled crew members can manage in an emergency," Thuban argued. "I will have no difficulty finding a single volunteer."

"What is going on?" Laura asked. Both men broke off their angry discussion to stare at her.

"So, there you are," Marica said with an unpleasant smile for Laura. "While the rest of us are forced to rise at dawn, you sleep làte. What have you done to deserve special treatment?"

"Yes, Laura, you are late," Kentir said, his voice unexpectedly cold.

"But I thought you said—" Laura stopped, took a deep breath, and continued in a quieter tone. "I must have misunderstood you, Kentir. I apologize for not being here on time. I'll get right to work." She started to leave the central room for the alcove where she usually worked and where she could see a pile of reports awaiting her attention. They had accumulated during the night, and Kentir would want to know at once whether they contained any new information. In the last few days he had left all of the reports for her to handle, an act of trust that Laura appreciated, for it made her feel useful. At the moment, however, she felt only frustration at the change in Kentir's mood since she had last seen him.

"Don't go, Laura," Thuban said, catching her arm. "Stay and help me convince my brother that I am right and he is wrong."

"Oh, yes," Marica said. "If anyone can convince Kentir, Laura can."

"Right about what, Thuban?" Laura asked. Doing her best to ignore Marica, who was watching her with a nasty gleam in her eye, Laura looked from Thuban to Kentir and said, "Wrong about what?"

"The first of the weapons I have been constructing is almost ready to use," Thuban said.

"That's good news," Laura said, still looking at Kentir. "Isn't it?"

"The way Thuban plans to deliver the weapon is bad news," Kentir told her.

"I want to modify one of the saucerships for space flight," Thuban explained to Laura. "I'll have the weapon installed aboard the ship, take it into space, get as close to the asteroid as I can, and then discharge the weapon far from Earth. It will be safer for Earth that way. We can destroy or divert the asteroid while it is still distant enough to prevent most of the deleterious effects that a nearer approach is bound to have on the planet."

"Shortly after Kentir found me and took me aboard his saucership," Laura said to Thuban, "I asked Imilca if the ship could travel into space. She told me it wasn't meant for space flight."

"We modified an entire fleet of saucerships for use in space, and sent thousands of people away from Earth on them," Thuban said, refusing to give up his argument.

"Because the saucerships offered the only chance, however slim, for those people to escape certain death," Kentir said.

"In the process of modification we used up our supply of suitable material, as you very well know, Thuban. If I agree to your plan, you will be forced to use substitutes for materials that we no longer have. As a result, the chances are good that you won't be able to achieve orbit around Earth or, if you do, you won't have the capacity to thrust out of orbit along the correct path toward the asteroid. It is possible that your ship will sink back toward Earth and burn up in the atmosphere. In that case, the ship's engines will explode and rain destruction over a large area. And you and your crew will be lost," he finished.

"What does that matter?" Thuban exclaimed.

"Kentir, you persist in talking as if there is going to be an Earth, with living people on it, after the asteroid arrives. You read the reports every day, so you must know that's not likely. Each new piece of evidence we receive indicates that we are going to suffer a direct collision. There is no safer way than mine, Kentir, and no better chance for Earth."

"And no surer way for Thuban to prove he is a hero equal to his older brother," Marica said.

"Marica, be quiet," Thuban ordered. "Your tongue is sharp enough to make anyone discount the few good ideas you do have. I am not in competition with my brother. We may on some occasions prefer different methods, but Kentir and I share the same goal. I will not allow you to promote additional conflict between us."

"Thuban," Laura said, breaking into his impassioned speech, "do you have any kind of remote-control system you could use in place of a manned ship? That's how my people deliver rockets containing weapons. An unmanned venture is less costly. And, of course, it doesn't risk lives."

"We know," Thuban said. "You told Imilca about unmanned rockets on the day she questioned you. Marica has greater knowledge of the subject than you, and she also suggested sending the weapon aboard a rocket." He gave the dark-haired woman standing next to him a long look, as if he was reconsidering Marica's opinion.

"For once, I agree with Marica," Laura said. "My next question is the obvious one. Do you have a suitable rocket? Since you are capable of space flight, you ought to have the technology available to send the weapon to the asteroid that way. It's a method that has the added advantage of conserving both of your remaining saucer-ships. You may need them later."

"Thuban, there is merit to Laura's suggestion," Kentir said.

"It was my suggestion first," Marica exclaimed. "I am the weapons expert, not Laura."

"What does it matter who thought of it first?" Laura asked. "The important question is whether the idea can be made to work. You will need the right equipment, Thuban. Do you have it readily available?"

"Let me think about it for a while," Thuban said. "Perhaps I'll have a useful idea."

"There were segments of four or five rockets left after we sent our people away," Kentir said to Thuban. "They are stored in the building at the airfield. You could try using them."

"You can't expect me to build a functioning rocket out of bits and pieces of space junk!" Thuban cried. "The guidance system alone—"

"It is exactly what I expect you to do," Kentir told him. "I have made my decision on this issue; the first weapon will be delivered by a rocket aimed directly at the asteroid and controlled from our building here. The second weapon will be kept in reserve, in case we need it later. Take your workers and get to it, Thuban. If you need extra help, let me know and I'll pull people from other jobs and reassign them to you."

"You are wrong, Kentir," Thuban insisted. "Our rockets have always been used to put passenger ships into orbit, not to deliver weapons. This plan won't work, not for a crystal-generated heat beam. Do you have any idea how intricate the controls will have to be to aim and time the beam correctly from such a great distance?"

"You had better make it work," Kentir said. "We have only two weapons and no time to construct more. Therefore, we have only two chances to divert the asteroid or destroy it entirely. Don't waste one of those chances."

"It's you who are wasting our best chance," Thuban declared.

"I take full responsibility for the decision I have made," Kentir said. With a stern look at his brother he added, "Stop wasting time. Get to it, Thuban."

Uttering a vicious curse, Thuban stormed out of the building. With a mocking glance at Kentir and a laugh every bit as nasty as Thuban's curse, Marica followed him.

Kentir turned to look at Laura. He rubbed a hand across his stubbled chin, frowning as he did so, as if he was surprised to discover he had neglected to shave.

"You are still late for work," Kentir said. Then he, too, headed for the door.

"Where will you be?" Laura asked.

"I am going to see Seret," Kentir said, "to make my daily report to her. She will want to know about my decision to mount our first weapon on a rocket."

176

Laura had expected him to treat her more kindly after the time they had spent together, and to thank her for raising an idea that had given him the opportunity to make Thuban do what Kentir wanted. Instead, Kentir looked at her as if he disliked her. But Laura thought that, while he might deny his feelings, where she was concerned Kentir's emotions were far from dislike.

Though Kentir was unaware of the revelation Laura had experienced while he slept in her arms, Laura believed in her heart that he was as drawn to her as she was to him. Why else had he followed her to the hilltop instead of returning to work as he did after almost every evening meal? His overheated kisses had proven his interest, and his soft words spoken in her bedroom when he imagined she was asleep had confirmed Laura's belief. It was suddenly very important to her that Kentir admit, to himself as well as to her, that she did matter to him.

Perhaps it was selfish of her to dream of romance while the fate of the world hinged upon a few desperate people, two untried weapons, some pieces of discarded rockets, and a pair of saucerships. On the other hand, stealing an hour of happiness might be the wisest thing two people who were meant to be together could possibly do at such a time.

But there was little time left to them, and Kentir was so dedicated to his project that he was capable of blocking out all distractions, however pleasant . . . unless Laura could think of a distraction he could not ignore. A distraction sanctioned by Seret ought to be just the thing.

"I agree with you," Imilca said to Laura. "All of us have been working too hard, with too little sleep. Tempers are flaring and, as you say, unnecessary mistakes are being made because people are tired."

The two of them were walking along the seawall, watching the sky turn purple and orange as the sun slowly set behind the distant mountains. Laura knew why the long, northern sunsets had turned so brilliant over the last few days. She had read the reports of volcanic eruptions that threw ash high into the atmosphere, there to be transformed into glorious hues when the slanting rays of the lowering sun touched the layers of ash particles each evening. Kheressian scientists were debating the significance of the eruptions with other scientists in the small outposts scattered around the world. All of them were questioning whether or not the approaching asteroid had caused the volcanoes to explode into violent life.

"Will you talk to Seret?" Laura asked. "She is the only one Kentir will listen to. You've seen how he is, Imilca. The man is driven; he's killing himself. When I try to convince him to stop for a few hours, he says there is no time for rest."

"Seret chose Kentir as leader of the project precisely because he is so responsible," Imilca said. "But I don't think she realizes what the burden is doing to him. Yes, I will speak to Seret. She trusts my judgment as a—what is the word you use, Laura? A psychologist?" Imilca's tongue stumbled over the unfamiliar term.

"That's right," Laura said. "It's what you are, though psychology hasn't been invented yet and everyone here refers to you as a teacher and questioner."

"Hua Te says I am also a healer," Imilca remarked with a smile. "A healer of troubled minds."

"You two are spending a lot of time together," Laura said.

"Only because we have been assigned to work together," Imilca said demurely.

"It's more than that," Laura responded to Imilca's quiet protest with a laugh. "Tell the truth, now, my friend."

"How strange it is," Imilca said, her gray eyes soft, "how very strange, to experience a renewal of happiness just as the world ends."

"I know exactly what you mean," Laura murmured.

"When my husband was killed testing one of the first saucerships converted for space travel," Imilca continued, "I thought my life had ended, too. When it was necessary to send my daughter away, I believed I would never laugh again. It is quite ridiculous, really, to discover a fresh source of joy now."

"I don't think it's foolish at all," Laura said. "Something similar has happened to me. But Imilca, I do think we all deserve one final party, especially since it won't last long enough to interfere with work for the project. A single evening can't make much difference, but I believe it will lighten all of our spirits."

"And perhaps bring relief to a few overtaxed minds. That is my area of concern, and you are right to raise the issue with me," Imilca said. Her voice took on a dreamy note as she continued, "A festival to celebrate the Issa that once existed, and to show our guests the joyous life that used to be. Flowers and music and good food, pleasant conversation and tender encounters, all accepted without the least twinge of guilt, because the festival will be organized at Seret's order. Yes, we do need such an evening."

"And afterward, I am sure we will all return to work in a better frame of mind," Laura said, adding her final argument to Imilca's delightful plans.

"Frame of mind," Imilca repeated. "You do have an original way of speaking. Many of your phrases are strange to me, yet they illuminate your meaning quite clearly." Imilca paused only long enough to hug Laura before she hastened across the lawn to the house, where she would make her request of Seret.

Laura lingered near the seawall for a while longer, her eyes on the colorful sky, and on a flock of seabirds that were gliding on the evening air currents. When she heard a soft step behind her she turned, hoping it was Kentir, but it was not.

"The birds are different here," Chac said, watching the flying shapes. "They have no feathers, and they are all black or dark gray."

"I know what you mean, Chac. They remind me of drawings I have seen of prehistoric birds, of pterodactyls and such. They aren't much like the brightly colored birds you know, that still exist in my time, too."

"The sky is the color of fire and blood," Chac said, his gaze still on the heavens. "The Kheressian calendar is perfect, you know, just as the calendar of my people once was perfect. However, there is a slight discrepancy in their calculations of the speed with which the asteroid approaches. As a result, the time left to us is shorter than the Kheressians first thought."

"How much shorter?" Laura asked.

"Three days less than we first believed," Chac said, "which does not seem to be much, but under the present circumstances . . ." He left the thought unfinished.

"Have you informed Kentir?" Laura asked.

"Of course I have. Are you returning to the house? Shall I walk with you?"

"Yes, to both questions," Laura said. She had not seen much of Chac in recent days. He had been working with the astronomers in rooms at the far end of the project building, where there was a small rooftop observatory. The three of them spent the better part of every night there. Laura thought Chac looked and sounded sad, as if the pressure and the lack of sleep were getting to him, too, just as they were affecting everyone else. Trying to cheer him up she said, "Chac, you do know, don't you, that Hua Te and Imilca are hoping to discover a way to reverse the action of the timestones, so we can return to our homes? Imilca says they are making good progress."

"You may return," Chac said. "I shall not."

"You can't be sure of that," Laura protested.

"I know it," Chac said, his voice conveying an absolute certainty. "Marica scoffs whenever I speak of sacrifice, but she is wrong. Beware of Marica. Hers is a dangerous soul."

They had reached the front entrance of the house. Chac excused himself with the grave courtesy he always displayed toward Laura, saying he and one of the astronomers were planning to use the strongest of the starlenses to see if they could sight the asteroid and recompute its path by direct observation, rather than by using the computer. After the Aztec had taken his leave of her, Laura glanced once more at the darkening sky. Silhouetted against a brilliant red streamer of cloud was the black shape of a bird without feathers.

Repressing a shudder, Laura hurried inside and shut the door.

Chapter Eleven

At Seret's order the party that Laura and Imilca had proposed was scheduled for the next evening. The weather was clear, as it had been since the day when Laura had first come to Issa, and all afternoon a balmy breeze blew over the lawn and through the open windows of the house, bringing with it the salty tang of the sea.

"I must remember to thank Kentir for freeing you from your usual duties this afternoon so you could help me," Imilca said to Laura.

"He wasn't happy about the idea of a party," Laura said, "but he could hardly quarrel with Seret."

"Nor was Thuban pleased when I told him of our plans. Yet those two are the team members most in need of recreation," Imilca said. "It is often so. When men fix their minds upon a task, they are unwilling to stop until the job is finished."

"I believe it's the same story at any time in history," Laura responded to Imilca's comments with a laugh. "Thank heaven Seret has better sense than the men. Imilca, you and Hua Te have done wonders with the lanterns."

"It was Hua Te's suggestion," Imilca said. "He tells me that, in his homeland, illuminated lanterns are a common sight at evening entertainments."

Small lanterns in cheerful colors had been hung from many of the trees, and a row of lanterns sat upon the seawall. When darkness fell, the garden and the lawn would be illuminated and a sparkling light would be cast upon the waves. The lamps did not have the exact appearance of the ornamental Chinese lanterns Laura knew from parties in her own time, for they were not paper, but thin, undecorated ceramic cylinders, and the light they provided was from a phosphorescent chemical, rather than from the candles of Hua Te's day or the electricity of Laura's time. Still, Laura expected the overall effect would be bright and festive.

Indoors, Laura and Imilca arranged vases of flowers they cut from the garden. They placed tall vases around the main room and on the serving ledge in the dining room, and then set the lowest bowls on the dining room table. By late afternoon the house was filled with fragrance and bright-colored blossoms.

Seret herself had seen to the table settings, using glassy-clear plates, bowls, and cups, and she supervised the preparation of special foods, including an enormous dish of baked sea creatures that was encased in a thin, flaky crust. The meals Laura had eaten in Issa so far had been simple ones, consisting of whatever fruits and vegetables were ripe in the garden, combined with preserved foods, grains, and roots that were stored in the cellar. Such dishes were occasionally supplemented by the catches of several project workers who chose to spend their few leisure hours fishing.

"We have Renan to thank for today's fresh seafood," Seret told Laura. "First he caught a large fish; then he discovered a colony of shelled mud dwellers and dug them out for us to use."

"They look and smell like clams," Laura said, watching Seret prepare the dish. "Is that seaweed you are adding?"

"It is," Seret said. She had wrapped a voluminous, sleeveless garment over her yellow robe like an outsize apron, and she appeared to be enjoying the opportunity to cook. The dignified leader of Kheressia reminded Laura of an aged grandmother preparing a holiday meal. Seret crumbled dried kelp into the seafood mixture with skilled fingers, as if she worked in the kitchen every day of her life. For Laura's benefit, as Seret worked she continued her lesson on the local cuisine. "At one time, seafood baked in pastry in just this way was the favorite meal in Issa, a dish so famous that every visitor felt an obligation to try it. The sea has always been so bountiful that no one here need go hungry when just a slight effort will produce at least one good-sized fish."

It saddened Laura to know that the meal they were preparing to eat would very likely be the last such feast enjoyed in Issa, and that never again would visitors from other lands carry home recollections of the famous seafood creation. But Seret did not look sad, and she hummed as she stirred a sauce or chopped ingredients. Laura admired the older woman's ability to lay aside her serious worries in order to make certain that others would enjoy the party.

With the house and grounds in readiness and the food prepared, Seret excused herself to rest until it was time for the party to begin. After she left them, Laura and Imilca made a final inspection of the dining room, to be sure everything was in order. Laura glanced out the window. The day was lengthening toward evening, and as the sun began to sink behind the mountains, the sky once again assumed brilliant hues as the fading light was reflected from the volcanic ash high in the atmosphere.

"Just for this one evening," Laura remarked to Imilca, "the sight isn't disturbing. A long, orange and lavender twilight will only add to the festive appearance of the grounds."

"So it will," Imilca agreed. "Now, my friend, you and I have not quite finished our personal preparations. Come with me, Laura. We are going to beautify ourselves. I have found a dress for you to wear, and I will display it for your approval as soon as both of us have bathed and washed our hair."

An hour or so later, Imilca knocked on Laura's bedroom door, holding the promised dress over her outstretched arms. The gown was a simple column of bronze-colored fabric that fastened at either shoulder with circular gold pins. The pins were set with stones that looked to Laura like real amethysts and topazes, though, not knowing much about the formation of gemstones in such a remote time, she could not be sure that was what they actually were. It was enough for her that the pins, and the gold-and-amethyst earrings Imilca also provided, were perfect complements to the gown, which had gold and purple threads woven into the material. With each movement Laura made there was a faint sparkle of gold, and deep purple shadows revealed themselves in the soft folds of the cloth.

"Imilca, thank you. This is easily the most becoming gown I have ever worn," Laura exclaimed, seeing herself in the mirror for the first time as Imilca finished securing the shoulder pins and stepped away from her. Laura hoped Kentir would approve of the way she looked, though she did not voice her desire to Imilca. For her own pleasure Laura sprinkled Imilca's flower-drenched perfume over her bare shoulders and arms. As always, the fragrance lightened her mood.

Imilca was already dressed in a gown similar

187

in style to Laura's, but icy blue in color. The pins at Imilca's shoulders were silver, set with blue stones. Instead of wearing earrings, she had woven tiny blue and lavender flowers through her thick, reddish blond curls, which she had left unbound.

"You look like a lady in a Pre-Raphaelite painting," Laura said, admiring her friend's appearance. "Hua Te will be stunned at the sight of you, though he'll be too polite to say so—in public, anyway."

"Do you think so?" Imilca blushed a little at the compliment, then stole a last look in the mirror, as if to reassure herself that Laura was right.

"I left a dress for Marica in her room," Imilca said. "I hope she will decide to wear it."

"So do I," Laura said, "but you never can tell what Marica will do. She is perfectly capable of refusing to wear a dress out of sheer spite."

Laura and Imilca met Seret in the upper hall and descended the stairs with her. Seret's yellow evening robe was trimmed with blue and green embroidery, and she wore a large pair of gold earrings as her only jewelry.

When the company gathered in the flower-filled main room, the men proved to be as splendidly garbed as the women. Renan had on a turquoise tunic and trousers. Hua Te was in a blue robe of vaguely Oriental design that blended remarkably well with the color of Imilca's gown.

Chac had found a sleeveless, belted tunic and matching trousers in a fabric of bright red, woven with a zigzag pattern of equally bright blue and yellow, and he had topped his eye-catching outfit with a brilliant red cape. There wasn't a single feather on the man, yet the effect of his costume was every bit as exotic as the priestly garments he had worn when Laura had first seen him.

"I like it," Laura said, greeting him. "It suits you well."

"That is what Seret also said," Chac responded. "If my clothing pleases her, and you, then I am happy." Chac moved away to join the two astronomers, who were more soberly clad in dark green, the man in tunic and trousers, the woman astronomer in a gown similar to Laura's, which seemed to be the favorite style among Kheressian women.

Left to herself, Laura surveyed the colorful gathering. She nodded and smiled at Arad when he appeared with a woman on each arm, and at Nirod, who came in alone a few minutes later. Listening to snatches of cheerful conversation, hearing laughter, accepting compliments on the flower arrangements and thanks for the original idea to have a party, Laura began to understand what life in Issa had been like in happier days.

Then Kentir arrived. He was clad in a jacket and trousers of dark purple-red, trimmed in gold. Laura caught her breath when she saw him descending the stairs to the main room. No other man in that gathering was as tall as Kentir; no one else could boast of shoulders so broad or display such a commanding presence.

Not even Thuban could outshine Kentir in

189

Laura's eyes, though Thuban came·in directly behind his brother, wearing black and silver and looking remarkably handsome in a dark, hard-edged way. Laura spared only an instant to admire Thuban's striking appearance before she returned her attention to Kentir.

He was looking about the room with a restless gaze, as if he was searching for someone. He saw Laura, and she had the impression that he, too, caught his breath. He came directly toward her. He did not mention her gown, but the way his eyes kindled with gray-blue fire as they swept over her from head to toe made Laura think he was appreciative of the effort she had made with her toilette. Kentir's compelling gaze made her feel decidedly weak in the knees. She could not breathe naturally again until he turned slightly away from her to answer a question that Renan had asked.

In the first moment when Kentir's attention was not fully on her, Laura admitted to herself the irony of her fate. She, who had sworn to learn everything she could find out about the next man she got involved with, had fallen head over heels in love with a man whose heart and soul must remain forever alien to her, for he was not of her time, not of her world. His childhood and his early years were a mystery to her, because she did not know enough about normal Kheressian life to put the facts Kentir revealed about his youth into their proper context. And she must seem as foreign to him as he was to her.

Laura reminded herself that Seret trusted Ken-

tir completely, that every member of the project
regarded him as an honest and exceptionally responsible man. From her own conversations
with him, Laura believed him to be a lonely man.
Though she knew he was not indifferent to her,
Laura suspected that some part of Kentir's heart
remained bound to his fiancée and always would.

But even if he did care for her, what future
could there be for them? They had only a brief
time before the approaching asteroid changed
everything. It was possible that everyone living
in Issa could die, including herself. It was also
possible—assuming Hua Te and Imilca were
successful in their efforts to devise a way to reverse the mechanism of the timestones—that
Laura would be returned to her own time. If that
were to happen, she would be separated from
Kentir by thousands upon thousands of impass-
able years.

*If I had any common sense at all, I would close
my heart to him,* she thought. *I'd remember the
promise I made to myself when I broke up with
Roger.*

And then Kentir looked away from Renan, toward Laura. The warmth in his eyes and the
slight smile curving his firm lips told her he was
far from indifferent to her.

*Why did I imagine that love, when I found it,
would make sense?* Laura asked herself. *If the
next few weeks are all I am going to have with him,
then I'll accept whatever life has to offer, and I
won't complain when it ends.*

Kentir's warm gaze slid from Laura's face to

her shoulders. Laura could not help herself; she moved her shoulders and arms, changing position under his heated look. The motion stirred a faint whiff of the perfume she was wearing, allowing it to waft upward to her nose. Laura took a deep breath, inhaling the scent, and her mood changed.

There was nothing mysterious or sinister about the effects of the perfume. Imilca wore the same fragrance every day; she had created it as a way to lift her spirits in a dark time. Since the evening's entertainment was designed for the same purpose, Laura saw no harm in the perfume. She decided to enjoy it, along with whatever pleasures the night had to offer.

The party began on a pleasant note, the twenty or so project members who were gathered in the room agreeing that the evening was a welcome respite from long days of constant work. Wine was poured, the first alcoholic beverage Laura had tasted since coming to Issa. The wine was clear amber in color and slightly fizzy on her tongue, with an agreeably sweet taste. They drank it from small crystal cups. Kentir came to Laura with a cup in each hand. He gave one to her and waited expectantly until she had tasted and approved it.

"I am told that we have you to thank for this evening," Kentir said to Laura. He did not look directly at her when he spoke, though he was standing so close beside her that the soft fabric of his sleeve brushed her bare arm when he lifted his winecup to his lips.

"It was a joint endeavor," Laura responded. "Imilca and I suggested it, and Seret agreed it was a good idea. I wish you would smile," she added, noting his serious expression.

"You have a remarkable effect on those around you," Kentir said. "Never before has anyone suggested that we ought to rest from our labors. I was amazed to learn from Seret that she approved of your idea."

"Perhaps someone should have suggested such an evening long ago," Thuban said, joining Laura and Kentir as he spoke. He gave his brother a mocking look, as if to emphasize his next words. "It's just possible that we could have found a solution to the coming disaster by now, if only we had occasionally lifted our heads to look around us. Nor should we stop living before our doom strikes. And, speaking of living—and of doom . . ." Thuban's voice trailed off. He stared at the staircase.

Marica stood on one of the steps, keeping well above the group in the main room while, with a haughty air, she looked over the partygoers. The sleek, narrow gown Imilca had chosen for her was as black as the night sky, with just a few silver threads for trimming. Glittery black jewels dripped from Marica's earlobes in long strands, and her close-cropped hair shone with blue-black highlights when she moved her head. Her restless gaze found Chac and swept over his splendid attire. Marica's lip curled.

"Well, Chac," she said in the scornful tone she always employed when addressing the Aztec, "I might have known you would decide to wear bloodred. It suits you, but where is your precious obsidian knife? Ah, good evening, Thuban. So you have also been coerced into attending this ridiculous and unnecessary gathering." Dismissing Chac in favor of Thuban, Marica tilted her head to look directly into the eyes of the tall man who had hastened to her side to escort her down the final few steps.

"Marica, you are the last of our company to arrive," Seret said, breaking the momentary silence. "Let us adjourn to the dining room."

As if embarrassed by Marica's undisguised hostility, and relieved to have something to do to avoid a confrontation with the perpetually angry young woman, the company moved in some haste to the next room. At Laura's urging the food had been set out buffet style so no one would have to act as server, a task that was alternated among all of the project members. Having filled their plates, people sat wherever they wished at the long table.

Laura was pleased to see Chac in animated discussion with the couple who were the astronomers of the project. Watching the three of them laughing together, she realized that the astronomers did not share Marica's aversion to Chac. Apparently they had chosen to ignore Chac's past priestly activities in order to establish a camaraderie with him that was based on their mutual interest in what happened in the skies.

"May I join you?" Kentir asked, appearing beside Laura's chair. At her assent he took the seat next to her. "This is my favorite dish," he said, and proceeded to consume the seafood pastry on his plate with an open pleasure that delighted Laura.

"Perhaps you and my brother are right," Kentir said to her a few minutes later. "This is a pleasant interlude. For most of us at this table tonight, it will be the last such evening. Perhaps the last such evening for all of us," he ended on a more somber note.

"Just for a couple of hours, don't think about the asteroid," Laura pleaded, surprised to discover that his thoughts were so similar to the ones she had found herself dwelling upon while helping to prepare the party. But she had banished her own worries for the evening, and she had originally suggested the party in the hope of helping Kentir to forget his burdens. "Please, Kentir, just relax and enjoy yourself."

"You cannot know how difficult it will be for me. But I will try. How could I do otherwise, when you and Seret command me?" he said.

Forgetting about the oncoming asteroid, if only for a single evening, appeared to be the goal of everyone at the table. Seret, Laura, and Imilca received many compliments on the food, the flowers, and the glowing lanterns that could be seen through the wide windows. Even the lingering sunset was praised, as if the three women had arranged it, too. When the sky darkened and the meal ended, couples began to drift out of the house.

Imilca had promised Laura that the project

members would provide their own entertainment, and so they did. From the direction of the garden came the haunting sounds of a stringed instrument and a man's voice lifted in song. His music was soon blended with a woman's voice, and then with another man's, the three singers creating a strange, beautiful harmony that Laura knew she would never forget.

The sweet sound wound itself through her mind until she began to believe that she recognized the song and knew the words to it. Laura was reminded of "Londonderry Air," and of "Greensleeves," both songs so old their origins were lost in the ancient shadows of past history. Then the tune spun into another, less plaintive strain, and she dismissed the hint of familiarity. Surely her brain was trying to make connections that weren't there—or were they? Finally she stopped questioning and let the music fill her mind and heart, for while it continued she felt as if she truly belonged to the wonderful, soon-to-be-lost city on the edge of the northern sea.

Kentir sat back in his chair, a cup of wine in one hand, listening to the music with a faint smile on his face. Hua Te and Renan were still at the table, discussing the differences between Chinese and Kheressian medical practices in voices too low to interfere with the music. Seret added an occasional comment, while Imilca listened to the two men in silence, very likely memorizing every word they said. Farther down the table, Chac and the astronomers fell silent under the influence of the sweet sounds drifting through the open windows.

Even Thuban seemed content, looking relaxed while he nursed his own recently refilled cup of wine. Laura and Imilca exchanged pleased looks across the table, the mutual acknowledgment of women in any era of history who have worked together to arrange a successful dinner party.

Only Marica could not let the evening finish in a peaceful way.

"Seret," Marica said from her place beside Thuban, "when all of your spaceships left, evacuating most of the population of this planet, why weren't you among the passengers?"

"How could I, an elder, insist upon taking a berth on an overcrowded ship?" Seret asked. "Such a place is better occupied by someone younger and stronger than I, perhaps a woman who thus need not suffer the anguish of separation from her children, or a man who will be able to offer physical protection to his family when they finally reach a strange, new world and begin to settle it."

"You're crazy," Marica declared with a look of disgust for Seret's altruism. "If I were you, I'd have been the first person to set foot aboard the first ship leaving. What's the point of being the leader if you can't get a ride out of danger?"

"It is the duty of a leader to set aside her desire for personal safety and, instead, act for the benefit of all. Who can say what good will be accomplished by the person who went off-world in my place?" Seret spoke with the serenity of one who knows she has done the right thing.

"Yes," said Chac from the far end of the table. "You made a sacrifice for the benefit of your people. It is an act I can understand and admire, Seret. A willing sacrifice is always a worthy deed."

"Chac, you idiot, will you please just stop talking about sacrifice all the time?" Marica said, raising her voice. "The smartest thing anyone can do is preserve her own life. Nothing else matters, except getting rich if you can, but unfortunately, I haven't seen much chance of doing that while I'm in this place."

"I can think of a lot of things that are more important than saving my own life, or making a fortune in earthly goods," Laura said. "Marica, don't you feel any responsibility at all to help the Kheressians?"

"Why should I?" Marica demanded. "Did they show any responsibility toward us when they brought us here?"

"The Kheressians feel a larger responsibility, to save their world from destruction if they can, and, in the process, to teach us how to save our own world if we should encounter a similar situation in some future time," Laura answered. "If you had been paying attention when Seret spoke to us on our first day here, you wouldn't need me to remind you of that obvious fact." Laura's temper was flaring, as it so often did when she was dealing with Marica. She struggled to keep her irritation with the woman under control.

"You are as bad as the Kheressians are," Marica said, sneering at Laura. "Thanks to what you call their sense of responsibility, we four involuntary time-travelers are as good as dead."

"Is everyone in the twenty-second century like you?" Laura asked. "I'd hate to think so, because I find your attitude incredibly selfish."

"It's the only attitude I have," Marica said. "And I don't care about your opinion."

"If you can bring yourself to cease worrying about your own demise," Chac said to Marica, "you may then be able to understand a point of view different from your own."

"Oh, be quiet!" Marica shouted at him. "I'm sick of all of you." She leaped to her feet as she spoke, and rushed out of the dining room and up the stairs toward her own room. Thuban set down his winecup and followed her.

Seret watched them go. Then, rising, she said to Renan, "I find that I am tired. Renan, would you escort me to my room? The rest of you, remain as long as you wish. Imilca and Laura, thank you for an evening I shall not forget. Until tomorrow, my friends."

Chapter Twelve

With Seret's departure the party came to an end. Chac left with his fellow astronomers, saying they were planning to spend the rest of the night watching the stars. Imilca and Hua Te decided to walk in the garden and admire the lanterns while they listened to the music. Within a few minutes Laura and Kentir were the only ones remaining at the table.

"I fear my brother is fast becoming ensnared by Marica," Kentir said, pouring more wine for both of them.

"He does seem to be fascinated by her," Laura agreed. "I cannot imagine why. I have seldom met anyone so unpleasant and self-centered. I can only hope Marica doesn't represent the future of the human race."

Winecup in hand, Laura rose to stand by the window, to look out at the soft lantern lights and the shadowy figures of the partygoers who were strolling about on the lawn. The late-evening air remained warm, and the scent of night-blooming flowers floated from the garden into the room as if borne on the notes of the continuing music. A faint, low-lying mist hung over the calm sea. If she had not seen Issa pointed out on a holographic map, Laura would have found it impossible to believe the city lay so close to the North Pole, for the darkness outside the open window was that of a soft, summer night in a more southerly clime.

"Though you and your companions have been of great help to us," Kentir said, "I now regret the decision that brought you here."

"Why?" Laura asked. She turned from the window, thinking to find him still at the table. But Kentir had moved quietly until he was standing beside her. Laura took a guess at the reason for his unexpected remark. "Is it because your brother is sleeping with Marica? Or soon will be sleeping with her? Surely it is his own, personal business. Thuban is an adult. In the short time we have left, if they can be happy, why shouldn't they be together?" Laura could not imagine Marica making anyone happy but, as Marica herself would say, that was Thuban's problem.

"You do not understand," Kentir said. "Thuban's interest in Marica has little of the intellectual in it, and nothing spiritual at all. It is entirely physical. In fairness to my brother, I must wonder if perhaps the three years of uninterrupted, intense work he has dedicated to the project have made Thuban vulnerable to the lure of a woman like Marica. Yet in the lives of Kheressians, sex is only a minor factor. Traditionally, intellectual inquiry and spiritual development have been our primary goals."

"What about love?" Laura cried. "Love does include sex—or it ought to." Recalling her own distaste for the sexual act she stopped.

"True," Kentir said. "Yet there should be more to mating than mere physical joining. There ought to be joy and a sense of emotional union. I do not think Thuban finds that kind of closeness with Marica. I fear he never will."

"The kind of closeness you experienced with Nivesa." The thought of Kentir in the arms of another woman was painful to Laura, and the bitter pang that stabbed her heart told her beyond any doubt that he was the one and only man for her. If only she could be equally certain of his feelings for her.

"My betrothal to Nivesa ended more than two years ago," Kentir said with quiet finality.

"And now?" Laura asked, her voice barely above a whisper. "What about the here and now?" Setting her winecup down on the sill, she leaned back against the window frame and looked up at Kentir. His gaze was on the faintly illuminated landscape beyond the house, on the lawn, the misty sea, the sky, and the distant stars. Then, slowly, Kentir turned his head and looked directly at her.

"Here and now," he said, "you are the most disturbing woman I know. Until I saw you standing alone in the desert, I experienced no difficulty at all forgetting that I am a man."

"I'm glad to hear it," Laura said.

"You should not be glad. Nor should I. You have made me hope again, and that is a dangerous thing. All of my hopes, my entire concern, ought to be focused on the project, not on a woman."

"What are you afraid of, Kentir?" Reaching up, Laura touched his face, skimming her fingertips over his cheekbones and his hard jaw. With the lightest pressure she outlined his lips. She was rewarded by his swift intake of breath.

"You distract me from my work." His voice was a low growl.

"Perhaps you need distraction," she whispered. Her hands were on Kentir's shoulders, so she felt the shudder that went through him when she moved closer to press herself against him. "This evening has been designated as a time for pleasure and relaxation. If the others can accept Seret's decree, why can't you?"

"Laura, don't," he said, as if in warning.

She paid no attention to his frown. She was not a seductress by nature; in fact, she had been left unmoved by her few previous sexual encounters. But Kentir affected her as no other man ever had. She feared that for the two of them there might be no night but the present one, no other opportunity so beckoning. She was determined to make the most of what little time they had.

Laura linked her fingers together behind Kentir's neck and smiled at him.

"Don't," he said again, his voice low-pitched and throbbing with intensity. He stood perfectly still, not moving away from Laura, yet not embracing her, either.

"Don't what?" she asked. "Would it destroy you to put your arms around me?"

"It might." He took another long, shuddering breath. "Do you know what you are doing to me?"

"Yes," she whispered, her lips still curved into a smile. She met his eyes squarely, certain for the first time in her life that she wanted a man—this man, and no other. A heated melting began deep within her. "Yes, Kentir, I know exactly what I am doing."

With a groan, he put his arms around her and bent his head to kiss her. Laura stood on tiptoe, her fingers moving through his thick, dark hair. Her breasts were crushed against his broad chest, her thighs were forced tight along his thighs when his hands reached down to catch her hips and pull her against his burgeoning masculinity. She opened her mouth beneath his, deliberately tempting him to enter. He did, not in a swift surge but in a slow, tantalizing process of possession that left her shaken and weak. Kentir made her his with that kiss, and Laura understood that the kisses and caresses they had shared on the grassy hilltop on two previous occasions had been the most casual of preliminaries. What she was experiencing now was something else entirely, and she was overwhelmed by the fierce flame of Kentir's barely banked desire.

"This is not all I want of you," he murmured into her ear. "I need more than a kiss or two, more than a brief embrace."

"I want more, too," she whispered. With her face buried against his shoulder, she breathed in the scent of him, a fine, masculine odor spiced with the salt of the sea. His mouth had tasted of amber Issian wine and of hot, manly desire. She wanted his lips on hers again, wanted to taste desire grown out of control. "Make love to me, Kentir."

He drew back a little, so he could look into her eyes. Laura saw in his gaze the longing he could not hide. She saw something else, too. In the gray-blue depths of Kentir's eyes lurked a grief so terrible that Laura marveled how one man could bear it. She wondered how she would have handled the violent loss of her entire world, of the person she loved most, and of her dearest family members. She knew her parents, and the world in which she had grown up, still existed in some other part of time, even though she was no longer with them. She had that much, and she found the knowledge comforting, but Kentir was bereft of all he held dear, for he could not be certain whether or not Nivesa and his parents still lived. He was certain only that the world into which he had been born would end soon.

"For us, there can be no past," Kentir said, as if he were listening to her thoughts. "And, very

likely, there will be no future. For you and me,
Laura, there is only the present. We must ask no
more of the fates than this one precious night."

"It's enough for me," she told him, and pulled
his head down so his mouth met hers again.

Kentir swept her into his arms and carried her
out of the dining room, through the deserted
main room, and up the long staircase to the second floor. Laura was no light burden. She was
tall, with a well-rounded figure, and she was
fairly muscular for a woman, the result of regular
exercise. Kentir held her as if she weighed nothing at all. With Laura in his arms he climbed the
stairs and headed along the corridor to her room.

Once there, he laid her on the bed and bent
over her. Laura was glad he didn't expect her to
stand while he undressed her, because, as usual
when she was dealing with Kentir's disturbing
closeness, she was trembling. She began to shake
even harder when he unfastened the pins holding
her gown together at each shoulder and drew the
loosened fabric down to expose her breasts.

She desperately wanted him to find her lovely
and to appreciate what she was offering him,
without making comparisons to his beloved fiancée.

Then his mouth was on hers, his hands were
stroking her breasts, and Laura fully expected to
die from the heat that surged along her body in
response to his caresses. When Kentir continued
to kiss her without ceasing his knowing atten-
tions to her breasts, the warmth began to coa-
lesce somewhere deep inside her, at the very core

of her being. The heat grew and expanded, threatening an imminent explosion. Swept up in desire, Laura forgot her fears of not measuring up to Kentir's expectations, or to his memories of another woman. All that mattered to her was Kentir and the warmth he generated in her body and her mind.

Laura tore at the gold fastenings of his jacket, her fingers trembling. With a broken laugh Kentir brushed her fumbling hands aside and pulled off the jacket. A moment later they were both unclothed, were lying flesh to naked flesh, and Kentir's hands and his mouth were driving Laura to the brink of madness. He roused erotic sensations from places she had not imagined could tingle and ache and burn. No sooner had his hands moved on to some other unexpected area of her body than she wanted him to return to where he had already been. She heard someone moaning and gasping and did not know she was making the sounds until Kentir gave her what she was pleading for, until he touched her again and again—and urged her to touch him in ways she had always thought were forbidden. With Kentir she quickly learned that nothing was forbidden.

He was so large that she was glad it was not her first time with a man. Yet she did not fear his size or his strength. She knew he would never hurt her. Kentir would only give her pleasure.

She was sobbing with need when he finally entered her. She felt her body give way to him, and then close around him. She clutched at his shoulders and smiled into his eyes. He had brought her so close to fulfillment that she shivered into ecstasy as soon as he began to move in her. The ecstasy ebbed, only to be renewed when Kentir, aware of what was happening to her, loosed all restraint and, with a wild cry, plunged into her moist heat over and over again, seeking his own passionate release.

By the time Kentir held her gently under his arm and whispered to her of the pleasure he had found in her, Laura was his, body and soul.

"That never happened to me before," she said, her own voice unfamiliar to her, so soft and husky was it in the aftermath of great emotion. "I was always left wondering what all the fuss was about."

"Hush," he whispered, his large hand smoothing her hair. "We are sworn to live only in the present. The past does not exist for us, nor does the future. We are agreed that we have only the present. Only this night."

"In this night," she told him, "I am more richly blessed than any woman has a right to expect."

"So am I blessed with the gift of your unfettered passion," he said.

He made love to her again later, when the lanterns on the trees and the seawall had been extinguished, and the only light remaining was the blue-green glow of the aurora. In that magnetic glow Kentir was like a ghostly dream-lover created out of shadows and invisible fire. Laura, delirious with love and desire, unable to withhold anything from him, offered herself up to varia-

Thrill to the most sensual, adventure-filled Romances on the market today...

FROM  LOVE SPELL BOOKS

As a home subscriber to the Love Spell Romance Book Club, you'll enjoy the best in today's BRAND-NEW Time Travel, Futuristic, Legendary Lovers, Perfect Heroes and other genre romance fiction. For five years, Love Spell has brought you the award-winning, high-quality authors you know and love to read. Each Love Spell romance will sweep you away to a world of high adventure...and intimate romance. Discover for yourself all the passion and excitement millions of readers thrill to each and every month.

Save $5.00 Each Time You Buy!

Every other month, the Love Spell Romance Book Club brings you four brand-new titles from Love Spell Books. EACH PACKAGE WILL SAVE YOU AT LEAST $5.00 FROM THE BOOK-STORE PRICE! And you'll never miss a new title with our convenient home delivery service.

Here's how we do it: Each package will carry a FREE 10-DAY EXAMINATION privilege. At the end of that time, if you decide to keep your books, simply pay the low invoice price of $17.96, no shipping or handling charges added. HOME DELIVERY IS ALWAYS FREE. With today's top romance novels selling for $5.99 and higher, our price SAVES YOU AT LEAST $5.00 with each shipment.

AND YOUR FIRST TWO-BOOK SHIP-MENT IS TOTALLY FREE!

IT'S A BARGAIN YOU CAN'T BEAT! A SUPER $11.48 Value!

Love Spell ✦ A Division of Dorchester Publishing Co., Inc.

Get Two Books Totally
FREE —
An $11.48 Value!

▼ Tear Here and Mail Your FREE Book Card Today! ▼

PLEASE RUSH
MY TWO FREE
BOOKS TO ME
RIGHT AWAY!

Love Spell Romance Book Club
P.O. Box 6613
Edison, NJ 08818-6613

AFFIX
STAMP
HERE

tions that tormented and then delighted her, until she was too weak to do anything more than lie across Kentir's heaving body and weep for joy.

In the pale early morning light he took her once more, this time with a slow tenderness that told Laura it was the last time, though he did not say so. But in his smoky eyes she saw grief mingled with his desire, and she gave herself to him as if they were saying farewell for all time. The ecstasy, when it came upon her, was bittersweet, though no less intense for that. And when Kentir shivered and went rigid in her arms, she held him close and wept again, but not for joy.

She held him till he fell asleep, his legs still tangled with hers, his breath warm upon her cheek.

"Wake up, Laura."

Hearing Kentir's voice, Laura rolled over in bed, reaching for him. When she did not find him, she reluctantly opened her eyes.

The tangled bedclothes were dragging on the floor, two pillows were pushed to the foot of the bed, and in the middle of the rumpled chaos of the sheets Laura lay, alone. And naked.

Pushing her hair out of her eyes, she sat up and looked around. Her evening gown and her bronze sandals were on the floor where Kentir had dropped them, and her earrings were tossed carelessly onto a table. There was no sign of Kentir's gold-trimmed dress uniform.

Kentir stood by the window, his back to Laura, his fists planted on his hips. He was once again clad in his everyday red tunic and trousers, and his dark hair was damp, as if he had just come from his morning bath.

"What time is it?" Laura asked, yawning and stretching as she spoke. She could tell by the way the sunlight was shining on the tree outside the window that it was not very late. "I expected to wake up in your arms," she whispered, hurt that he was not beside her in bed.

"Of course you do understand, don't you, that last night was a night out of time? It will not ever happen again," Kentir said, keeping his gaze on the landscape beyond the window.

His tense stance and the way he moved his shoulders showed Laura just how impatient he was to be gone—impatient to leave her, to be back at work, to be discussing the weapons on which Thuban was working, to be reading the reports Laura would compile for him, and, above all, to listen to the astronomers' accounts of the most recent location of the asteroid.

"No, I do not understand," Laura cried. "I thought you cared about me. My God, Kentir! How could you make love to me the way you did and not care?"

"The misunderstanding is yours alone," he said, his voice so cold that a shiver went up Laura's spine at the sound of it. "It was you who offered yourself to me, Laura. I cannot allow myself to give way to deep emotion for you, or for anyone else. There is simply no time left to waste on the complications that inevitably ensue from intense romantic relationships."

"I never heard such idiotic double-talk in all my life!" she yelled at him. "Either you care, or you don't. Either way, you owe it to me to say so in plain language. Furthermore, it's not human to lock up your emotions."

"Human or not, it is what I have done for the last three years, and it is what I must do now. I agreed to last night's party because Seret asked it of me, saying she believed many of our people were overly fatigued and that everyone would work more seriously after an evening of recreation."

"And what was I?" Laura cried, unable to conceal the pain his words were causing her. "Am I no more to you than that? Just an evening's recreation? A cure for your personal fatigue?"

"We agreed," he said, speaking slowly and evenly, "that for us there could be neither past nor future, but only the one night. I was honest with you. Of your own free will, you consented to spend the night with me. And now the night is over."

"You bastard." Laura's voice broke on the words. She choked back the tears, refusing to allow them to overcome her.

Kentir was still facing the open window. He had not so much as glanced at her while he broke her heart. After the tenderness and the sadness of their last lovemaking, Laura could not believe he was untouched by what they had done together. Not even her growing rage could make her believe he had felt nothing while they had soared to the heights of passion in each other's arms.

"Look at me," she ordered. "Look me in the eye and say you don't want me anymore."

He turned from the window to stare at her, and Laura reared up on her knees, naked as she still was, daring him to claim there was nothing more between them than one single night's pleasure. Kentir looked into her eyes as she had demanded, but he said nothing. Nor could she read desire in his cool and shuttered gaze. Then his glance moved to her bare shoulders, and to her breasts. Her nipples grew taut at the gleam in his eyes when he looked at them for a long, silent moment. When he let his gaze move downward to her hips and her thighs, and when he lingered on the mound of brown hair between her thighs, Laura began to tremble as she had trembled on the previous night, when he had first carried her to her room.

Kentir's lips parted as he stared at her. Laura saw him moisten his lips with his tongue just before he clamped his mouth shut in a hard line.

"Cover yourself," he said, and headed for the door.

"Don't you dare walk out on me!" Laura shouted. She got out of bed and ran across the room to plant herself between Kentir and the door.

"Don't do this to me, or to yourself," he said, his voice as hard as his expression. "We had an agreement. Honor it with dignity."

"*You* had an agreement," she told him. "I refuse to believe there is no future for us."

"There will be no future for anyone," he said, "if we do not return to work at once. Don't you understand yet, Laura? Must I say it again? There is no time left for what we might have had together in another time or another place. There is very little time left at all, and what time there is must be given to the project. From now on the project must be our only passion."

She wanted to say she loved him, but she could not. Not in the face of his implacable determination. She had known before their first kiss that Kentir's full devotion was given to the project he headed. For the sake of the project he had given up the woman he loved, sending her away while he remained behind, to work toward a solution to the oncoming peril. Now he was giving Laura up, too.

And he was right. Laura could not deny it. The survival of Earth and of humankind was far more important than the love she felt for Kentir and the affection—or whatever emotion it was—that he felt for her. Nothing was more important than the success of his project.

But she could not give him up. She had never truly loved a man before, and so she had never dreamed the power of love could be so strong that it could bind one woman to one man for all eternity. As she and Kentir were bound, whether he wanted it to be so or not. Because she loved Kentir, she would do what he required of her. For the moment. Until she could think of a way to save them both.

"I'm sorry," she said, keeping her voice as quiet and calm as she could. "I shouldn't have made a scene. I will dress and join you in the project building as soon as I can." She stepped away from the door.

"Thank you." He hesitated before leaving, and when their eyes met Laura saw his pain at what he had just done to her. In that instant of revelation she knew that he did care about her, though he might not admit it to her, or to himself.

Kentir touched her cheek. It was the lightest of grazing contacts, lasting only a moment. And then, for a fraction of a second, his hand brushed across her breast.

"Thank you," he said again, and left her.

Chapter Thirteen

Other people were also tardy in arriving for work on the morning after the party. Others were quarreling, too, as Laura discovered a short while after Kentir had gone, when she left her room and stepped into the corridor. What had been no more than a murmur of sound as long as her door was closed suddenly became distinguishable as loud, angry voices coming from the direction of Marica's room.

"Just because I allowed you a favor or two, don't think you own me, Thuban," Marica shouted.

"A favor?" Thuban's voice roared. "Is that what you call it, you selfish bitch? A favor is something one person gives to another. You don't know how to give. You only know how to take."

"You didn't mind what I took from you last night," Marica said, adding in a malicious tone, "though it was so small I scarcely knew I had it and, therefore, I did not miss it at all after you so hastily withdrew it."

A sudden and complete silence emanated from Marica's room. Laura stood perfectly still in the corridor, not daring to move a single step for fear Marica and Thuban would hear her and know she was an unwilling witness to their argument. At the same time, she was afraid to stay where she was, lest Thuban should leave Marica's room and discover her standing there and know she had heard Marica's insult. A few tense minutes passed, with no further sounds from the room where Marica and Thuban were.

Then someone closed a door down on the first floor and laughter drifted upward as two women walked into the main room, talking about the party. They were on cleanup duty and were giggling and chattering as they piled the previous night's dirty dishes and winecups onto trays for removal to the kitchen. Under the cover of their cheerful voices Laura fled down the stairs and out the front door.

She did not make her usual stop in the dining room for the Kheressian morning meal of fresh fruit and a hot herbal beverage. Instead, she headed directly for the project building. After what she had just heard, she would rather live with a growling stomach until midday than chance a meeting with either Thuban or Marica.

"There you are," Hua Te said as soon as Laura

entered the building. "I have been looking for you."

"I'm late," Laura responded. "I can't stop to chat right now, Hua Te. Kentir will want to know what is in the reports that have come in during the night."

"Kentir is with Seret and will be for some time," Hua Te said. "Laura, what I have to discuss with you is important. May we talk in the alcove where you work? We should be undisturbed there."

Seeing how serious he was, Laura nodded and led the way to the alcove. There was no door to close it off from the central room, but most of the project workers were elsewhere. Those who were in the building were busy at their own jobs, and Laura had learned over past weeks that the Kheressians had a finely tuned sense of privacy. Those who withdrew from a group to speak quietly together were seldom interrupted, and eavesdropping was considered to be among the worst forms of rudeness.

Once she and Hua Te were within the alcove, a quick glance at the table that served Laura as a desk showed only a few reports awaiting her attention. She could spend a short time with Hua Te and still have the information Kentir needed ready for him when he expected it.

"All right," she said, turning around to look directly at Hua Te. "What's going on?"

"Laura," Hua Te said, "are you in good health?"

In her present emotional state his question, and the solemn way in which he asked it, brought

217

her close to hysterical laughter. For a minute or two she imagined that Hua Te knew all about her night with Kentir and the abrupt way in which Kentir had left her in the early morning and, as a result, Hua Te was worried about her. Only after she reminded herself that he and Imilca had probably spent the night together, that he had no way of knowing what she had been doing, and that Hua Te's innate sense of discretion would prevent him from making such a personal inquiry, did she understand what he meant.

"You're talking about my physical health. I am fine," Laura said.

"When I asked him, Chac said the same thing," Hua Te informed her. "Not wishing to be subjected to a lecture about transdimensional disorder, I have refrained from questioning Marica."

"Hua Te, are you ill?" Laura asked.

"Not at all. If anything, my health has improved since I came to Issa," he answered. A hint of amusement lurked in his eyes when he continued, "I feel years younger and far more vigorous than I once was. I do believe there is less gray in my hair. Neither you, nor Chac, nor I, exhibit any symptoms of the time traveler's disorder that Marica has described to us in such vivid detail."

"Do you think the scientists of her time are wrong in their theory, and the disorder doesn't exist?" Laura asked. Eager for Hua Te to get to the point, she did not mention her suspicion that Marica might have been lying about the illness.

"Our physical conditions do suggest a mistake

on the part of those future scientists," Hua Te responded. "From what Marica said about the theory during our first evening meal with her, all four of us ought to be dead by now. There is no doubt that we endured great stress upon learning what had happened to us and where we were, but so far as I can tell, we have all recovered and accepted the transportation through time. I cannot think any harm will occur to us as the result of a return journey."

"Hua Te, what are you saying? Have you and Imilca found a way to reverse the action of the timestones?" Laura asked, her voice sinking to a hushed whisper. If her friends had been successful, then she and the other three time travelers could go home again. If they wanted to go home. Laura wasn't sure she did, and she thought Hua Te might have some doubts, too. He and Imilca had been growing closer, and making no secret about it, so there was always the possibility that he might decide to remain with Imilca.

"We believe we are close to a solution," Hua Te said. "However, the mechanism within a timestone is both intricate and delicate. Therefore, we cannot be certain our calibrations are exact."

"I see. You are saying that if we try to return to our own times, we may return later—or earlier—than we left."

"That is so," Hua Te said, assuming a serious expression. "You will perceive the difficulty. Kheressian science holds that a person cannot exist in two places at the same time, that if such a situation occurs, one form of the person must instantly perish."

"That's pretty much what American science says, too," Laura told him. "Which means that anyone using a timestone to get home, and hoping to live through the process, will have to arrive at the same moment he left, or a bit later. That will call for precise timing."

"Just so," Hua Te said. "As you know, in addition to attempting to recalibrate the four timestones that have already been used, Imilca and I have been making new timestones. Kentir's goal is to have one available for every member of the project, in case the weapons fail us and we are left with no other means of escape. As you know, Seret and Kentir believe it is the duty of the Kheressians to prevent as much damage as possible to Earth. Their only fear is that they will miss an opportunity to alter what now appears to be inevitable. Thus, they will wait until the very last moment to give the order to use the timestones."

"I understand," Laura said, "and I agree with Seret. Hua Te, can you make enough of the stones?"

"Not in the time we have left," Hua Te answered, shaking his head. "But there are those who will choose not to employ the device. Seret will refuse to leave, and a few others will feel the same way. Chac has already expressed to me his certainty that he is destined to remain in Issa."

"He mentioned something similar to me, too," Laura said. "Hua Te, what about Imilca? Will she decide to stay, or to go with you?"

"Ah, therein lies yet another problem," Hua Te said. "If Imilca wants to, will she be able to go with me and reach the same place where I arrive?"

"I see what you mean, Hua Te. Is it possible to construct one timestone with a mechanism strong enough to move two people in the same process?" Laura asked. "Or, alternately, can you make two separate mechanisms so carefully synchronized that they will send their holders to the same time and place? If so, you and Imilca could be sure you would be together, wherever you land."

"It is an intriguing problem." Hua Te looked thoughtful. "Given enough time, I believe it can be done."

"I suppose some people will want to go back into Kheressian history, so they can live in a familiar culture," Laura said, turning over in her mind all that Hua Te had told her. "But others, aware of what we four time travelers have revealed, will want to see the far-distant future. Think what they will be able to teach the people of future centuries, Hua Te! You and I have just barely begun to learn about the Kheressian culture. Imilca tells me it has existed for thousands of years, and Kentir has mentioned a little about the philosophy and the religions of his people. What wonderful contributions the Kheressians still can make!"

"They will all be in grave danger in the future," Hua Te said. "Even with their implanted translators, which will enable them to understand and

221

speak any language, still, they will not belong to the times in which they find themselves. They may be persecuted for their knowledge, rather than honored for it."

"Or burned as sorcerers, or as heretics," Laura added when Hua Te fell silent. "I'm afraid you are right. Whether the Kheressians reach the future individually or in a group, they are sure to face misunderstandings, ridicule, and danger. The world that you and I have lived in has never been kind to those who are different from the average. I don't think attitudes will change by Marica's time, either. You have only to listen to her to know as much."

"We will have to issue a strong warning to those who choose to avail themselves of the time-stones," Hua Te agreed. "For I have no doubt that, if Imilca and I can construct a sufficient number of them, they will be used. I am familiar enough with the Kheressians by now to believe they will want to keep alive through all the centuries to come the story of their lost world that was so beautiful, and that vanished in a single day."

"The civilization we call Atlantis," Laura whispered, awed by the possibilities Hua Te was suggesting, "and the people of Atlantis, scattered throughout time, telling the story again and again, and offering the knowledge they possess, however cautious they will have to be about revealing their knowledge."

"You see cause for hope," Hua Te said, smiling at her.

"I do," Laura said. "Hope for all of us. These people have given up war. They treasure the land on which they live. They almost never get sick. Renan tells me his medical practice consists almost entirely of repairing accidental injuries. And as far as I can tell, the Kheressians don't care about age, except to value the wisdom it brings, or about gender or any other differences between groups of people. Just consider the way they have accepted the two of us, not to mention Chac and Marica, who are even more different from them than either you or me. The Kheressians have a lot to teach us, Hua Te."

"So I also believe," Hua Te said.

"Is there anything I can do to help you with the timestones?" Laura asked, her enthusiasm for Hua Te's project spilling into a broad grin and a desire to begin working on it at once.

"Imilca and I, and her two assistants, are the only ones at Issa who are trained for such delicate work," Hua Te said. "It will take too long to train others to do it."

"Have you spoken to Kentir about all of this?" Laura asked. "What does he say?"

"Kentir wants the timestones used only as a last resort," Hua Te answered. "His hope is to divert the asteroid before it approaches close enough to cause the terrible effects we all fear. But if all else fails and it is certain the world, and most especially the land of Kheressia, will be obliterated, then Seret and Kentir will offer the timestones to the project members in hope of saving their lives and of transmitting the knowl-

edge the Kheressians possess into another time.
Until then, neither of them want this information
to become common knowledge. Seret and Kentir, Imilca and I, and now you, are the only ones
who know."

"I won't tell anyone," Laura promised. She
could not help wondering why Hua Te, who
seemed to her to be the very soul of discretion,
had chosen to tell her about his work on the timestones, but she decided not to ask him for his
reasons. Perhaps later, after she had taken time
to think about the revelations he had made, she
would ask.

"I should return to my work," Hua Te said. He
moved toward the open arch leading out of the
alcove and into the central room. Before he got
that far there came the noise of a scuffle. An instant later Chac appeared, grasping a furious and
squirming Marica by both her arms. Still holding
her in front of him, Chac shoved Marica into the
alcove.

"I caught her eavesdropping on your private
conversation," Chac said to Hua Te. "You know
how the Kheressians feel about such behavior. I
suggest we turn her over to Seret for punishment."

"Let me go, you bloodthirsty barbarian!" By exerting a fierce effort, Marica managed to pull herself free from Chac. She tried to leave the alcove,
only to find Hua Te and Chac standing shoulder
to shoulder in the archway, preventing her. "I
said, let me out of here!"

"How much did you hear of what Hua Te and I were saying?" Laura asked.

"I don't know what you are talking about," Marica declared. With a furious glare at Chac she added, "I was on my way to assist Thuban when this disgusting creature assaulted me."

"I found her flattened against the wall outside your alcove, listening so intently to what was being said within that she did not hear me approach," Chac explained to Laura. "Let us take her to Seret and tell our story."

"Thuban!" Marica raised her voice to an ear-splitting shout. "Thuban! Come at once!"

Almost immediately, Thuban appeared in the archway. He looked at the two men, who were still blocking Marica's exit, looked next at Laura, and finally turned his cold, measuring eyes on Marica.

"What have you done?" Thuban said to Marica.

"I haven't done anything," Marica answered. "Chac attacked me, and now he and Hua Te are conspiring to drag me before Seret and accuse me of a crime I haven't committed."

"That's not exactly what happened," Laura said, looking straight into Thuban's eyes. Something flickered there, far inside his dark gaze. Laura could not tell if it was anger at her for contradicting Marica, or outrage at Marica's behavior.

"I will see to Marica," Thuban said. "Move aside, Chac. You, too, Hua Te."

When the men obeyed him, Marica tried to push between them and make her escape. Before she could do so, Thuban caught her by her wrists, holding her so tightly that she winced.

"Come with me, Marica," Thuban said. "We have work to do. And you have an explanation to make."

"Are you going to let them treat me that way and not punish them?" Marica cried. "I expected more from you, Thuban."

"I said, come with me." Thuban tugged on her wrists. Marica was not a weak woman, but Thuban's strong fingers were clasped around her wrists in an unbreakable grip, giving her no choice in the matter. She was forced to let him drag her out of the alcove and toward the room where he worked, but she complained every step of the way.

"I cannot stand that woman," Laura said. "She's a born troublemaker and totally selfish. Unfortunately, Thuban is infatuated with her."

"Perhaps," Hua Te said, looking after the pair with a thoughtful frown. "Perhaps not. Or perhaps not any longer, after this morning's incident."

"I do not know how long she was listening to you before I saw her," Chac told them. "I do know that, while I was creeping up on her, I overheard a fair portion of your words. I will not reveal to anyone else what you said. But let me warn you to keep the timestones well hidden. If Marica discovers where they are, she will surely steal as many as she can carry before she uses one of the stones to return to her own time."

"I don't even want to think about the kind of

power the timestones would give her," Laura said, aghast at the prospect Chac was suggesting. "She could destroy the future, and the past."

"And never regret it," Chac added. "Marica would take pleasure in the destruction. There are few hearts not acceptable to the gods. Marica possesses one of those hearts."

Laura swallowed hard, thinking about Chac's words, and recalling what the sacrificial duties of an Aztec priest entailed.

"I will warn Imilca and her assistants about Marica," Hua Te said. "And I will advise Imilca to tell Seret what has happened here. Please excuse me now, Laura. I want to find Imilca."

"At least I've been distracted from my personal problems for a while," Laura muttered to herself when she was at last alone in the alcove that served as her office. She glanced at the machine beside her desk, where another series of notes from other project leaders around the world was being printed even as she watched. "If there are no more interruptions, maybe I can compile the report for Kentir before his meeting with Seret ends."

She was granted no more than an hour of quiet before yet another argument erupted. Again, Marica was one of the combatants.

"I will do it my way!" Thuban shouted, his voice so loud that Laura leaped up from her chair and ran to the archway to see what was happening.

"You don't know what you're talking about," Marica shouted at Thuban. "I know more about crystal-generated light beams than you do, and more about explosives. You have never been involved in warfare, but I have. For those reasons, I can produce a better weapon than you."

"Be quiet, both of you." Kentir had entered the project building. He spoke to his brother. "Thuban, would you care to explain the nature of this latest dispute?"

"He is an ignorant savage," Marica said before Thuban could answer. "I know how to make his weapon work more accurately, but he won't listen to me."

"I asked Thuban for an explanation," Kentir said in a quiet, deadly tone. "Marica, I wish you would be silent and let my brother respond."

"Respond is just what Thuban is incapable of doing," Marica said with a sneer. "Nothing about Thuban responds properly, including his *weapon*." With that, she stalked back to Thuban's workroom, leaving Thuban with a face as dark as a thundercloud.

"We both know that's not true," Kentir said, clapping his brother on the shoulder, "as several Kheressian woman would happily bear witness, if only they were here to speak of your exploits."

"Thanks for your confidence in me, Kentir." Thuban's face cleared a little at his brother's words, and he returned to the subject of his dispute with Marica. "Marica is insisting she can set up a crystal-generated light beam that will be more effective against the asteroid than the weapon I have been working on. I think we are too far along in production to change the weapon now. I need not tell you, Kentir, how short the time we have left is."

"Thuban," Laura said, "I admit I don't know much about lasers, but I don't understand how a light can destroy a large, solid body that is hurtling through space, or even change its path."

"The weapon I have invented is complex," Thuban said. "At Marica's suggestion, we will use explosives as well as a light beam. I am convinced that the weapon I have been working on will be effective, but Marica claims that she knows how to produce a stronger beam than Kheressian technology allows."

"She could be right," Laura said. "Her people have an extra two centuries of practice over the scientists of my time, and I do know American scientists have done some amazing things with lasers. But, Thuban, I wouldn't trust Marica with anything so dangerous, not unless you can monitor every move she makes."

"There, we are in full agreement," Thuban said.

"Be careful, Thuban. Your life is too valuable to your brother and your friends for us to want to risk losing you." Once again, Laura looked deep into Thuban's eyes as she spoke to him. This time she saw no anger in him, only a friendly warmth.

Thuban looked from Laura to Kentir and then back to Laura again. One corner of his mouth tilted upward, the closest Laura had ever seen him come to a real smile.

"You be careful, too," Thuban said to her. To Kentir he added, "Don't worry. I can use Marica's

229

knowledge and still keep her under control. In the last night and day, I have taken the true measure of that coldhearted woman, and I promise you I won't make the same mistake twice. I never have; I never will."

"I believe you." Kentir was smiling as the brothers parted. He swung around to face Laura and ask a question of her. "Is the latest report ready?"

"Yes. I'll get it. There has been another volcanic eruption." Returning to the alcove, Laura reached across her desk for the report.

Kentir followed her on silent feet. When she turned to offer the report to him, she discovered he was standing so close they were almost touching. His tall figure and broad shoulders seemed to fill the tiny alcove to overflowing. She could feel his warmth, and she had to fight the urge to reach up and stroke his face. Kentir did not move. He simply stood there, looking at her, and she had no idea what he was thinking. To distract herself from his disturbing proximity she began to chatter.

"There is a group of scientists on the other side of the world, near the site of the latest eruption, who are arguing that all the recent volcanic activity and the earthquakes are caused by the approach of the asteroid," she said. "Another group of scientists claims the asteroid is still too far away to cause such severe disturbances. That's about the sum total of all the data I have here; you've heard the same discussion before, several times." She thrust the report into Kentir's hands.

"Laura," he began.

"If there is nothing else you want," she interrupted him, "then I'll ask you to excuse me. As you know, I was delayed this morning, so I'll have to hurry if I'm going to catch up on my work. And there is nothing more important than our work, is there?" She regretted the words as soon as she said them. There was no point in throwing Kentir's devotion to the project up to him, not when she endorsed what he was trying to do, but the pain of his rejection was still fresh in her heart.

Kentir paused in the archway to look back at her, his expression bleak. Laura wanted to run to him, to feel his strong arms holding her close.

"It isn't easy," he said.

"Really?" she said. She knew what he meant. Still, injured pride made her speak with all the sarcasm she could muster. "I thought you found it remarkably easy." She saw him clench his jaw before she looked down at her desk, refusing to meet his eyes again, afraid of what she would find there. She heard him mutter a curse beneath his breath, and when she finally looked up, he was gone.

231

Chapter Fourteen

Six days after the evening party, the first of Thuban's weapons was ready. It took a full day to move the weapon to the launching area that had been constructed at the airfield outside Issa, and another three days to install it in the rocket Thuban's workers had hastily pieced together.

When Laura, who was standing in the project building more than a mile away at Issa, first saw the holographic image of the launch site, she could not believe that anyone imagined the ramshackle construction would actually get off the ground. She feared Kentir was of the same opinion, for he looked remarkably grim. He walked around the table several times, viewing the hologram from all angles.

"I wish we had sturdier shielding for the work

crew," he said, frowning at the single stone building on the airfield. It was the same building that
housed the control tower and that could serve as
a passenger lounge when necessary, though
there were no longer any passengers flying in and
out of Issa. Only the two saucerships used the
airfield anymore.

"You're the one who refused to allow Thuban
enough time to build a better shelter," Marica
snapped at Kentir. "Furthermore, the way the
rocket was patched together defies all the rules
of missile construction. I'm just glad you didn't
expect me to go out there and stand on that open
field to help Thuban try to control the cursed
thing. He'll be lucky if he's not killed when it lifts
off."

"There are four other men and women out
there with him," Laura reminded Marica.

"That's their problem," Marica said. "Let them
risk their lives. I'm staying here."

"If you will all be quiet now," Kentir said, "Thuban is about to start and I want to hear every
detail."

Seret had come to the project building to observe the launch of the first Kheressian weapon-
carrying rocket. She sat in a chair near the hologram table, and she never took her eyes off the
image projected there. Everyone on the project
team who could possibly get away from pressing
work was there as well. No one spoke as Thuban's voice was heard calling off items on his
checklist of final preparations. One by one his
assistants answered him.

As the moment to launch the rocket approached, the tension thickened in the project building, and Laura could hear the strain in the voices of those out on the airfield. She held her breath, praying the hastily constructed rocket and its engines, as well as Thuban's weapon installed in the rocket, would all work as they were supposed to. Laura glanced across the room to where Hua Te was standing perfectly still with his hands tucked into the loose sleeves of the blue Oriental robe he wore in preference to the red project uniform. Hua Te's eyes were fixed on the holographic image of the airfield that was hovering above the table. Beside him, Imilca twisted her fingers together and chewed on her lower lip.

Renan had positioned himself behind Seret's chair, ready to offer medical aid if the strain became too great for her. Kentir stood beside Seret, watching the hologram with his jaw clenched tight. Chac was next to Laura, his head bowed, as if he was praying to the Aztec gods. Only Marica looked bored. But even she showed some interest when Thuban began to call out the final directions to his assistants.

"We are ready," Thuban said, his voice carrying clearly to the group in the project building.

"Understood," Kentir responded to his brother's report. "Proceed on your own count, Thuban. We are all depending on you."

"Now!" Thuban's shout resounded through the speakers in the project building.

Within a few seconds a mechanical roar began, a noise so loud it was transmitted through the communication system not only as sound, but also as a continuous, strong vibration. The holographic image showed the rocket beginning to move upward. The cheering of the men and women out at the airfield briefly rose above the noise of the rocket engines, to reach the ears of those who had gathered around the table in the project building.

The roar of the rocket quickly rose to an ear-splitting crescendo that drowned out every other sound. The rocket lifted a little higher. Steam and flames began to billow from its tail section, as the propellant system came on to full thrust.

Kentir leaned forward, bracing both his hands on the hologram table, his eyes on the dramatic images being projected just above the table. Incredibly, through all the noise of the rocket's lift-off, Laura heard what sounded like a choked-off scream. Then sound and holographic image both abruptly disappeared, shut down in an instant.

No one in the project building moved. The sudden silence was terrible. It stretched on and on until, finally, Laura heard Chac take a shaky breath and mutter an oath. She glanced at him in surprise; she had not heard Chac curse since the day of his arrival at Issa. Laura quickly looked back at Kentir, who appeared to be frozen in place, staring at a nonexistent image.

"Kentir," said Seret, "what has happened to the transmission?"

"I don't know," Kentir said, shaking himself as if he were trying to awaken from a bad dream. He began to press the buttons on the hologram table, attempting to regain the image. Nothing happened. The space above the table remained blank.

"Kentir," Seret commanded, "tell me the truth. Where is the rocket? More important, where are our people?"

"We have lost all contact with the airfield," Kentir said. "The problem is in the transmitters out there. I can't answer your questions, Seret."

"If the rocket has actually been launched and is flying into space, then we should be able to hear it," Laura exclaimed.

She ran for the open door, with Kentir following just behind her. Both of them stopped when they reached the lawn. Laura could hear the squawking of birds, the buzz of insects among the flowers, and the gentle sound of surf breaking on the shore. She was aware of Kentir's soft intake of breath and of the movements of the other people who were leaving the building to join her and Kentir. But there was nothing in the sky, nothing to see, nothing to hear.

"In my time," Laura said, her voice breaking, "we have had some rockets blow up on the launch pad. Of course, it could just be that we have lost the transmission. The vibrations we felt were so strong; perhaps at the airfield they were violent enough to disrupt the transmitters." She could not bear to see the desolate look in Kentir's eyes, or the way the color had drained from his face.

"Kentir," Seret said, coming out of the building to face the group gathered on the lawn, "this is a time to use the land vehicles. On this occasion do not concern yourself about burning valuable fuel. Take the vehicles out of storage, drive to the airfield, and discover the truth of what has happened."

"Seret, please," Renan said, touching her arm in a gesture meant to be comforting, "let me escort you to your room."

"Not yet." Seret shook off Renan's hand and continued to speak to Kentir. "You will need more than one vehicle, so you will have the space to bring Thuban and the rest of his team home with you when you return. Whatever has happened, I want all of them brought back."

"I understand," Kentir said.

Laura understood, too. Seret was afraid Thuban and the others were dead, and she did not want their remains left at the airfield.

"Take Renan and Imilca and four or five volunteers with you," Seret said to Kentir. Seeing the first two to come forward and offer themselves, she said, "No, not you, Laura and Hua Te. I thank you for your thoughtfulness, but I prefer to have you stay here at the compound, to help me make arrangements to care for anyone who may be injured. You will be more useful in that way."

"I will go with you, Kentir." Chac stepped forward at once.

"Of course he will," Marica said. "Chac loves blood, and he will never faint at the sight of a dismembered body."

Laura felt like slapping the woman. She settled

for an angry glare that silenced Marica, perhaps because it was coupled with similar hard looks from Imilca and Hua Te. Laura was only glad that Kentir hadn't heard Marica's insensitive remarks.

"Come along, then," Kentir said to Nirod and Arad, who had just volunteered. "Let's not waste time." He nodded his acceptance of their offers to Chac and Renan, then rested his hand on Imilca's shoulder for a moment, adding her to the group he was assembling. At Kentir's signal, they all ran together toward the compound gate.

"Marica, I want you to remain in plain sight and stay always with a project worker," Seret ordered. "Hua Te, will you close and lock the project building door?" She held out the key for him to take.

"What's the matter, Seret?" Marica asked, her customary rudeness unaltered by the possibility of tragedy. "Are you afraid I might steal something from the building if you leave the door open?"

"I am not certain what you might do," Seret told her. "However, I notice that you alone have shown no distress over what has occurred."

"We don't know what has occurred," Marica said. "All we know for certain is that the hologram and the sound shut off. I can think of several possible explanations."

"The rocket wasn't launched," Laura said. "We'd have seen it and heard it if it had gone up."

"Not if the compass went awry and the rocket flew toward the mountains instead of heading straight up," Marica said in a haughty way that suggested Laura did not know what she was talking about. Speaking to Seret as well as to Laura, she continued, "Are either of you aware of how complicated the compass on that rocket was, not to mention the stabilizers it controlled? Of course not. Thuban did not bother himself to explain minor details to you, because neither one of you has the scientific knowledge to understand what he was doing."

"Don't say *was*, as if Thuban is dead!" Laura cried. Seeing the distress on Seret's lined face, she bit back the additional angry words she wanted to speak in response to Marica's unfeeling remarks. Instead, in the absence of either Renan or Imilca, she went to Seret, to offer her arm for the older woman to lean on as they made their way back to the house.

Laura did not look at Marica again. She was certain that Hua Te and the few Kheressians who remained at the project building would see to it that Marica was conducted to a secure place. There she would be kept until Seret and Kentir could interrogate her to discover if Marica had had anything to do with the malfunction of the rocket. Far more important than Marica were the questions of what had actually happened to the rocket, and of Thuban's safety, along with that of the other project members who had been working with him.

Kentir, and the men and women who had rushed to the airfield with him, returned several hours later. As Laura had feared, Kentir reported that the rocket had exploded just as it left the ground. Two of Thuban's assistants were dead and another was badly injured, though the fourth assistant, a young woman, was only slightly hurt and was able to provide a full account of events up to and immediately after the explosion. Thuban himself lay unconscious, his left arm and leg mangled by the blast.

"He saw what was happening and tried to stop it," Kentir told Seret and Laura. "When he realized he couldn't prevent the explosion, Thuban tried to drag one of the women away to safety. The blast knocked them down and the woman fell on top of Thuban. That's why he lived. The woman died when jagged metal debris struck them. There are more details, told to me by the woman who survived, but I think you won't require a full report, Seret. No report, however eloquent, can bring back those who have died, or change failure into success. There is nothing left of Thuban's weapon that can be salvaged."

Kentir's crisp, clipped delivery of this speech revealed his despair at the loss of the rocket and the weapon that might have saved them if only it had reached space. Worse, each word he spoke told of his deep anguish over the deaths of two whom he called friends. In the aftermath of the accident he was left to deal with worry for his brother's life and with the need to find an infallible way to use the one remaining weapon. Laura's heart ached to see his grief and pain, but at the moment there was nothing she could do for him. Kentir immediately plunged into activity that Laura was certain was intended to keep his darker emotions at bay.

Thuban and his two injured assistants were put to bed, with Renan and his medical personnel to care for them. After a brief discussion with Renan, Kentir returned to the project building, to the work that consumed him.

"Will Thuban live?" Laura asked Hua Te, who had gone to Renan and Imilca immediately upon their return to offer his assistance in caring for the wounded.

"Thuban will recover, in time," Hua Te said, "though Renan fears he will never regain complete use of his left hand and never walk well again, either. The woman has only minor cuts and a broken rib. She will not require much care. Renan says she can return to work on the second weapon after a single day's rest and after a long talk with Imilca to discuss her fears about the incident. As for the badly injured man, his survival is doubtful."

"Poor man," Laura said, "and poor Thuban."

"Poor Kentir, too," Hua Te said, voicing Laura's chief concern. "He was depending on the weapon contained in that ruined rocket. As were we all. Now we have only one chance left to alter the course of the asteroid, or to destroy it."

"And not much time," Laura added.

"As you know, Imilca and I have been working long hours on the timestones," Hua Te said. "In the end, if we can produce enough of them, they may prove to be the best hope for the Kheressians to live beyond the fatal day."

"After the accident this morning, there are two timestones you won't have to make," Laura said, not trying to conceal the sorrow she felt at the loss of team members whom she had begun to think of as friends.

She was not the only one coping with grief. Those who had chosen to remain at Issa to help Kentir with the project were a dedicated group, and their comradeship ran deep. They were also strong men and women who, for the most part, kept their emotions in check, yet no one tried to hide the tears that were being shed over the accident.

If it had been an accident. Laura could not escape the suspicion that Marica had done something to the weapon to make it explode. As Marica had so contemptuously informed her, Laura did not have the scientific knowledge to guess what had gone wrong, nor was she able to imagine what Marica's motive could have been.

Over the next few days Laura watched Marica, hoping to discover a clue to what had happened to the rocket. She learned nothing new from Marica, who was not confined as Laura had expected. Laura did discover that, despite the illusion of freedom granted to Marica, two of the Kheressians had apparently been assigned to keep her under continual surveillance. Wherever Marica was, one or the other of the Kheressians was also present. Laura thought it was on Seret's orders, though she did not have nerve enough to ask Seret about the discreet guards.

On the second day after the explosion, Laura visited Thuban. He was in a first-floor chamber at the rear of the house, part of the suite of rooms that Renan used as a clinic. Thuban's room was ascetically bare, with pale green walls and a single window opening on a limited view of lawn and sky. The bed where Thuban lay was high and narrow, and the only other furnishings were a stiff-looking metal chair and a shelf projecting from one wall. Bottles of medicine were arrayed on the shelf, along with a few instruments and several rolls of bandages. Renan had just finished changing the dressing on Thuban's left arm and hand and was rolling up the leftover bandage when Laura appeared in the doorway.

"Well, at least it doesn't smell like a hospital," Laura said, looking around the room. She inhaled a breath of fresh, slightly leafy air. "Do I detect Imilca's fine hand with fragrances?"

"She says clean aromas can raise a patient's spirits and hasten a cure," Renan said. "All of my experience indicates that Imilca is correct."

"I don't need perfumes to make me feel better," Thuban declared with remarkable fierceness, considering the fact that he was flat on his back with a frame over the lower half of his bed to keep the weight of the blanket off his injured leg. "All I need is for Renan to let me have a bit more painkiller and then to stop coddling me."

"I am surprised to hear you ask for painkiller this soon after your last dose," Renan said, taking a closer look at Thuban. "Are you really experiencing so much discomfort?"

"Would I ask for help if I weren't?" Thuban snarled. Looking from the departing physician to Laura, Thuban asked, "Did you come with a message from my brother? I haven't seen him yet today."

"No," Laura answered him. "I came for my own reasons, to discover how you are feeling and to ask if there is anything I can do to help you."

"You can tell me what Kentir is planning to do with the remaining weapon," Thuban said. "Has he talked to you about it?"

"Kentir doesn't say much to me these days," Laura said. "I do know he is very upset about what happened. He has ordered an investigation of the accident. Nirod is in charge of it. I'm sure you will learn what the results are as soon as Kentir knows."

"We don't need an investigation," Thuban said. "There isn't time for administrative delays. Am I the only one who understands that simple fact?"

"I believe Kentir's intent is to avoid another accident with the second weapon," Laura said. "To do that, he has to find out exactly what happened at the airfield."

"Just let me out of this bed, and I'll discover what went wrong," Thuban said in a growl. As he spoke, he pushed himself up on his good arm and tried to swing his legs over the edge of the bed. At once his face paled and sweat broke out on his forehead.

"Thuban, lie down at once!" Laura exclaimed.

She rushed forward to push on his shoulders, trying to make him do as she ordered.

"There is no time to rest," Thuban said. "Help me, Laura. I have to get up. You must see that. I can lean on you; I'll go back to work—"

"You will not," Renan said, returning to the sickroom with a syringe in his hand. "You asked for more painkiller, Thuban. Here it is." With that, Renan injected the medication into Thuban's right arm. Thuban lay back and closed his eyes.

"I wanted the stuff I have to swallow," Thuban muttered in a drowsy voice. "This other works too fast."

"He'll sleep for the rest of the day," Renan said, escorting Laura from the room. He ran his fingers through his light brown hair, leaving it in a sadly disordered state. "Thuban is easily the worst patient I have ever had to deal with.

"Laura," Renan said suddenly, looking into her eyes, "have you been feeling ill?"

"No. I'm a little tired and a bit overstressed, but so are we all. It's nothing out of the ordinary for an extraordinary situation." She grinned at Renan to show him she really was healthy and then asked, "Are you worried about transdimensional disorder, too? Hua Te asks me every other day or so if I'm sick, though neither of us has suffered any symptoms at all."

"Oh, that nonsense," Renan said. He shook his head in a disparaging way. "There is nothing to that supposed disorder. It's only that Marica speaks so forcefully that most people assume she knows what she's saying."

"And doesn't she?" Laura asked.

"I'm sure she is wrong, and the time traveler's disorder she talks about is a mistake on the part of the scientists of her time," Renan said. "My belief is based on continued observation of you four visitors. But Marica will use any idea to her own advantage. In fact, this idea of transdimensional disorder may be her own invention, intended to make us feel guilty for bringing her here, and thus convince us to return her home promptly."

"With a handsome profit for herself," Laura said, grinning again. "Renan, you aren't the only one to suspect Marica of lying about the disorder. And I have also been wondering what she had to do with the accident."

"I would not be Marica for all the stars in the sky, if Kentir discovers she caused the explosion that killed two of his friends, may have killed a third friend—for I do not expect my other patient to survive longer than another day—and almost killed Kentir's brother. No," Renan said, "most of the time Kentir is a gentle man, but there is a determination lurking in him that will allow no interference with his duty."

"Yes," Laura said with a sigh. "I know what you mean."

It was not until later that she thought again of Renan's question about her health and wondered what had made him ask if she was ill.

* * *

On the fourth day after the accident Kentir called a meeting, which was held in Seret's most private room. It was in a separate wing from the guest rooms, in an area of the house where Laura had not previously ventured. Imilca was her guide, and when they reached Seret's suite of rooms, Laura discovered that she and Imilca, Seret and Kentir, Hua Te, and Thuban's friend, Nirod, were the only ones present.

Laura had seen Seret only once or twice since the day of the accident. The Kheressian leader was sadly aged in that short time. Whereas before Seret had been the picture of mature vigor, now she seemed fragile, and her steps were slow and unsteady. Seret lowered herself into a large chair as if every muscle and bone in her body ached.

Kentir was hollow-eyed and pale. When he began to speak, Laura quickly understood why he was so haggard and, also, why there were so few participants in the meeting.

"Thanks to Nirod's thorough investigation," Kentir said, "we have proof that the weapon— not the rocket, but the weapon itself—was sabotaged."

"But why?" Imilca cried. "It's self-defeating behavior. The weapon was our best chance to save all of our lives by destroying or altering the course of the asteroid. Who among us would undertake such a senseless action?"

"I don't mean to insult you by saying this," Laura spoke up, "but you Kheressians are remarkably trusting people. Perhaps it's because you are all basically honest. Didn't it occur to any of you when you decided to bring strangers to your world from distant times, that at least one of us might prove to be a criminal? Or a destructive personality? Or crazy, or just plain rotten in character?"

"If you are speaking of Marica—" Kentir began.

"I am," Laura said, cutting off his next words. "Marica knows that Imilca and Hua Te are working on the timestones. She acquired that supposedly secret piece of information by blatant eavesdropping on a private conversation. My guess is that Marica hasn't been able to discover where the timestones are hidden, so she rigged the weapon to make it blow up. The rocket wasn't sabotaged because it was constructed at the airfield, where Marica hasn't been since the day she arrived in Issa. But the weapon was built here, in the project building, where Marica had easy access to it, because she was supposedly helping Thuban."

"There's no question Marica has the technical knowledge for sabotage," Nirod said. "I worked with her on the weapon. Thuban and I were both impressed by how much Marica knows on the subject of weaponry. But Laura, how would destruction of the weapon help her in her search for the timestones?"

"By narrowing our range of options," Kentir said before Laura could answer. "If the rocket had been successfully launched and the weapon had eliminated the threat posed by the asteroid, we wouldn't need the timestones. In that case, we would have destroyed them to prevent misuse of them, whether by accident or intention."

"We would, of course, offer to return our visitors to their own times," Seret said. "But the once-used timestones that Imilca and Hua Te have repaired and recalibrated for that purpose have been slightly altered from their original form. Each of them will function only one more time, after which the inner mechanism will automatically destroy itself, leaving only a pretty—but useless—crystal."

"I didn't know that," Laura exclaimed. "I'll bet Marica doesn't know it either."

"We Kheressians are not quite so naive as you imagined," Seret said, a faint smile crossing her weary face.

"Even so," Laura insisted, "if Marica can get her hands on a few extra timestones and take them with her, unused, to her century, then the scientists of her time can probably figure out how they work and how to make more of them. I don't think I need to describe to you the destruction a bunch of people similar to Marica could cause if they began to roam through history, heedlessly changing events."

"I agree," Kentir said. "Marica does present a danger. However, there is little we can do about it, except to keep the timestones safely locked away. We dare not alter the completed ones, for they must be kept ready for immediate use."

"I am having Marica watched," Seret said, thus confirming Laura's observations.

"Lock her up, instead of hiding the time-stones," Laura suggested.

"The simplest way to deal with Marica is for everyone to be aware of her evil tendencies, while she is ignorant of the extent of our knowledge of her," Kentir said. "Thus, we can learn more about her schemes and prevent her from doing further harm.

"Now," Kentir went on, changing the subject abruptly, as if Marica had been disposed of to everyone's satisfaction, "the most urgent question for us to consider is how to use our one remaining weapon."

"Thuban's original plan was to convert a saucership for space flight and use it to deliver the weapon," Nirod said. "His argument for that method was that it allowed a close approach to the asteroid, so a misfiring of the weapon would be almost impossible. We could return to that first plan."

"It does seem to be our best chance," Seret said, nodding her approval. "Thuban had the conversion plans for the ship prepared before Kentir decided to use the rocket instead. Nirod, can you do the conversion?"

"I'll start at once, and I'll work in secret, under the guise of repairing minor damage done to both of the saucerships when the rocket exploded," Nirod said. "I doubt if anyone will question that excuse, since I have been in charge of maintaining the ships. Kentir, when I talked to Thuban an hour ago, he insisted he would be out of bed in another day. He may not be recovered enough to do the actual work himself, but I will be glad of his knowledge to guide me."

"Thuban will regain his health sooner if he's constantly occupied," Kentir said, agreeing at once with Nirod's suggestion. "Then there's the weapon itself. It's almost ready to use, so I can handle the job of completing it, using just one or two assistants to help me."

"Take my advice, and keep Marica well away from your work sites," Laura said.

"Don't worry, we will," Seret assured her.

"Who is to pilot the ship?" Imilca asked. "Thuban wanted to be the one, but I question whether he will be able to handle the controls. It's a task that will require an expert pilot. Kentir, you know we have less than thirty days left. If Thuban were here, he would tell us we need to stop the asteroid as far from Earth as possible."

"We will decide later who is to be the pilot," Kentir said, brushing aside Imilca's question as if it were of no consequence. "Nirod, how long will it take to make the conversion to space capability?"

"Some preliminary work has already been done on the saucership," Nirod answered. "I think we can complete the conversion within ten days, twelve at the most. If you will excuse me, Seret, I'll go talk to Thuban about this. He may have some ideas on how to shorten the time we need."

"Go, then," Seret said. After Nirod had left, she looked from Laura to Hua Te. "You are both free to return to your own times at once, if you wish.

251

Timestones have been prepared for you."

"I'm not leaving," Laura responded, her eyes on Kentir. "I am staying here until everyone else leaves—or until your second weapon destroys the asteroid or sends it away into space, so no one has to leave."

"Imilca will need my help to continue making new timestones if we are to have one for each person," Hua Te said. "I, too, will remain in Issa, not only to complete the work I have undertaken, but also because I am curious to learn what the outcome of this most remarkable adventure will be."

"Thank you," Seret said. "Chac has already informed me of his intention to remain with us until the end. He believes it is the plan of his gods that he is to witness what he calls the end of the Age of the Fourth Sun. Who can say he is wrong?" Seret ended on a sigh.

"You could send Marica home and be rid of her," Laura suggested.

"Not until nearer the final time," Kentir objected. "Marica has acquired knowledge while she has been here that might be detrimental to us. For example, since she remains healthy, she has surely realized by now that it is possible to travel through time without developing the transdimensional syndrome of which she has repeatedly warned us. When she returns home she will report that fact, and it is possible the scientists of her time will decide to join us."

"If those scientists are like Marica, they will not come to offer their assistance," Hua Te said.

"Exactly," Seret said, nodding her agreement with Hua Te's statement. "So long as we keep a close watch on Marica, I believe we will be safer for her continued presence in Issa."

Chapter Fifteen

As they all left Seret's room after the meeting ended, Laura hung back, letting Hua Te and Imilca go ahead and hoping Kentir would catch up with her before she returned to the project building. He did not. Instead, he went into a room some distance down the corridor from Seret's suite. Laura hesitated only a minute or two before she retraced her steps and knocked on the door. Hearing Kentir's voice from within, she entered. He wasn't there, but Laura heard water running in the next room. Kentir called through the door, saying he would be out in a moment.

The red tunic tossed at the foot of the bed told Laura she was in Kentir's private room, but she could see by the lack of personal belongings that he was seldom there, a fact that did not surprise her, considering the long hours he spent working in the project building and meeting with Seret.

The walls of Kentir's bedroom were unadorned white plaster, the windows looked out on the garden, and the wide bed was covered with a dark blue cloth. A typical, low Kheressian clothing chest pushed into one corner, a light globe hanging over the bed for reading, and a table beside the bed were all the furniture. Nothing in the room spoke of Kentir's tastes or his interests—except for the pile of books on the table.

Laura had seen many books throughout the house, and there was a large library in the project building. The Kheressians were proud of having invented books, and Imilca had told Laura of their rich literary heritage. Many books had gone off-world in the luggage of fleeing Kheressians, who could not conceive of life without them.

Curious to discover what Kentir was reading, Laura reached for one of the books on the bedside table. The binding was made from a silky fabric with geometric designs woven into it. The pages were the Kheressian version of paper, a thick, creamy material created from the bark of a special tree. The book fell open to a page marked with a narrow, dried, blue-green leaf. Laura stared at the printed lines. Thanks to her implanted translator, she was able to understand the words. She recognized that she was reading a poem, but the subtle images and the mythological allusions the poet had used made little sense to her. To appreciate Kheressian poetry she would have to know more about Kheressian history and literature.

With a sigh she replaced the book on the table, almost knocking over the object set next to the pile of books. A rounded green glass vase holding a single spray of white, orchidlike flowers tilted precariously as Laura's knuckles hit it. She grabbed at the vase, her hand brushing against the blossoms. A spicy fragrance drifted upward, delighting her senses.

"Why are you here?" Kentir stood at the bathroom door. He was naked above the waist, with a pale blue towel slung over one shoulder. He did not appear to be angry, just curious at her presence in his bedchamber without an invitation.

Looking from the flowers and the books to the man, with his broad shoulders and muscular arms, his thick, dark hair, and his searching gray-blue eyes that were fixed on her face, Laura was suddenly conscious of how little she still knew about him, or about the world in which he lived. She had spent a passionate night with Kentir and she did not doubt her romantic feelings for him, but in many important ways he remained a stranger to her. Perhaps he would always be a stranger.

He kept sweet-scented flowers on his bedside table, he read poetry, and he had a past he did not want to discuss, except in the briefest possible sentences, because it was too painful to remember. And he belonged to a history and a culture that remained almost totally foreign to Laura. Kentir could, in fact, be the alien, other-

worldly visitor she had first imagined him to be—
except that she was the alien in Kheressia. He
belonged here; she did not, and her sudden consciousness of all that separated them tore at
Laura's heart.

"I'm sorry to disturb you, Kentir," she said in
a whisper.

"Then why did you?" He took a step toward
her.

"I was worried about you." Laura wished she
could think of something sensible to say, instead
of sounding like a foolish, lovelorn schoolgirl.
The questions she wanted to ask him were un-
askable, for there was not time enough for her to
learn everything about his world. And the things
she wanted to tell him were equally unspeakable.
Kentir did not want to hear that she loved him
and would not leave him. He would probably regard her devotion as just one more burden he
was forced to assume at a time when duties and
problems already overwhelmed him. He had
made it plain enough after their first night together that he did not want another romantic interlude with her. And yet, night or day, Kentir
filled her thoughts.

"I am in the best of health. You need not worry
for my sake," he said, and took one more step in
her direction. "If you want to worry about someone, visit Thuban again."

"I think you must feel very much alone just
now," she said, unable to stop the words that rose
directly from her heart. "I thought you might
want company. I know I would, if I were you."

There was a slight softening of Kentir's expression, a gentler look in his eyes, as if her honest words had touched a chord in him.

"You were reading my book of poetry," he said, and reached past her to straighten the book, which was about to tumble off the top of the stack on the table.

He had just washed his face. The edges of his hair were damp and there were droplets of moisture on his shoulders and chest. Laura inhaled the remembered scent of him and felt her heartbeat quicken.

"I did read the poem you had marked," she said, "but I couldn't understand it. Your frame of reference, your entire culture, is so different from mine." She sounded just the way she felt, breathless and a little frightened.

"Your world would be equally foreign to me," Kentir said, his voice very low and a bit uncertain. "Yet we did achieve mutual understanding, did we not?"

"For a while, we did," Laura whispered. Unable to resist her desire to touch him, she placed a hand flat on his bare chest, over curly dark hair and warm skin. At once she regretted what she had done, for she could not bring herself to remove her hand, though she was aware of a flash of fire in Kentir's eyes that surely indicated anger.

With a sound that might have been a growl of vexation at her bold gesture, Kentir took hold of the hand that lay on his chest. She was sure he meant to move it away, to break the physical contact he had warned her he did not want again. His fingers curled around her hand. Laura stared at his tanned skin against her paler flesh. And then he pressed her fingers harder against his chest, so she could feel the steady throbbing beneath the hard muscle.

"There beats a heart that longs for you," he said. "What am I to do? There is nothing left to offer you, no time, and precious little hope. Why did you come into my life when it was almost over?"

"As I recall, you sent for me," she said.

"A grievous error."

"I prefer to think of it as a quirk of fate. Someone else might have found the timestone and come into the past in my place, in which case we would never have met. I'm glad to be here, Kentir." As she said it, Laura knew it was true. She did not want to be in any time or place where Kentir was not. She laid her hand over his, which still held her other hand against his heart. He stared down at their hands, sandwiched together, and he did not pull his hand away.

"Issa is a dangerous place to be," Kentir said. "It will grow more dangerous with each day that passes, until the last day."

"Never have I felt so brave," Laura told him, "or so sure of myself."

"Never have I been so uncertain," he responded. "Never so filled with unwanted emotions. When I undertook the earth-saving task Seret required of me and sent Nivesa and my family away, I set tenderness aside and swore I would not allow softer feelings to weaken me."

"That's not entirely true. I've seen how you treat Seret, as if she were your beloved grandmother. Your affection for your brother is undeniable, and I've watched you with the project workers. You are a kind man, Kentir, and your kindness does not weaken you. It makes you the wonderfully strong man you are."

"There is no time for kindness." His mouth closed firmly on the words, and he set his jaw in the familiar hard line Laura was beginning to know too well.

She saw the raw emotions he was trying to deny. And she knew what her own feelings were. Kentir talked constantly about how little time was left, but a woman's heart functioned in a different way, ignoring the artificial construct called time, understanding what was more important. Instinctively, she knew what both of them needed.

"You can stand here and argue with me," she said, "or you can put your arms around me and make a memorable experience out of the time we do have left."

"You would tempt a statue to passion," he said, all but growling the words. A shudder went through him, and then he stood very still, watching her.

"I would rather tempt you." She was fully aware of the conflict raging within him. Kentir's chief characteristic was his strong devotion to duty. Upset over his brother's injuries and the deaths of friends, possessed by an unrelenting sense of urgency, he found it almost impossible to consider taking even a single hour away from the project. Laura told herself he would work better if he were relaxed and if she could give him some measure of contentment.

In addition, there was her own desire, which heated her thoughts each time she saw Kentir, the same desire that was making her tremble as they stood by his bed, surrounded by the scent of flowers, with their hands locked together on his naked chest.

She knew the instant he surrendered to what she was offering. She saw the tenderness in his eyes deepen to longing. His arm slipped around her waist. Laura lifted her face to his.

"I cannot resist you," he muttered, and kissed her hard, as if he feared he would never have a chance to kiss her again.

They tumbled onto the bed, Kentir pulling Laura down and pinning her beneath him. He stripped off her clothes so quickly that Laura gasped out a warning about torn seams. Kentir gave no sign of having heard her. It did not take Laura long to understand that, while she had spent days fighting her desire for him and pretending to be annoyed with him for his apparent coldness, Kentir had been dealing with all the pent-up longing of a healthy male who had been celibate for several years. His one night with Laura had not been enough. Their passion had only whetted his appetite for her.

"This is a form of madness," he said with his face buried in Laura's hair. "We should not be here like this. My brother is injured, Marica is devising wicked schemes for reasons of her own, our time grows ever shorter, and yet, when I look at you, when I hold you in my arms and kiss you, I forget everything that ought to matter to me, and I want only to lose myself in you."

"You need relief from all the stress you are under," Laura said. "You need comfort. And tenderness. So do I."

Kentir lifted his head to look into her eyes. Laura was intensely aware of the flexing of the strong muscles in his shoulders and upper arms. She wrapped her fingers around his hard biceps, enjoying the contrast between the surface of smooth skin and the hardness just beneath that surface. There was hardness elsewhere, too, pressing insistently against her thigh.

"You must know," Kentir said, "there is more to our coming together than my need for a respite from duty, or for comfort."

"There is my need, too," Laura whispered. She shifted under him, so he would know that she was as eager for him as he obviously was for her. She was a little surprised when he still held back.

"There can be only one reason for the uncontrollable desire you evoke in me," Kentir said. "I have tried to deny what I feel for you, but I find I no longer can. Perhaps there is no further need to deny it, for, when the world is about to end, what is left but love?"

"What did you say?" Laura stared at him, into eyes lit with a warm inner fire that she suddenly perceived was the result of something more than sexual desire and, certainly, more than a weary need for an hour of forgetfulness. "Kentir, did you just say 'love'?"

"I do love you," he responded, smiling. "I have loved you since I first saw you standing alone in the desert, terrified and yet braver than any woman left on this planet, for you were determined not to show your fear to strangers."

"I was afraid of you then, Kentir. I didn't know who, or what, you were. But I think I know now."

"Do you?" he whispered. "Tell me, Laura. Tell me how you feel at this moment."

Never had Laura seen a look so intense in any man's eyes. Or a gaze so beseeching. This strong, courageous man, who literally bore the burden of the world's survival on his shoulders, had just put his heart into her keeping.

Kentir's declaration of love gave Laura a sense of power. It also shifted some of his burden to her, for if she accepted what he was offering, they would stand together, shoulder to shoulder, until the very end of the present crisis, whatever the end might be. In that moment of comprehension Laura saw what the substance of Kentir's love was. They would be equal partners. Together. Till the day they died.

"I love you, too," she said, returning his intense gaze, willing him to believe each word she spoke. "I can't say it started when I first saw you, but it did begin the moment you took off your desert suit and offered me a cup of water. That was the moment when I looked into your amazing eyes and knew I was where I belonged. With you.

Since I was a little girl, I have believed I was destined to love only once, and forever. I lost track of that certainty for a while, but I found it again when I found you. When you found me," she corrected herself.

"I never loved at all until I met you," he said. "You are and always will be my only love."

"And you will be mine," Laura whispered, knowing they were speaking solemn oaths that would never be broken, no matter what happened to them in the days to come.

Kentir stirred against her, and bent to touch his lips to hers. Their kiss represented a sealing of their promises to each other. When it was over, Kentir raised his head to meet her eyes again. He shifted position, and Laura felt his hardness pushing against her. He entered her slowly, his face serious, never taking his eyes from hers. Laura offered herself to him in love, accepting Kentir's gift of loving masculinity in return, until he was fully buried in her and she was part of him.

In some secret room of her heart Laura had always known that when true lovers came together they did actually become one being, an entity beyond the mere joining of bodies. It was the inevitable consequence of discovering one's soul mate. Youthful mistakes had led Laura to believe she had forfeited her chance to experience that wondrous melding of two selves in her own life. Yet, in the moment when Kentir possessed her completely, she knew the dreamed-of, soaring, spiritual joy that only true lovers can experience.

Nor was there any lack of healthy lust between them, for their bodies were strong and eager and they craved each other with a mutual longing for physical release. Hearts and souls and bodies combined to produce a prolonged state of intense ecstasy, until their lovemaking ended on a wild burst of delight and laughter and, on Laura's part, in a few tears as her happiness spilled over, even as Kentir's seed spilled into her. She had a sense, in that last, blinding moment of glory, that together they were defying all the forces of nature, defying fate itself.

Chapter Sixteen

"Where does Nirod take Thuban each day?" Marica demanded of Laura. She stood in the open archway of Laura's work alcove with her feet planted far apart, fists on her hips, and the frown on her face boded ill for anyone who crossed her.

"Hasn't Thuban told you?" Laura asked, to gain time while she seached her brain for an excuse that Marica would accept.

"I have not been allowed to see Thuban since the day of the accident," Marica said.

"Really?" Laura tried to look surprised. "Do you think he's avoiding you?"

"I think you are avoiding an answer." Marica's frown deepened. "I think you know why Thuban and I are being kept apart and why I am under constant surveillance."

"Do you care whether you are permitted to see Thuban?"

"Answer my questions!" Marica took a threatening step toward Laura.

"I suppose we could argue all day about whether you have the right to give me orders," Laura said, keeping her voice calm by sheer force of will. She did not want to reveal her mistrust or her dislike of Marica, but the woman was making it difficult. Laura decided to placate Marica with a half truth. "The fact is that I don't know where Thuban and Nirod go or what they do when they get there. Perhaps it's some kind of therapy, to help Thuban regain full use of his arm and hand."

"Nirod is not a physician," Marica said in the same falsely patient voice she might have employed when speaking to a not-very-bright child. "Nirod is the Kheressian equivalent of an engineer, who most recently has been copilot of Thuban's saucership."

"Well, there you are, then," Laura said, finally seeing a way to an acceptable excuse. "That explains what they've been doing. They've been flying supplies to the cave in the mountains."

"Cave?" Marica looked as if Laura had just spoken in a language she could not understand. "What cave? What are you talking about?"

"Don't you remember?" Laura asked. Perhaps, if she added enough details that were common knowledge, Marica would believe the excuse she was offering. "When you made the suggestion, shortly after we came here, that the Kheressians find a safe place to hide until the asteroid has come and gone, Seret told you the plans were already under way. There is a cave in the distant mountains, and the Kheressians have been flying food and medical supplies to it, in the hope that at least a few of them will be able to reach it at the last moment and take shelter there. When we first arrived in Issa, Thuban and Nirod were making trips to the cave almost every day. I wouldn't be at all surprised if Nirod has asked Thuban to go with him again, to boost Thuban's morale and make him feel better."

"Do you actually believe what you are saying?" Marica asked, her mouth twisting in derision.

"It seems perfectly reasonable to me," Laura said.

"If you are telling the truth," Marica said, "then you are a bigger fool than I thought." She spun around on her heel to leave. She almost collided with Hua Te.

"I suppose you also believe this nonsense about a cave?" Marica said to him.

"The Kheressians have never lied to me," Hua Te said, his quiet voice a reproof to Marica's constant, loud rudeness.

Marica's response to his statement was a silent scowl. She stalked away from the alcove, heading for the table in the middle of the central room. Once there she stared for a few minutes at the holographic images of Earth and the approaching asteroid, before she began questioning the woman who was working at the table.

"Hua Te," Laura said, "I do admire the way you

have of making honest statements without actually answering questions. It's something I have never been able to do. I tend to get hung up on details."

"It does take a certain attitude of mind," Hua Te said, his eyes twinkling, "and many years of practice. Marica is becoming annoyed because no one will provide the answers she seeks. And I begin to fear that an annoyed Marica is a dangerous Marica."

Laura repeated Hua Te's remarks and Marica's questions to Kentir later, while they walked together at sunset. Since their passionate interlude in Kentir's bedroom, he had taken at least an hour out of every busy day to spend with her, usually after the evening meal. It was as if, having made his declaration of love, Kentir had decided there was no longer any point in denying his need to be with Laura.

Whenever fear of the near future threatened to engulf her, Laura wondered if Kentir believed they were all going to die, no matter what the project team did to try to avert disaster. If that was the case, perhaps Kentir had chosen to seize what happiness he could before the end arrived. Laura did not ask him if it was so; she simply accepted the gift of his presence, treasuring the time he devoted to her because she knew its value.

As they approached the seawall Laura began to tell Kentir about her conversation with Marica, but she halted in midsentence at the sight of

Thuban and Renan coming from the direction of the project building.

Until they noticed Laura and Kentir, the two men were engaged in a vigorous discussion. Thuban, who steadfastly refused to use either a crutch or a cane, was limping heavily on his injured left leg. His left arm was still bandaged and it was supported in a sling. Nevertheless, Thuban plowed awkwardly on across the grass, occasionally stumbling and then righting himself, while Renan walked backward facing him and speaking urgently, perhaps in an attempt to get a word in, for Thuban was talking at the same time, and he kept cutting right through Renan's frantic pleas.

"You must listen to me," Renan insisted, putting out an arm to aid Thuban, who had just tripped on a tuft of grass.

"I don't have to listen to anyone, least of all you, *physician*," Thuban shouted back. With his good right arm he pushed Renan to one side, rejecting his help. Thuban regained his balance and hobbled onward.

"I have lost three good friends because of the rocket explosion," Renan said. "Two of them I never had a chance to help, and the third died despite my best efforts to save him. I don't want to lose you, too, Thuban."

With a resolution quite at odds with his normally gentle manner, Renan stepped in front of Thuban again, blocking his path. But Thuban refused to be stopped, and the two of them continued their crablike progress across the lawn.

Renan tried his best to stay with Thuban, but he was pushed aside each time he got directly in front of Thuban and began to impede the other man's movements. When Renan caught sight of Laura and Kentir he waved, signaling them to wait.

"I'm glad to see you," Renan called to Kentir. "I am justifiably concerned about Thuban's condition, but he refuses to heed my advice. Perhaps you will be able to convince him to listen to me."

"What's wrong?" Kentir turned from the agitated physician to his brother, who, from the disheveled, furious look of him, was not much calmer than Renan. "Thuban, if you have been working beyond your physical limits, I want you to listen to Renan. There is no point in killing yourself—"

"Do you hear what you are saying?" Thuban asked with a croak of bitter laughter. "In another fifteen days we will all be dead. What will it matter then if I work beyond my physical limits?"

"I cannot give him the extra medication he wants," Renan said, speaking to Kentir. "It would be irresponsible of me, and dangerous to Thuban. Instead of taking stimulants and painkillers, he ought to spend half of each day in bed, to allow his body to heal itself."

"I keep telling you, it doesn't matter!" Thuban yelled. "Nothing matters now but finishing the conversion of the saucership as quickly as possible. Renan, I thought you would understand the urgency of the situation and have the decency to give me the medicine I require, so I can work without the distractions of pain and exhaustion. But medicine or not, neither you, Renan, nor you, Kentir, will stop me. I know what has to be done and I intend to do it."

Unnoticed by the group on the lawn, Marica had come out of the house with Eliel, a young woman who was one of Marica's ever-present guards, at her side. With catlike grace Marica stalked forward.

"Did I hear you correctly, Thuban?" Marica asked. "Are you working on the saucership? I did wonder how you would decide to deliver the second weapon. Tell me, have you recovered enough to deliver anything at all? When I asked about your condition, I was told that you are now—shall we say, totally incapacitated?"

"What do you want?" Thuban demanded, turning to her with a snarl.

"I have taken note of your continued absence from my bed, Thuban," Marica continued, sending a seductive gaze in his direction. "What a shame. Issa is a boring place, so I deplore the lack of nightly entertainment now that you are gone. It was a minor affair, you understand, but briefly interesting. Entirely too brief, too *short*, of course, and therefore never completely satisfying. Nor was it profitable to me in any way."

Thuban did not deign to answer the remarks which Marica plainly meant to be insulting. The look he sent her was one of frustrated desire mixed with burning hatred. Seeing the expression on Thuban's face Laura shivered, and she shivered again when she glanced from him to

Marica and noted the cold contempt in Marica's eyes. Whatever had actually happened between the two of them, it was clear that affection had not been a part of it.

"Renan," Thuban said, with his gaze still on Marica, "I find myself in need of a particularly strong painkiller this evening, and I have no intention of listening to your excuses and denials." Taking Renan's arm with his uninjured right hand, Thuban pulled the physician away from his brother and Laura and began to hobble toward the house.

Marica started after the two men, but Kentir stopped her by laying a firm hand on her shoulder and turning her around to face him again.

"Eliel," Kentir said to the guard, "you are to escort Marica to her room and keep her there. Under no circumstances is she to see or speak with my brother."

"What would I want with that inadequate fool?" Marica asked with a disdainful toss of her head. "I have no more interest in Thuban."

"You are interested enough to play crude mind games with him," Laura said.

"I don't know what you mean," Marica responded, laughing at her. Marica shrugged to remove her shoulder from Kentir's restraining hand. Then she heaved a dramatic sigh and turned to the waiting guard. "Well, come on then, Eliel, you tiresome girl. Obey your orders. Conduct me to my cell. Bind me hand and foot if you must. As if keeping me prisoner will change anyone's fate."

With Marica gone, Kentir and Laura resumed their walk toward the seawall. Laura's tranquil mood had vanished, and Kentir's face was dark with a worry that Laura was sure had to do with his brother. It was then that Laura told him about Marica's attempt to learn from her where Thuban was going when he left the compound with Nirod each day.

"I have said it before," Laura finished her account, "but I am going to repeat myself. You Kheressians are remarkably naive. Or perhaps you lack the paranoid point of view of most people of my time. Marica is obviously up to something, yet you allow her to roam the compound at will."

"She is not as free as you—or Marica—believe," Kentir said. "I want to know what she is 'up to' as much as you do. Eliel and the other guards I have set to watch Marica report to me, or to Seret, everything she does and says. So far, Marica has done nothing more than make unpleasant and inappropriate remarks to everyone she meets, as you have just heard. I admit, I wish she would treat Thuban with compassion, but I do not think Marica possesses so sweet a characteristic. She is full of anger and thinks only of herself."

"Among people living in my country in the late twentieth century," Laura said, "there is a deplorable trend in public life, in business, and too often in personal relations, toward rudeness and a lack of concern for anyone except oneself and one's own advantage. Whenever I listen to Marica talking, I think the situation has only worsened between my time and hers, and I hear in her disgusting remarks to Thuban the final result of that trend. It's as if people just got ruder and more self-centered as time went on until, a couple of centuries later, someone like Marica finally appeared. I want to feel sorry for her, because I believe someone so nasty cannot be a happy person. But I find I can't. She's too despicable for pity."

"There I agree with you," Kentir said, "and I wish my brother did not desire her. But Thuban has promised he will keep away from Marica."

Kentir broke off all discussion of Marica then. He and Laura had reached the seawall, and the calm northern sea stretched before them. The sun was about to sink below the mountains, and the sky was glowing with shades of pink and lavender. A few bright stars were beginning to shine. Kentir put his arm around Laura. They stood close together, watching the water and the sky, waiting for the moment when the aurora would begin to glow.

Laura nestled against Kentir's shoulder, taking comfort from his strength and telling herself to be content with each precious hour they shared. While Kentir was with her she would be able to push aside the new fear raised as a result of the dispute between Renan and Thuban. After too short a time Kentir stirred, kissed her gently, and released her from his loving embrace.

"I have to meet privately with Thuban and Renan," he said. "I'll join you later if I can."

After a long and tender kiss he strode off through the twilight, leaving Laura to worry over what was being said at the meeting, to recall Thuban's reminder that there were only fifteen days left until the advent of the asteroid, and to think about what the reminder meant.

The last remaining hope the Kheressians had of saving their world lay in the saucership that Nirod was converting for space flight. The two best pilots were Kentir and Thuban. But in Thuban's present, injured condition he was physically unable to act as pilot. His constant need for painkillers and stimulants so he could act as overseer of the work proved he was unfit for any more challenging task.

Which left Kentir to do the job. As soon as the conversion of the saucership was finished, the weapon Kentir was working on would be installed in it. Then Laura did not doubt that Kentir would lose no time in piloting the saucership on the dangerous flight into space. It was almost certainly a suicide mission.

There was nothing Laura could say or do to stop him. Kentir would love her less if she tried to prevent him from doing his duty. The only chance she had of keeping alive the love she had found with him lay in letting him go into space, possibly to his death, without argument.

Laura went to bed an hour or so after Kentir had left her, but she did not sleep. He came to her in the middle of the night, and when he took her into his arms, Laura clung to him desperately, as if it were the last time they would ever be together.

"Gently," Kentir said with a delighted chuckle. "You are attempting to ravish an exhausted man."

"Sometimes I'm afraid," she whispered, and then bade her tongue be still. If she could not generate real courage in her heart, she must pretend, for Kentir's sake and for the sake of the precious love that lay between them.

"We are all afraid," he told her. "It's how we know we are alive."

"I love you so much," she said.

"Let me show you how I love you," he murmured. He did not wait for her assent before proving how rapidly he could recover from exhaustion. His mouth held hers, his tongue playing along the margin of her lips, teasing her until Laura opened her own mouth and gave him the entrance he sought. No other man had ever kissed her with Kentir's passionate ardor; no one had ever stroked her breasts while kissing her, or let his hands trail slowly across her abdomen and down, down. . . .

When he finally removed his mouth from hers, Laura gasped for breath and caught his hands, pulling them away from the place where his fingers had strayed to press and torment and nearly drive her mad.

"Too soon," she whispered. "Too fast."

"Do you think so?" A twist of his strong wrists and suddenly it was her hands being held captive. Kentir drew her fingers to his erect manhood. "Here's proof I am alive. Do with me what you will, Laura. If I am too fast, then you set our pace." He lay back upon the bed, smiling at her.

Left with her hands wrapped around his hot, throbbing masculinity, Laura could only stare, first into his smoky, teasing eyes and then at the rigid flesh she held. She moved her fingers, rubbing softly, and felt him leap at her touch.

"You trust me," she whispered, awed by the sight of his great strength laid out for her to use in any way she wanted.

"With my life," he said at once. "With my manhood. As you see, my love."

"Oh, Kentir." Tears ran down her cheeks. Kentir had given her all she had ever wanted from a man—complete honesty, openness, and trust. His love filled her with a soaring joy. That it also filled her with pain and the terror of impending loss seemed irrelevant at such a moment. "What can I say, Kentir? What shall I do?"

"Improvise," he said, and gave her the wickedest grin she had ever seen.

Under the influence of his humor she forgot her cowardice and did as he commanded. She stroked and teased, sucked and nibbled, and found delightfully sensitive places where she could put her fingers or her mouth and tongue. Finally, when Kentir was gritting his teeth and clutching at the mattress to try to keep himself under the last traces of self-restraint, when Laura's own need had grown so great she could scarcely move for desire, she mounted him as if he were the finest thoroughbred stallion.

The sensation of Kentir's great size filling her and stretching her body brought with it a fresh burst of energy. Laura rode him hard, and harder still, until his sudden, totally uncontrolled shout of release broke upon her eardrums. It was the sign she awaited. She sank down, impaling herself upon his hardness one last time, and her own pleasure came upon her in ripple upon ripple of explosive heat. She fell across Kentir's heaving chest, to lie there in panting delight, still filled with him, still consumed by the tremors racking her body. After a moment his arms came around her, holding her close, and even in her ecstatic state she noticed how his muscles trembled, too.

"I suppose all men wonder from time to time what it would be like to be ravished by a beautiful woman," Kentir said after a long, silent while. "Now that I have had the pleasure of learning how wonderful it can be, I may ask you to do it again."

"Did I truly please you?" she asked, her face still pressed against his chest.

"Everything you do pleases me, Laura. You are my heart, my soul, my hope. My dearest hope," he repeated, pulling her closer.

"I can't bear the thought of losing you," she cried. Unable to conceal her fear from him, she clutched at his shoulders. Panic filled her. In only a few days—too few, too precious—they would be torn apart, separated by death or by the intervening centuries. She did not think she could live without him.

"I depend on you," he said.

"Don't. I am weak," she told him.

"On the contrary. You are the bravest of women." Kentir's hand caught her chin, lifting her head until they were face-to-face and she was looking directly into his eyes, into the warmth and tenderness he always extended to her.

Laura saw his love for her in his gaze, and she could not look away, though she was ashamed of her cowardice when he was so courageous. Kentir thought she was as brave as he was. She knew she wasn't; still, because she loved him, she would try for his sake to discover whatever courage there was within her fearful heart.

"I'll do whatever you want me to do," she said. She tried to keep her lips from trembling and her voice from cracking. It wasn't easy, but it was worth the effort, for Kentir smiled at her.

"Stand with me till the end," he said. "Love me. Believe in me. No man can ask more of his woman."

"Yes, I will," she whispered, and meant it with all her heart.

Kentir pulled her closer and kissed her. It was a gentle kiss, with no promises in it. They had no need for promises, and no time for them, either. They had only the present moment, and their love. It would have to be enough.

He made love to her again, tenderly, sweetly, in contrast to the pulsing passion of the last time. And yet, when the climactic moment came, when their bodies were joined and their hearts beat as one, the ecstasy was hotter and more piercingly sweet than before. In that moment, to Laura, the future became irrelevant. So long as Kentir loved her, and was with her, nothing else mattered.

She would worry about time and consequences—and death—later, after he was gone.

Chapter Seventeen

"We have no choice," Kentir said, countering Thuban's continued angry protests.

It was midmorning and they were once again gathered in Seret's private rooms. Marica was confined on the other side of the house, as she had been for many days, with Eliel guarding her door, so there was little concern that they would be overheard.

It was a good thing that Marica was so far away, Laura reflected, since Kentir and Thuban were arguing rather noisily. Renan interjected a few surprisingly stern statements into the contentious atmosphere, speaking out of his medical knowledge and from his desire to treat Thuban, who was both friend and patient, in the way that would best speed his recovery.

"I am certain I can do it," Thuban said for the third time. "All I need is a little more painkiller and another day or two of exercise for my injured arm."

"A year of therapy won't improve the movement in your arm," Renan said bluntly, "nor in your leg. And I refuse to add your death to my already overburdened conscience by providing any more medication. With all of the painkillers and stimulants filling your system at this moment, you couldn't walk in a straight line even if your leg were in normal condition."

"I don't have to walk," Thuban said. He spoke through gritted teeth, as though all of his bottled-up impatience over his injuries would pour forth if he unclenched his jaw. "The only thing I have to do is sit in the pilot's chair and fly the saucership."

"The mission will require the most exacting skills," Renan argued, "and instantaneous reaction times. Face the truth, Thuban. You are unfit to drive a land vehicle, let alone fly a saucership."

"How dare you say such a thing to me!" Thuban's patience snapped and his voice rose to a fearsome roar.

"I will not grant you medical permission to pilot a ship," Renan said, facing down Thuban's fury with his own quiet firmness. "Kentir must be the pilot."

"I agree with you completely, Renan," Seret said. With undisguised sympathy she added, "Accept our decision, Thuban, and try to control your disappointment. It's not as though you are

283

entirely useless to us. We need you here, to take Kentir's place."

"No one can take my brother's place, least of all me, and all of you know it." Thuban's harsh-featured face was a study in frustration, rage, and—after Seret's firmly stated declaration—the very picture of reluctant resignation. Obeying Seret's advice to control himself, Thuban continued in a quieter tone, "I am too impatient, too quick to use sharp words. Never will I be the leader that Kentir is. Nor do I want to be leader. Seret, you will have to choose someone else to act as your second in command. All I want to do is fly my saucership. I belong in the air, and in space, not in diplomatic meetings.

"Great God of the Sea!" Thuban shouted, his anger surfacing again, as if he could not keep it contained, not even at Seret's wish. "Here we are, talking as if there is a future for us, when we all know that in a few days the world of Kheressia will cease to exist."

"Not if I do my job right," Kentir said.

"At least let me go along with you as a crew member," Thuban begged. "You will need another person to act as navigator."

"I also volunteer," said Nirod.

"No," Kentir told them. He looked away from his brother and his friend, to glance in Laura's direction. His eyes met hers, and he must have seen the request that she, too, had been about to make. Shaking his head, Kentir silently refused Laura, as he had refused the men. "I must go alone. With the most recent modifications Nirod has made to the ship's controls, one person can serve as both pilot and navigator until the moment when the weapon is fired."

"Ha!" said Thuban, fairly crowing as he detected the flaw in Kentir's logic. "Now I have you, brother. After the weapon is fired, you will have only a second or two in which to get away from the asteroid before pieces of exploding rock smash the saucership to bits. All of your attention will be occupied with the actual piloting, Kentir, and you will require a second crew member to keep track of your exact location while you navigate through an area of fast-moving debris. Then, once you have escaped from the immediate vicinity of the asteroid, who will guide you home again? You cannot answer those questions, can you?" Thuban finished triumphantly.

"When the time is right," Kentir said, not bothering to respond to his brother's challenge, "the rest of you will have in your hands the timestones that Imilca and Hua Te are making. I will not order you to use them. It will be a decision you must make for yourselves, though I prefer that all of you choose safety over the dangers you will face if you remain in Issa."

"I don't want to live in another time," Thuban declared. "Not in any world as different from Kheressia as the places our time-traveling visitors have described. I don't belong in any of those other times."

"Nor do I," Nirod stated.

"This is not a matter to be argued in a meeting," Seret said. "It is a question best decided in each individual heart." Her firm tones silenced that particular discussion.

"How long do we have?" Laura asked the question, dreading the answer.

"We will begin installing the weapon in the saucership later tonight, as soon as we can move it out to the airfield," Kentir answered her. "It will take two full days of work before it is ready." His eyes held hers, and in them Laura saw a lifetime of love. Nor did Kentir hide his regret for what they were going to lose, though she knew he would not speak aloud of it while others were present.

"So soon," she whispered, wishing she dared to challenge Kentir's decision as his brother had done, but knowing she would not defy him. She would not waste what little time they had in fighting Kentir. The best thing she could do for him was simply to love him, as he had asked her to do.

"Actually, converting the saucership has taken longer than we expected," Thuban said, "but I have an idea for shortening the time required to install the weapon and ready it for use."

Thuban paused for a moment, staring down at his bandaged left hand as if he was forcing himself to accept the decision to send Kentir into space instead of him. His next words revealed how dedicated he was to the project to which he and his brother had devoted their lives for almost three years. Disappointed though he was at not being allowed to fly the ship that carried the weapon he had invented, still, Thuban was not

286

going to walk away until the project was completed and the saucership was in the air.

"Kentir," Thuban said, "let me make a suggestion. Instead of transporting the weapon out to the airfield to install it in the saucership, and possibly damaging it along the way, why don't Nirod and I fly the ship here? There is plenty of room to set it down on the lawn near the project building, and the final takeoff will be no more difficult from here than from the airfield."

"In fact," said Nirod, breaking into Thuban's remarks, "it might be easier to send the ship into space from here. The grass at the airfield has grown pretty high, with no one left to care for it. Certainly installation of the weapon can be done here at the compound with no problem. Nor will there be any danger, since the explosive device is set on a timer."

"We can have both ship and weapon ready to go by tomorrow evening," Thuban said, with a nod of thanks for his friend's support. He continued, speaking to Kentir. "Doing it the way I suggest will cut at least half a day off your expected schedule. That will allow you a bit of extra time to maneuver in space, if you need it."

"You're right," Kentir said, after giving the idea a moment's thought. "It will be faster and simpler to do the job your way, Thuban."

"You will have to keep Marica under extra-tight guard," Laura cautioned.

"We will," Kentir promised. "Marica will be confined to her room until I have left in the saucership."

287

"Then, after all of the guests and project members who wish to leave Issa have done so," Seret said, "when there is no further harm that Marica can possibly cause in this time and only the one timestone left for her to use, I will send her on her way, knowing that the instant she reaches her own time, her timestone will automatically destroy itself beyond the ability of anyone to reconstruct it. Thus, we will attempt to ensure the integrity of all future history, from this time until Marica's day."

Laura heard Seret's confident words, but her gaze, and her thoughts, were on Kentir.

Two more days at the most; that was all the time she would have with him. She wondered if they would have a few hours to themselves for a private farewell, or if the requirements of the last, desperate attempt to avert disaster would keep Kentir from her.

She need not have worried. The passion flaming in Kentir's steely blue eyes reassured her. He would find a way for them to be together, if only for a short time. She regarded his tall, strong frame, while she considered his intelligence and courage, his dedication to the duty that had been laid upon him, his gentleness toward Seret, and his love for his brother. Laura marveled that a man as fine and true as Kentir should love her, and she almost wept then and there at the realization that he would very likely die in his heroic attempt to stop the asteroid.

Laura understood the precision that would be required when the concentrated light beam employed in the weapon was turned upon the asteroid. Kentir had explained to her how close the saucership would have to fly to the huge rock to determine the exact target for the light beam. And Thuban had just restated with frightening clarity the probability that, if the light beam shattered the asteroid, large fragments of it could, in turn, destroy the saucership. As Thuban had noted, there would be only a few moments during which the pilot could maneuver the ship out of range, and it was possible that there wouldn't be enough time to do so.

Though she knew very little about actually flying a saucership, Laura agreed with Thuban when he said having a second crew member along would increase what little safety factor there was. No matter what arguments Thuban made, Laura knew Kentir well enough to be certain he wasn't going to put anyone else's life at risk if he could avoid it.

Recalling Chac's repeated insistence that sacrificial victims were going to be required, Laura thought she knew how those whom the Aztecs sacrificed felt in their last moments of awareness, for as she contemplated Kentir's death, it seemed to her that her heart was being ripped out of her bosom. And she reflected that there was more than one kind of sacrifice. With a timestone being prepared for her to use, the chances were good that she would live on after Kentir died, to grieve for him every day for the rest of her life, a life she would live without the love that meant everything to her.

She knew there was nothing she could do to stop Kentir from his chosen path. Much as she wanted to, she wasn't even going to try. Kentir would not be the man she loved if he were not willing to make his own sacrifice, and he would love her less if she tried to prevent him from undertaking his mission. From Kentir's duty-bound point of view, some things were more important than the desire of two lovers to be together. To him, the tragedy of his parting from Laura would, in fact, be a triumph.

In Kentir's attitude Laura saw the foundation of a long tradition of men who were willing to set aside their personal desires in order to do what they perceived as the right and honorable thing. Trying to stop Kentir would dishonor both of them and sully their love beyond redemption. Accepting his decision to fly the saucership, Laura took a long breath, willed her voice to be steady, and looked from Kentir to Seret.

"Tell me what I can do to be most helpful to you in the next two days," she said.

Kentir knocked on Laura's door late at night, barely an hour after she had obeyed Seret's command to retire. It had been a long and intense day of steady work. Though the asteroid was still several days away from Earth, frequent reports were coming in from all over the world, telling of volcanic eruptions, earthquakes, and peculiar magnetic phenomena. Several bases where companion projects to the Kheressian efforts had been under way were now abandoned, the project teams escaping into space in saucerships if they were available. In some cases, taking advantage of the technology the group based at Issa willingly shared, team members had fled by means of timestones to the future or to the distant past.

Reading the reports, Laura marveled at the lack of panic among the people who remained. At Issa, members of the project were calm, though the strain showed in all of them. Kentir's face was pale with fatigue and there were dark circles under his eyes.

"Seret sent me away to rest until midday," he said. "Thuban and Nirod are supervising the final work. Thuban wants to make a few last adjustments to the weapon. I will leave Issa at the hour of sundown," he finished.

"Then by this time tomorrow—" Laura's brave intentions failed her. She choked on the words she meant to say and fell silent instead.

"By this time tomorrow," Kentir took up the thread of her thought in an even voice, "it will be done. Kheressia, and the world, will be safe—or not, if I fail."

"You will succeed," Laura cried, throwing her arms around him. "I know you will."

"How I value the trust you put in me," he murmured, his cheek resting on her hair.

"Trust and love," she responded, holding on tightly to him, not wanting him out of her arms for an instant of the time Seret had granted to them. For Laura was certain the wise and kindhearted Seret had deliberately sent Kentir from the worksite, knowing he would come to her on what could very well be his last night of life. Laura believed Seret was depending on her to make Kentir's last hours a time of peace and rest.

Laura refused to think about what would happen after the present night, just as she refused to spend the next few precious hours in tears and grief. She would think only of her love for Kentir and of the miracle of fate that had allowed them to find each other across the endless reaches of eternity.

Kentir lifted her into his arms. He gazed at her for a long time before carrying her to the bed. It was as if he wanted to memorize every line of her face, to burn the sight of her into his mind and heart, so he could never forget her.

Laura understood his need, for it was a reflection of her own longing to make Kentir so much a part of her that she would never forget anything about him. She wanted to remember every detail of his handsome, strong-boned face, his dark, curly hair, and the warmth that lit his remarkable eyes. There was no trace of flinty hardness in Kentir's eyes at the moment. What Laura saw when she met his gaze was tenderness, a building desire, and a trace of sorrow. She made herself smile at him, and Kentir smiled back.

He laid her gently on the bed and began to undress her. It took a long time. Kentir paused to kiss and caress each inch of skin he unveiled, from her waist as he lifted her tunic, to the sensitive place where her throat met her shoulders. A slight detour to express his appreciation for both of Laura's ears and the nape of her neck left her shivering in delight. Then he moved on to her shoulders, her upper arms, the insides of her elbows, her wrists, and each of her fingers in turn.

She knew what he was doing. He was memorizing her body by touch. As soon as Laura was uncovered from her waist up and Kentir reached for the waistband of her trousers, to pull them down, she put her hands over his, stopping him.

"It's my turn," she said. "It's only fair to give me equal time, Kentir." She unfastened his tunic, then pulled it over his head and flung it aside.

"Not fair at all," he groaned, catching his breath as Laura sucked at his nipples. "Maddening. Arousing. But definitely not fair."

"Ah, well, a man must just endure what a man must endure," she said, surprised to discover she was capable of teasing him at such a time. She placed a hand on each of his shoulders and pushed him down onto the sheet. Kentir chuckled at what she was doing, then caught his breath when she bent over him and began to rub her breasts against the dark hair on his chest. If the sensation startled Kentir, it electrified Laura. She believed her actions were more arousing to her than to Kentir until, in her increasingly vigorous wriggling atop his body, she made contact with an impressive hardness.

"Oh." She gasped, and pushed harder against him.

"I do believe it's time for self-control," Kentir said. He lifted her up and laid her down beside him, turning to her with a smile that told her he was fully aware of her growing need. "Let us not be hasty, my love. And let us be very, very thorough in what we are doing."

He was. He spent an inordinate amount of time in simply kissing her. Of course, Kentir's kisses were not so simple, for they ranged from the first soft, quick, almost teasing touching of their lips to long, deep, drugging conquests of her mouth that ought to have sated Laura, but only left her hungry for more of his kisses. And all the time that he was kissing her, his hands were busy, stroking, caressing, now and then pinching in a way that elicited soft cries of pleasure from his willing accomplice.

Laura touched him, too, paying homage to his tight arm muscles, to his broad shoulders and his wide chest. With trembling fingers she traced the long, straight line of his nose, ran her knuckles along his square jaw, and outlined his generous mouth. The fires of passion leapt high, searing their hearts, leaving Laura weak and aching for what would inevitably come next.

And through it all they both remained clothed from waist to toe. The rising heat low in her body made Laura twist and writhe as she tried to get nearer, to press herself against Kentir's hardness. She could see the way his body strained against the fabric of his trousers. His face was taut with the self-control he had advocated. Surely he yearned for immediate completion, just as she did.

"Please," she begged, twisting her hips toward him while Kentir held her wrists in a firm grip at either side of her head, keeping her immobilized so he could rain kisses on her breasts. His tongue flicked out to circle a nipple. Laura moaned, gritting her teeth against the wonderful, sensuous torture he was inflicting on her. "Kentir, you are driving me mad!"

"It was my intention," he murmured, his voice thick with desire. "But now I think it is time to provide the cure for your madness. And my own." His hands worked at the waistband of her trousers.

Incredibly, for a man so obviously aroused, Kentir proceeded to take his time, to kiss and caress the lower half of Laura's body as he had done the upper half. He nibbled each of her toes in turn and then, having finished with her toes, he ran his hands along her calves and thighs, gradually working his way upward until his skillful fingers molded the supple curves of Laura's hips and waist. After moving her into a slightly different position, Kentir traced the length of her spine, finishing his loving exploration of her body by cradling the rounded firmness of her buttocks in both his hands.

There was one exception, one area he carefully avoided. There were moments when he came temptingly close and then retreated. Equally incredibly, Laura did not expire of the madness she had warned him about, or even of her increasing desire. Instead, she found herself reaching a new level of excitement. Her intense awareness of Kentir was so complete that she was not sure where she ended and he began.

And still he was half clothed.

Finally, when the world and everything in it had receded to a hazy, barely perceived distance in Laura's consciousness, when nothing existed for her but Kentir, he reached down and unfastened his trousers. Slowly he slid the red fabric downward and kicked the trousers away. Naked at last, he turned back to Laura and gathered her into his arms with an unmistakable purpose in his movements.

She scarcely noticed that he was undressed. Visual details no longer mattered to Laura. She wanted only to be one with Kentir, though she did have a quick impression of hardness and great size, and a remarkable sensation of heat as he slid into her.

"Don't leave me!" she cried, pulling him closer, and closer still, taking him fully into her own moist and eager warmth.

"We can never be separated," Kentir said. "We are in each other's hearts for all time."

"I love you, Kentir."

"And I love you, Laura."

In the next instant speech became impossible. The passion Kentir had so carefully nurtured while keeping it under restraint, he now set free. Laura was drowned in sweet desire and in the still sweeter, rapidly approaching fulfillment of that desire. They were together every step of the way, Kentir smiling into her eyes, or kissing her, Laura gasping and holding him tight, telling him just how much she loved him with each eager movement of her body, each passionate thrust of her hips to meet his forward surges at exactly the right time.

And when it was finished and Kentir held her against his heart, Laura discovered to her surprise that she had no tears to shed, no fears left, and no regrets at all. She had only a deep, warm joy and a sense of completion.

Chapter Eighteen

"I cannot ask you to wait here in Issa for me," Kentir said to Laura, fastening his tunic as he spoke. They were together in Laura's room. It was midday; the sun had just passed its zenith, and Kentir was preparing to make his final inspection of the saucership and of the newly installed weapon before beginning his flight into space. Kentir's appearance was calm, though Laura was aware of the emotion he kept banked below the impassive surface.

"We both know how slight is the chance that I will return," Kentir continued. "The last thing I want is to put you into danger. The latest reports from Chac and the other astronomers warn that the asteroid is approaching more rapidly than we believed. The closer it comes to Earth, the faster it moves."

"Is that because of Earth's increasing gravitational pull on it?" Laura asked.

"That is the astronomers' explanation," Kentir said. "Because of the asteroid's increased speed, the astronomers say that merely diverting it won't change the course of events. It is already so close to Earth that, unless our weapon shatters the asteroid into small pieces, the few people who survive the next day or two will be forced to endure an indescribably harsh existence. I cannot, and I will not, put you into such terrible danger or subject you to so bleak a future."

"I don't care," Laura said. "I will wait."

"Go home, Laura." Kentir's voice took on a darker shading, slipping perilously close to command. "Return to your own time. You belong there."

"I belong with you, my love," she insisted. "I am not going to try to stop you from doing what you must, but I won't leave. I don't care how hard life becomes. I don't care if we are fated to live through an ice age. So long as I am with you, I will be happy."

"But I cannot be happy, knowing I have inflicted hardship on you," Kentir said.

"You haven't inflicted it; not if I have chosen it freely, with love, because I want to be at your side." She smiled brightly, to show him she meant every word.

"Laura, this is my last wish. Do not deny me."

Kentir took her by the elbows, holding her so she could not turn away from him. "My soul will love yours through all eternity. But I cannot die in peace if I know you are in danger because you want to take one last risk for my sake, to exercise one final hope that I may survive tonight's mission. I want you to swear to me that when the time comes, when Seret decides you must go, you will accept the timestone she offers you and use it."

"Kentir, I can't," she protested, fighting back tears. "How can I return to the future, not knowing whether you are alive or—or not?" she finished, unable to say the dreaded word, *dead*. She discovered that, for all her good intentions about letting him go with a smile, she could not bear to think of Kentir's death.

"It may be that you will know," he said. "It may well happen that Seret will have definite news of me. But, whatever the news is, still you are to leave Issa."

"No. Don't ask it of me," she whispered.

"Swear it, Laura. Swear that you will obey me, and Seret, in this."

"Kentir, please—"

"Swear it!" His eyes were cold, hard, silver-blue steel.

Longing to see the warmth of love in his gaze one final time, Laura bowed her head, swallowed her tears, and then lifted her eyes to meet his.

"I swear," she said. "On the love I have for you, I swear that I will do what Seret tells me to do."

"Thank you. Now I can leave with an easy

heart." He was smiling at her, bending his head to kiss her, and Laura thought her own heart would stop from the pain of his leaving.

"I love you, Laura," he said as his mouth claimed hers.

It was such a brief kiss. Laura wanted to clutch at him, to hold him tight and beg him not to go. She wanted him to kiss her again and again. It took all the strength she had to smile at him when he released her.

"Will you come to the ship later?" Kentir asked.

"I'll be there as soon as I bathe and dress," Laura promised, knowing she would need some time in which to cry a bit and then to disguise the signs of her tears. She would keep up the pretense of bravery, though her heart was breaking.

"I'll be expecting you." After delaying only long enough for a quick, final kiss, Kentir left her.

When he was gone, Laura collapsed onto her bed, unable to control her tears any longer. Never again would she hold Kentir in her arms; never again would they make love. They would say their last farewells in front of Thuban and Seret and the others. And then Kentir would fly off on his suicide mission. The thought of Kentir dying alone in a tiny saucership in cold, black space made Laura feel ill. A sick feeling rose in her throat. Nausea threatened to overcome her. She fought it back, refusing to give in to it.

She thought about stowing away on the saucership, so she could be with him at the end. The idea lasted only an instant. Seret would surely insist on keeping Laura with her during the lift-off, so she could offer emotional support to Laura. And even if Laura succeeded in hiding aboard the saucership, Kentir would be furious with her when he discovered her presence. He would most likely return to Issa, there to have her removed from the ship. The delay might well be fatal to Kentir, but it would not stop him.

Overcome by a fresh burst of tears, Laura reminded herself yet again that she must not interfere with Kentir's plans. She could only be there, at the saucership, to say farewell to him in a way that would show him how much she loved him. She must honor his bravery by being brave herself, and by carrying out his wishes, as she had promised to do.

Her final decisions made, Laura experienced a feeling of melancholy peace. She lay quietly on the bed for a few minutes until, worn out by weeping and by another wave of queasiness, she drifted into sleep.

Laura wakened abruptly, roused from slumber by a loud cry. Lifting herself up on her arms, she listened, but all she heard was the sea and the wind and, once, the calling of a bird. When she scrambled out of bed and opened the door, the corridor was silent and shadowed.

But it should not be shadowed, not in the middle of the day. Laura went to the window first, before she glanced at the timepiece beside her bed. Both the light outside and the clock told her the same thing as the shadows in the corridor: it was late afternoon. She had slept for several hours. It was time wasted, time when she could have been with Kentir. She would have to hurry so as not to waste the shortened time still left to them.

The bathroom mirror showed her a woman who looked as if she had wept the day away. Her eyes were red and puffy. Her face was drained and pale, and marked by creases from the bed-covers. Her short hair was tangled, with the ends sticking out in all directions. She looked, and felt, distinctly unwell.

"I'm sick," she said to her reflection. "No doubt about it. Can it be that Hua Te and Renan are wrong and Marica is right? Does transdimensional disorder actually exist and, if so, am I developing it?

"No," she told herself. "I won't believe Marica. It's only nerves. The past quarter-year since I came to Issa has been enough to drive anyone around the bend from stress. I am not sick. I won't allow myself to be sick.

"I can't let Kentir see me like this," she said. "His last memory of me ought to be of a composed woman, who has taken the time to wash her face and comb her hair, a woman who is brave enough to smile as he leaves. His last memory. Oh, Kentir, my love, I can't bear to lose you. How can I let you go?"

Sudden dizziness struck her. Laura leaned against the bathroom wall, closing her eyes tight, fighting the sensation. After a while the dizziness receded. Aware that time was passing too quickly, Laura stopped herself from sobbing, choking back the tears, refusing to cry again. She didn't have time left for tears. She had to pull herself together for Kentir's sake. She stepped away from the wall, testing herself for steadiness.

"All right," she said. "I think I can do it. I *will* do it. I'll just keep telling myself I feel fine, and I'll keep smiling until Kentir has gone."

Never in her life had she bathed and dressed so quickly. She was glad her hair was short; it could dry while she applied lash darkener, a dash of lip color, and, because she was so terribly pale, a faint dusting of rose on her cheeks. She pulled on a clean red tunic and matching trousers, fastened her sandals, and hastened out of her room, heading for the stairs and the front door of the house.

Something about the silence in the corridor made the hair on the back of her neck stand up. Laura halted in her rush toward the stairs and looked around. The corridor appeared to be perfectly normal and shadowy in the late-afternoon light, with the sun halfway down the sky and shining into windows on the western side of the house. The doors along the corridor were closed as usual, with only one door open a crack, letting a narrow beam of sunlight shine across the polished stone of the floor.

Laura stared at the line of sunlight. It was coming from the door to Marica's room, a door that ought to be closed and locked. And where was Eliel, who should be standing guard outside Marica's room? Laura moved forward as quietly as she could, until she reached the door that stood ajar. There was no sound from within, no indication at all that the room was occupied. Uncertain what she would find, and with every sense alert for danger, Laura gave the door a tentative push. When it swung inward she took a step back from it, fearing that Marica would come bursting through to confront her.

"Hello?" Laura called, not really expecting a response, not with the door left open and Eliel gone from her post. All of Laura's instincts told her something was very wrong. She called again, "Marica, are you here?"

"Ohhh," came a moan from within. "Help— please, help me."

"Eliel?" Thinking she recognized the muffled voice, Laura stepped cautiously into the room. A fast look around showed the chamber to be empty, with no sign of either Eliel or Marica. However, a heavy vase lay on the floor, as if it had been thrown down in haste, and a few sprays of flowers were scattered nearby. With a glance toward the open door leading to the bathroom, Laura called, "Eliel, where are you?"

"In the chest," the muffled voice responded. "Please, Laura, let me out."

"Oh, my God!" Laura exclaimed, forgetting all caution.

The Kheressians did not keep their clothing in drawers or in closets with hangers. Instead, all of the bedrooms had beautiful carved chests made of aromatic wood. The lids of these chests swung upward, so folded clothes could be stored inside. Laura had once teased Imilca that the

Kheressians kept their garments in hope chests. The chest in Marica's room did not look large enough to contain a person, but Eliel's voice came from inside it, pleading again to be released.

Laura lifted the lid. Eliel was, indeed, in the chest. She was bent forward at the hip, at a most uncomfortable angle. Her wrists were tied together and bound to her ankles, with her head pressed against her knees. A wrapping of fabric that had been used for a gag hung around Eliel's chin. Tossed into the chest on top of her was the coverlet from which strips had been cut to make her bindings.

"I suppose you are lucky she didn't kill you," Laura said, working at the knots that held Eliel's wrists to her feet. "It was Marica who did this to you, wasn't it? I can't think of anyone else who would want to tie you up this way. I assume she bashed you over the head with the vase I found on the floor."

"She tricked me," Eliel said. "Marica called through the door that she had cut herself and needed my help to get to Renan's clinic for treatment. When I entered the room she was behind the door, waiting for me. I saw her standing there with the vase in her hand and I tried to give the alarm, but there wasn't time before she struck me."

"I thought I heard someone cry out, almost an hour ago," Laura said. "When I didn't hear any other sounds, I discounted the noise. I'm sorry, Eliel; I should have investigated sooner. There, your wrists are undone. They were tied pretty tight, so rub them to get the circulation going again while I work on your ankles." She began to tug at the second set of knots that fastened Eliel's ankles together.

"Marica didn't actually hit me very hard with the vase," Eliel said, "but I was too groggy to fight her when she trussed me up like this and gagged me. I did manage to get the gag off by scraping it against my knees, and then I called for help, but I was afraid no one would hear me. I know just about everyone is out of the house today, working on the ship or the weapon.

"I've failed in my duty," Eliel said as Laura unfastened the last of the knots and helped her to stand up. "How am I going to explain my stupidity to Seret and Kentir?"

"I don't think there is going to be any time for making excuses, or for placing blame," Laura said. "Come on, now, Eliel, try to step out of the chest. Just lean on me."

Eliel nearly fell and, once out of the chest, she had to sit down on the closed lid to rub her ankles until the feeling came back into them. Laura did not want to leave her, but she was consumed with impatience. She wanted to get to Kentir, to warn him that Marica was loose. Laura was certain Marica had something planned that would prove detrimental to Kentir's mission and to the other Kheressians.

"Did Marica say anything to you?" Laura asked of Eliel. "Did she mention where she was going? Thank heaven, she doesn't know about the saucership being here instead of at the airfield. The ship can't be seen from this room."

"She'll discover where the ship is as soon as she leaves the house and walks toward the project building," Eliel said. Grabbing Laura's arm, she continued, speaking with a new note of urgency. "I remember now. Just before she closed the chest lid on me, Marica mentioned the time-stones."

"Of course!" Laura exclaimed. "That's what she has wanted all along. Marica thinks she can make a profit from selling the timestones. But they are in a secret place inside the project building."

"Imilca and Hua Te are probably there right now," Eliel said. "Surely they are still working on the last of the stones. Imilca told me only yesterday that she feared there wouldn't be time to make enough of them. Laura, don't worry about me. I'll be able to walk in another few minutes. You have to find Imilca at once. Tell her what has happened. Stop Marica if you can. That wicked woman will think nothing of stealing all of our timestones and leaving us here to deal with the asteroid, with no hope of escape."

"Eliel, the moment you can walk, go to the saucership," Laura said. "Warn Seret and Kentir that Marica has escaped. And, Eliel . . ."

"Yes?" Eliel looked up from rubbing her ankles. "Is there something else?"

"If Seret decides that Kentir ought to leave before I get there, tell him . . . tell him I wish him good luck."

"I will." The look in Eliel's eyes told Laura that she understood what Laura could not say over the sudden thickness in her throat.

"Go on now, Laura," Eliel said. "Hurry, please. Our survival depends on you."

Laura ran from the room, along the corridor, and down the steps. She flung open the front door, then stopped for an instant, gazing in the direction of the saucership. She could not see it from where she stood, but it drew her with a magnetic attraction because Kentir was there. It was so unfair that she could not go to him, to say a final farewell. But, like Kentir, Laura understood what her immediate duty was. If she did not stop Marica from taking all of the timestones and using one of them to return to the twenty-second century, then Kentir's brave sacrifice might well be in vain. The timestones were the only hope the Kheressians had of escaping the effects of the asteroid's close approach.

And worse, far worse than what would happen to the Kheressians, was the use to which Marica would put the stolen timestones. Marica would have no hesitation about changing the course of history. She would not care if she caused the deaths of millions of innocent people in the intervening centuries. If she saw some advantage to herself or a chance to make a profit, Marica would stop at nothing.

With a final glance in the direction of the saucership, Laura said a silent good-bye to her love. Then she turned and began to run in the direction of the project building.

Chapter Nineteen

The door of the project building stood wide open. There was nothing very unusual in that but, after what had happened to Eliel, Laura wasn't going to take any chances. She approached the doorway at an angle so no one who was inside the building could see her, and when she was nearer she hugged the wall, moving closer to the door, listening for voices from within. When she heard Marica, Laura was glad she had been so cautious.

"Do as I say," Marica commanded someone whom Laura could not see from where she was standing, "or Imilca will die."

"What difference can it make whether I die now or in the next few days?" came Imilca's voice. "If I tell you where the timestones are hidden, if I let you steal them, then it is very likely that all of us who are left in Issa will perish—and some of us slowly and painfully. I would far rather die quickly at your hands and, by my death, give my friends a chance of survival."

"Imilca speaks for me, also," said Hua Te.

"And for me," came a third voice, that of a young male.

Laura did not recognize the voice at first. Not until she moved closer to the doorway and poked her head around the edge of the frame, was she able to identify the young man as Arad. With the saucerships not flying and his navigational skills not required, Arad had been put to work monitoring the holographic images.

At the moment, however, there was no image of the planet turning in the air above the hologram table in the center of the room. Arad, Imilca, and Hua Te were the only project members in the room, and they were all standing at the far side of the table. Marica faced them, with her back to the door. She appeared to be holding a weapon. From where Laura was, she could not tell what kind of weapon Marica had, though she was fairly certain it was stolen from Eliel.

Imilca and Hua Te could not see Laura from their positions, but Arad could. When he glanced around, as if looking for a way out of his predicament, Laura waved to him. Arad tilted his chin just a little and his eyes widened. Then he turned back to Marica, his expression so completely bland that Laura knew he had seen her.

Laura ducked back outside the building, hiding there while she waited for the right opportunity to intervene without endangering her friends. Without warning, the sick feeling came upon her again. Fighting it, Laura leaned back, resting her head and shoulders against the wall. She took deep breaths while she made herself concentrate on the conversation going on within, and after a few moments she felt a little better.

"I am sick of hearing your constant Kheressian protestations of altruism," Marica said. "It is unnatural to give up one's own life for someone else. I don't believe any of you are as brave as you pretend." She sounded edgy and more than a little impatient.

"The Kheressians mean what they say," Hua Te told her. "I have been impressed by their courage and decency—and by their concern for future ages."

"Be quiet!" Marica ordered. "Do not attempt to distract me, Hua Te. I intend to return to my home, taking with me as many timestones as I can carry. The bidding will be high for those unique treasures. I have been inconvenienced beyond all tolerance during this kidnapping, so it's only fair for me to realize a profit that will allow me to live where and how I please for the rest of my life.

"Now, understand me and make no mistake about my intentions," Marica continued. "I will waste no more time arguing with you. If I am not told where the timestones are by the time I count to three, I will kill one of you. Then I will give you another chance to tell me where the stones are,

before I kill a second person. And then the one remaining alive will have a final chance to speak."

"We will not tell you," Imilca said, "and if you
kill all of us, you will never find what you seek."

"You can't even be sure the timestones are hidden in this building," Arad said. "They could be
someplace else."

"I told you to be quiet!" Marica exclaimed. She
pointed her weapon directly at Arad. "Or, better
yet, since you are so eager to talk, Arad, tell me
what I want to know. If you refuse, you will be
the first to die, on my count of three. One."

Frantically, Laura looked around for a stone to
throw into the project building, to distract Marica from her murderous intent. She could see no
readily available object, just the lawn of rough-
cut grass, which did not even have a stray branch
laying on it. Nor was there time for Laura to begin a search for something to throw. With a sense
of utter frustration she heard Marica continue
the deadly count.

"Two," Marica said.

Laura did not doubt that Marica would carry
out her threat. The woman had no sympathy for
anyone but herself, and she would have no compunction at all about killing if she thought it
would get her what she wanted. Laura decided
there was only one way to save Arad. She would
have to go through the door, yelling to startle
Marica. Laura just hoped she could duck fast
enough to avoid being hit when Marica used her
weapon. Moving as quietly as she could, Laura
stepped into the arch of the doorway.

"Three," Marica said.

"Marica!" Laura shouted at the same instant that Marica's finger began to tighten on the button of her weapon. Marica whirled around. Laura gave Marica just a split second to see who was confronting her, and then dove for shelter beneath the hologram table.

She wasn't quite fast enough. A blast of flame flared from the weapon in Marica's hand and seared along Laura's left cheek. The pain was so shocking in its severity that Laura lost consciousness for a few minutes.

She returned to full awareness with her head resting on Hua Te's shoulder while Imilca held a silver vial beneath her nose. A sharp, minty aroma wafted from the vial into Laura's lungs with each breath she took. Her wits cleared with remarkable speed and she was amazed to find the pain in her cheek growing faint. When she put her hand to the place where Marica's weapon had burned her, she felt the wound, but it no longer hurt and it wasn't bleeding.

"Where is Marica?" Laura asked, looking around. She was surprised to discover that the three who had been menaced by Marica were all still alive. Laura had fully expected Marica to carry out her deadly threat, and to take pleasure in doing so.

"She's gone," Arad answered. He was sitting on the floor a few feet away from her. The left sleeve of his tunic had been cut away and a bandage was wrapped around his upper arm.

"What happened to you?" Laura asked him.

"Marica tried to kill me, as she had threatened to do," Arad answered. "When you burst through the door and distracted her, Hua Te knocked me aside, out of weapon range. He was just in time, for Marica shot me immediately after she fired at you. I must thank both of you for my life," Arad finished, looking from Laura to Hua Te.

"Why didn't Marica stay long enough to kill all of us?" Laura asked.

"Hua Te convinced her that you had certainly alerted Seret and Kentir to the fact that she had escaped from her room," Imilca said.

"Then she didn't get the timestones after all," Laura said with a sigh of relief.

"I gave her one," Hua Te said.

"You did what?" Laura exclaimed, staring at him in disbelief.

"It was the stone we intended for Marica," Imilca said. "We had just finished it when she appeared and began to make her demands of us."

"She can use it only once," Hua Te added to Imilca's explanation. "When Marica reaches her destination, the stone will automatically destroy itself."

"Will the stone return her to her home as she wants?" Laura asked.

"I hope and believe it will restore her to the exact time and place from which she left," Hua Te said. "It would be a pity for Marica to live in any other time but her own."

"Personally, I'd like to think of her living in the age of the dinosaurs," Laura said. "She deserves to be punished for what she tried to do to you

315

three, not to mention what she did to poor Eliel."
Quickly, she explained how Marica had managed
to escape from confinement. "I'm sure that's how
she got her hands on a weapon, too. She stole
Eliel's," Laura finished.

"A person so inherently violent will surely
bring about her own punishment, and perhaps
her own destruction as well," Hua Te remarked.
"It is a sad thing to see intelligence so misused."

"I sent Eliel to warn Seret and Kentir that Marica is free," Laura said. Then, praying she still
had time enough to say good-bye to him, she
asked, "Do you know if Kentir has left yet?"

"I don't think so," Arad told her. "I haven't
heard the ship's engines."

"I have to go to him," Laura said. She tried to
stand, only to discover to her dismay that she
could not. The room spun around her, and Laura
was sure she really was going to be sick this time.

"Put your head down," Imilca advised. She
opened the stopper on the silver vial and held the
vial under Laura's nose for a second time. "This
will help. Just remain still for a few moments."

The minty aroma quickly restored Laura to a
normal state. Her stomach settled down and the
room stopped spinning. She took Imilca's advice
and stayed as she was, with her head against Hua
Te's shoulder, while she fought off her mounting
fear of an encroaching, unknown illness. She
told herself that Hua Te did not look the least bit
sick, and Marica had certainly not been unwell—
or was she? Perhaps it was the effects of transdimensional disorder that had spurred Marica's

desire for immediate escape to her own time.

"Are you feeling better now?" Imilca asked.

"Yes, I am. Much better, thank you," Laura lied. With Hua Te and Imilca helping her, she slowly got to her feet. She was still light-headed, but she wasn't going to tell Imilca or Hua Te about it. She had to get to Kentir, to see him one last time, and she wasn't going to let her friends prevent her with their good intentions. She would worry about her physical condition later. She had a perfectly good excuse for the way she staggered when she tried to walk, and she took full advantage of it. "Good lord, what did that woman do to me? My head is still spinning."

"Marica repositioned the control on Eliel's weapon to the highest setting," Imilca said. "Ordinarily our weapons are set only to stun, and they are rarely used. But they can be tuned to kill, if necessary. That is what Marica did. You and Arad are fortunate to be alive. Laura, you are still very pale. Are you sure you can walk? Why don't you take a few moments more to recover?"

"I'll be just fine," Laura said. "We don't have time to waste. Heaven only knows what Marica will do next. Come on." Refusing to give in to the last vestiges of dizziness, she started for the door.

The four of them left the project building and headed for the saucership. As they drew nearer to the spot, Laura left Hua Te and Imilca to support Arad, who also complained of feeling dizzy. Imilca paused to administer a dose of the aromatic concoction in her vial to the young man. Laura wished she could stop long enough to inhale the vapors. The mixture was better than smelling salts for clearing the mind after a faint, but she didn't want to stop. She just wanted to find Kentir.

When she reached the ship, Marica was nowhere to be seen. A group of project workers, including Nirod and Chac, had gathered around the entrance ramp of the ship, where they stood gaping in amazement at the scene before them. Eliel was there, too, standing just behind Seret. And Seret, that wise, quiet, and gentle lady, who seldom raised her voice, was engaged in an angry confrontation with Thuban.

The reason for the dispute was obvious. Kentir lay on the ground at the bottom of the ramp, unmoving, a winecup by his outstretched hand.

"Kentir!" Laura rushed toward him, but Seret and Thuban blocked her way and Eliel caught her arm to prevent her from going any farther. Laura wasn't going to let them stop her. All she could see was Kentir, and she was sure he needed her. With a rough gesture, she pushed past Eliel and knelt beside Kentir, taking his head onto her lap. Kentir looked as if he was asleep. When Laura touched his face his skin was warm and dry. His color was normal, but he did not waken when she leaned closer and whispered his name into his ear.

When she looked at the group gathered around the saucership ramp, Laura saw that Seret was openly angry with Thuban, yet the Kheressian leader displayed no concern for Kentir's condition. That fact told Laura that Kentir was in no great danger. If he were in danger, Seret would be issuing orders to have him removed to Renan's clinic at once.

Brushing a lock of Kentir's black, curly hair off his brow, Laura wrapped her arms around him in a protective way while she listened to the ongoing argument between Seret and Thuban.

"I am appalled by your foolhardy actions," Seret said to the dark, harsh-featured young man standing before her. "You had no right to make such a decision on your own. We all agreed that Kentir should be the pilot."

"You and Kentir agreed," Thuban said. "I did not."

"Thuban!" Laura cried, "what have you done to your brother?"

"I put a painkilling medicine into some wine," Thuban replied. "Then I suggested that we drink a farewell cup before the saucership lifted off. As you can see, Kentir won't be acting as pilot. He will awaken in a little while, after I have gone from Issa. He won't be harmed by the medicine, Laura. I made certain there was just enough in the wine to put him to sleep. The purpose of my deception was to keep Kentir safe, not to hurt him."

Imilca, Hua Te, and Arad arrived on the scene as Thuban was explaining to Laura. Imilca left her companions and went to check on Kentir's condition. Satisfied that Thuban had spoken the truth, she faced him with her hands on her hips and an expression almost as angry as Seret's on her face.

"A painkiller?" Imilca exclaimed, shaking her head in disgust at what Thuban had done. "Now I understand. That is why you wanted the extra medicine, and why you repeatedly asked for the liquid instead of accepting an injection. You haven't been taking your medicine, Thuban; you've been saving it to dissolve in Kentir's wine. You lied to Renan when you claimed to be in great pain. And you made me a party to your deception when you pleaded with me to intercede with Renan for you."

"Now that your scheme has been discovered, I hope you are properly ashamed of yourself for what you have done," Seret said to Thuban in a reproving tone of voice.

"Not a bit," Thuban responded, grinning at her like a naughty boy who has gotten away with mischief.

"And I suppose Nirod has aided you in this nefarious plan?" Seret's voice remained sharp, but the look she gave Thuban held a certain respect for his cleverness.

"Nirod is my best friend," Thuban said. "Of course he helped me."

"In your injured condition, you cannot pilot the ship," Seret said. "That's why I chose Kentir over you for the mission to the asteroid, and you are in no better health now than you were a few days ago, when I made my decision."

"We have made a few decisions of our own, Seret," Nirod said, stepping forward from the group of project workers. "I am going with Thuban. I will act as pilot, following Thuban's instructions. Seret, you know I am almost as skilled as he at flying a saucership."

"I see." Seret looked from Nirod to Thuban, and it was to Thuban she spoke next. "I do not approve."

"You can't stop us," Thuban said.

"If you fail—" Seret began, but Thuban interrupted her.

"We won't fail," he said. "We can't. Failure is unthinkable. So is any further delay. We must leave at once."

"Give us your blessing, Seret," Nirod begged, going to his knees before her. "We will undertake this mission whether you approve or not, but I would far rather go into space with your blessing than without it."

Still angry at the subversion of the plan she and Kentir had agreed upon together, Seret stared at the two men for a long moment. She looked at Kentir, who still lay unmoving in Laura's arms. Seret's shoulders slumped as the anger went out of her, and she nodded.

"It is clear to me that nothing I can say or do will sway you from the course you have chosen. It is also plain to see that Kentir will not be able to fly a saucership until it is too late for him to do any good. But, oh, my dear children, how I grieve to lose you—as much as I sorrowed to know I would lose Kentir," Seret said. A tear ran down her lined cheek when she placed her hand on Nirod's bowed head. She looked from him to Thuban, and Thuban also went to his knees. Seret put her other hand on his head.

"I'll go, too," Arad said, stepping forward. "They will want a holographic expert to navigate for them. If I am in the crew, Thuban and Nirod will have a greater chance of success." It was not a boast on Arad's part, just a simple statement of an obvious fact.

"I won't let you leave without me," said a young woman, who came forward to link her hand with Arad's. He did not object, but instead smiled at her and kissed her cheek.

"Nor will I be left behind." Another man stepped up to stand beside Arad, and a second woman joined him.

"You cannot all go," Seret said, regarding them with tear-filled eyes.

"Though a single pilot can handle a saucership with the modifications I have introduced to the controls," Nirod said, "still, a crew of six will fly it with greater ease. We can make good use of these volunteers."

"Be aware that, if we survive our mission, Nirod and I do not intend to return to Earth," Thuban said to the group standing around Arad. "While we converted the ship for space flight, we also stocked it for a long voyage. Seret, we took some of the supplies intended for the cave. I do not think it will make much difference to the lives of any people who reach the cave."

"How deceptive you have been, and I never guessed," Seret said, adding with a sigh, "Considering the future you will face on Earth should you return here, I cannot blame you for searching elsewhere for a place to live. Thuban, where will you go?"

"When we have finished with the asteroid, we will head for far space," Thuban said. "We'll follow the route taken by the others who went offworld, and hope to join them at one of their settlements. Or perhaps we will discover our own new world."

"Good fortune and happiness to all of you," Seret said, regarding the little group with an affectionate gaze. "Now, my dear, brave friends, you have a most dangerous task to complete."

"Yes, and the sooner we leave, the better," Thuban agreed. He bent to touch Kentir's shoulder, then looked at Laura. "Tell him I said farewell."

"Good-bye, Thuban," Laura said. "Good-bye, Nirod. Arad." Gently she laid Kentir's head down on the grass. Rising, she began to shake Thuban's hand. She changed her mind and embraced him instead, and then embraced Nirod and the rest of the volunteer crew as well.

"Thuban," Seret said, "I want to have a few final words with you."

"Nirod, get the crew aboard and begin the takeoff checklist," Thuban ordered. "I'll join you shortly."

"Eliel," Seret said, turning to the young woman, "you will find Renan in the clinic. Tell him what has happened and ask him to bring a stimulant to waken Kentir."

Eliel started for the house. Seret drew Thuban aside and began talking to him in a low voice. Nirod disappeared into the saucership with the other crew members, and the entrance door slid shut behind them. Laura, Imilca, Hua Te, and Chac were left in a group, standing a short distance away from the unconscious Kentir.

Laura took a step in Kentir's direction. Having said her farewells to Thuban's crew, Laura focused all of her thoughts on her love. She was overjoyed to know he would not be piloting the saucership. A renewal of hope flared in her heart. Kentir would be angry when he wakened and discovered what had happened, but she could deal with his anger as long as he was alive and well and safe. Together she and Seret would make Kentir understand Thuban's need to go in his brother's place.

In the meantime, Laura wanted to be absolutely certain he was unharmed by the drugged wine. It was possible that Thuban had somehow misjudged the medication and given Kentir an overdose. Laura hoped Renan would come quickly to revive him. Before she could reach Kentir, a frightening interruption occurred.

Seret and Thuban were still talking, standing side by side near a thick clump of bushes.

"How very convenient you are making this for me," said Marica, stepping out from her hiding place among those same bushes. With a swift motion she wrapped her arm around Seret's throat and pressed her weapon against Seret's head. With a curse, Thuban froze, watching Marica intently.

"Don't move, Thuban," Marica warned him. "And you stay where you are, too, Laura. Don't go near Kentir. No one else move, either, unless you want me to kill Seret. Now, Thuban, I have an interesting proposition to make to you."

"Don't expect me to trust you," Thuban replied. "Especially not if you hurt Seret in any way."

"Marica, this is quite unnecessary," Seret said. She was standing perfectly still in the grip of Marica's arm. Her calm blue eyes surveyed those who were staring in horrified astonishment at her and at Marica. Seret continued to speak to Marica in a voice as quiet and soothing as that of a mother who was trying to reassure a disturbed little girl. "We have prepared a timestone for you that is set as closely as our technology allows to the exact moment when you left your time. You will be able to return to your home, and you may do so as soon as you wish. I promise you, my child, there is nothing for you to fear. Only release me and I will get your timestone and give it to you."

"I'm not afraid of anything, you old witch! And I am not your child!" Marica exclaimed, visibly tightening her hold on Seret as she spoke. "I already have a timestone in my pocket, and Hua Te swears it is the one meant for me. But I have only the one stone. I want more of them. I want as many timestones as I can carry, to take with me when I leave this time. You, Seret, are going to tell me where the rest of the stones are hidden."

Seret did not respond, but Thuban began to move, slowly circling Marica. To keep him directly in front of her where she could see him,

Marica was forced to move, too, pulling Seret with her as she turned.

"Hold still!" Marica yelled at Thuban, "or I'll kill Seret."

"If you do, I won't be interested in that proposition you mentioned," Thuban said. "And a dead Seret can't tell you where the timestones are. Give it up, Marica. Surely you know by now that Kheressians don't respond to threats of violence. Use the timestone Hua Te gave to you, and go home."

"Listen to me, Thuban," Marica said. "Help me get all of the timestones and we'll go together to my time. We can be rich beyond dreaming! And we'll be safe there. In my century you won't have to worry about asteroids crashing into the earth."

"Won't I? How can you be certain of that?" Thuban asked, moving another couple of steps, still circling Marica. "And how do I know you won't kill me once you have the timestones and don't need me anymore?"

"Marica!" Laura cried, hoping she could divert the woman's attention from Thuban long enough to give Thuban a chance to rescue Seret. "Are you beginning to feel sick? Is that why you are so eager to go home right now? Are you developing the symptoms of transdimensional disorder, just as you predicted all time travelers will?"

Marica laughed, but she did not take her weapon away from Seret's head, and she never removed her eyes from Thuban's constantly moving form.

"I am not sick," Marica said.

"Yes, you are," Laura insisted, eager to say anything to keep Marica distracted. "You just don't know it yet."

"I cannot be sick from transdimensional disorder," Marica said, "because it doesn't exist. As soon as I understood how tenderhearted the Kheressians are, I invented the illness, thinking I could frighten them into sending me home quickly, so I wouldn't get sick."

"What?" Laura gasped. "Are you saying it has all been a lie?"

"In your time, I believe you would call it a scam," Marica said, a smile of genuine amusement curving her lips.

"Then why do I feel so ill?" Laura whispered the question, not wanting Marica to hear it. She needn't have worried. Marica had dismissed Laura and returned her full attention to Thuban.

"I know you want me," Marica said to Thuban. "That night we spent together, you told me you couldn't get enough of me. Help me now, and you can have me whenever you like, and in any way you prefer."

"I wanted you before I knew what you really are," Thuban said, still moving, step by slow step. "I have no desire left for you, Marica. Not for a creature who can hurt decent souls like Seret or Eliel, or invent an illness that doesn't exist, just to make others feel guilty. How could I want a woman who would steal the timestones from the people who will need them to reach safety, whose lives will depend on those stones if I cannot stop the asteroid? What happiness can I hope for with a lover who expects me to betray my friends just when they need me most?"

"Thuban, you are a fool!" Marica exclaimed. She gave Seret a brutal shove, pushing her aside.

Laura caught Seret in her arms, steadying her.

"Stop this violence at once!" Seret commanded.

Marica spun around, as if to strike Seret with her weapon. Thuban had been gathering his strength during the long conversation with Marica. He knocked the weapon from her hand and grabbed at her. But Thuban's range of motion was still restricted by his injuries, and Marica possessed a wiry strength. She fought Thuban off and, breaking free of his grasp, she headed for the beach. Thuban picked up the weapon Marica had dropped and hobbled after her.

In the group with Laura, Chac had been muttering imprecations against Marica under his breath. Now he hastened after Thuban. As he ran, Chac pulled a dark, shiny object from his tunic pocket.

"Let Marica go," Seret called to the two men. "She can do no more harm."

Her words did nothing to halt the chase across the grass to the seawall and the beach. Thuban continued to limp along, and Chac soon caught up with him. Laura could hear them speaking, but she could not make out their words. Then Chac ran ahead of Thuban.

"Stop them," Seret cried. "Laura, Hua Te, go after them."

"I don't think they'll listen to me," Laura said.

"Thuban is too angry with Marica to pay heed to anything I say, and Chac—oh, good heavens, what is Chac planning to do?" she exclaimed, her eyes on the man who was following Marica with a speed and grace that reminded Laura of a fleet jaguar chasing its prey.

Fear stabbed at Laura's heart. Knowing that something terrible was going to happen unless the men were stopped before they reached Marica, Laura handed the trembling Seret into Imilca's arms. She took a quick look at Kentir's unmoving form and told herself there was nothing she could do for him. Renan would come soon to care for Kentir. Then, certain it was what Kentir would do if he were conscious and able to act, Laura ran for the seawall. A moment later she heard Hua Te running behind her.

Marica reached the seawall. She leapt onto it and waited there, crouching in a warrior's stance, watching as Chac approached. Chac ran right up to Marica and jumped onto the wide, stone wall to face her. Without warning he swung his right arm at her, aiming his blow with the deadly precision of long practice. Only then, with Chac's arm in midswing, did Laura clearly see what he was holding and recognize the object he had pulled from his pocket. The sun gleamed on a long, shiny black blade. Chac was using his obsidian sacrificial knife as a weapon.

Marica was well trained in self defense and in the use of weapons. With split-second reflexes she countered Chac's movement, stopping his arm before the razor-sharp blade reached her.

329

Marica fastened her fingers around Chac's wrist and bent his hand backward until his fingers were forced to relax their grip. The obsidian knife clattered onto the seawall.

In one fluid motion Marica scooped up the knife and jumped off the seawall. She stood on the beach, with Chac's knife in her own hand, and she laughed at him.

"If you want it," Marica said in her mocking, taunting way, "then come and take it, Chac. If you can." She moved the knife casually, as if she were playing with it.

With a cry of dismay and of outrage at the sight of his sacred blade in the clutches of such a person, who was handling it so irreverently, Chac followed Marica off the wall and onto the beach. Without hesitation, he closed the distance between them.

Marica stabbed him twice—swift, hard blows to the abdomen. The bloody knife still in her hand, she danced away a few steps, then stopped on the sand, poised as if ready for a second encounter. With a surprised expression Chac looked down at the blood spreading across the front of his tunic. He staggered backward until he came up against the wall. There he stayed, bracing himself upon the stone.

"Now you know how it feels, you Aztec barbarian," Marica yelled at him.

"He's not the barbarian. You are!" Thuban shouted. He reached the seawall, with Laura just a few paces behind him and Hua Te immediately behind her. Thuban stopped, panting, his face pale from the exertion of running.

"Great God of the Sea, Marica!" Thuban gasped. "It wasn't necessary to kill Chac. You have your timestone. Go home. Go away from here and leave us alone. We want no more of your wicked violence."

"Not yet," Marica said. Her eyes narrowed, she watched Chac, who had slumped into a sitting position on the seawall, with his dark head bowed and his sturdy frame weaving from side to side. "He's not dead yet. I'm going to finish the job before I go." Once more raising the hand that held Chac's knife, she took a step toward him.

"Don't," Thuban warned. He lifted the weapon he had picked up near the saucership and pointed it at Marica. "Don't force me to use this. Please, Marica. Stop now. You've done enough harm."

"You won't use that on a woman," Marica said, taunting him. "You aren't man enough. You lack the most vital element of masculinity— ruthlessness. You have too many moral scruples and they make you weak, Thuban. You'd never succeed in my world."

"Then I am glad I will never see that world," Thuban said.

"You won't stop me from putting an end to this barbarian." With a mocking laugh, Marica took two more steps toward Chac. The Aztec lifted his head to meet her eyes. Marica bared her teeth in a feral grin and continued her advance.

"Stop, Marica!" Thuban cried. "Heed my warning!" But Marica did not stop. He set his jaw, and, when Marica took another step in Chac's direction, Thuban pressed the button on the weapon he held. It was still on the highest setting, where Marica had tuned it after stealing it from Eliel. A blast of white-hot flame leapt from the barrel and caught Marica in the chest. The front of her blue jumpsuit flamed and smoked. Marica went down without a sound.

Chapter Twenty

"Marica!" Thuban clambered awkwardly over the seawall and limped to her. Marica was still conscious. She glared up at him, defiant as ever.

"It didn't have to happen," Thuban said, looking down at her. "You could have stopped it, but you would not. Why is your heart so violent?"

"It's the way I am," Marica whispered. "The way all of my people are. Thuban?"

"Yes. I'm here." He bent over her.

"I want to go home," Marica said, her voice barely audible. "I don't want to die here, in this hateful, foreign place. I don't want that stupid barbarian, Chac, gaping at me when I breathe my last."

"You could have gone home without forcing

me to kill you," Thuban said. "You have the time-stone that will take you home."

"I can't—can't reach it." Marica's words were little more than a weak moan.

Thuban fumbled at her scorched jumpsuit, searching for the pocket. He pulled out the time-stone and placed it in Marica's hand.

"Hold it up to the sunlight," he said.

"I can't," Marica whispered with a grimace of pain. "You do it."

"No." Thuban stepped away from her. "I am not going into the future with you."

"Thought I'd try," Marica said with a choked laugh. "Just . . . one last . . . opportunity to . . . to trick you." She raised her hand slowly, as if hand and timestone together were unbearably heavy. She lifted the timestone high and held it there for a moment. Her eyes went wide, staring at it. Then her hand fell back and the timestone rolled away across the sand. Marica lay still.

"I am sorry," Thuban said, reaching to close her eyes. "Had you possessed a gentler soul, I might have loved you, for there is no doubt you were intelligent. And beautiful." He sighed, then, straightened and looked around as if waking from a bad dream.

"Chac!" Thuban cried, sighting the wounded man. At once Thuban hurried to the seawall, where the Aztec sat motionless, staring at Marica. "It's all right, Chac. I see Renan coming from the house now. It will take only a moment for him to inject Kentir with a stimulant, and then I will bring him here to help you. Renan will know how to treat the wound Marica inflicted."

"The age will end in fire and blood," Chac said, speaking as if he were reciting from a memorized text, "I by blood, and Marica by fire. So it is written. So it shall be, as the gods have ordained. Leave me as I am, my friend." Chac raised red-stained hands as if to ward off Thuban and any help Thuban—or anyone else—would have offered.

By this time, Laura and Hua Te were standing beside the seawall, too horrified by the scene before them to speak or to take any action at all. They were quickly joined by Seret, with Imilca supporting her. Incredibly, Kentir was hurrying across the lawn to reach them. He was barely awake, even after receiving the stimulant Renan had given him, but he stumbled along with an arm over Renan's shoulders. Nirod came last down the grassy slope, passing Kentir and Renan in his haste and skidding to a halt at the seawall.

"Great God of the Sea!" Nirod gasped, looking in awe from Chac sitting on the seawall, to Marica's body on the sand, and then to Thuban. "What has happened here?"

"I'll tell you later," Thuban said, his own gaze on the approaching Kentir. "If you and I are wise, Nirod, we will take the saucership into space before my brother recovers fully from that pain-killing medicine I gave him."

"As usual, you perceive both the problem and its solution," Nirod responded. He turned to the group gathered by the seawall. "Farewell, dear

Seret. Imilca, live happily. Good-bye, visitors. May you return safely to the times where you belong." With that, Nirod spun on his heel and headed back to the ship. He paused only to say a word to Kentir and Renan.

Thuban left more slowly. He bowed low to Seret, but said nothing to her, perhaps feeling that everything they needed to say had already been discussed between them.

"Kentir." Thuban laid a hand on his brother's shoulder.

"Don't go." Kentir sounded as if he was still not fully awake. "Wait, Thuban. We'll talk. This is wrong. I should be the pilot."

"There is no time left for further delay," Thuban said, his fingers tightening on Kentir's shoulder. "This is the way it was meant to be. Until tomorrow, Kentir." With the words of the traditional Kheressian farewell still on his lips, Thuban removed his hand from his brother's shoulder and began to limp toward the waiting saucership.

"No!" Kentir tried to follow him, but the aftereffects of the painkilling medicine that Thuban had given him still lingered in his system. Kentir stumbled and would have fallen if Renan had not caught him on one side and Laura on the other. "Thuban, wait!"

"Let him go," Renan said. "It's what he wants to do, what he has wanted all along."

"Thuban," Kentir whispered. Then, accepting what he was powerless to change, he said, "Farewell, brave soul, and luck go with you. Until tomorrow, dear brother."

Laura put her arms around Kentir's waist. She felt his arm encircle her, drawing her close to his side, though he did not look at her. Kentir's attention was on the saucership, which Thuban had just entered. The entry ramp was retracting and the door was sliding shut for the last time.

Never would Laura have expected a man as strong as Kentir to shed tears, but his face was wet with them. The three of them stayed where they were, Laura and Kentir arm in arm, and Renan supporting Kentir on his other side, while the saucership engines roared into life and the ship began to lift straight up into the air.

Once it was clear of the house and trees the ship hovered there for a little while, just above the compound. Suddenly it performed a tilting, side-to-side maneuver, as if experimenting with a dance step—or as if the crew was bidding a final, cheerful farewell to Earth. Then the engines came on to maximum force and the ship soared skyward and out of view. The last glimpse Laura had of it was a flash of silver as the sun's rays caught it for a moment, just before it vanished.

"Thuban always was a dreadful show-off," Renan said in an oddly thick voice.

Kentir said nothing. He was watching the sky. After inhaling a few deep breaths he rested his cheek on Laura's hair, and his arms tightened around her.

"Laura, tell me what has happened," Kentir

said, turning with her to face the scene of carnage on the beach and the seawall.

"First, Marica knocked Eliel over the head, stole her weapon, and stashed her in a clothes chest," Laura began. She told the story quickly, in the order in which she had observed the events unfolding. As she talked, she, Kentir, and Renan moved toward the seawall, where everyone who still remained at Issa had gathered, all of them drawn by the sound of the saucership engines.

"There are only twelve Kheressians left," Seret said to Kentir, "and our visitors. Imilca tells me that she and Hua Te have finished their work on the timestones. Those of us who wish to use them may leave now, since there is nothing more that we can do. The end of the asteroid lies in Thuban's hands.

"Any among you who prefer to test the safety of the cave we have prepared ought to begin your journey there at once," Seret continued, speaking to the dozen Kheressians who clustered around her. "From our last reports on the position of the asteroid, I believe the full effects of its approach will be felt within the next day. And there will be severe effects, whether Thuban's mission is successful or not. Issa must be evacuated, for we are living too close to the sea. This compound, and the city itself, will be destroyed when the great waves begin to roll across the land. Imilca, please bring all of the timestones here."

Seret placed a key into Imilca's hand. Imilca and Hua Te returned to the project building together.

"They knew where the stones are hidden and they refused to tell Marica," Laura said, looking after Imilca and Hua Te. "They preferred to die, rather than help Marica."

"Which proves that I have chosen my confidantes well," Seret said with a quick smile. "Had Marica gotten the timestones she wanted and returned home with them, a greater catastrophe than an asteroid can cause would certainly have ensued upon this planet. For, from what Marica has told us of the time in which she lived, no one there would suffer the least moral qualm about disrupting the ordained path of history. I grieve for the unnecessary waste of any human life, but I think the world is fortunate that Marica did not survive to report what she had learned of us." Seret ended this speech with a long sigh and a glance toward the spot where Marica's motionless form lay.

Hua Te and Imilca quickly returned to the seawall with the timestones in a wooden box, which Hua Te carried. Imilca held in her hand a small bundle containing the few possessions she wanted to take with her when she left Issa. Hua Te handed the box of timestones to Seret.

Most of the Kheressians had already decided what they wanted to do, so there was little discussion among them. A few of the Kheressians were determined to remain in their own, familiar time and to try to survive the coming catastrophes in the cave. Even so, Seret gave to them the timestones that had been prepared for each person.

"In case you discover later that a change of mind is advisable," Seret said to them.

The members of this first group bade a tearful farewell to Seret, to Kentir, and to the friends whom they would never meet again. Then they hurried off to the house, to gather their belongings before they left for the airfield, there to board the remaining saucership and fly it far inland, to the cave hidden in the distant mountains. Their hope was that, once the most violent effects of the asteroid's approach were over, they would be able to make contact with the few other groups around the world who had also chosen to retreat into caves, and to join forces with them.

The remaining Kheressians had elected to use their timestones immediately, and most of them had brought to the seawall bundles similar to Imilca's, which contained their most treasured possessions. From what she knew of the people of Issa, Laura was sure there was at least one book tucked into most of the bundles, and a musical instrument in many of the others.

Two couples intended to travel to a future century in pairs, but the rest were going as individuals. Seret handed a timestone to each of them. They said their farewells to their friends, then turned as a group to Seret.

"As you live your new lives," Seret said to them, "do not forget the old life. Tell the story to your children, and to your children's children in those later centuries, so the world of Kheressia, and of the beautiful city of Issa, will never be forgotten.

Keep alive the memory of a land where kind-hearted souls once lived together in peace, where every day brought music and joy and laughter. Sing the songs of Issa. Teach them to your children. Impart to others the learning you have gained while living in this glorious place, so that future generations may benefit from our knowledge. If you do this, Issa will never die, though it be destroyed, for it will live on in the hearts of the men and women who know the story." Seret stopped for a moment, overcome by emotion. Then, in a firm voice, she said, "Until tomorrow, my dear friends."

"Until tomorrow, Seret," they responded in unison.

One by one, the Kheressians held their time-stones up to the rays of the setting sun. One by one they shimmered into invisibility and were gone. At last only Laura and Kentir, Imilca, Hua Te, Seret, and Renan stood on the lawn.

"Imilca and I will go together, of course," Hua Te said to Laura. He put out his hand, but Laura threw her arms around him.

"I am going to miss you so much," she said, fighting back tears. "How can I be sure you will get home safely and find your friends again?"

"We won't know if you reach home again, either," Imilca said. She embraced Laura, and the two women shed a few tears over a valued friendship that must end too soon.

"There is a way for you to learn how Imilca and I will fare after we leave Issa," Hua Te said to Laura. "I have told you of Wroxley Castle in England, where I once spent a most interesting year. If Imilca and I are successful in reaching the twelfth century, we will journey to Wroxley, to see my friends who live there and reassure them that I am alive and well. I may even decide to tell one or two of those friends the truth about my sudden disappearance and my great adventure.

"In the chapel of Wroxley Castle," Hua Te went on, "among the paving stones next to the altar, there is one stone that can be lifted. The space beneath it has occasionally been used as a hiding place for valuables. Should I return safely to Wroxley, I will leave a message for you there. Not many know of the secret place, so I dare to trust that my message will survive the centuries until you find it."

"Hua Te," said Seret, "it is time for you to go, before the sun sets."

"May you be happy always, Laura," Hua Te said. He and Imilca then said their good-byes to Seret, Kentir, and Renan.

Imilca fell upon Seret's shoulder, weeping, but at Seret's urging she wiped her eyes and smiled at her friends. Hua Te took Imilca's hand. Together they lifted their matched timestones to the sun and, a moment later, their figures shimmered and were gone.

Laura could contain her emotions no longer. She leaned upon Kentir and let his strong arms support her until she had herself under control again.

During all this time Chac had been sitting quietly on the seawall, watching everything that happened. He was breathing with obvious difficulty, and his face was as pale as the seawall stones.

"Chac, I have neglected you and I am sorry for it," Renan said, moving toward him. "Please let me help you now. It's possible that there is still time for me to repair your wound."

"No, my friend." As he had done with Thuban, Chac put up his hands to halt Renan's advance. "I thank you, but I do not wish your help. The moment of my end draws near, and I have no desire to change what has happened. Believe me when I say that I am in no great pain."

"Leave him alone," Seret said. "Let him do this in his own way."

Renan turned away from Chac, swallowing hard, and Laura sensed his frustration. It was Renan's nature, as well as his duty, to offer his medical skills to anyone who needed them. He had been greatly disturbed over the death of the friend who had been seriously injured in the rocket explosion, whom even his best efforts could not save. Now he could not help Chac, either, and as a result, Laura believed, Renan was suffering his own kind of pain.

Slowly, grunting with the effort, Chac stretched himself on his back upon the seawall. There he lay, struggling for breath and clutching at his midsection, his hands clasped over the wounds Marica had inflicted. After a time Chac moved his limbs until one arm and one leg hung down on each side of the seawall, in the same fashion as Aztec sacrificial victims were laid upon a stone altar. Finally he turned his face toward the setting sun, to a sky streaked with lurid shades of red and orange and purple.

"Oh, Chac!" Laura cried, wanting to touch him, aching to offer him comfort, and knowing she must not.

"Do not weep for me, Laura," Chac said, not looking at her, his eyes fixed on the brilliant sky. "I am a fortunate man. I have dwelt for a time in the abode of the gods. For a priest of my people there can be no greater honor." He drew a long, shaky breath.

"I am willing to give up my life," Chac said. "I freely offer my blood to the earth, that the earth might continue to live and be fertile. Kentir?"

"I'm here, my friend," Kentir said. He released Laura from his arms and stepped forward so Chac could see him.

"I have one last request," Chac said.

"Name it and I will carry it out," Kentir responded.

"Speak my full name as I die," Chac said. "Cast my name upon the wind, so it will be carried over the earth and never be forgotten. Do it now, Kentir."

Kentir lifted his head, took a deep breath, and in his loudest voice shouted, "Chacatlipichi!"

Chacatlipichi's last breath sighed away on the wind as Kentir fell silent.

"Truly a worthy death," Seret said in a low, reverent voice. "I hope I can do as well when my moment comes."

"There has been too much death," Laura cried. "Too much loss." Her voice broke on a sob.

"She's right," Renan said. His face was hard and set in lines of grief. Unshed tears glittered in Renan's eyes, yet he spoke with calm purpose. "Seret, there is a timestone for you. Though you did not wish it, Imilca prepared one. You have only to say the word and I will go with you wherever you want, and I'll take care of you in whatever time we find ourselves. I can do no less. You have been like a dear grandmother to me."

"Chac was correct, you know," Seret said, as if Renan had not spoken. "He believed we were witnessing the end of one of the great ages of the world, and it is so." Walking the few steps to the seawall, she seated herself a short distance away from Chac.

"Seret, please, let us leave now," Renan begged. "As you have said yourself, the time is growing short."

"If you will not go with us," Kentir said, "then Renan and I will stay with you."

"Why?" Seret asked, smiling at him. "To what purpose, Kentir? Issa is finished and I am old and weary. Our time is over. My work is done."

"No, it's not," Laura cried. She crouched in front of Seret, taking the older woman's wrinkled hands into hers. "There is still work for you to do. Let us all go into the twentieth century together. When I think of the wisdom you possess and the good you might do in a century yearning for greatness of spirit—oh, Seret, don't refuse to help a world that needs you."

"You will do that work for me." Seret pulled her hands out of Laura's grasp. Her fingers traced along Laura's cheeks in a caress as gentle as the touch of rose petals. "Stand up now, Laura. I have something to say to you and Kentir and Renan."

They stood before her in a row, like schoolchildren before their teacher. And like obedient schoolchildren, they listened to Seret without interrupting her.

"Kentir and Renan, you have been my most loyal and devoted followers," Seret said. "Laura, though a recent friend, you are a faithful one. As you have obeyed my wishes in the past, I expect all of you to obey me now. I want you to use your timestones to travel together into Laura's century. I privately asked Imilca to prepare timestones that will send the three of you to the same time.

"I had a specific reason for my request," Seret continued. "Kentir, you have lost a brother today, but you need not lose your dear friend. Renan, with a companion like Kentir, you will not be isolated in a strange, new world. Laura, I know you love Kentir with your whole heart. I bid you for my sake to love Renan as a brother and friend."

"I will. I already do." Laura could barely speak for emotion, but she whispered the words she knew would give Seret a last, small measure of joy.

"Do you truly expect us to leave you here, alone?" Renan cried. "Seret, I cannot."

"It is what I wish," Seret told him. "I shall not be alone. The spirit of my friend, Chacatlipichi, is here. And I have many happy memories to review while I wait."

"I can't do this," Kentir said. "Seret, consider Laura's suggestion. Come with us. Use the timestone Imilca prepared for you. Or, if you do not want to live in a different time, let us hurry after those who are traveling to the cave. I'm sure they haven't left the airfield yet. They will welcome your presence."

"Obey me in this, Kentir," Seret said quietly, yet in a voice filled with the authority that had once been hers, when she had organized the great effort to save a planet that was fast approaching violent destruction.

"Don't ask it of me, I beg you, Seret." Kentir stood for a long moment, looking deep into Seret's eyes. She looked steadily back at him, communicating without words. Suddenly, Kentir's figure drooped. Then, slowly, he straightened again and raised his head. And Laura, understanding much of what he was feeling, slipped her hand into his and felt the firm pressure of his fingers around hers.

"Very well, Seret," Kentir said. "I have never disobeyed you; I will not do so now."

"I am glad to hear it," Seret said, a smile in her eyes, though not on her lips. "I want you to go now, before the sun sets, while there is still a ray of sunlight to activate the timestones."

"We could wait until morning," Renan suggested. "We could spend the night with you, and keep you company."

"Who knows what the morning will bring?" Seret asked him. "Who can say if the sun will still be shining when morning comes? You must go now, Renan. At once." She handed them the timestones meant for them.

Again they stood in a row facing Seret. Kentir held Laura's hand so tightly that she feared he would crush her bones. She suspected that he was afraid of losing her as they traveled through time. She was glad of his touch. Her first use of a timestone had occurred without any understanding on her part of what was happening, and she remembered the darkness and the pain with revulsion. But if they could make a successful transition, if she and Kentir and Renan could reach her time together, then countless possibilities for happiness stretched before them. Years of love, like glowing pearls strung upon a beautiful necklace, awaited them at the end of their journey.

"Thank you," Laura said to Seret. "Thank you for the gift of time."

"Use it well," Seret said.

"I will. I promise," Laura said, and found the strength to smile through her tears.

All three at the same time, Laura, Kentir, and Renan lifted their timestones toward the setting sun, which was just about to sink below the horizon.

A mist was rising off the purple-blue sea. Twilight gathered softly around the beautiful, doomed city in the distance, around the house and the garden and the lawn that sloped down to the seawall where Seret sat in serene calmness. A single star twinkled in the western sky. Soon the nightly aurora would unfold its glowing drapery across the heavens. Already Laura could see the first, faint tint of greenish light.

As if to mock the Earth-altering horrors soon to come, a slight breeze stirred, carrying to Laura's nose the fragrances of delicate flowers and lush, green leaves, all the sweet scents of a garden that would vanish in a single day, a single hour, never to be enjoyed again.

Then a last, golden ray of sunlight touched the timestone Laura was holding. She heard the click and whir of the timestone's mechanism and she knew she had only a moment or two more left of her time in Issa.

"Until tomorrow," Seret said, smiling at them.

"Until tomorrow," Kentir and Renan responded in unison.

Laura wanted to answer Seret's farewell, too, but she discovered she could not form the words. She was immobilized, as she had been once before. She could only hope that Seret saw on her face and in her eyes the affection and the sorrow she felt.

Seret's figure and the landscape around her—Chacatlipichi's unmoving form, the seawall, the ocean, the orange and purple sky, and the beginning glow of the aurora—all dissolved into thousands of tiny, sparkling particles. Then even the particles were gone from Laura's vision, and there was nothing but the darkness and the firm grasp of Kentir's hand holding hers.

Chapter Twenty-one

The land that had once been a desert lay scoured and bleak beneath the radiant blue sky. The fierce winds of global upheaval had blown all the sand away, and the fire generated by cosmic catastrophe had scorched the underlying bedrock. The fire had burned until it was extinguished by waves that towered miles high as they swept across the ruined terrain.

Debris churned up and carried along by the waves lay in gigantic heaps wherever it had dropped when the waters withdrew. The bones of animals were spread out across the landscape, where they lay bleached white and dried by the sun.

Earth had acquired a satellite during the great calamity, for the approaching asteroid had been forever captured by the planet's gravitational force. Earth's orbit around the sun, along with the length of each day, had been changed by the cataclysmic effects of two heavenly bodies in a state of near collision. As a result, the sun appeared smaller when seen from Earth, and farther away than it had been before the asteroid had come so close.

Many of those new, longer days had passed; centuries had passed, and during those dark centuries of constant cloud cover, the snow and ice had piled up, foot by cold foot of it, all of it pressing heavily upon the land until, finally, the age of ice passed away as so many other ages had done, and the glaciers began to melt. The water contained in the ice ran off into the sea, causing ocean levels to rise until they settled within new boundaries. Under the old weight of ice the land had broken apart in many places, to reform into new continents.

There was little of life left on Earth after so much upheaval and change, yet not all was dead. In the land that had once, tens of centuries before, been a desert beneath a brazen sun, a seed borne upon a great wave moving southward from the polar region had fallen upon a patch of broken, fertile soil.

When the glaciers retreated and the weather began to warm, the seed sprouted and grew into a small tree that was periodically watered by the new, gentle rains that fell upon the earth. At last, a sweeter spring arrived to warm the land still further, and the tree put forth buds and began to bloom. Delicate pink and white blossoms quivered in each sudden breeze, and newborn insects, resurrected from the remnants of previous life, flew from flower to flower.

There were ghosts abroad under the spring sunshine, for not all specters cling to dark and storm-tossed midnights. The spirits of two who had known a more ancient time floated together across the awakening landscape.

"Look, Chacatlipichi," murmured the first spirit, "you and I were right. All is not lost. The earth begins to revive. There, on a little hill, blooms a single almond tree, not unlike the trees that once bloomed in the garden at Issa."

"After so many harsh centuries, the new age has finally begun," Chacatlipichi whispered in awe. "But Seret, where will it end? In fire and bloodshed, as the last age did?"

"Who can say, dear friend?" Seret murmured. "Even you and I cannot guess at the future. We can only remember the past we once knew. But we can hope that those whom we sent into the future will offer their knowledge to the new age. We can hope that, if so dreadful a catastrophe ever threatens Earth again, men and women will know how to prevent it."

"We can also hope," Chacatlipichi said, "that when future ages demand it, there will again exist brave men and women who are willing to risk their own lives that Earth might continue."

"They saved this," Seret said, making a ghostly motion that produced a faint stirring of the air. It was just enough to ruffle the almond blossoms, sending a sweet fragrance into the warm day. "Before Thuban and his crew fled the oncoming disaster, they gave their home planet a second chance, a chance for life eventually to renew itself. Perhaps, one day, their descendants will return, to see Earth for themselves and meet their distant cousins still living here."

"Come now, Seret," Chacatlipichi whispered. "It's time for us to go."

"Yes," Seret murmured. Then, wistfully, she said, "How beautiful the springtime is. There were no seasons in Issa, only constant sunshine and long, warm days. Days like this one. And, until the end of our time approached, we took such days for granted."

"Come," Chacatlipichi murmured again. "Come, my friend. Our visit is over."

A moment later there was a brief disturbance in the air. Then all was still again.

The little almond tree trembled slightly in the aftermath of the disturbance, before it quieted to stand as it had before, lifting its flowery branches to the kisses of the buzzing insects and the warmth of the gentle sun shining upon an Earth returning to life.

Chapter Twenty-two

Ventnor, New Jersey
August, 1998

Salty waves swirled around Laura's calves. The clear blue sky stretched above, and the late August sun was warm on her head. She still held the aquamarine glass egg in her fingers, lifting it toward the sunlight. In the center of the blue stone a small, golden mechanism suddenly glowed hot, then melted and flowed into a solid, egg-shaped mass that congealed within the stone. With a sigh, Laura lowered her hand, but she did not drop the timestone.

In a state approaching total bewilderment, Laura took in the scene before her, only gradually accepting what her eyes revealed. Hua Te and Imilca had promised her that the timestone prepared for her would return her to a moment shortly after the time when she had left the beach at Ventnor. Nonetheless, Laura had expected to notice at least some subtle changes, and to experience a sense of major disorientation similar to what she had felt after her first journey through time. Instead, she was amazed by how familiar everything was.

At the lifeguard stand a short distance away from her, a teenage girl in a bikini was flirting with the younger guard, Ben, who sat high above her on his wooden bench. On the sand next to the lifeboat, Jim, the older lifeguard, broke off his conversation with his wife, Kathy, to kneel and accept the sand crab offered by his little daughter, who played at his feet.

Farther up the beach, past the sunbathers and the bright umbrellas, two figures began to climb the steps leading to the boardwalk. One of the figures, a man in a navy polo shirt and tan trousers with the cuffs rolled up, placed his hand on the elbow of a blond woman in tan slacks and pale blue polo shirt. It took several moments for Laura to recognize the figures ascending the stairs as Roger and Marlene.

So much had happened since the conversation with Roger, during which Laura had broken their engagement. And yet, so little had changed. It was as though Laura had left the beach only an instant ago, as though the quarter of a year she had spent in Issa had never occurred, as if it had been only a dream.

But she was wearing a dark red tunic and trousers, not the gray sweatshirt and white shorts in which she had begun her adventure through time. There were sandals on her formerly bare feet. She was holding a timestone in one hand. And she was not alone.

"Great God of the Sea!" said a masculine voice from directly behind her. "What a ride. I once crash-landed a saucership, and I tell you, Laura, a timestone journey is far more exciting."

"Kentir!" She turned to him just as an incoming wave surged around her. When she staggered from the force of the water, Kentir caught her at her waist to steady her with both of his hands. Laura stuffed the timestone into her tunic pocket and then flung her arms around him. "You're here! We made it. We're together."

"So we are," Kentir said, and planted a salty kiss on her lips. "And half-drowned, too. I suggest we wade to shore before we are dragged out to sea by these waves."

With Kentir's arm around her, they left the water. The older lifeguard and his wife stared at them as they walked onto the damp sand in their dripping-wet tunics and trousers, and their sandals that squished with every step they took.

Laura and Kentir didn't care how they looked. They only cared that they were together, alive, and safe. Until—

"Renan!" Kentir exclaimed. "Where is he?"

"Our timestones worked, so his should have worked, too," Laura said. In haste she scanned the relaxed beachgoers scattered across the sand.

357

There was no one who seemed out of place, no one in a red tunic and trousers.

"Renan!" Kentir spun about, searching both the beach and the water. Cupping his hands around his mouth he shouted, "Renan, answer me!"

At once the older of the two lifeguards left his wife and child to join Laura and Kentir.

"Is something wrong?" the lifeguard asked. "Someone missing?"

"Kentir," Laura said, "this is Jim, who knows my family. He'll help us find Renan."

"My friend is missing," Kentir said to Jim. "He ought to be with us."

"What were you doing in the water with your clothes on?" Jim asked. He looked from Kentir to Laura. "I remember seeing you standing in the water a few minutes ago, Laura, but you were alone, and you sure weren't dressed like that. What the heck is going on here?"

"There!" Laura cried. She grabbed Kentir's arm with one hand and pointed with the other. "Out there, in the deep water. I just saw an arm in a red sleeve."

"No one is supposed to be out that far," Jim said. He looked seaward, following the direction of Laura's pointing finger. "I don't see anything."

"I do." With that, Kentir was off, running through the shallow water, then plunging head-first beneath a wave to rise on the other side of it. With strong strokes he propelled himself into deeper water.

Ben, the lifeguard sitting on the bench high on

the wooden guard's stand, did not have his complete attention focused on the girl who was talking to him. He was keeping his eyes on the bathers in the water as he was supposed to do, and from his vantage point he saw the struggling, red-clad figure at the same time that Kentir did. With a warning shout to Jim, Ben leapt over the head of his startled girlfriend and onto the beach. Kathy snatched her daughter out of the way, and Ben began to push the lifeboat on its log roller. Jim joined him at once, and the two lifeguards gave the boat a hard shove. Then both of them were in the boat and rowing through the waves.

They reached Renan a moment after Kentir did.

"They'll get him out," Kathy said, coming to stand with Laura. "Your friend will be all right."

"I hope so. Renan has come so far. If he were to die now, it would be so unfair." Laura could not tear her gaze from the drama taking place in the smooth, deep water beyond the surf. Kentir was still in the water, supporting Renan and holding his head up. As Laura and Kathy watched, Kentir lifted Renan's limp figure to Jim, who hauled him aboard while Ben used the oars to keep the boat steady. Then Kentir was climbing over the side and into the boat, too, and Ben was rowing back to shore.

"It's okay," Kathy said, smiling. "I knew Jim would get them out."

"Thank heaven." Overcome with relief and assailed by a sudden wave of dizziness, Laura staggered.

Kathy caught her, holding Laura upright until she could regain her balance.

"Those fellows in the boat may be all right," Kathy said, "but you sure aren't. Laura, you are awfully pale, and that's a nasty burn on your cheek. Are you sick, or have you been in an accident?"

"Neither. I'm just feeling a bit light-headed," Laura said. She hoped whatever was wrong with her wasn't contagious, hoped she had not returned from Issa with a terrible illness. Her stomach was definitely becoming unsettled again.

The sight of the lifeguards making a rescue generated considerable interest along the beach. Spectators in swimsuits gathered around to see what was happening. A tall man in a navy blue polo shirt left the boardwalk and crossed the sand to push his way through the crowd to the water's edge. He halted when he reached Laura and Kathy.

"What in heaven's name have you done?" Roger demanded. "What happened to your face? And where did you get those peculiar clothes? Good God, woman, Marlene and I left you only a couple of minutes ago!"

"A friend of mine got into water too deep for him," Laura answered. She did not respond to the questions about the burn on her face or about her change of clothing.

"What friend?" Roger asked. "There was no one here with you when I left."

"I just told you," Laura said, somewhat impatiently. "He was in the water."

"What the hell?" Roger exclaimed, staring at the men in the lifeboat that was just being beached. "Who are the two guys in the red outfits? Did they jump off a passing boat? I hope you haven't gotten yourself involved in bringing illegal aliens into the country."

"Don't be ridiculous," Laura exclaimed. "You ought to know me better than that. You've scolded me often enough about my too-rigid sense of honesty. I told you; they are friends of mine." Dismissing Roger, she went to where Renan stood. He was taking deep breaths and hanging on to the bow of the lifeboat as if he would fall without its solid support.

"Renan, are you all right?" Laura asked. "What happened to you?"

"I don't know," Renan said to her. "Perhaps there was a slight error in the calibration of my timestone."

"What are you talking about?" Jim, the lifeguard, asked of Renan. "Have you been drinking? Or shooting up drugs?"

"Drinking?" Renan repeated, as if he did not understand. Then he laughed. "Only seawater, though I admit, I did imbibe a bit too much of it. But nothing stronger, I assure you. Drugs are only for people who are ill, and I am in excellent health. Sir, I am grateful to you. Without your help, I fear I could not have reached the shore."

"Why were you swimming with your clothes on?" Jim asked. "And where's your beach card?

You're not allowed on the beach without a valid card."

"What card?" Renan asked.

"You don't have a beach card pinned on, either," Jim said, staring at the chest of Kentir's tunic. "The cards are supposed to be displayed in plain sight. Laura, where is yours? You know there is a fine for coming onto the beach without proper ID. I'll have to report you. I'm sorry, but you know the town ordinance as well as I do."

"Oh, good lord," Laura muttered. She couldn't decide whether to laugh or cry at the situation. After traveling through time for uncounted centuries, she and her companions were about to be hauled off to the police station and fined on a twentieth-century technicality.

"Come on, all of you," Jim said, looking from Laura to Kentir to Renan. "It's only a couple of blocks to City Hall."

"Roger, get us out of this," Laura said, staring her ex-fiancé squarely in the eye.

"What do you expect me to do?" Roger asked.

"You owe me one," Laura said. She glanced from Roger to Marlene, who had come across the beach to stand in the front row of spectators. Then Laura returned her gaze to Roger. "I give you my solemn word, there is nothing illegal going on here. Fix this. Fix it *now*, Roger. You know you owe me one, for Marlene, and for all the lies you told me."

She had not realized that Roger was unaware that she knew about his affair with Marlene. She saw realization come to him, saw Roger, the clever politician, looking for a brief instant like a small boy caught with his hand in the cookie jar. She watched him closely, understanding exactly what was going on in his mind, while Roger quickly considered all the possible ramifications of her knowledge and what might happen to his career if she went public with it. Then the persona of the smooth politician took control again.

"Jim, isn't it?" Roger said to the older lifeguard. He thrust out his hand, and Jim took it. "Perhaps you don't know me. I am Roger Greydon, and I'm running for the United States Senate. I want to commend you for the valiant rescue work you've just done. Our country's greatness was built upon the efforts of brave men like you and your assistant, here.

"What is your name, young man?" Roger said, turning to the other lifeguard and shaking hands with him, too. "Ben? Well, congratulations to you, too, Ben.

"Now, what do you say, my fellow citizens?" Roger asked the crowd still gathered about the lifeboat. "Let's have a round of applause for these two courageous men. I'm sure all of you feel safer when you come to the beach, just knowing Jim and Ben are on duty every day, watching over you and your children whenever you go into the water."

The requested applause followed, and then the crowd began to disperse, though a few people lingered to speak with Roger or to shake hands with Jim and Ben.

"Thanks for your appreciation," Jim said to

Roger. "But you can't change the fact that these three people don't have beach cards, or the fact that one of my duties on this beach is to see to it that everyone obeys the rules."

"They didn't know the rules," Laura said. "They've never been to Ventnor before. They come from . . . from . . ."

"From England," Roger said, picking up the thread of Laura's lie with every appearance of honesty, "where beach cards aren't required. It's a simple misunderstanding, and I can promise it won't happen again. I'm sure you don't want these gentlemen to return home to England and tell their friends over there that Americans are inhospitable," Roger ended with a smile, turning all of his considerable charm on the lifeguard.

"Well, no, I wouldn't want that," Jim said. Then, making up his mind, he added, "Okay, we'll skip the fine this time, but I expect you people to consider this an official warning. Laura, get your friends off the beach right away, and don't any of you come back without valid cards."

"Thank you, Jim," Laura said. "Come on, Kentir. Renan, can you walk? It's not far to my parents' house."

"Just a minute," Roger said, stopping them. "In return for what I've just done for you, the least you can do is introduce your friends to me."

Laura hesitated just a moment too long in complying with his request. Frowning, Roger looked from her to Renan and Kentir. His glance held on Kentir as the two men assessed each other.

"Who are you?" Roger said to Kentir. "And where did you come from? You were not on the beach half an hour ago, when I was talking with Laura. I don't forget many faces, and there is no way I'd have forgotten yours."

"Roger, please, just drop this," Laura begged. "Renan needs to lie down and rest."

"Renan," Roger said slowly, as if he were testing the word on his tongue. "What an unusual name."

Laura caught her breath, hoping Roger wasn't going to cause any trouble. They had already brought too much public attention to themselves. She was afraid someone from the press would show up to see what Roger was doing and would begin to snap pictures at any minute. All she wanted to do was get Kentir and Renan off the beach and away from curious eyes. As if he sensed her fear, Kentir took control of the situation.

"You are Laura's former betrothed," Kentir said to Roger. "She has told me much about you."

"Betrothed?" Roger repeated, frowning and looking a bit uncomfortable as he met Kentir's eyes. "That's an old-fashioned word."

"I am an old-fashioned man," Kentir said, grinning. In contrast to Roger, he appeared to be completely at ease. "I am delighted to meet you, Roger, and I thank you for your assistance, but Laura is correct about Renan's condition. He was close to drowning, and I think it's best if we get him to a place where he can rest. We will meet again, Roger."

"Will we?" asked Roger, now looking thoroughly bemused.

"I am certain of it," Kentir responded. He put an arm around Renan's shoulders and the two of them started for the steps to the boardwalk.

"Thanks, Roger," Laura said. She was so relieved that there hadn't been a quarrel between him and Kentir that she actually smiled at him. "We're even now."

"Are we?" Roger's eyebrows rose. "I wish I knew what has really happened here this afternoon. I must say, I am glad to discover that you aren't above twisting a rule to your own advantage. We'd have made a good team, Laura, better than you think."

"No," Laura said, "we wouldn't. But thanks, anyway."

She caught up with Kentir and Renan just as they reached the boardwalk. Renan was still pale, though otherwise he appeared to have recovered from his unexpected swim. Both men were looking around them in wonder. Recalling her first impressions of Issa, Laura gave them a few minutes to get used to the idea that they were in a new time and place. But when Renan sagged and caught at the boardwalk railing, Laura decided it was time to move on.

"My parents' house is just ahead," she told Renan. She put an arm around his waist, lending support on one side, as Kentir was still doing on the other. "You can lie down there."

Together she and Kentir got their friend down the ramp and along the sidewalk. There were quite a few people about, either going to or leaving the beach. Dressed as the three of them were, in soaking-wet red tunics and trousers, they met a few curious stares, but no one questioned them. When they reached the house, they had to lift Renan up the steps and across the porch.

Laura hadn't had time to think about the explanation she was going have to make to her parents for bringing a pair of strange men into the house to stay. As the screen door swung shut behind them, she decided that, while she would be as brief as possible with her mother, she ought to tell her father everything. He was the one person she knew who might believe her fantastic tale. She had forgotten about her sister's planned visit to the beach house. It was with great relief that she saw Susan standing in the front hall.

"I just got here a few minutes ago," Susan said, hurrying forward to kiss her. "Dad told me you went to talk to Roger. I'm glad you've come to your senses about him. Hello, do I know you?" she said to the two men with her sister.

Quickly Laura introduced the men, saying only that they were friends. When she noticed the sharp, professional look Susan was casting upon Renan, Laura added that he had been pulled out of the ocean by the lifeguards.

"Come into the living room and sit down," Susan said to Renan. "Let me examine you. I'm glad I brought my bag along. I can put some ointment and a bandage on Laura's cheek, too. What have you people been doing, anyway?"

"Bag?" Renan said.

"I'm a doctor," Susan told him. "You don't have a problem with female doctors, do you?"

"None at all," Renan said. "I am a physician myself."

As Susan guided Renan into the living room, William Morrison appeared from the other end of the hall. His sharp eyes took in the bedraggled strangers and his younger daughter in a dripping-wet costume that matched the clothing worn by the men.

"Do you want to talk about it?" he asked Laura.

"Definitely," Laura responded. With her eyes on Susan, who was listening to Renan's heart, she added, "I want Susan to hear, too. Where's Mom?"

"She left for the grocery store shortly after Susan arrived," Mr. Morrison said. "She'll be gone for at least an hour, and longer if she meets someone she knows and starts talking. Which should give you and your friends time to get into dry clothes before we talk. Some of Bill's things are still in his old room. They won't be a perfect fit, but they'll have to do," he said, appraising Kentir's muscular shoulders.

It was less than an hour later when Laura and her sister joined the men in her father's study at the back of the house. Laura had taken a quick shower and donned a flower-printed dress and flat shoes. She had also let Susan treat her burned cheek, though she hadn't revealed how it had happened. In deference to Susan's concern over her, Laura had allowed her sister to examine her, to be sure she was healthy. Under Susan's questioning, Laura had admitted to the nausea and dizziness that had been plaguing her. She was a little surprised when Susan didn't seem to be overly worried about the symptoms.

"One of the advantages of a big, old house like this," William Morrison said to those who were gathered in his private retreat, "is the provision that was made for the men to withdraw from their womenfolk. We won't be disturbed here."

"So many books," Renan said, moving along the shelf-lined walls that were crammed full of books and pamphlets and piles of scientific journals. "So much knowledge is gathered here. How I would like to read all of these." He appeared to be fully recovered from his near-drowning, and he smiled at Laura in greeting, but his gaze lingered on Susan.

While Laura was showering and dressing, William Morrison had seen to the needs of his male guests, providing jeans and a pale blue shirt for Kentir to wear, and giving Renan tan trousers and a blue-and-green plaid shirt. Both men had rolled up their sleeves and had left the top buttons of the shirts unfastened. Their hair was a bit long, but otherwise they looked remarkably modern.

Laura noticed how her brother's shirt tightened across Kentir's shoulders each time he moved his arms. At the moment, Kentir was bent over the globe resting in a mahogany stand beside William Morrison's desk. With a light touch of his fingertips, Kentir sent the globe spinning.

"Laura," Kentir said, "I begin to understand what your feelings must have been when you first saw our holographic globe."

"A holographic map of the entire world?" William Morrison said. "We've been working on that idea. Why haven't I heard about your success?"

"Kentir," Laura said, knowing there would never be a better opening for an incredible tale, and also knowing they would have to be prompt in the telling, if everything was to be recounted before her mother got home, "you tell the story. Renan and I will fill in any details you leave out. Dad, Susan, I want you to know in advance that every word we are going to say is the absolute truth. I'll leave it to you, Dad, and to Kentir and Renan, to decide if it ought to be kept in strict confidence."

"It sounds earthshaking." William Morrison settled himself in a big leather chair and motioned to his daughters and his guests to be seated.

"That's exactly what it is, Dad," Laura said. She took a seat next to Kentir. It did not escape her notice that Susan and Renan sat together on the leather sofa.

"Three years ago," Kentir began, "my people became aware of a terrible threat to the future of Earth." He left nothing out, pausing only to let Laura describe how she had been carried through time and, later, to allow Renan to add a few details about what had happened while Kentir was unconscious after Thuban had drugged his wine. At the end of Kentir's recitation, he,

Laura, and Renan all produced their timestones for Laura's father to see.

"There were rumors, decades ago," William Morrison told them, "that the United States government was experimenting with time travel and that some people involved in the experiments died or went mad as a result, so the experiments were stopped. I don't find it impossible to believe what you have said. What a fascinating story! Laura, what an adventure you have had! And all of it in the space of a single afternoon of our time."

"If you have any sense at all," Susan cautioned them, "you won't tell another soul about this. I mean it, Dad. If the tabloids get hold of the story, none of you will have a moment's peace."

"For the time being, I agree with you, Susan. We do need to think very carefully about all of this," William Morrison said. He looked at Kentir and Renan. "You two men will blend in with present-day society easily enough. We can just introduce you as summer visitors. No one will question that explanation of your presence here."

"Dad," Laura said, "they will need Social Security numbers, driver's licenses, birth certificates, all the papers that most present-day people acquire automatically as they go through life."

"You'll need to learn how to drive a car," Susan said to Renan. "That should be an interesting experience for you."

"I am not without contacts in the government," William Morrison said. "I'm sure we can work something out. Identification papers are not that difficult to obtain. People in witness protection programs get new papers; so can Kentir and Renan. In the meantime, gentlemen, you are welcome to remain here as my guests. As you can see, there is plenty of room in this old house."

"Thank you, Will," Kentir said, using the name Laura's father had said he preferred. "However, there is an important matter that I want to settle at once. I wish to marry your daughter."

"Oh, Kentir," Laura whispered, her eyes misting with happy tears.

"I could not in honor ask you before, when I had a dangerous mission to perform and when we all feared the world was about to end," Kentir said to her. "But this is a new world, and a new beginning for me. Will, I do not have much to offer Laura just yet, but all that I am, my whole heart and soul, belong to her. Everything I become, every possession I may gain in the future, will be for her sake."

"Laura is of age," her father said. "She will have to make the decision for herself."

"Yes," Laura said, smiling into Kentir's eyes.

"Do it soon," Susan advised. "As soon as you possibly can."

"Ah," said Renan, nodding, "you have also noticed the look about Laura's eyes. Recently I have observed that she has alternated between eating very little in the mornings and eating large meals."

"She complained to me about occasional nausea and light-headedness," Susan said. "Isn't it nice to know some things never change?" With that, she and Renan began to laugh together.

"Susan, are you saying what I think you're saying?" Laura asked.

"I sure am, little sister." Susan grinned at her. "I'm going to be an aunt."

"So that's why I've been sick? And here I thought I was incubating some awful germ!"

"Laura," said Susan, "I will thank you not to refer to my future niece or nephew as a germ!" She was obviously trying her best to appear as the stern and mature elder sister. Since she was still grinning, the attempt was a miserable failure. Abruptly, Susan collapsed into all-out laughter, in which Laura joined.

"Ahem!" William Morrison cleared his throat. Unlike his older daughter, when he tried to look stern, he succeeded. Susan and Laura sobered at once and an uncomfortable silence fell until Kentir broke it.

"Sir," Kentir said to Laura's father, "I assure you, I love Laura with all my heart."

"It is obvious that you have already loved her," said Mr. Morrison. "Too well."

"I intend to marry her as soon as possible," Kentir said.

"You're damned right, you will," Mr. Morrison said, using a tone of voice that made his displeasure perfectly clear.

"Dad," Laura protested, "you did say it was my choice."

"Yes, indeed," Susan said to Renan with a smothered laugh, "some things never change, especially the attitudes of fathers of unmarried daughters. But Mom is going to love having a wedding to plan." Susan could hardly get the next words out for renewed laughter. "In fact, I'm sure she'll be thrilled."

"Thrilled about what?" said a new voice. Alberta Morrison stood in the study doorway, gazing with a puzzled expression at the group gathered about her husband.

"I hope you bought extra shrimp, my dear," William Morrison said to her. "We have guests for dinner."

It was nearly midnight, and Laura and Kentir were strolling through the garden Laura's mother had created at the back of the house. The lots in Ventnor weren't very large, so it was a small garden, but Alberta Morrison had done wonders with it.

"There are sweet fragrances in this time, too," Kentir said. He paused to sniff at a flower.

"That's a rose you're smelling," Laura said. "And the white flowers on this vine are called moonflowers. They only bloom at night."

"Lovely." Kentir moved from blossom to blossom, inhaling the fragrances.

Remembering the vase of white, orchidlike flowers he had kept beside his bed in Issa, Laura was overcome by the realization of all Kentir had been forced to leave behind. Unlike her when she had first been moved through time, Kentir could have no hope of ever returning to his original home. Laura was thankful that they shared some common memories of Issa; it might help to banish a small portion of Kentir's inevitable home-sickness.

"I will never forget the scents of Issa," Laura said. "It was the sweetest-smelling place I've ever known."

But, while she was feeling sorry for him, Kentir had discovered a reason for astonishment. She heard his gasp and saw him looking upward, at the glowing object in the sky.

"Is that your moon?" Kentir asked. "Could it be the asteroid that menaced us? You once mentioned the possibility of the asteroid being caught by Earth's gravity and held forever in a permanent orbit around Earth."

"I don't know for certain," Laura said. "We may never know. You could talk to Dad about it; he could tell you if my idea is plausible. Kentir, I am ashamed to say I never gave a thought to how you and Renan would adapt to this time and place."

"I did," he told her. "I knew it would be very different from my world. But as long as you are by my side, I will be content."

"I'll help you all I can," she promised. "Dad will help, too. He has already forgiven you for making love to me without marrying me first."

"Your father is a fine man, to believe and trust in two very peculiar strangers."

"Why shouldn't he?" Laura asked. "After all, his daughter has believed and trusted you from the first day she met you. Although it's true that I still don't know enough about you."

"Nor I about you," Kentir said. With a smile

that flashed white in the darkness, he added, "We will simply have to spend the rest of our lives learning all there is to know about each other."

She was in his arms; the moonlight shone upon them, and the scents of roses and moonflowers were all around them. Laura could hear the roar of surf in the distance. She also heard Kentir's sigh as he gazed up at the moon once more.

"In spite of all our help and love, you will be homesick," Laura said.

"I am sure the other Kheressians who went into different times, or into space in search of new worlds to settle, were also homesick from time to time," Kentir said. "Like them, I have found a new world. This is my home now. Nor will I be alone. Renan and I can remember the older time, you can also recall Issa with us, and your father and sister believe our story and understand.

"Best of all, I have you," Kentir said, lowering his head to kiss her. Silver moonlight gleamed on his dark hair and his harshly molded face, making him appear to be a statue out of the distant past. But no mere statue could be as warm or as loving as Kentir was.

"I will love you forever," Laura whispered, just before his lips claimed hers.

Epilogue

Lincolnshire, England
Two years later

Wroxley Castle was a deserted ruin, albeit a romantic ruin. The moat had long been silted up and turned over to pastureland, though the faint indentation remaining in the land revealed to a sharp-eyed observer just how large the boundary of Wroxley once had been.

Most of the encircling walls had disappeared over the centuries, as the stones were carried away piece by piece by the local folk, to be used for building materials. The tower keep still jutted skyward, its jagged edges like broken teeth where the pounding of cannonballs had broken through twelve feet of solid stone during the civil wars of Cromwell's time. But the lower levels of the keep remained intact after nearly eight centuries and, in an attempt to enforce some measure of safety upon visitors to the old castle, a sturdy wooden door had recently been installed to block the entrance to the keep.

The door presented only a minor impediment to the four American travelers who arrived at Wroxley in late afternoon after a long day of hiking. All of them had overcome too many obstacles in their lives to be stopped by a mere padlock and chain.

The castle grounds were empty of visitors. Tourist season was over; the September shadows were growing long, and the dinner hour was nearing. While Renan and Susan stood guard in case some early evening passerby should decide to question what they were doing, Kentir crouched down before the door and began to pull tools out of his backpack. He laid a chisel, a mallet, and a small crowbar in a neat row on the ground before he found what he was looking for—a long locksmith's pick.

"It won't be long now," Kentir said, smiling up at Laura. "This is a simple lock. It will take only a minute or two to open it."

"I know," Laura said. "I have learned that you can do anything you want to do."

She watched his dark head bent over the lock and knew she had spoken only the truth.

Once upon a time, she had sensed that something was missing in her life and in the lives of her family. It hadn't been simply a lack of love;

without question, her parents had always loved each other and their children. It was more a matter of love misdirected.

Now that she had Kentir by her side and knew he would be there for the rest of their lives, Laura finally understood that the missing piece she had been seeking was not a controlling or manipulative love, such as her mother had once displayed toward Laura and the other children, but an unconditional love that set free the object of its affection.

Kentir had always known how to give that kind of love. He had loved his fiancée and his family enough to send them away from Issa so they could find a safe, new life. Laura could still recall her amazement when she first learned what Kentir had done, and when she understood the courage and self-sacrifice such an act demanded. Kentir had loved his homeland enough to stay behind when his family left, so he could do what was needed to avert total annihilation. Kentir's loving heart had seen what was good and decent in Chac. He had even been willing to give Marica a fair chance. It wasn't Kentir's fault that Marica's heart was immune to love.

"Will you hold the chain away and shine the flashlight on the lock?" Kentir asked.

Laura knelt beside him. Their fingers touched for a moment and Kentir smiled at her. The bold lines of his face were only partly lit by the flashlight Laura held, but the beam illuminated his eyes, and Laura could see both love and humor glowing in their gray-blue depths. Once again, as she did at least a dozen times a day, Laura considered how incredibly fortunate she was to have met him. She hoped she would never forget the difference Kentir's presence had made and was still making to so many people.

Upon reaching the twentieth century, Kentir quickly created a strong emotional connection with her family, and by doing so, he had forever changed their lives. He had gone into business with Laura's father. The two men had developed a line of laser-powered inventions for use in space vessels and, also, for more earthly products. Later, Renan joined with them to create a collection of extremely precise surgical instruments, which Renan used in the research he was doing.

As a result of their work, both Kentir and Renan were now wealthy men, and Laura's father, already well-to-do, had discovered a fresh interest in life in his middle age. When Kentir prevailed upon Bill Morrision to return from Texas, to join his father and his new brothers-in-law as permanent legal counsel for their company, the older William began to look ten years younger.

Meanwhile, Renan's work on regenerating the nerves of patients with spinal-cord injuries brought him fame, along with the occasional suggestion he might be considered for a Nobel prize. But it was Renan's marriage to Laura's sister, Susan, and the knowledge that he would become a father in another few months, that had made the physician from Kheressia a truly happy man.

As for Kentir, his continuing delight in the daughter, Imilca Marie, who had been conceived in Issa and born in the twentieth century, and his pride in the beloved wife who worked with him as his closest assistant, were obvious to everyone who knew him.

William Morrison was greatly amused by Kentir's suggestion that he approach Roger Greydon for help in getting government approval for several Morrison Corporation products. Roger had won the election and he was proving to be an effective and surprisingly honest senator. His outspoken support of William Morrison's latest inventions only enhanced his image as a man on the cutting edge of modern technology. Roger and his wife, Marlene, were the new power couple in Washington. More important to Laura, Roger and Kentir had established a cordial relationship. Laura felt certain that Kentir's influence would keep Roger on the right path.

The most amazing change of all since Kentir's arrival in the present time had taken place in Laura's mother. Thrilled to have both her daughters happily married to successful men, Alberta Morrison ceased trying to manage her children's lives and instead devoted herself to her new role of indulgent grandmother. She was at present caring for Laura and Kentir's daughter while they were on this brief vacation in England, and she was awaiting with great excitement the birth of her older daughter's first child.

As a result of all these changes, the world as a whole seemed to Laura a brighter, happier place.

And it was all because of one visionary man, who had once taken on the burden of trying to save Earth from cosmic destruction, Laura thought, stretching out her hand to run her fingers through Kentir's thick hair.

"If you don't stop that," Kentir warned her in a low, seductive voice, "I'll be forced to give up trying to pick this lock and it will be midnight before we get into the keep. Are you willing to spend the night here with whatever bats and ghosts inhabit the place?"

"No," Laura said, shivering a little at the thought. "I just wanted you to know how much I love you."

"You showed me how much last night," Kentir said with a grin. "And, if you behave yourself for the next hour or two, I may allow you to demonstrate your affection later this evening."

"How generous of you." Laura could not repress a giggle. She, a woman once supremely indifferent to sex, continued to be deeply and passionately enamored of her romantic husband. Laura wondered if this was the right moment to tell Kentir of her suspicion that they had started another baby. She decided to wait. One exciting event per day was quite enough, and Kentir had just succeeded in opening the lock.

"We can go in now," Kentir said, helping her to pull the chain away from the door.

All four of them had brought flashlights. In single file, with Kentir leading, they made their way into the keep and down a debris-clogged stone staircase, to a wide area at the bottom of the steps, which appeared to be an anteroom.

"The crypt will be down there," Laura said. She motioned with her flashlight to show her companions another set of steps that led downward from the anteroom to a dark and musty vault.

"These stairs are surprisingly wide," Renan noted, shining his flashlight first up the way they had just come, and then downward to the crypt.

"They had to be wide," Laura said. "The lord of the castle and all his family were traditionally buried in the crypt, sometimes with large marble tombs erected over them. So coffins, slabs of marble, and craftsmen with their tools all had to get up and down these steps—not to mention priests in their vestments with candles and probably a cross or two, and all the mourners who would come to witness the interment of the noble dead."

"It sounds like a busy place," said Susan. "You have been making a serious study of castle architecture, haven't you?"

"I thought I ought to, if we were going to locate the chapel without a long search that might well draw unwanted attention to us," Laura responded. She walked across the anteroom to a rounded arch where pieces of a battered door hung from iron hinges. "This will be the chapel," she said. Pushing back the remains of the door, she entered.

The chapel was only dimly lit by the fading daylight coming through the narrow windows. There was light enough for Laura to see that the stone floor was clear of debris, though it was covered by years of dust and marred by bird droppings underneath the window niches.

"Looks like someone stole the stained glass," Susan remarked, looking up at the long, open spaces where glass had once been. There were birds' nests in the window niches, and a faint fluttering and chirping indicated that the nests were occupied.

Laura gave the windows scarcely a glance. She was interested in them only because they shed just enough light into the chapel to enable her to see where to search.

"There's no altar left," Susan said.

"Perhaps it was taken away during the Civil War, after the castle was slighted," Laura suggested. "But here is where the altar once stood." She mounted the two broad, shallow steps at the end of the chapel, and with a sweep of one hand indicated the marks on the stone floor that outlined an oblong structure. Laura knelt, feeling along the dusty stones, searching for the one stone Hua Te had told her about, that concealed a hiding place.

"Let me help." Kentir was beside his wife, running his sensitive fingertips over the places where the stones were joined together. "Here, I think. Renan, hand me the chisel and mallet."

Taking care not to damage the stone, Kentir chipped out a small piece of mortar. Then he inserted the crowbar.

"In the old days," Laura said, "the stone rose easily if a person knew exactly where to press on it. Hua Te told me there was a spring set below to move it."

"Need I remind you that we are far removed from the old days?" Kentir asked. He grimaced and grunted with the effort he was exerting. "No doubt the spring Hua Te spoke of is long broken and useless."

"It's moving!" Renan exclaimed. Squatting beside Kentir, he caught at the slightly upraised edge of the stone. A few minutes later they lifted the stone out of its place to reveal a rusted, broken spring laying at the bottom of the cache beneath the stone.

Through the dust and cobwebs of centuries, Laura saw below the broken spring a square packet. When she reached to lift it out, the leather thong securing the packet disintegrated. The oiled parchment wrapping remained in place, tightly folded around the contents of the packet.

"Amazing," Susan said in a voice filled with wonder. "After all the wars of the Middle Ages, and bombardments during the Civil War, and all the other disasters that might have destroyed it, that little packet has survived."

"Open it now," Kentir said to Laura. "Do it here, where Hua Te left it for you to find."

She had to pull hard on the parchment. It was stuck together, but finally it came apart. Underneath the parchment was an inner wrapping, a square of linen that was only slightly yellowed by age. Inside this second wrapping was a folded parchment with writing on it, along with yet another square package of linen enclosing an object that made a slight metallic noise when Laura lifted it. She opened the little package and a glitter of gold and amethyst tumbled into her dirt-smudged palm.

"What is it?" Susan asked, peering over her sister's shoulder.

"Earrings," Laura said. "These are the earrings Imilca lent to me to wear on the evening of the last party ever held in Issa."

She could not speak another word. Tears choked her voice, so she lifted up one of the earrings between her thumb and forefinger, holding it by its wire, letting the joined sections dangle free. The gold shone untarnished and the cascade of amethysts sparkled when Renan turned his flashlight on the piece.

"What lovely workmanship," Susan whispered.

"I remember those earrings," Renan said to Laura. "And the night you wore them," he added with a sigh.

"So do I," Kentir said, "and especially what happened after the party ended."

His eyes met Laura's, their gazes holding in love and memory.

"When the time is right," Kentir said to Laura, "you ought to give them to our own Imilca, for by the reckoning I have done, it was on the night when you wore those earrings that she was conceived."

"Oh, my," Susan said, with a catch in her breath. "This is getting awfully personal, isn't it? Look, it's growing darker and the air in this chapel is much too stuffy for me. Besides, Laura, you may want to read that letter in private. Renan and I should leave."

"I think Renan wants to know what is in the letter," Laura said, with a glance at her brother-in-law.

"I do," Renan said. "Hua Te was a good friend, and Imilca and I knew each other from childhood. I want to know what finally happened to them."

"In that case," Kentir said, "let's close up the cache and go outside before some curious soul intrudes on us and demands to know what we are doing here."

"Right," Susan agreed with a nervous laugh. "We don't want to have to turn over our fabulous loot to the British Museum, do we?"

The two men slid the movable stone back into place and smeared the dust around on the floor, to cover the traces of its opening as best they could. Then they all climbed up the steps and into the pale light of evening.

A short distance from the castle they sat down beneath a gnarled old oak tree. There, Susan poured hot tea from the thermos jug she carried in her backpack and passed the cups around, while Renan brought forth a selection of slightly crushed sandwiches from his pack.

"Will you read the letter now, Laura?" Kentir asked, his voice gentle in deference to her nostalgic emotions.

"Yes," Laura said. "It's time." Setting aside her cup of tea, she unfolded Hua Te's letter and began to scan the words written eight centuries before. Kentir held his flashlight so she could see in the growing darkness.

To my dear friend, Laura,

If you have found this packet, then you and Kentir and Renan have survived your long journey through time.

Imilca and I arrived safely in Baghdad, the city from which I departed when I visited Issa. There was some slight, and as yet unexplained, discrepancy in the mechanisms of our timestones. So while we arrived together as planned, we appeared in the same room ten days after I had left it. My prolonged absence led my youthful pupil, Warrick of Wroxley, to fear that one of his magical spells was responsible for my disappearance. He left Baghdad before I returned, but I am happy to say we were finally reunited upon my arrival at Wroxley some months later, with my beautiful wife, Imilca, by my side.

We have enjoyed a long reunion at Wroxley with old friends, during which I have revealed much, though not all, of our great adventure— for what purpose would it serve to alarm these good folk over events history assures us they will not have to face?

Now the urge to travel has come upon me again, and I long to show the wonders of the Middle Kingdom to Imilca. Therefore, I have undertaken to fulfill my promise to you. This letter, and the earrings Imilca wants you to have, will be deposited tomorrow in the cache beneath the chapel altar, where I hope they will remain undisturbed until you find them.

Since Imilca and I remain in excellent health, we believe you, Kentir, and Renan have also reached the twentieth century in health and safety.

Imilca and I wish for you the same happiness that we have found in each other. Every day we remember the friends we once knew in Issa, and we know that you will never forget us, either.

Farewell, beloved friend.

Hua Te
Imilca

They sat in silence for a long time after Laura finished reading the letter, until Renan spoke in tones of great sadness.

"Except when we speak of it among ourselves, that is the last we will ever hear of Issa," Renan said.

"Not so," Kentir responded. He shut off his flashlight and got to his feet, to look at the sky, where the evening star was shining. Then he shifted his attention back to the three who still sat under the old oak tree. "We can discover traces of the men and women of Kheressia in this remade world. Think of the pyramids in Egypt, of the sudden appearance of writing in Sumer, the mechanical inventions of the last two centuries, even the ability to travel into space. So much of this world is founded on inspiration provided by our people, then refined and improved upon by the great thinkers of this present age. It makes me proud to know we have been a part of it."

"There may be more to come, Kentir," Laura said, getting up to stand next to him. "The descendants of the Kheressians who went off-world are still out there. I refuse to believe they all died in space. The recent discovery of planets orbiting around stars that are not far away in astronomical terms makes me believe there is a chance the Kheressians could have found more than one world where they could settle. Someday, their descendants may contact us."

"My distant cousins, my nieces and nephews, out there," Kentir said. "One thing I have learned since meeting you, my love: we live in a world filled with marvels. Who can say what will happen in the next year, or the next decade?"

Putting his arms around Laura, Kentir gazed upward, and Laura followed his gaze to the darkening sky, to the twinkling stars that were just beginning to shine, and to the unseen worlds orbiting around those stars.

"Until tomorrow, children of Issa," Kentir said softly.

"Until tomorrow," Laura repeated, just before she wrapped her arms around his neck and kissed him.

Heart's Magic

Flora Speer

Bestselling author of *ROSE RED*

In the year 1122, Mirielle senses change is coming to Wroxley Castle. Then, from out of the fog, two strangers ride into Lincolnshire. Mirielle believes the first man to be honest. But the second, Giles, is hiding something–even as he stirs her heart and awakens her deepest desires. And as Mirielle seeks the truth about her mysterious guest, she uncovers the castle's secrets and learns she must stop a treachery which threatens all she holds dear. Only then can she be in the arms of her only love, the man who has awakened her own heart's magic.

___52204-7 $5.99 US/$6.99 CAN

The Magician's Lover — Flora Speer

Determined to locate his friend who disappeared during a spell gone awry, Warrick petitions a dying stargazer to help find him. But the astronomer will only assist Warrick if he promises to escort his daughter Sophia and a priceless crystal ball safely to Byzantium. Sharp-tongued and argumentative, Sophia meets her match in the powerful and intelligent Warrick. Try as she will to deny it, he holds her spellbound, longing to be the magician's lover.

___52263-2 $5.99 US/$6.99 CAN

Dorchester Publishing Co., Inc.
P.O. Box 6640
Wayne, PA 19087-8640

Please add $1.75 for shipping and handling for the first book and $.50 for each book thereafter. NY, NYC, and PA residents, please add appropriate sales tax. No cash, stamps, or C.O.D.s. All orders shipped within 6 weeks via postal service book rate. Canadian orders require $2.00 extra postage and must be paid in U.S. dollars through a U.S. banking facility.

Name_____
Address_____
City_____ State_____ Zip_____
I have enclosed $_____ in payment for the checked book(s).
Payment <u>must</u> accompany all orders. ❑ Please send a free catalog.
   CHECK OUT OUR WEBSITE! www.dorchesterpub.com

FLORA SPEER
Rose Red
A Faerie Tale Romance

Once upon a time...they lived happily ever after.

"I HAVE TWO DAUGHTERS, ONE A FLOWER AS PURE AND WHITE AS THE NEW-FALLEN SNOW AND THE OTHER A ROSE AS RED AND SWEET AS THE FIRES OF PASSION."

Bianca and Rosalinda are the only treasures left to their mother after her husband, the Duke of Monteferro, is murdered. Fleeing a remote villa in the shadows of the Alps of Northern Italy, she raises her daughters in hiding and swears revenge on the enemy who has brought her low.

The years pass until one stormy night a stranger appears from out of the swirling snow, half-frozen and wild, wrapped only in a bearskin. To gentle Bianca he appears a gallant suitor. To their mother he is the son of an assassin. But to Rosalinda he is the one man who can light the fires of passion and make them burn as sweet and red as her namesake.

_52139-3 $5.99 US/$6.99 CAN

THE FOREVER BRIDE — EVELYN ROGERS

"Evelyn Rogers delivers great entertainment!"
—Romantic Times

It is only a fairy tale, but to Megan Butler *The Forever Bride* is the most beautiful story she's ever read. That is why she insists on going to Scotland to get married in the very church where the heroine of the legend was wed to her true love. The violet-eyed advertising executive never expects the words of the story to transport her over two hundred years into the past, exchanging vows not with her fiancé, but with strapping Robert Cameron, laird of Thistledown Castle. After convincing Robert that she is not the unknown woman he's been contracted to marry, Meagan sets off with the charming brute in search of the real bride and her dowry. But the longer they pursue the elusive girl, the less Meagan wants to find her. For with the slightest touch Robert awakens her deepest desires, and she discovers the true meaning of passion. But is it all a passing fancy—or has she truly become the forever bride?

_4177-4 $5.50 US/$6.50 CAN

Dorchester Publishing Co., Inc.
P.O. Box 6640
Wayne, PA 19087-8640

Please add $1.75 for shipping and handling for the first book and $.50 for each book thereafter. NY, NYC, and PA residents please add appropriate sales tax. No cash, stamps, or C.O.D.s. All orders shipped within 6 weeks via postal service book rate. Canadian orders require $2.00 extra postage and must be paid in U.S. dollars through a U.S. banking facility.

Name_____
Address_____
City_____ State_____ Zip_____
I have enclosed $_____ in payment for the checked book(s).
Payment <u>must</u> accompany all orders. ☐ Please send a free catalog.

FLORA SPEER

Bestselling Author Of *Love Just In Time*

Falsely accused of murder, Sir Alain vows to move heaven and earth to clear his name and claim the sweet rose named Joanna. But in a world of deception and intrigue, the virile knight faces enemies who will do anything to thwart his quest of the heart.

From the sceptered isle of England to the sun-drenched shores of Sicily, the star-crossed lovers will weather a winter of discontent. And before they can share a glorious summer of passion, they will have to risk their reputations, their happiness, and their lives for love and honor.

_3816-1 $4.99 US/$5.99 CAN

APOLLO'S FAULT

MIRIAM RAFTERY

Taylor James's wrinkled Shar-Pei, Apollo, is always getting into trouble. But the young beauty never expects her mischievous puppy to lead her on the romantic adventure of a lifetime—from a dusty old Victorian attic to the strong arms of Nathaniel Stuart and his turn-of-the-century charm. One minute Taylor and Apollo are in modern-day San Francisco, and the next thing Taylor knows, a shift in the earth's crust, a wrinkle in time, and the lovely historian finds herself facing the terror of California's most infamous earthquake—and a love so monumental it threatens to shake the foundations of her world.

_52084-2 $4.99 US/$6.99 CAN

THE MASK
DONNA LEE POFF

Sitting in the moonlight at the edge of the forest, she appears to him as a delicate wood elf, but Anne of Thornbury is no spritely illusion. A fresh-faced village girl, Anne has no experience with love, until she meets the brave yet reclusive lord with the hidden face and mysterious history. She soon realizes that only with her love can Galen finally overcome the past and release his heart from the shadow of the mask.

___4416-1 $4.99 US/$5.99 CAN

Dorchester Publishing Co., Inc.
P.O. Box 6640
Wayne, PA 19087-8640

Please add $1.75 for shipping and handling for the first book and $.50 for each book thereafter. NY, NYC, and PA residents, please add appropriate sales tax. No cash, stamps, or C.O.D.s. All orders shipped within 6 weeks via postal service book rate. Canadian orders require $2.00 extra postage and must be paid in U.S. dollars through a U.S. banking facility.

Name_____
Address_____
City_____State_____Zip_____
I have enclosed $_____ in payment for the checked book(s).
Payment <u>must</u> accompany all orders. ❏ Please send a free catalog.
         CHECK OUT OUR WEBSITE! www.dorchesterpub.com

Panther's Prey
Doreen Owens Malek

BESTSELLING AUTHOR OF
THE PANTHER AND THE PEARL

He rides from out of the Turkish wilderness atop a magnificent charger. Dark and mysterious, Malik Bey sweeps Boston-bred Amelia Ryder into an exotic world of sultans and revolutionaries, magnificent palaces and desert camps. Amy wants to hate her virile abductor, to escape his heated glances forever. But with his suave manners and seductive charm, the hard-bodied rebel is no mere thief out to steal the proper young beauty's virtue. And as hot days melt into sultry nights, Amy grows ever closer to surrendering to unending bliss in Malik's fiery embrace.

_4015-8 $5.99 US/$6.99 CAN

THE OUTLAW HEART

VIVIAN KNIGHT-JENKINS

Bestselling Author Of *Love's Timeless Dance*

A professional stuntwoman, Caycee Hammond is used to working in a world of illusions. Pistol blanks firing around her and fake bottles breaking over her head are tricks of the trade. But she cannot believe her eyes when a routine stunt sends her back to an honest-to-goodness Old West bank robbery. And bandit Zackary Butler is far too handsome to be anything but a dream. Before Caycee knows it, she is dodging real bullets, outrunning the law, saving Zackary's life, and longing to share the desperado's bedroll. Torn between her need to return home and her desire for Zackary, Caycee has to choose between a loveless future and the outlaw heart.

_52009-5 $4.99 US/$5.99 CAN

Dorchester Publishing Co., Inc.
P.O. Box 6640
Wayne, PA 19087-8640

ATTENTION ROMANCE CUSTOMERS!

SPECIAL TOLL-FREE NUMBER
1-800-481-9191

Call Monday through Friday
10 a.m. to 9 p.m.
Eastern Time
Get a free catalogue,
join the Romance Book Club,
and order books using your
Visa, MasterCard,
or Discover®

Leisure
Books

Love
Spell

GO ONLINE WITH US AT DORCHESTERPUB.COM